Our Fathers

Our Fathers

Karin Brynard

Translated from the Afrikaans by Linde Dietrich

PENGUIN BOOKS

Published in 2016 by Penguin Random House South Africa (Pty) Ltd
Company Reg No 1953/000441/07
The Estuaries No 4, Oxbow Crescent, Century Avenue, Century City, 7441, South Africa
PO Box 1144, Cape Town, 8000, South Africa
www.penguinbooks.co.za

First edition, first printing 2016
1 3 5 7 9 8 6 4 2

ISBN 978-1-4152-0692-8 (Print)
ISBN 978-1-4152-0670-6 (ePub)

Cover design by Georgia Demertzis
Author photograph by Ansie du Toit
Text design by Fahiema Hallam
Set in 10.5 on 13.5 pt Minion Pro

Printed by **novus** *print*, a Novus Holdings company

MIX
Paper from
responsible sources
FSC
www.fsc.org
FSC® C022948

This book was printed on FSC® certified and controlled sources. FSC (Forest
Stewardship Council®) is an independent, international, non-governmental organisation. Its
aim is to support environmentally sustainable, and socially and economically responsible
global forest management.

For Rien

Prologue

A vast expanse of barrenness, this landscape with its sparse vegetation as far as the eye could see lay basking in the late-summer sun. No sign of life besides a bateleur eagle gliding lazily on air currents.

Leaning against the bonnet of his car, Captain Albertus Markus Beeslaar surveyed his surroundings. He had stopped at the viewing point on Van Rhyn's Pass to eat the breakfast he'd bought at Nieuwoudtville, the last town before the road winds down the eight-hundred-metre-high Bokkeveld escarpment to Vanrhynsdorp. And then to the Cape. As he chewed, Beeslaar gazed across the bleak plain spread out below him. The Knersvlakte. In the distance, the Hardeveld region and the Maskam Mountain. Black straggly bushes dotted the landscape, like flecks on an old man's scalp.

As a starter, he tucked into a fresh, hot chicken pie. Then the bacon-and-egg sandwich, which he washed down with a mug of sweet black coffee. For the first time, he was really looking forward to his trip to the Cape. Till yesterday, he had been too busy to give it much thought. But this morning, indeed ever since shaking off the Kalahari dust in last night's darkness, a speck of excitement had settled behind his ribs.

He had never been to the Cape. Table Mountain and Robben Island and Bloubergstrand were just pictures to him, images with pleasant associations. Mandela walking out of prison, the cable car on one of the world's most famous mountains, the beaches with their penguin colonies, the playground of millionaires and film stars. And he had never seen Stellenbosch either. All that wine, the culture. A Disney wonderland to anyone who'd grown up amid the toxic mine dumps of the East Rand.

But now he'd be able to see all of this. And, best of all, he'd be exploring the sights with Blikkies, his sole remaining pal after more than twenty years in the South African Police Service. Who had chosen to retire in Stellenbosch, of all places. Because his daughter lived there, he'd explained.

When he'd finished the sandwich, and downed a second mug of coffee, Beeslaar got back into the car and began to navigate the steep descent of the mountain pass.

His cellphone rang, and he groped around, his fingers feeling for it among the scattered articles on the passenger seat. A fleece jacket thrown into the car at the last moment – just in case. A newspaper, to inspect the Cape weather forecast.

The caller was Blikkies, he saw before answering.

"Yes, yes, yes! Has the oom got the wine on ice?" he asked before Blikkies managed to get a word in.

"Albertus?" An unfamiliar voice.

"Yes?"

There was something in the voice, something broken, he realised.

"It's Tertia here, Albertus. I'm afraid I have bad news."

"Yes?" He felt a chill. Goosebumps.

"He's dead, Albertus, my dad. Three days ago. I'm sorry I'm only phoning now, but things were … it happened so suddenly, early morning and—"

Beeslaar cut out. He didn't hear the rest of her sentence.

1

"O death, where is thy sting? O grave ... *where* thy victory?"

The dominee looked heavenwards, as if addressing someone seated in the rafters. He closed his eyes, his old head shaking slightly.

Beeslaar looked around him. Old people, he observed. Ooms in jackets the shade of a faded tortoiseshell, which hung loosely on shrivelled bodies. Tannies with saggy bosoms, dim eyes fixed on the preacher high above the congregation in his eyrie. Beeslaar surmised that the mourners were residents of Blikkies's retirement home, Great Gables. All except Tertia, the daughter. She sat huddled in the front pew, next to the varnished coffin: Blikkies's wooden overcoat. A stiff bouquet of white flowers on top. And a framed photograph of "The Departed", as the dominee referred to Blikkies.

"All of us," began the dominee as he looked down mournfully at his tiny flock, "all of us fear death. Down the ages, this has been the one appointment none of us can cancel. Consider what Job tells us in the Old Testament, chapters thirteen and fourteen. Man is a windblown leaf, a dry husk; his days are few and full of trouble. He blossoms like a flower and withers, flees like a passing shadow, decays like an old tree stump in the ground."

Beeslaar stared at the photograph on the coffin. A recent one, no doubt. He recalled fewer liver spots. Fewer furrows around the severe mouth. Ears that were less droopy, firmer skin. When was the last time they had seen each other? Three years ago, four?

"But, beloved brothers and sisters," the voice registered in his consciousness again, "today, here where we are gathered to commemorate the life of Balthasar van Blerk, today we can be glad. Yes, we should be *joyful*."

A pause.

"Joyful in the knowledge that God sent his own Son to conquer death on our behalf."

Beeslaar shifted his weight, and the wooden pew creaked loudly. Someone turned around and gave him a sharp look. A woman with a thick white plait. Her glance was more inquisitive than disapproving, he noted.

"Because, friends, the good news is this: after Christ had breathed his last on Golgotha, he descended into the nethermost regions of the earth."

He didn't know any of the people at the funeral service, Beeslaar realised. Save for Tertia – though they were barely acquainted. After Blikkies and his wife divorced, Tertia had broken off all contact with her father for a while, and Beeslaar never got to know her.

On his arrival at the church, she had come up to him and introduced herself. Grief stricken, her face grey and tired, her nose a feverish red. Beeslaar realised with a shock: this woman had really cared. Bliksem van Blerk had someone who was mourning him with all her being.

"My dad was so excited about your visit," she'd said with a wan smile. "He had so many plans lined up. A cricket match at Newlands, the cable car on Table Mountain, maybe a trip to Robben Island." She held out a slim white hand, which he took in his own. "He was convinced he'd be able to persuade you to apply for a transfer."

Her voice petered out.

The muted notes of an organ floated out of the church and she turned to go inside. Beeslaar tugged at his collar and entered the building.

Would the shop take back the jacket, he'd wondered as he sat down, squeezing his two-metre frame into the end of a pew. The jacket was too tight around the shoulders. It had been a rushed purchase the day before, his mind elsewhere. Dwelling on the bitter irony of his life: innocently driving down to the Cape to pay a visit to his old pal. Only to arrive – ha ha, how bloody funny – at the "dooiemansdeur". Dead man's door, no one at home. He had brought along kudu biltong. Wine from the Gariep vineyards. Tiger's eye, the most beautiful gemstone from that part of the world, cut and polished so that its yellow and gold bands glowed. He'd chosen a stone that had been converted into a pretty table lamp. Had reckoned that old Blikkies would like something like that.

But then Blikkies was not there any more. He'd simply checked out.

"*I hold the keys of hell and of death*, Jesus states in Revelation one, verse eighteen," the old minister suddenly said with renewed energy, new enthusiasm. "Because you see, dearly beloved, He took those keys away from Satan. When He descended into hell. Yes, Christ was in hell, *before* his resurrection, *before* his ascension to heaven. And because of this, I'm promising you here today, *for this* we should be joyful. Oom Balthazar wouldn't have wanted us to grieve. Because today he is in the arms of his Maker, the …"

Oom Balthazar.

This dominee had definitely not known the "oom". Otherwise he'd have known: Blikkies never allowed anyone to address him by his proper Christian name. And secondly: he hadn't believed in either heaven or hell. Heaven, he used to say, was a boring place dreamt up by old women. And hell by the church's own big shots – guys who'd long known that it'd be tickets for them and their church if people ever found out there was nothing behind the curtain. Church fathers and politicians. Birds of a feather: the kind of people who let others do their dirty work.

Others. Just like this oom: Balthazar "Bliksem" van Blerk. A blue-blood policeman whose daily task it was to wrestle down this so-called sting of death. Who, throughout his life, had taken on this sting, this sin. Take it on, and take it out. But in turn it took its toll. Broke you down, bit by bit. Slowly, unnoticed. Crushed you in the corners of your heart. Externally, of course, you hardened. That went without saying. But it was on the inside that you died a little each time. Day in, day out: the relentless register of brutality. The things human beings are capable of.

"This world," Beeslaar heard the dominee say, "is not our home. It is only the trail – the trail each of us follows to eternity. Death, my beloved, was instituted by Satan. In Paradise, when Eve yielded to the snake and brought death upon humanity. But *we*, beloved ..." A sip of water. "*We*, children of Jesus, need not fear death. Yes, people die every day. It stops us in our tracks, shocks us into reflecting on our mortality. But Christ has redeemed us. Brought us the road map to eternal life."

Beeslaar had trouble with the picture in his mind. Blikkies atop a little cloud, along with the estimated eighty-five billion people who had died since the first ape walked upright. How do you cope with such a multitude? He folded his arms across his chest, heard the seams of the jacket complaining. He unfolded his arms again, reached for the funeral card instead – for the umpteenth time. A purple lily graced the front, with Blikkies's full name and the date of his death, four days ago. Printed below: *Say not in grief "He is no more" but live in thankfulness that he was – Hebrew Proverb*. The text of the sermon appeared on the back, together with the words of a hymn that presumably still had to be sung. *My morning song is thankfulness*. He put the leaflet back into the Bible holder in front of him. The sheet of paper slid out and fluttered to the floor. Beeslaar bent down and grabbed it. The pew creaked again. This time the woman with the plait frowned as she looked at him over her shoulder.

The mourners filed out and assembled for tea at a stately old Cape Dutch house adjacent to the Mother Church.

Unsure of himself, Beeslaar joined a queue at the tea table. He felt like a giant among this group of grey-haired Lilliputians. He was easily twice as tall and twice as heavy as any of the oldies around him. Had these people always been so tiny? Or was it age, he wondered. Had Blikkies also shrunk? His phone voice still sounded the same. And, in fact, he'd still been fairly young, on the right side of seventy.

"Are you the policeman?"

The woman with the plait was behind him in the queue. She didn't give him a chance to reply. "Blikkies told me a lot about you. I'm Trula, by the way."

"Pleased to meet you," Beeslaar mumbled and stood aside to let her go first.

She thanked him and then waited before accompanying him to the shade of an oak tree.

"When did you arrive?" she inquired.

"Day before yesterday."

"To think he had to go like that …"

Beeslaar raised his cup, tasted the bitterness in the tepid liquid. Clearly, the service had lasted longer than anticipated.

"So damned suddenly." She blew gently on the tea, her lips pursed. It was a pretty mouth in an otherwise ordinary face. A pointy nose, grey-blue eyes behind gold-rimmed glasses, her skin white and soft. Her hair was combed flat with a neat middle parting and pulled back tightly into the plait.

"Blikkies and I were good buddies," she said, sipping cautiously. "We were perhaps also the youngest of the residents – both of us still in our sixties." She glanced around her to prove her point. "He was my salvation, you know? Otherwise I may also have been hobbling around with a walker by now. An old age home tends to—"

One of the oldies had come up to them, and was standing next to her.

"So this is Balthie's son." The woman blinked, her head thrown back as if she were peering up at a cat in a tree. He guessed she was in her mid-seventies. Well preserved, hair immaculate, a black-and-white two-piece suit finished with an expensive brooch, old-fashioned white gloves.

"No, Rea, Balthie only has the daughter, Tertia. This is Albertus. He's from the Kalahari. He and Blikkies used to work together."

Beeslaar inclined his head.

"And this is Reana du Toit," said Trula. "She's one of the residents."

"Then *you* are the policeman," the older woman declared. "The one who was coming to visit him?"

"That's right, Mevrou. Blikkies and I go back a long way."

The woman edged a bit closer to Beeslaar. "Tell me, do you perhaps do private work too?"

"Rea, no! He's a policeman. Full-time. He's only here for the funeral," Trula interjected. Her voice was impatient, slightly too loud, as if the older woman had a hearing problem.

"But it's precisely because he's a policeman," Rea du Toit retorted. "Maybe *he* can help us. There is death among us here at Great Gables, prowling around like a roaring lion."

Trula wiped her forehead with the flat of her hand. "Heavens, Rea, that's really melodramatic. And your Bible text is wrong. It's the devil that prowls around like a roaring lion – not death. Please excuse me," she continued. "I'm going to give Oom Dolfie a hand. He's shaking too much to handle a cup of tea."

Rea du Toit sidled up to Beeslaar. He caught a whiff of mothballs, hairspray and cough medicine.

"She can mock all she wants, but there is an evil prowling around there." She lowered her voice. "At the old age home. It's been happening for a while now. Small things, if you take them one by one. But ..." She came nearer. "It all started with Jan van Riebeeck."

"I beg your pardon?" This slipped out before he could stop himself.

"He disappeared, see? And we think he's – well, that he's been murdered!"

Beeslaar took another sip of the bilious tea and regretted it immediately. He turned around, looking for a way to get rid of the cup.

"You have to help us, Albertus. Balthie didn't want to listen to us. But when Jan van Riebeeck ..."

He cast around for help. But Trula was standing next to an oom with an egg-shaped paunch and braces, assisting him with his tea. "Tannie Rea, I assume we're talking about ... er?"

"Ag, nobody knows his real name. He actually lives in the flat next to us. He visits all of us in the corridor. And everyone gives him a saucer with a little something."

Beeslaar smiled with relief: a cat! "Perhaps he's visiting the rooms in another corridor. Where the saucers are bigger."

"It's not a joke, you hear? We're not allowed to keep pets. Jan van Riebeeck was an important visitor. Our matron tried to ban him from visiting us, but he's only an animal and understands just two things: food and love. And he comes every day, because he gets so much love from us. And now he's gone. All of a sudden. And that's not all." She looked up at him with wide eyes.

"Other things have been happening. Just last week, old Dominee Potgieter, bless his soul, was kicked out of his cactus box."

Beeslaar coughed into his fist.

"He's Antoinette's late husband," she explained, tilting her chin in the direction of an attractive woman in her early seventies. "They were both crazy about gardening. But then he was struck down by cancer. She cared for him on her own in their flat. Until he died in her arms. The children wanted to scatter his ashes in the mountains, but Antoinette refused to let him go. She buried the ashes at the bottom of a huge flower box and then planted cactuses on top. An aloe, some vygies, desert roses and bokpootjies. He loved those plants. But then someone kicked the box over. It was probably the same thief who broke into old Arnold Sebens's place the very same day. Made off with his collection of Kruger-rands. And it was at that point that Jan van Riebeeck went missing too."

Beeslaar raised his hand to stop the flow.

"Tannie Rea, hold on. Let me ask something first. Did you report the burglary and the vandalism to the police?"

"Old Arnold reported it, but nothing came of it. Just yesterday he—"

A phone had been ringing in her handbag for a good few seconds. Beeslaar gestured towards her handbag and she unclipped it.

"Hello!" she bellowed across the gathering of mourners. "Who's speaking?" She paused, gave the phone a shake, and then handed it to Beeslaar. "You take it, son. See if you can make anything out."

"Captain Beeslaar speaking, may I help you?"

Silence. Then: "Are you from the police? She … er, knows already?"

"I beg your pardon?"

"My mother. You've informed her? My wife's … her death?"

Beeslaar felt the hairs rise on the back of his neck. He knew that tone of voice all too well. "Sir, you mother and I are at a friend's funeral. She handed me her phone because she couldn't hear very well. What is it that she has to know? Should I pass the phone to her?"

"Something terrible has happened to us. My wife, my mother – my wife …"

"Hello?" Beeslaar stepped away from the buzz of the funeral-goers.

"It's my wife, Elmana. She's been murdered. Just now. Here at our home."

He could hear from the man's voice that more was to come.

"Burglars—"

"Are the police there? And are you safe?"

"What?" The man seemed to be slowly processing the questions.

"The police. Did you call the police?"

"Yes, of course. But our daughter, Ellie. She's still in the house. She's locked herself in and I can't get to her. My mother must please come and help us. Please can you track down the matron and tell her to help break the news?"

"Of course. I'll do what I can. Where are you?"

"At home, here. Right here …"

"You live in Stellenbosch."

"Our son is okay. It's only – it's just my wife. And our daughter."

The line went dead.

Beeslaar stood motionless, stared at the bright white church next door, registering the peals from the clock tower – half past four. The sounds jerked him back to the present.

Rea du Toit was still standing there, her handbag gaping, her face questioning. It was only when he came closer that he saw the trembling, the nostrils white and taut. She had guessed already, he realised, and stretched his arms out towards her.

Death, Dominee. The thought grated in Beeslaar's mind. This is what it looks like. Not a trace of joy or jubilation.

2

Ghaap was jogging lightly along the base of a low dune. Pausing for a moment, he scooped up a handful of fine dry sand and tossed it into the air. His eyes followed the flow. Good, he was still safely downwind.

Around him, the sandy savannah veld stretched away to a never-ending horizon. Here and there the monotony of grass was interrupted by a red dune, the dark-green embroidery of a haak-en-steek bush or the umbrella of a camel thorn tree.

He was following a spoor in the red sand. A blood trail. That of a wounded animal.

A gemsbok.

There was resentment in Sergeant Johannes Ghaap's heart. It should have been a kill shot.

He had taken aim with such care, the 30-06 rested in the fork of a sweet thorn. Two hundred metres, according to his estimation. Upwind. Close enough. It should have been the perfect shot. The animal had been clearly visible. The black-and-white mask, the powerful neck. The massive shoulders and chest. Horns more than a metre long, two deadly spears above the abstract mask of the face.

He'd been able to plan his shot at leisure. There was a slight breeze, nothing to worry about. A neat shot behind the shoulder, smack into the giant's engine room, making allowance for the downward trajectory of the lead.

He had taken aim, the butt of the Musgrave rifle cool and smooth against his cheek, the K98 Mauser action lock cocked. Loaded with only the best: three 180-grain bullets. Cartridges he'd hand-loaded himself in Norma cases. They packed a proper punch: Sonchem's S365 powder behind the pricy Nosler Partition bullets. Bullets that wouldn't splinter against the shoulder bone and sinews of such an enormous animal. The Rolls-Royce of bullets. He'd saved them specially.

He had to get a move on, the sun's eye was starting to redden.

But this day, he knew, was not yet at an end. Not before there was blood on the sand. It would either be him – slashed by the bull's lethal blades – or the prince of the desert himself.

Ghaap was travelling light.

Like his ancestors. Just the bare necessities. His velskoene functioned well, tied tightly around his ankles to keep out sand and grass and devil's thorns. He wore only khaki shorts, with a knife and a water bottle attached to his belt. For the rest, it was only him, his rifle and this majestic antelope.

It was a matter of honour. Of gaining the elders' respect.

His naked torso was toughened against the sun. His heart was strengthened by the blood of a snow-white cock poured over his head early that morning. Straight from the pulsing heart of the bird. The smell lingered in his nostrils and he could still taste it in the saliva at the back of his tongue.

He squatted at the next dune. The antelope's spoor had been dragging here. There was a small lump of mud next to the trail. He picked it up carefully and squashed it between his fingers. He smiled, the crusts of blood cracking at the corners of his mouth and along his cheeks. The ancestors were satisfied. They were showing him the—

"Hey, dushie! It's *your* turn!"

Sergeant Ghaap's head jerked upright, and he woke up with a snort. For a moment he didn't know where he was. Then he remembered. And his heart sank. Fuck, he'd had it up to *here* with being a skivvy. And being called dushie by these two darkies. Angrily, he clicked his tongue.

"Basop! Maye wena! Show some respect for your warrant officers. Remember, we could leave you right here! Let the jackrollers ukuhlaba you!"

The speaker was Sibusiso "S'bu" Mthethwa, who was drawing his finger across his throat to demonstrate Ghaap's likely fate. He was the funny guy. Bandile Mabusela, the older cop, wasn't much of a joker. Ghaap was given the "privilege" of being "shown the ropes" in Soweto by these two seniors from the Orlando East police station. But they weren't "showing" him anything apart from the fact he was never going to make it out of this place alive and in one piece.

Mabusela's hair was greying. He was in his late forties, Ghaap guessed. A broad chin and big ears. He was originally from KwaZulu-Natal, and Zulu-speaking, he had told Ghaap when they were introduced.

S'bu was a lot younger. He was more energetic, more into arsing around, playing pranks and making kak. He was spiteful, and suspicious of anything new and unfamiliar. He was pure Model D – township born and bred. And pissed off as hell about it. He refused to speak ordinary English to Ghaap, got a kick out of making him look stupid by sticking to his township slang, generally known as Kasi.

S'bu was also the big brain behind Project Ghaap: breaking him in, putting him through the mill, so that the skebengas of the kasi won't injini him – to prevent the township thugs from taking him for a ride.

Mabusela was okay. But he didn't intervene in S'bu's taunting.

And with Ghaap being so green, it hadn't taken them long to discover his weak spots. The day before they had tried to get him to eat smileys and s'kop – boiled sheep's heads and cow's heels, the sinews and hooves that the people in the township hawk around in plastic buckets, selling bits and pieces in Jiffy sandwich bags. Last night they said they'd take him for a shisa nyama – a township braai. But *he* had to buy the meat. They sent him to a guy with one of those buckets. He shuddered with revulsion.

And if it wasn't the food, it was the language. Kasi is a concoction of just about all eleven official languages, but mostly Afrikaans, English and Zulu. At least Ghaap knew by now that "basop" meant "pas op" – Afrikaans for "beware". And "ukuhlaba" was "to stab with a knife". He still didn't have a clue what a "jackroller" was. But he suspected it was the type of criminal you didn't ever want to bump into, not even in broad daylight. One who'd roll him. And he had no desire to be rolled. Not in *this* place!

Ghaap disentangled his limbs from the Toyota Corolla. The chill of the late-afternoon Highveld air hit him, and he reached back into the car to grab his parka. Almost lost his balance, because he forgot he was wearing the bulletproof vest. An extra twenty-two kilograms on his tall, rangy frame.

This place really sucked. His superiors treating him like a blougat mampara, fresh from the farm. Having to do all the shitty work, like going to buy the min'ral, the cooldrink. And being told to bring along a qota – a quarter loaf of white bread filled with slap chips and French polony. Jirre! And having to wear the bulletproof at all times.

He felt as if he'd landed on an alien planet, like in the movies – Denzel Washington in *The Book of Eli*, the DVD Beeslaar had given him as a Christmas present. Except that Ghaap wasn't really the hero in this story. But he felt just like old Denzel, trapped in hell itself. It was a world where the line between children's laughter and lunacy was blurred, unfathomable. He shivered and lowered his hand to the z88 on his hip, his fingers on the safety catch. There was always a round in the barrel. Here you didn't issue warnings. You first fired fifteen shots, *then* you warned. As you reloaded.

He started walking. It was their third afternoon here, parked on the koppie the locals called Motor Mountain. A hill of stones and garbage. Paper, dead dogs, tins and glass – household waste. His two seniors loved this spot, though he hadn't been able to figure out why. Maybe because they could sit here peacefully and while away their time. Fooling around with their cellphones, WhatsApp, talking shit. It was Ghaap's third day-shift in Soweto. In the company of the Big M's, as they referred to themselves: Mabusela and Mthethwa. It was the third day he'd had to go and buy food. Down the koppie, crouching as he headed towards the little spaza shop in the dip below.

Further away lay the boundless expanse of Soweto. Millions of shacks and matchbox houses as well as bigger, grander abodes connected by thousands of kilos of roads and power lines. Hazy in the coal smoke that hung in the late-afternoon air like a cloud of doom. Here and there, the high masts of the Apollo lights towered above the smog, each one illuminating several street blocks. They were apparently a remnant from the apartheid years – when war had raged here.

The smoke came from millions of fires. People who were preparing food or simply trying to keep warm. On street corners and at taxi ranks, fires burnt in empty petrol drums and tins. Made with anything that came to hand – coal, cardboard, paper, plastic. As long as it produced heat. Pinned to the ground by the cold early-evening air, the smoke glowed ominously in the dirty yellow light of the setting sun and the Apollo giants. Everything smelled of anthracite and soot, a dry, acrid smell that pervaded your hair and clothes and nose.

So, *this* was Soweto, Ghaap thought, as he lengthened his stride over the uneven track. The place he'd heard so much about. SOWETO – an acronym for South Western Townships. The most dangerous city in the world. Worse than Baghdad. Prior to his arrival, Ghaap had been given a whole lecture on the place and its history. And one thing was impressed on him repeatedly: this joint *chowed* cops. For breakfast, lunch, dessert – you name it. Only the ysters, the seasoned veterans, survived here. Blougatte like him died like flies.

Behind him the Corolla gave a roar, and he whipped round. If those two scumbags were playing another dirty trick and leaving him here, he'd hand in his papers.

But this time jokes were not on the menu.

"Car theft in Dube!" Mabusela shouted as Ghaap scrambled into the back. He groped around in vain for the safety belt, his eyes on the smoke-filled city they were heading back to. The road down the koppie was bad. Mabusela rode screen saver – local jargon for a front-seat passenger. Mthethwa took no chances with the bumpy track. But the moment they hit the tarred road, he stepped on the gas. Ghaap's Kevlar-clad chest slammed into the back of his seat. He peered at the dashboard. The needle shot up to eighty, then a hundred and ten kilometres per hour. Ahead of them, a red traffic light emerged from the smog, but Mthethwa's foot remained flat on the accelerator. Mabusela had meanwhile got hold of the blue light and stuck it to the roof. Ghaap guessed that visibility was limited to fifty metres at most, the smog thick mustard-coloured fumes. On either side of the road, houses and shacks were packed together, tight as pips on a mealie cob. Ramshackle vibracrete and wire fences, with razor wire along the top. Everything a blur in the haze. Ghaap had the door handle in a death grip and his arse was just about chewing up the seat.

The police radio was crackling incessantly, but he couldn't make head or tail of what was being said.

Mabusela was clutching the hand grip above the window as the Toyota zigzagged to avoid a pothole. Then he picked up the mike and called out something, ending by repeating a registration number: "Citi Golf, white! Victor, Pappa, Bravo! Six, zero, eight, seven!"

Mthethwa braked abruptly as the reflector lights of a vehicle loomed in front of them. Ghaap lost his grip on the door handle and his torso shot forward, causing his forehead to connect painfully with Mabusela's neck rest. "Hai, man!" he shouted before he could stop himself.

The two men laughed at him, their voices shrill, reminding him of ruttish stallions tripped out on adrenaline.

In the road before them lay the scattered parts of a donkey cart. Its axle broken, one wheel was lying in the middle of the road. Mthethwa sounded two short blasts with his siren, pressed his hooter non-stop. Then he shot past the cart and Ghaap's body jerked back once more, slamming against the seat. He felt a wave of nausea rise from his stomach, not sure whether it was fear, adrenaline or the day's excessive Coke consumption. Whatever it was, he didn't give a fuck. He wanted to go home. He was fed up with this shit.

"Whoa!" Mabusela yelled suddenly, and the car came to a stop, its tyres screaming.

Ghaap saw the red eye of the traffic light further along the road – and a black blur with antennas on its roof flashed across their field of vision.

"Trackers!" Mabusela yelled again. "Follow!"

Mthethwa swung left and accelerated hard. Ghaap shut his eyes, but they flew open again when Mthethwa swerved sharply to avoid a greyish shape. "Jissus, S'bu," he shouted, "how do you know it's not a child!" The only reply he got was the frenzied light dancing in Mthethwa's eyes in the rear-view mirror.

Ghaap's phone rang. In his shirt pocket, under the bulletproof. Not a fuck was he going to answer now. "Your phone, Sergeant!" shouted the man behind the wheel. "It's djou mammie!" Big joke. Ghaap looked away, but every now and again he caught Mthethwa's mocking eyes in the mirror. God, he was gatvol with this whole show. He simply didn't have the balls to survive here. Beeslaar had warned him.

Fuck him too!

The car skidded. Ghaap wasted no time, flinging his door open before they came to a halt. Hell, he had to get out of there.

Then the door was yanked from his hands as something thudded into him.

It was a person!

Ghaap screamed and tried to pull himself back into the car, but his legs were held in a tight grip. He felt his buttocks slip on the seat. He struggled, tried to kick the figure away from him, saw a pistol in the whirl of arms and legs. Too late. The butt hit him on the jaw. He tasted blood and struck out blindly with his fists, punched the man in the ribs, heard the shriek of pain. The figure stumbled away from him, but Ghaap groped with both hands and caught hold of the man's clothes. Everything was happening fast, no chance to think.

He held on with every sinew and muscle in his body, wondering where the pistol was. Then he got his answer: a sharp pain that exploded against his forehead and jerked his body backwards. A dark fog descended on him. For a moment he saw a second person, two figures in the open door by his legs, limbs flailing as they struggled.

A shot rang out, and everything fell silent.

3

Trula Momberg was giving Beeslaar directions as they drove away from the funeral reception.

She sat in the back of the car, holding Rea du Toit's hand. Beeslaar kept his foot on the accelerator, only braking slightly at the succession of four-way stops on the way to the murder scene. They were going east, he reckoned, with the rocky mass of Stellenbosch Mountain on their right.

The road forked, and Trula told him to continue left.

Beeslaar glimpsed a street name: Jonkershoek Avenue. They drove over a series of mean speed bumps. More stops. Then he turned right. Another mountain came into view, with two lead-grey peaks shimmering in the midday heat. Right again, he was instructed, then straight, across several side streets, until the road ends in a T. "Just here, around the corner." He followed the directions and immediately saw the cluster of vehicles – police vans, an ambulance. Smaller sedans with flashing blue lights. "It's the big white one," she said, pointing to the huge double-storey house ahead on their right.

Beeslaar drove up to a uniform and rolled down his window.

"I have a family member with me," he said, flicking his eyes at the back seat. "She's elderly. I'm just dropping her off and leaving again immediately."

The man waved him past, and Beeslaar nosed the car through the vehicles. The place was a hive of activity, as if every cop in the province had assembled here. Damn nosy parkers. He gritted his teeth at the annoyance welling up inside him, his irritation with the casual officer in charge.

But he put his annoyance into his pocket. This wasn't *his* case. He was merely dropping his passengers off and then he'd be getting the hell out of there.

Back to the north. To the Kalahari, where he belonged.

The blaring ambulance siren right behind him jolted him out of his reverie. He got out of the car, sorely wanting to stuff the siren down the driver's throat. But he swallowed his anger.

His two passengers had also climbed out. "Won't you come with me," Rea du Toit pleaded, her eyes full of fear. The bag was still dangling from her arm.

"Trula will go with you, Mrs du Toit. I have to move my vehicle."

She shook her head.

He groaned inwardly, and walked with them towards the house.

"Oumaaaa! Help me!"

The voice was that of a young girl sitting in an open window on the second storey, covered in blood. She flung her legs outward, turned, and tried to climb down. But she lost her footing, hung by one arm from the sill.

"Oh, my God. Ellie!" Rea du Toit screamed as she started running. She dropped her bag, kicked off the church shoes and hobbled along in her stockings.

Beeslaar shot forward, shouldering frozen figures aside. The girl kicked against the wall, trying to get a foothold, but her feet kept slipping. Long blonde hair flying across her face, her hands losing their grip on the windowsill.

"Ouma!"

She fell, with Beeslaar not quite there yet. He flung himself forward, breaking her landing with his body.

He heard the panic around him as people tried to pick her up. He quickly ran his hands over her legs and arms. Nothing broken. But there was blood on her. Fresh blood.

Her eyes were open. She stared at him blankly.

"Give her to me!" A middle-aged man pushed through the throng and knelt down next to the girl, grabbed her away from Beeslaar. There was blood on him as well. "Ellie!" He pressed her tightly against him. "It's all right, my sweet, all right, all right. Everything's all right. Everything. Daddy's here now."

The man stood up, the girl in his arms. A black paramedic stretched out his arms towards her. "Fuck off!" the man snarled at him.

"Malan!" Rea du Toit had joined them. She was still wearing her gloves, wiped the girl's hair from her face and seemed shocked by the blood on her gloves.

"Ma, I'm taking her to hospital. You have to help Boeta inside, in my office. Ellie's going to be okay."

With that, he strode off towards a black Range Rover in the wide driveway leading to the house.

The powerful engine roared. The man reversed the car aggressively, cutting a path through the rubberneckers.

Beeslaar went to move his own car, and motioned to the ambulance driver behind him to do the same. As soon as the road was clear, he would leave. But he heard a knock, saw the white plait and rolled down the window.

"You can't leave," said Trula. "Rea needs you now. It's all black inside there." She threw him a meaningful glance.

He shook his head, pointedly ignoring the old lady's racism. "I have to get back. And the people here are sufficiently experienced."

"No! Please."

He hesitated.

"Please, Albertus. You don't know what it's like." She gave him another meaningful look.

Beeslaar put his car in reverse. His chest felt tight. Sweat was soaking into the stiff collar of his shirt. New shirt. Funeral shirt. He had to get away.

"Stay!" Now she had her hand on the door. "Just for an hour. Just until we know what happened here. You know that's what Balthie would have done."

Beeslaar swore under his breath. But he switched off the engine and got out. Ahead of him he saw Rea du Toit, searching for her shoes. There was a strange character standing close to her who had picked up her handbag. His pedigree was inscribed on his face and forehead in crude tattoos, with black teardrops under one eye. The typical stamps of prison. From his appearance, he seemed to be a member of one of the Cape's notorious Mitchells Plain gangs. Beeslaar walked purposefully towards him. The man noticed him and hurriedly put the bag down, pulled his hood over his head and slipped away in the crowd.

Beeslaar snatched the bag and looked around, but the man had vanished into thin air.

"Come, Mevrou," he said, taking Rea du Toit's hand. Her bottom lip was quivering. A drop of mucous landed on her lapel. She wiped her nose with her gloved hand, leaving behind a faint smear of blood. She was breathing like a frightened bird: shallow and fast.

Someone handed over her shoes, and Beeslaar knelt down to help get them on her feet. Her stockings were torn, he noticed.

The trio walked towards the house in silence. Rea with her head held high once more – holding her pose now that her dignity was restored. Trula was steering her by her elbow and an uncomfortable Beeslaar was bringing up the rear, feeling like a tame goose on a leash.

The garden path split into two pathways that ran on either side of an ornamental fountain. A cement fish rose from the water, spraying silver drops. Stately palm trees stood on the other side, where the two paths converged again, and led to the steps of the stoep.

A policewoman in a uniform was waiting for them at the top, her face grave, with eyes that surveyed the world calmly and soberly. Her pants were a tad tight around her thighs. Not fat. Generous. Her waist was small, cinched by a broad canvas belt from which her firearm, handcuffs and ammunition clips hung.

She held out her hand to Mrs du Toit in the traditional African way, the left hand touching the elbow of the greeting hand. A sign of respect.

"My sympathies, Mevrou." She bowed deferentially. "I'm very sorry about—" she began, but Rea spoke as if the woman had said nothing, ignoring the hand.

"Where's my grandson?" Her tone was peremptory, brusque. "Who's in charge here?"

Something shifted in the black policewoman's expression. Her eyes flicked up to Beeslaar and then back to the woman in front of her. She shifted her weight almost imperceptibly, blocking the door.

"Your grandson is safe," she replied quietly. "He's in his father's office, with a policewoman and a paramedic. I'll take you through."

"Where's Elmana? What happened here?"

"Come, Mevrou. Let's go inside, we can talk there. I'm Captain Vuyokazi Qhubeka. I'm in charge of the investigation." Her voice was pleasant and warm, despite the frosty atmosphere. The click with which she pronounced the first consonant of her surname sounded warm and soft, like a pebble dropping into a deep well.

"Beeslaar … er," he said uncomfortably, already cross with himself.

"A relative?" Captain Qhubeka prompted.

"No, er—"

"He's with me. He's a policeman. And he's going to assist the family," said Rea du Toit, a hint of defiance in her voice. "He's here on the express instruction of my son, the owner of the house. Come, Albertus!"

A hard light went on in Qhubeka's eyes. She turned around wordlessly and gave an instruction in Xhosa to a constable behind her. He indicated that they should follow him, to the left through the entrance hall.

Beeslaar glanced at Qhubeka over his shoulder. She stared back, her chin raised. He couldn't decide whether it was arrogance or annoyance he was reading in her gaze. Not that he actually cared a hoot, he was just seeing the old lady off, and then he'd be on his way.

The entrance hall looked expensive. A mottled marble floor. An Oriental carpet. Big modern paintings. Originals – one of an Nguni bull. A dining room came into view on their right. Beeslaar counted fourteen chairs. Two crystal chandeliers hung low above the table, a starlight ceiling.

A staircase. Probably leading to the bedrooms at the top.

Bloodstains on the wall. On the thick pile of the carpeting that ran up the stairs.

Beeslaar felt the stirring in the pit of his stomach. The string that tautened, a buzz, slowly awakening.

A murder scene. A human life had been taken here. Brutally. A family devastated.

What had happened here called for retribution. *That* was the message from his body.

4

The boy was squeezed into the corner of a two-seater couch, sitting as far as possible from the policewoman beside him. He held a mug of what looked like tea. The policewoman stood up to make room for Rea du Toit next to her grandson.

"Ag, my child!" Rea du Toit held him close. He did not resist, gazing into space with a stunned look. For a while the two sat like that, the woman's face twisted in a struggle to contain her emotions, the child's expressionless, his mouth gaping. He was at that awkward stage between child and man. Long, spindly limbs, knobbly knees and shoulders. The first hint of a moustache among the pimples.

Beeslaar hovered near the door as Captain Qhubeka pulled up a straight-backed chair and sat down next to the pair. She waited a moment before speaking, then leant forward, her palms on her knees.

"Won't you please leave us alone?" Rea du Toit's voice was brimming with hostility. There was a tremor in her powdered cheeks and her eyes glistened with tears.

"I'm sorry, Mevrou, but we have to talk to the boy. It won't—"

The boy suddenly moved. He pulled himself from his grandmother's embrace. "Pa said I don't *have* to talk."

"Your father's right," Qhubeka said calmly. "But you want to help us catch the perpetrator, don't you?"

The boy glanced around searchingly. His one leg started twitching, and there was fear in his eyes. He looked up at Beeslaar, then at Qhubeka who was seated right in front of him.

"I don't know what happened," he mumbled, focusing on the mug of tea in his hands. Big, clumsy boy's hands, with warts on one thumb. He reminded Beeslaar of a newly hatched ostrich chick: all legs.

"And he doesn't have to talk to you either," said the grandmother. "He'll talk when a *real* policeman arrives." She glared at Qhubeka, her mouth pulled down and her nostrils flared. She was no stranger to the boxing ring, Beeslaar decided.

"Mevrou, I *am* the real police. I'm leading the investigation. And it would really—"

"It won't *help* to talk to you – to any of you people," said Rea, cutting her short. "Because it's not *your* people that are being killed like flies. You couldn't care less if the whole lot of us are butchered and massacred. On the contrary, you people are *glad* when another white person dies!"

Qhubeka seemed about to respond but then clearly decided against it. Her mouth snapped shut and she sat back, letting the woman's venomous anger wash over her.

Beeslaar approached them. "I think it would be best if the boy could tell us what happened, Mrs du Toit."

"Yes, I know, Albertus. But I'll talk to *you*. Not to a – to one of *them*!" She ignored Qhubeka; her eyes were fixed on Beeslaar.

"Mevrou, I can really understand—" Qhubeka tried again.

"Go away! I'm not talking to you people. You … you … Get out, *you*!"

Qhubeka sat for a moment, as if she were waiting for the κ-word. Then she stood up abruptly and the older woman pulled the boy protectively towards her, something wild in her eyes.

"A word, please," Qhubeka said as she brushed past Beeslaar.

They walked through two big sliding doors onto a small stoep under a striped canvas awning. Two easy chairs faced the river. This, Beeslaar decided, was how the other half lived. To the left of the stoep, a lush garden. Flowering shrubs in bright orange and red. A long swimming pool edged with a deck of Cape teak, cypress trees in pots on the two far corners.

"What exactly are you doing here?" Qhubeka asked, stony-faced.

"Nothing. Absolutely nothing. I happened to be at the same funeral as the old lady. I just came to drop her off."

"Then there's no reason for you to hang around."

He was on the point of turning around when she spoke again: "I thought I'd be decent and respectable enough for the white people, but …" She looked up at him reproachfully, then past him to the office, where Trula Momberg now occupied the chair she had vacated.

Beeslaar tugged at the top button of his shirt collar. He didn't want to get involved, didn't know what to say. He actually just wanted to get the fuck away.

"Funeral, you said?" Her question caught him off-guard.

"Former colleague. He came to Stellenbosch to retire."

"Oom Blikkies."

"You knew him?"

"Get the circus on the road and remember not to forget the fleas on the trampolines."

One of Blikkies's sayings.

A hot flush rose in Beeslaar's chest, pushing the blood into his ears.

"So *you* must be The Kwartel," she remarked. "Albertus Markus Aurelius Kwartel. The fourth to the power of five, to infinity." It was old Blikkies's way of referring to Beeslaar's inglorious pedigree from the mine dumps of the East Rand.

Beeslaar averted his eyes, afraid that the pain would show.

"The very same." His voice was husky. He cleared his throat. "Did I hear correctly? This was a – what? A burglary gone wrong? House robbery?"

"Who told you?"

"The owner. Du Toit." He glanced at the scene inside, where Rea was still cradling the boy in her arms. "I happened to be on the spot when he phoned his mother with the news. At the funeral. She'd handed me the phone."

"And he said it was a house robbery."

"Something like that, yes. Was it something else, then?"

"Fuck knows. But that's not so important right now. The main thing is, it's a disaster. It looks as if—"

She hesitated briefly before saying: "Come and see for yourself."

For the second time that day, he was a tame goose. But this time he didn't mind. Because a stillness had descended in his head. A familiar silence. As if all his senses were quietly listening from somewhere deep within, probing the atmosphere for traces of evil that still lingered in the air. Gossamer-light spider threads, faint echoes of violence, invisible and intangible, unless you knew how to listen. It was as if his entire body became attuned to this, the strings between heart and head and body beginning to vibrate together.

She led him through the posh dining room. They tiptoed carefully, keeping to the wall. The forensic team was already busy with their marking and measuring. Dragonflies, Blikkies used to call them. They just land and look at the shit, then take off again. And you can forget about getting anything useful out of them. Takes them weeks. And you still had shit for results.

An arch separated the dining room from a big, informal living room. The wall was dotted with niches in which bottles of wine were gracefully aging.

The white dining-room carpet was dotted with blotches of blood that had been carried in from the living room. There were several footprints. Someone with a lot of blood on his clothes had walked along the wall around the dining-room table, smeared blood on the walls.

He followed Qhubeka past the dining table to the entrance of the living room, where the dragonflies were scurrying around in their plastic suits. There was a breakfast nook and bar on the left, and a TV area on the right. The floor was strewn with plants. Lots of them. And broken bits of pottery.

Then he saw the victim: a woman, sitting on a wide couch. The back of her skull had been smashed in so violently that grey brain matter oozed through splinters of bone and hair. He started when he registered the hair colour: red. Beeslaar shook his head to get rid of the shock. Not all redheads were Gerda.

"This scene has been tampered with," Beeslaar heard himself say. He was rewarded with a smile from Qhubeka. He liked the light in her eyes: a hound catching the scent of a springhare.

"Come," she said and turned around, "let's go have a look from the other side."

They returned to the front door and went outside, walking around the house to the back. There was another fountain. This time a tilted ceramic urn leaking a trickle of water. Blikkies would have had some caustic remark about that. He had a healthy contempt for rich people's fancies.

They reached a huge stoep area at the back of the house. There was a sandpit for making campfires and a gas braai stood in the corner, big enough to launch a missile to the moon.

The back of the house, Beeslaar saw, was actually the front. The part where the occupants spent most of their time – the stoep, partially covered and furnished with luxurious cane furniture with plush cushions and a large wood-and-chrome dining table, led onto a swimming pool with yet another fountain. Everything spoke of big money.

Most expensive of all: the private view of the Eerste River and Stellenbosch Mountain. It felt as if you only needed to reach out your hand to pick a handful of fynbos and proteas, or a bunch of late-season grapes from the red vineyards that ran up the mountain.

A row of French doors connected the living room to the stoep. Two of the doors were open. Qhubeka handed him gloves and a set of shoe covers. She called them "oortjies" – another term coined by Blikkies. Funny to find Blikkies's stamp on a stranger.

The coppery smell of raw meat and something chemical still lingered in the air. Fresh kill, was the thought that flashed through his head. And just below it, the musty cave smell of soil coming from the shattered flower pots that lay strewn across the marble floor.

Beeslaar's heart jumped again at the sight of the red hair. But there was no resemblance. The woman on the couch was tall and bony. Anorexically thin. The complete opposite of his Gerda. He followed Qhubeka to the couch. A giant television screen on the wall opposite the couch was switched on, the sound muted.

"Look," she said, pointing out the blood patterns around the couch: spots, tear-shaped spatters, jumbled shoe prints. Between the couch and the TV was a long glass-top coffee table. The glass was shattered. Amid the shards lay a bronze statuette. It was a Brahman bull, he saw, bloodstained and half hidden under some glossy coffee-table books. One of the books had a lion on the cover, spots of blood across its golden stare.

"She didn't die on the couch, did she?" Beeslaar asked once they were outside again.

"We found her like that."

"What time?"

"The call came in shortly after four. When the kids came home from school. The daughter, what's her name …" She squeezed her eyes shut. "Emmie, Evvie?"

"Ellie."

"Apparently she got home first. And then the boy. He phoned the dad."

"Who was where?"

"Late business lunch. The Volkskombuis restaurant."

"And he phoned you?"

"No, his lawyer did, he'd been at the restaurant with him."

Beeslaar said nothing. He stood surveying the garden, hands on his hips. Across the rivier, the grey rockface of the mountain. A bird of prey gliding on warm air currents above. Then he looked back at the house.

Decide, he said to himself, now. Before you ask the next question. Before you get hooked. Through the cheek, like one of the trout swimming in that river.

But she made the first move. "He was a full colonel, wasn't he?" she asked, her eyes also on the mountain. She was talking about Blikkies, he knew, and nodded.

"You were lucky."

She was actually damn attractive, he noted. Fine, smooth skin, the colour of dark chocolate. Prominent cheekbones. Arched eyebrows, like the wingspan of a graceful bird. A generous mouth. But it was her eyes that set her apart. Brown, with golden flecks. Clear eyes. Intelligent. He had a weakness for intelligent eyes. And big expressive mouths. Like Gerda's.

"To have had a man like Oom Blikkies in your life, I mean." She smiled. Sparkling white teeth. "I hear you're not in Jozi any more."

His shook his head, looked down at his shoes. "Thank God for that," was all he could come up with.

And then he did it: he crossed the line, succumbed to the pull of the puzzle. He asked the question.

"This scene – it's a bit *too* intimate for a house robbery, isn't it?"

5

The pain in his shin was excruciating.

It was from the struggle with the hijacker, the guy Ghaap had nabbed accidentally when he'd flung open his door before the car had come to a halt. The guy had run slap bang into the door, followed shortly by someone chasing him. A scuffle ensued, with two fighting men dancing around on Ghaap's feet and shins.

And then the shot went off.

The hijacker had fired blindly when he was overpowered. Right there, on Ghaap's shins. Ghaap himself had been blissfully unaware – he'd passed out, maybe from fright. He'd only come round when someone shone a torch in his eyes to check whether he was dead. He was still lying on the back seat of the car, his legs dangling outside, conscious of a jumble of voices and a lot of shouting. Afrikaans, English and probably Zulu. There were no Zulus in the Kalahari. So he found it hard to distinguish the language from other African languages. Mabusela and Mthethwa spoke Zulu, he knew. But that's as far as his knowledge went.

He felt like the doos of the century. Out of his depth, out of place.

"Get him out of the car," someone had shouted. "He took that bullet. And get the medics!"

Ghaap had pulled himself upright. "I'm cool," he'd squeaked. Then louder, "Leave me alone. There's nothing wrong with me!" And he was right, there was no blood and no bullet wound to be found on him. Just a bruised ego and a sore shin from being trampled on by two burly men.

It was almost six o'clock and growing dark fast, but they were still sitting in the same spot. Waiting for the scene to be written up. And waiting for the fingerprint guys to finish up with the stolen Golf so that everyone could bugger off and get on with their lives.

Mthethwa was the one who was supposed to do the paperwork. He was the most senior, promoted, Ghaap reckoned, far beyond his age and capabilities. Said to have come from the right family, with deep ANC ties that went back to the liberation struggle. It was an open secret that he believed he should have been the station commander. Not the Indian guy whose family ties apparently ran even deeper.

But Mthethwa had shifted the job onto Mabusela, who was busily writing and filling in forms under the bright cabin light of a colleague's bakkie, cigarette in the other hand, cellphone clamped between his shoulder and ear. Ghaap wondered how much writing he was getting done. Meanwhile the rest of them had to sit here twiddling their thumbs, in a tiny cul-de-sac in Mofolo, one of Soweto's many suburbs. Mthethwa himself was standing to one side, chatting to a small group of "ysterbaadjies", which was what the men here called the uniformed guys. From Mthethwa's gestures, Ghaap guessed he was recounting the story of the car chase. With himself in the starring role, of course. A darkie Vin Diesel, Soweto's own *Fast & Furious*.

Unable to make head or tail of the kasi slang, Ghaap kept to himself – seated on the back seat of the Toyota, the door open, his feet on the ground. He rested the right leg in particular because the pain was so bad.

Now and then he noticed Mthethwa motioning in his direction, eliciting guffaws from his audience.

Ghaap shoved his hands deeper into his parka pockets and hung his head. This was the last thing he'd needed: from zero to hero, and back to zero – flippin' fainted at the sound of a shot going off. Like an old woman.

He swallowed the bitter saliva that kept forming in his mouth. Wished for the hundredth time today that he was back home. For a moment he considered phoning Beeslaar. But he was on holiday, and ten to one he'd give him a tongue-lashing. Beeslaar had taken a dim view of Ghaap's sudden urge to experience Soweto. "Nowadays the place is just full of bullshitters chasing rank. They spend more time cooking the stats than catching criminals," he'd grumbled. When Ghaap told him he wanted to learn about "real crime" Beeslaar said, "Crime is the same everywhere. All it takes is one gatvol arsehole to stick a knife into his wife or his buddy – or a stranger, for that matter. The only difference is that there are more arseholes in Soweto because the place is bigger."

Ghaap tried to ignore the pain in his leg, and to his annoyance noticed one of the guys from the tracker company walking towards him.

"How's things, bro?" It was the trackie who'd finally brought down the hijacker. They were all over the place, these guys from a private company specialising in tracking down stolen cars. They looked to be damn good at what they were doing. Cowboys, the whole bunch of them, speeding around the place like bats out of hell in souped-up Golfs and Subarus. They wore their own uniform: loaded Glocks on the hip, with more than enough clips, tight-fitting jeans, stylish hunting boots. They were as much a part of the landscape of greater Johannesburg as the mine dumps and the SABC tower. And nobody's fools, either. They were a major subspecies in the greater net of law enforcement. Nearly all of them were ex-cops: old-school, hardboiled types, heads shaven or sporting military hairstyles. Smoked like diesel lorries. And they didn't take any shit from anybody.

The guy who had asked the question was short. Tough, though – judging by the forearms hanging over the open car door.

"What can I say?" Ghaap replied feebly.

"You donnered him big-time, boet!" The man's eyes twinkled in the dark. "Bugger's still bleating in the back of the van there." He indicated the police bakkie where Mabusela was working, completing his forms while a constable sat behind the wheel, engrossed in his own logbook scribblings.

"We've been looking for that meerkat for a very long time." He spoke calmly, as if he were a church elder and Ghaap a concerned member of his ward. "He's mos a specialist. Actually only goes for Lexus SUVS. He has his own starter pack and snake. He can peena any Lexus with that – and whoops, it's open! What possessed him to go for a le vora today … But I can tell you one thing – he made a fuckin' fat mistake. He's bad news, that oke. Two years ago he bashed an old antie's head in and took her Lexus. Since then he's been on the run. Till today." He produced a pack of cigarettes, lit one, and offered the pack to Ghaap, who shook his head.

"What's a 'le vora'?" asked Ghaap, desperate to be left alone. The pain in his shin was driving him mad and he wanted to inspect the damage in peace. He could swear something was cracked or splintered.

The trackie laughed. "Golf VR6. That's what they call it here in the district. And the skelms we call meerkatte. The way they crawl back into their holes the moment they see the law. Pure meerkat." He paused and peered at Ghaap, who just wanted him to bugger off. "You don't look all right, china?" The man kept his cigarette between his lips as he spoke – the words coming from a corner of his mouth. Like Popeye.

"I'm cool," Ghaap lied, heaving himself upright. But the pain that shot up from his leg made him gasp.

"Woza!" the trackie exclaimed, stepping around the car door. "Sit down, bru. Sit. Looks like you've been hurt. And you didn't even tune anything, hey?" He pushed Ghaap back against the seat and lowered himself to his haunches, gently probing Ghaap's calves with his fingers, left side first. It was when he touched the right calf that Ghaap almost jumped through the roof.

"Whoa, big guy, there's blood here. Wait. We need light!" He lifted Ghaap's leg carefully until it rested on his thighs. "Mauritius!" he called over his shoulder to the bunch of men standing around the hijacked car. "Bring me the torch! I think this laaitie caught that bullet!" Ghaap was just about to faint from the pain; his teeth started chattering uncontrollably.

One of the trackies came running. "Should we call the medics?"

The torchlight blinded Ghaap for a second, and he lifted his hand to protect his eyes.

"Jislaaik, bru. You really did catch that bullet. Must've been the ricochet. Lights! Hey, Mo! Shine the fokken torch *here*, so that I can see what I'm doing!"

Ghaap felt the man carefully untying his bootlaces. He heard a tearing sound and realised that the trackie was cutting open his trouser leg. But he was beyond caring. Right then he was fighting not to pass out. He lay flat on his back on the car seat, his jaws clenched.

He felt a sudden, searing pain. "Ouch! Fuck it, man, what the fuck you doing?"

"Relax, bru, it's out!"

Ghaap sat up and saw the trackie triumphantly hold something aloft, as if he'd just delivered a baby. "It's the bullet, bru. It's out," he called from the corner of his mouth, the cigarette still clamped between his lips. The tip created a red wavy pattern in the darkness as he spoke. More trackies and cops came running, and Mo, who'd held the torch, took the 9 mm bullet, held it between his fingers, and swung it around for all to see.

"He's bladdy lucky," Mo announced, clearly pleased. He had a hoarse, high-pitched voice that reminded Ghaap of a mafia boss in the old *Godfather* movies. "It's only a superficial wound. The bullet scarcely broke the skin."

Ghaap looked down at his leg, saw the spot just to the right of his shin bone where the bullet had lodged – between his boot and his trousers. The amount of blood was disappointingly small, he realised as he bent down to take a closer look, and the seated trackie obligingly held the trouser leg open to give him a good view.

"Shit, my china, you're lucky. If that bullet had jumped to the other side, you could have lost the old motor!" For a moment Ghaap didn't know what the man was talking about. Then he twigged. But his relief was only half-hearted, given the circumstances, even though he'd always had plans to take a wife and have some kids.

Ghaap took out his handkerchief and wiped at the trickle of blood from the small open wound. He suspected there'd be a helluva bruise tomorrow. But yes, he'd had a lucky escape, he supposed.

"That meerkat's problems has just tripled," Mo informed the bystanders. "Attempted murder of a policeman!" His announcement was greeted with the expected applause. Only one person sighed: Mabusela, whose paperwork had just doubled.

"So, how did that bullet manage to get into the rookie's leg?" he asked, noticeably irritated. He pushed his way through the crowd towards Ghaap. "Show me your leg. I want to see for myself!" He was standing so close that Ghaap could smell his breath. Behind him, the trackies shook their heads and exchanged glances. Typical of the cops of today, said the look on their faces: police work had become just another job. Eight to five, nothing more.

Ghaap kept his mouth shut and pulled his trouser leg open.

Mabusela peered at the wound. "Hai man, that's not a bullet wound. It's a scratch! Where'd that bullet go?" The tracker showed him the mark in the metal doorframe where the bullet had ricocheted before ending up at Ghaap's shin. Ghaap showed him the hole in his trousers. "Shit!" Mabusela exclaimed and clicked his tongue. Then he walked away, shaking his head.

"Let me help you up," said the short-arse trackie as he reached out his hand to Ghaap. "I'm Ghalla, by the way. Ghalla Kruger. I ride with these okes." He gestured over his shoulder to where Mo and another man in khaki fatigues were standing. "We all drive for Trackers." There were several tracking companies operating around the crime hub of Gauteng, Ghaap knew, but Trackers was the biggest, specialising in carjacking and car theft. "This is Mauritz van Schoor," Ghalla said and fisted the biggest of the three on his bulging upper arm. "His mom calls him Mouwie. But it's safer to stick to 'Mo', preferably 'Docta Mo'. And this," he said as he pointed to the third man, "this is old Dawid Vermeulen. You can call him Duif – he races pigeons, even sleeps with the bladdy birds!" Duif was a huge guy. Tall and brawny, yet lithe. Looked as if he spent hours in the gym. His shaven head was as round as a plover's egg – complete with speckles.

He didn't say anything. Nor did he offer to shake hands. Merely raised an eyebrow.

With the bullet out, Ghaap was feeling better and he introduced himself.

"Jannes," Mo repeated the name as he sized him up. "I hear you're from the Kalahari. Lion country, they say. No wonder you're not scared of the meerkats of this district!"

Ghaap laughed sheepishly.

If the big man only knew.

6

Beeslaar pushed his plate aside in disgust. God, he hoped he wasn't going off meat too. If so, he'd die of hunger. Already he couldn't face rice, and even spaghetti was starting to be a problem. Thanks to his years and years of digging up corpses. Bodies crawling with maggots.

Too many bodies. For too long. It was getting so bad that he couldn't face an underdone steak. One of these days he might turn into a bladdy vegetarian. A vegetarian in the Kalahari. Ja, right.

He'd been in this business far too long. What was it, just over twenty years? A lifetime. Too long, working for the dead.

But that's not what had messed up his appetite. It was everything about this day, starting off with the most depressing funeral sermon he'd ever had to endure. Then the redhead on the sofa, together with the fact that he was itching to get involved in the case. Right from the start, when he'd arrived at the crime scene with the two old ladies in the back of his car, suppressing the urge not to tell the bunch of rubberneck policemen standing around to bugger off. They'd heard on their radios that a rich white madam had been murdered. And the whole world and his wife had come to gawk. From far and wide. And apart from them, the place was jammed with rubberneck civilians. He recalled the guy with the crude prison tattoos. Definitely a gangster. Hands, forearms, neck, everything covered in tattooed symbols. Even his eyelids decorated with two crosses. And those teardrops under his eye. They said each drop stood for a life taken.

Qhubeka wasn't too bad. Even though she had a bit of a superior air.

She probably had problems of her own to deal with. Too young, for one. In her early thirties, he guessed. Climbing the ranks without the benefit of experience or a solid mentor. She was smart, though. And how the hell she'd linked up with Blikkies was a mystery. He'd forgotten to ask her.

Because the SC had suddenly arrived at the scene.

Lieutenant-Colonel Prometius Baadjies, Station Commander. A coloured guy in his early fifties who'd swept over the scene like a breaking wave, the paparazzi following in his wake. He had summoned Qhubeka to pose with him for the photographs. And then he'd led his entourage into the house to where Rea du Toit and her grandson were consoling each other. He had presented his moving condolences in English, so the mainstream TV news programmes, the English papers and the big shots higher up would all understand. Then came the heartfelt barrage of assurances ... the full might of the law ... right to the top, with the Minister himself ... no stone left unturned ... and all the other platitudes that were regularly trotted out on such occasions.

Beeslaar had kept a low profile and slipped away unobtrusively. He'd driven back to his guesthouse to pack his things. To go home, where he belonged.

But he didn't go. Instead he found himself wandering through the streets of the town in the late-afternoon sun, kicking up oak leaves to rid himself of the day's excess adrenaline.

But the Du Toit murder had kept preying on his mind. The peculiarity of the scene. Too much blood. Too much drama. As if the murderer had wanted to leave a message.

A burglar?

No way. A house robbery often looks like this, he had mused. When things go wrong. When the residents don't cooperate. But in broad daylight? Maybe the housebreakers' modus operandi was different here in the Cape. Usually the thugs wait for daddy to come home. Because *he* carries the keys to the safe. He would hand over the firearms. And the cash. Easy prey, a rich businessman like that. With his soft hands, who reckons his money will keep the ugly side of life outside his walls. But he was putty in their hands.

They'd just hold the gun to little Jannie's head, or the wife's, and he'd fold. He would unlock everything, even pack up his possessions for them, give them all his treasures. If they would just leave his family unharmed.

All these thoughts had rolled around Beeslaar's head as he walked. At some point he'd found himself on a winding footpath along the river, on a wide bank under giant oak trees.

It was surprisingly busy – strollers walking their dogs, people jogging in trendy sportswear. Long-legged girls with shiny ponytails, wearing skimpy maroon sports skirts and swinging hockey sticks, laughing and chatting loudly.

The maroon skirts made him think of the daughter, Ellie. She hadn't been dressed in school clothes – or had she? Maybe she was the type that detested a uniform and took it off the moment she got home. Who would put on make-up. Lots of it.

He'd crossed a narrow paved bridge and suddenly found himself in a charming formal garden with the statue of a man at the centre. He'd walked up to it to see who it was: Doc Danie Craven, the old Stellenbosch rugby legend. A replica of his famous dog was seated at his master's bronze feet, the pair staring into eternity together. The dog's name was Bliksem.

He had fondled the dog's head, unconcerned about what passersby might think, tried to detect any bliksem-like quality in the animal. Which could be spotted a mile off in the case of old Blikkies – what with his perpetual cantankerous look and his thunderous voice.

Oom Bliksem.

His thoughts returned again to Qhubeka, someone who'd obviously been fast-tracked because she was both female and black. Would she be able to stay the course? From an investigation perspective, she was already faced with a nightmare. That scene had been trampled so extensively, it looked as if a herd of cattle had wandered through it. It would take forensics years to make head or tail of all those footprints.

The boy had been barefoot, he'd noticed. And there were no barefoot prints at the scene, at least not from what he'd seen at first glance. But … it was possible they'd been erased by all the others.

The girl: she'd worn tackies, a style that was trendy among teenagers – American basketball types. North Stars, or something similar, which laced up to above the ankle.

If his memory served him correctly, he had seen blood on the tackies.

And the father? He only had a hazy recollection of the man: average height, sturdy build. A greyish-brown circlet of hair around a broad bald pate. Intense blue eyes behind glasses. The eyes brimful with bewilderment. And panic.

Beeslaar had roamed around in the golden autumn afternoon, kicking up leaves, until it grew dark and he had to ask for directions to get back to his guesthouse. The one Blikkies had booked for him.

"I can't offer you accommodation, but one of our residents has a child or some other relative who owns a guesthouse in the town. I can ask her to give us a special price. Then you come and visit for a few days. I'll show you what civilisation looks like."

And now Blikkies was sitting around in a totally different dimension – never mind civilisation.

It struck him that he was already on his way home, but still hadn't seen a proper Cape wine farm. Those in Upington didn't count. They were in the box-wine category. But a historic Stellenbosch wine farm had been a must-see on the holiday agenda.

Beeslaar had looked forward to the sightseeing trip. And the reunion. Because Blikkies had actually been the closest thing to family he'd had over the past twenty years. Everything he knew, he had learnt from him.

He'd last seen the old guy shortly before his departure from Johannesburg. When Blikkies had taken the package. Early retirement, facing a lonely old age. And then his daughter's dog, old Toffee, went and died on him. Old Blikkies and the daughter, Tertia, were not on speaking terms back then. And Toffee was the only thing old Blikkies still had left of her.

"To think that a person can get so cut up about a dog," he'd said. But they both knew that it was about more than the dog. It was about a lifetime of stuff that had built up. All the stuff you had dealt with during your life in the police service. And then something happened. Not even a big thing. Just Toffee dying. And the dam wall broke.

He'd picked up Blikkies at the old police flats on the koppie in Triomf – that's how his friend still referred to Sophiatown. The two of them had sneaked into the Westpark Cemetery that night and buried the dog. In an isolated spot high against the hill near the Jewish graves.

On the way home they'd stopped at the Seven Oceans bar in Westdene and bought a bottle of brandy. Had emptied it together.

Beeslaar's reverie was broken when the waitress removed his uneaten plate of food and asked if he was having dessert. He shook his head, asked for the bill and took a sip of the lukewarm tea he'd ordered with his meal. Unimpressed by the vinegar they passed off as wine here, he'd resorted to this.

But the tea tasted of dog piss.

He pushed the cup aside. What now?

He could stay for a few days, he had plenty of leave owing to him. He could have a proper holiday for once.

But he wouldn't.

Unless … He thought fleetingly of Gerda. Their last meeting – her soft neck and full breasts. So soft. Filling your hand with warm happiness. To walk with her in the winelands—

No, Beeslaar, forget it.

7

Ghaap really wanted to phone someone. Share the story of the evening's events. The carjacker he'd caught by accident. The fact that he had taken a bullet.

But who? His mom? It would cause too much drama.

He called the only other person he knew he could tell. But, just as he'd expected, the party at the other end of the line wasn't exactly thrilled to hear from him. "Do you know what time of the fokken night it is?"

Ghaap laughed into the phone. It was vintage Beeslaar: rude.

"And good evening to you too, Boss Beeslaar. Glad to hear you're well. I'm fine too, thanks for asking. Except that I took a bullet tonight!"

"What? Where? Are you hurt?"

"Of course I'm hurt. It's bladdy sore. And, yes, I nabbed the guy who did it, and thank you very much for asking after my health too!"

"Jokes aside, Ghaap, have you genuinely been shot?"

"'S true's Bob. But it was a stray bullet, so the damage was minimal."

"A *stray* bullet? What are you talking about, man? Did one of the gattas of that place shoot you by accident?"

Ghaap laughed. "No, it was a hijacker. We were chasing him. And then his shot hit me."

"Kak, man. If you'd really been shot you wouldn't have called me. You would've checked in at Avbob!"

Ghaap told Beeslaar the whole story. When he'd finished, there was silence at the other end.

"Hello?"

"I'm still here. I'm just trying to recover my breath. Who are the guys you were driving with?"

"Two warrant officers: Mabusela and Mthethwa."

"Mabusela, as in Bandile? Busi, they call him."

"The very same. And—"

"Is he still so fat?"

Ghaap chuckled. "I'll tell him you send your warm regards."

"He's not so bad. Who's the other guy?"

"Mthethwa."

"Any relation?" Beeslaar was referring to the current Minister of Police with the same surname.

"Can't say that I know," Ghaap replied. "He's not easy to get along with. The senior of the two, but he hates any kind of exertion. You know him?"

"Jesus, Ghaap," was the only response he got.

"His name is Sibusiso, but they call him S'bu. Used to be a helluva soccer player. Had apparently been groomed for Pirates, but buggered up his knee."

"Nah, he's from after my time there. But I know old Mabusela. Honest guy, I recall. We worked together at one stage."

"Partners? You and him?"

"No, not like that. We were just at the same station. Back when I was still in uniform."

"Doing what?"

"Dog unit. What station did you land up at?"

Beeslaar had warned him against going to Soweto, told him he was still too wet behind the ears. He first needed to gain more experience. But Ghaap had set his sights on promotion. And he believed he'd get promoted more quickly there than in the bundu of the Northern Cape, where his job highlights were breaking up booze parties and catching knifers.

"Orlando East," he replied. "Since last Monday. I'd only been at the station for a day when the SC put me with Mabusela and Mthethwa. We're supposed to be on patrol, but we've been doing more damn sitting than driving. From day one. Whole fokken time parked at Motor Mountain. And guess who's the doos that gets sent to the kuka shop each time to buy food and drink? Of course, the two gents don't contribute a cent of their own."

He heard Beeslaar laughing at the other end. "Hey," he chuckled, "that used to be my pozzie!"

"Where are you, Beeslaar? It sounds as if you're running."

"Ryneveld Street, I think. But I'm not moving. It's the wind that's making such a racket. The famous Cape southeaster. They say it can get so strong, it rips up trees, roots and all. But other than that, I think I'm getting hopelessly lost in this damn town. But where are you dossing?"

"With my cousin Charlie, in the flats in Riverlea. But he's getting on my tits, that oke. A party pig who jols all night, drinking and smoking ganja, and loafs around during the day. By the way, is it lekker by the sea? Caught any fish yet?"

"Listen here, what do you want? Are you missing your mom, or something?"

"Relax, man, relax. I actually just wanted to check something with you. And I didn't realise it was so bladdy late."

Ghaap heard Beeslaar say something, but the wind was so noisy he couldn't quite catch it. Then the line went dead.

He called again immediately. The phone rang until he reached Beeslaar's curt voicemail: "Captain Beeslaar. Leave a message." Ghaap redialled the number.

"It's late, Ghaap. And I'm not in the mood for talking shit. Phone me tomorrow." The line went dead.

Ghaap sat looking at the phone in his hand for a while, thinking. Was it his imagination, or had Beeslaar sounded a bit down? More remote and stand-offish than usual. Bladdy hell, Beeslaar better not get all soft and cosy down there in the Cape, getting ideas of staying there. Because back in the Kalahari, things just wouldn't be the same without him.

8

Beeslaar shoved his hands deeper into his trouser pockets and wished he was wearing his new, too-tight jacket. Earlier that evening the weather had been windless and warm. He stopped walking and blew his nose, irritated with the blustery wind that was making his eyes water and his nose run.

Usually, he liked wind, but this was something else. It was wild, this southeaster, fiendish. Another good reason to hit the road at the crack of dawn tomorrow. Going home. Funny that he no longer thought of Johannesburg when he thought of home. These days it felt as if he'd been in the Northern Cape all his life.

But when Ghaap had talked about Soweto earlier …

He'd *felt* the place, rather than just seeing it in his mind's eye. A dreary place, at the best of times. But people lived there. All kinds. Almost two million. Lowlifes, some of them, but mostly good, ordinary people – the majority by far. People whose lives had been harshly ruled by apartheid, who'd suffered most during the liberation struggle. These days they were still worst off when it came to crime.

He had spent a long time in Soweto, when he was still with the dog unit. Had grown to love it, in a way, the endless rows of two- and four-roomed houses. Fenced off by anything that could stand upright – ramshackle barricades against the crime. And in suburbs where there was more money, there were sky-high vibracrete walls protecting the houses. He smiled as he recalled the township name for those vibracrete walls: stop-nonsense walls.

And the thousands of tin shacks – mkhukhus, more numerous than the hairs on a dog's back. At least one in each backyard, but mostly three or four. They looked like crows' nests, cobbled together from scraps of wood, corrugated iron, black rubbish bags. And in between, scores of children, with snotty-nosed toddlers playing in the streets. And chickens. White Leghorns. Rocks, the locals called them, chickens for the pot.

When he'd arrived in Soweto in the late 1980s, early 1990s, their duties still mainly involved riot control. He remembered how they used to criss-cross the township at night – when the young comrades who controlled the streets morphed into com-tsotsis in their reign of terror. The kangaroo courts, where pipsqueaks as young as fourteen put community members on trial for alleged crimes, and administered the punishment themselves. Parents, teachers, ministers – anyone who had annoyed the comrades. With punishments ranging from beatings to necklacing.

Beeslaar shuddered and turned up the collar of his shirt. He found himself on the corner of a street that looked vaguely familiar. There were stately historic buildings, bright white gables lit by fancy street lights that resembled antique gas lamps. To his left he saw lanterns flickering outside a restaurant. The streets were quiet. Nine o'clock on a Tuesday evening. Where would the watering holes be? You'd expect a town with a university and a college to have bars. Or maybe this place was too posh?

From somewhere, he heard the thudding beat of dance music. Following the sound, he turned left and saw a bunch of young people on the pavement. It looked like some kind of club. He decided against it, crossed the road instead.

Hell, this town must be awash in money, he mused as he passed the umpteenth public sculpture on a pavement. This time it was a bronze cheetah, lit from below. It cast an ominous shadow against the white gabled wall of one of the old buildings.

These residents are the cream of the Afrikaner nation, Blikkies once told him. But he'd probably meant it sarcastically. In Blikkies's book, money didn't buy intelligence or virtue. "You're as good or as bad as your parents have moulded you – rich or poor," had been his motto. Once Beeslaar had inquired: "But then what about someone like me, Colonel? *My* dad wasn't exactly a role model."

"That's why I'm here," Blikkies had said after a long silence. "To straighten you out whenever you're out of line."

Beeslaar smiled at the thought. Blikkies hadn't been a big man. He used to call Beeslaar a "sore thumb" – with his two-metre frame he stuck out wherever he happened to be. He had dwarfed the old man, but only physically. Because many years' hard experience and wisdom were locked up inside old Blikkies. And, yes, common humanity too.

"Oubaas," a wheedling voice suddenly sounded from somewhere in the darkness. He saw a giant sculpture of a naked man, two horns on his forehead, crouched like a stalking devil. A ragged figure was leaning against the statue's massive buttocks and stretched out a cupped hand towards Beeslaar, who promptly lost his cool. He couldn't fathom why drunks everywhere were attracted to him like blowflies to cowshit. Once they'd finished talking to the fence or fighting the old lady, they turned their attention to him.

"Ja, boet. You just go back to sleep, nè?" he replied, turning around in his tracks.

"I looked nicely after the car, boss!" the voice called out behind him. "How about a few cents for a half loaf! So a man can at least have a little something to eat!"

"Bread, my arse," Beeslaar muttered and quickened his pace. He was also hungry, he realised. Maybe find a place that served fried eggs – a cheap place where the varsity students went.

He walked down a long street with an imposing white building on the right-hand side. A hall of some kind, he reckoned, maybe the town hall. There was another artwork in front, this time of Mandela's head. He turned right into a side street and kept walking. When he reached a t-junction, he heard music, which came from an old house that had been converted into a bar. *Mystic Boer* was written on the signboard outside. A student bar: the place was packed to the rafters with loud young people drinking and laughing. He had to shout to make himself heard, asking the youngster behind the counter for a coffee. Then he changed his mind and ordered a double brandy. More appropriate for launching a life without Blikkies.

He paid for the drink, added a splash of water, then looked around for a seat. A bearded guy with a ponytail slid off his bar stool and Beeslaar grabbed it. He sat down, emptied the glass in one gulp, and signalled to the barman he was ready for a refill.

This time he sipped more slowly while he mulled over the day's events. The conversation with Ghaap earlier that evening. He just hoped the young fool would survive Soweto. For a moment he wondered if he shouldn't try to get Ghaap stationed in a suburb like Westbury instead. Among his own people. He would at least understand the language. His introduction to police work in the big city would be less harsh. But Ghaap would never forgive him.

Anyway, first he was going to drink a toast to Blikkies. He took a substantial sip, his thoughts slipping back to Captain Qhubeka and to the fury he had witnessed at the murder scene. He had a nagging feeling that the crime had come from inside that house. Not from outside.

He swallowed the rest of the drink and ordered another. What the hell, he thought, this case was no concern of his.

9

Ghaap was tossing and turning in his bed.

What with his sore leg and the lumpy old mattress, he couldn't get comfortable. This place would be the death of him, he thought resentfully. Never mind Soweto, he wasn't going to make it here in Riverlea. The noise was incessant. It seemed as if the locals never went to bed. He could swear they operated in shifts to ensure an ongoing racket.

He had managed to score a lift back home shortly after midnight – a constable had dropped him off in the police bakkie. At least he could walk again, although his leg still hurt. He'd inspected it thoroughly once he was home. His shin was already blue. The 9 mm copper point had come to rest right between his trousers and his boot. He would survive. That's if he managed to sleep, because his cousin Charlie's party was only getting into full swing now. The air in the flat was already heavy with dagga fumes when Ghaap arrived. Beer bottles strewn everywhere, an American gangsta rapper's voice blaring through the loudspeakers, and Charlie's pals shouting, "Hey, watch out, the gattas are here!" Ha ha, very funny.

He had barely entered when Charlie tried to foist a female on him. She had a passion gap where her front teeth should have been. High as a kite, her eyes glassy from some or other shit drug smoked by the locals. Ghaap fled to his room and pushed a chair underneath the door handle to make sure the toothless bitch couldn't get her hands on him. He was beyond gatvol. In fact, he felt like getting into his car and buggering off back home.

On the other hand … if he returned home after only ten days in the big city he'd never hear the end of it. And he could forget about promotion for sure.

He thought about the trackies he'd met that afternoon. All three of them were ex-cops. Mo, the giant with the pinched voice, had told him he'd served for twenty-five years. In this very Soweto. But he hadn't said in which of its nine police stations. It was a vast city, Ghaap had discovered in the past couple of days. Some people estimated that, if you added the illegal immigrants, there were far more than two million inhabitants. And the numbers were growing by the day. Ghalla, the guy who'd taken the bullet out of his leg … Hell, strictly speaking, he'd taken the bullet *off* his leg, not out of it! Ghalla had left the SAPS even earlier. He was like a ratel, but with the cunning look of a hyena and a face like a bowl of scrambled eggs – coarse skin covered with scars. At first he'd worked in transit, as a security guard in the armoured vehicles that transported cash to and from banks. Dangerous work, because cash-in-transit robbers did the job with AKs and they took no prisoners. He'd left transit after one particular heist where he was the sole survivor. The robbers had pushed the heavy armoured vehicle over in order to cut through its underbelly. And when the reinforced steel plates of the chassis wouldn't give, they'd poured petrol over the vehicle and set it alight. Four guards who were trapped inside had burnt to death. Ghalla had managed to get out, and apart from everything else, lost his looks.

The youngest of the three trackies, Duif, had also left long ago. He was the laid-back, quiet Chuck Norris of the trio. The least talkative, but perhaps the most knowledgeable. Of the three, he'd been with the tracking company the longest. Smart okes. You could tell they were old school from the way they spoke.

And when he asked why they'd left the police, their replies were vague. Mo said he'd left because the time had come to resign. "But I'll go back to the cops at the drop of a hat," he'd added. "My blood is still blue. But you know how it is …"

Ghaap knew what the guy was getting at. A limited future for white men, the salaries were still pathetic, and the meerkats were winning the war.

His two "mentors" at the Orlando police station – Mabusela and Mthethwa – weren't exactly what you'd call inspirational. Mabusela was all right, but Mthethwa called the shots. And he was a lazy bugger. Except when it came to showing the blougat rookie the ropes in "the district". The blougat being Ghaap, of course.

The sounds coming from the lounge signalled that the party had shifted gear. The music had grown so loud Ghaap could feel his iron-framed bed vibrate.

He jumped up and yanked his door open, strode furiously towards the two big loudspeakers under the TV. He pulled the cords out of both and flung them aside. In the stunned silence that followed, he walked back to his room, pushed the chair under the door handle, and collapsed on his bed.

10

It was almost two o'clock in the morning when Beeslaar finally arrived at his guesthouse.

By rights he should have arrested the guy who gave him a lift. It wasn't far, just down the road, but still. He had matched Beeslaar with the Klippies, shot by shot. At some point they'd switched to Sambuca, which was obviously a mistake. Because Sambuca was invariably followed by tequila. And tequila left you thirsty. So you needed something "softer", like cane for the pain. And so on.

He fumbled around in his trouser pocket for the front-door key. His hand touched the damp handkerchief. Somewhere in the course of the past four hours he and his new young pal had swapped sob stories about life and shed a few surreptitious tears.

He struggled to see where exactly the keyhole was, as he was standing in his own shadow.

At the sound of a voice behind him, he jumped.

"Good evening, Captain Beeslaar. Do you need a hand?"

Qhubeka.

He turned around and was blinded by the bright light of a torch. "Um … are you also staying here?"

"I was on my way home from work," she said, lowering the torch. "Thought I'd drive past to see if you were awake. But you were busy elsewhere. Very busy, it seems. Give that to me."

For a moment he was confused.

"The key!"

He tried aiming for the keyhole again, but dropped the key instead.

She bent down and picked it up. "Seems like your aim is a bit off tonight. Come on, stand aside." There was laughter in her voice. A lovely voice, he decided.

"There we are!" she said as the door opened.

He held on to the door frame, afraid that he was looking as drunk as he felt. "But why were you looking for *me*? Is there a problem?"

She shook her head. "No, I just thought I'd come past. You'd better get to bed," she said.

"Sorry, I'm a bit drunk," he mumbled. He wanted to say something more, but she had already turned around and walked off. A moment later, he heard a car engine start.

11

"Albertus, it's Rea du Toit. From Great Gables. I hope I haven't woken you up."

Her voice cut through his brain like a meat saw. Why did old people always have to shout on a phone?

He sank back and tried to see what the time was.

"Is it convenient for me to talk?"

Beeslaar cleared his throat. "Go ahead," he managed to croak.

"It's about – we are – it's been a terrible shock. I can't tell you." She sniffed loudly. Began again: "You always think it can't happen to you. I don't know why. But you never imagine it. We – I wasn't myself yesterday."

"I understand, Mrs du Toit."

"I just didn't want you to think ... I was a bit sharp with the poor little black woman. It was the shock. Malan is my only son."

Beeslaar rubbed the sleep from his eyes and suppressed a yawn. *Poor little black woman.* He wondered how Captain Qhubeka would react to that.

"But that's why I'm calling you. Balthie isn't here any more – we can't go to him like we used to, you know?"

She paused.

Beeslaar tried to yawn soundlessly. He had slept like a three-ton ox.

"It's just that we – we don't know whether the local police – how can I put it. That they ..."

"It's understandable to feel like that, Mrs du Toit."

"I'm not a racist, Albertus. But I don't have much faith in the people here. You'd think that this town was still decent. But just the other day a man died *inside* the police cells. A family man, respectable. Who'd been locked up because ... Ag, he'd been drinking. But then they put him in a cell with a career criminal. Now he's dead. It's a nest of corruption there, and you dread what could happen! What if they locked Malan up? If Balthie were still here, he could have advised us. Told us what we can do. My son, Malan. He's—" Her voice choked up.

Beeslaar waited for her to compose herself.

"He wants to – he's talking about private investigators. Because ..."

"Mrs du Toit, I suppose it's his right to appoint private investigators. But maybe you should just—"

She didn't give him a chance to finish: "I don't know if you're aware of the student who was murdered here in Stellenbosch a few years ago. A pretty young girl, I've forgotten her name. But the story was all over the news. Her murder was just like Elmana … just like what happened to her. In the girl's case, the local police immediately accused her boyfriend. And then it turned out that it hadn't been him after all. It all came out in court. They'd fabricated evidence to make the boy look guilty!" Lowering her voice, she went on: "And now we're faced with something similar. And I'm worried. Because those two grandchildren of mine … They can't lose their father as well!"

Beeslaar sighed inwardly. In the course of the night he had also wondered how long it would take before someone drew a connection with that sensational case. Rea du Toit wouldn't be the only one. She sounded out of breath, tense. She'd probably been haunted all night, he reckoned, already visualising her son lying in a pool of blood in the police cells.

"Mrs du Toit …" Beeslaar had a splitting headache. And he was nauseous, as last night's cane and lemonade kept repeating. What had possessed him? Then he felt his stomach heave.

"I'll call back soon," he blurted, and fled to the bathroom.

It was only when he stood under the shower a few minutes later that he realised what the woman had actually asked him. If you could call it asking, because it had been closer to blackmail. And she sounded as if she didn't easily take no for an answer.

He soaped his whole body. Then he suddenly remembered the front-door episode with Captain Qhubeka in the early hours. Hell, he'd made an absolute arsehole of himself.

He got out from under the shower and wrapped the towel around his body, wiped the flat of his hand across the fogged-up mirror. Qhubeka would have been busy last night. Along with the dragonflies and the fingerprint guys. Would they have any clues yet? Malan du Toit was probably one of the town's best-known millionaires. The case was likely to attract a lot of attention.

By the time the phone rang again, he had finished shaving and was dressed in a creased pair of jeans.

"Mrs du Toit," he answered, as calmly and politely as possible. Outside, the day was breaking and he was keen to hit the road.

"Qhubeka," said the voice at the other end. "Ready for some breakfast?"

He was still gulping in surprise as she continued: "In half an hour, at Julian's, at the Eikestad Mall. Your hostess will be able to give you directions." The line went dead.

Beeslaar stared at the phone in his hand before putting it down slowly. This was the last thing—

But his musings were cut short when the phone rang again. This time he answered with a cautious "hello". For all he knew, the caller might be the chief commissioner himself, since all of a sudden everyone seemed to be looking for him.

"Albertus, it's Tannie Rea." This time she got straight to the point: "What I still wanted to ask was whether you couldn't please keep an eye on matters for us?"

"Mrs du Toit—"

"Just call me by my name. Or tannie. I don't stand on ceremony."

"Tannie, with the greatest respect, I really have to be on my way today."

"What about us, Albertus? Should we now …" She took a deep breath. "We'll just have to muddle along on our own. Balthie would've helped us. I *know* he would. He would have understood, known what it feels like. The – the – powerlessness! You have no idea. Being at the mercy of … And the people who're supposed to protect you are, in a word, incompetent! And they don't give a damn, because we're white!" She started crying.

He gave her time to calm down so that his words would sink in.

"Tannie Rea, I can't do what you're asking of me. I'm not allowed to do private work. I could be suspended—"

"Malan will *pay* you!"

"Then he should rather get a professional private investigator to assist him. Someone like Piet Byleveld, for instance. He has retired from the police and does private work, not so? This is what I—"

"It didn't help in the case of the student, Albertus. And it won't work in our case either. With her murder there were dozens of private investigators, from as far as America, but the police still tried to pin it on the boyfriend. Meanwhile the *real* killer is still at large. And now he – now he has struck again!"

"Tannie Rea, honestly, if I were in a position to help you, I would gladly do so. But I'm not allowed to get involved."

"Not even as a friend of the family?"

"But Tannie, I'm not exactly—"

Without giving him a chance, she cut in: "*I* consider you a friend of the family, Albertus. Balthie spoke a lot about you. He always told me he regarded you as the son he never had."

Beeslaar felt his heart expand, knocking against his ribs. Reluctantly, he agreed to stop by before leaving for home.

"Remember to come to Willem Bester's house, directly to the left of my son's home. He's putting us up for the time being. Willem is a family friend and also my son's lawyer."

It was a pleasant morning, and Beeslaar decided he'd walk to Julian's. According to his hostess, the coffee shop was quite close.

His phone rang. Blikkies's daughter, Tertia: "Albertus, good morning. I'm sorry I'm bothering you so early." She sounded dazed. "Mynhardt and I were wondering whether you'd like to accompany us for the – to scatter my dad's ashes?"

Mynhardt. That would be the son-in-law. He hadn't had a chance to meet him at the funeral.

"I'd actually planned on returning home today," he replied guardedly, but his heart contracted. She was Blikkies's only child. Who'd probably seen far less of her father in her childhood years than Beeslaar and the rest of the boys had. Because the old man was always on the job. "I'm the sweeper," he used to tell new recruits. "Because I've been put on earth for one thing only: to sweep the rubbish from our streets. Me and my baby: Miss Darling Deadly." Then he'd put his hand on the z88 holstered on his belt.

"I think," Tertia said, "I think it would be nice if you ..."

Beeslaar stopped walking so that he could hear better. Her tremulous voice was getting softer, and he was surrounded by noisy traffic. His head felt as if an army tank had gone over it. He glanced at his watch. It was still too early for a pharmacy, but there might be a shop in the Mall that stocked Panado.

"Mynhardt agrees, it would've meant a lot to my dad if you were there. Yesterday was a bit ... We didn't really have a chance to talk properly. My dad was so fond of you, you know." Once again he felt the jolting of his heart.

"When did you think of doing it?"

"Sunday?"

How was he going to occupy himself between now and Sunday? "Look," he said. "I'd really love to, but ... Do you mind if I call you back? I've sort of ... I must actually get back to the Northern Cape. And, er, I'll come and say goodbye before I leave."

He started walking again. Maybe the breakfast would help his hangover. His last bit of solid food had been a koeksister at the funeral yesterday. The midnight snack at the bar didn't count. And the restaurant food earlier last night didn't count either. He had barely touched it.

The morning air was a bit chilly, and he lengthened his stride to get warm. He was constantly aware of the mountains that encircled the town. Probably more so because there weren't really any high buildings. In Merriman Avenue, he turned right, as the guesthouse owner had directed him. It was a busy road, full of cars and taxis. People on their way to work, some transporting children to school: dolled-up mommies in big suvs, the obligatory cellphone to the ear. In the back, the little head of a kid, bobbing inquisitively from side to side.

He walked until he reached the crowded intersection at Andringa, and veered off to the left.

Qhubeka was already seated inside, he saw through the window. He hurriedly wove his way through the tables outside on the pavement – for the smokers.

"I've ordered for you," she said when he reached the table. "A full-house breakfast and a jumbo coffee. Plus a few Panados."

He sat down opposite her.

"And? How do you feel?"

Her face was solemn. He couldn't read her expression.

He shrugged. "Sorry about last night," he mumbled sheepishly. He must have been totally motherless, because the only thing he could recall was that she'd been at the guesthouse. Had he made some or other gaffe? Or, even worse, tried to chat her up?

She added sugar to her cappuccino and started stirring. Her hands were slender, the long nails a bright red. No wedding ring.

"I don't know what exactly your role is with the Du Toit family," she said, "but I'd like to warn you in advance: I don't tolerate freelancers in my investigations. Especially not if you're going to prejudice the family against me."

"What? Me?" He remembered the grandmother's outburst the day before. "I'm on my way home, Captain. I just need to say goodbye to a few people and then I'm skedaddling."

She said nothing, merely regarded him steadily. Then she lifted the cup to her mouth, took a sip, and wiped away the fine white line on her upper lip.

"Captain, honestly. I haven't been interfering, really and truly."

She put the cup down slowly. "You think I'm not up to this, don't you?" A slight smile played around the corners of her mouth, but her eyes glittered dangerously. "And," she added, "in case you didn't know, I've already seen this morning's papers."

"Did the family speak to the media?"

She nodded.

"And they said they didn't believe they would receive fair treatment?"

Another nod.

"The gogo," he said, "she phoned me this morning. She wants me to lead an independent investigation."

"And you said what?"

"That I'd drop by before driving back north."

She seemed satisfied, but then she surprised him: "I wouldn't be in such a hurry."

"What do you mean?"

"You're on leave, aren't you?"

"Ja, but I want to be back at work tomorrow."

She raised an eyebrow. "I wouldn't drive off today if I were you. For all practical purposes you're not sober yet, number one."

52

Beeslaar glanced at a bunch of students, cigarettes at the ready, who were traipsing out to smoke on the pavement. "And number two?"

"You could come in handy."

"*Handy*?"

"Be useful."

"Useful."

"Is there an echo in here, Captain Beeslaar?"

"There's *something*, Captain Kewbeka."

She laughed suddenly, her eyes dancing. The laugh was warm and deep. She reminded him of something regal, the long, elegant neck of an impala. But her eyes were pure panther.

"Qhubeka," she corrected him, emphasising the plopping click of the "Q". "That's how my colleagues address me. And I want to make a deal with you. That you will keep me informed."

"Informed of what?"

But he knew exactly what she was talking about. And he wasn't going to take the bait, that's for sure. "My car is already packed. And I've checked out of the guesthouse."

She didn't respond. Her focus was on the two plates of food that had arrived: fried eggs, deep-fried Vienna sausages, bacon and baked beans. And a basketful of white toast.

She surprised him again, bowing her head in what he suspected was a silent prayer.

"Eat, before it gets cold," she said when she had finished, and as she caught him staring, she tucked into her breakfast with relish.

12

His car was gone.

Ghaap was apoplectic with anger; he was way beyond words.

He stared at the empty space where his car should have been. Where he *knew* it was parked the night before because he'd checked on it first thing after being dropped off. He had hobbled, sore leg and all, to this very spot to make sure it was still there. The very spot where his car was now *not* parked. His brand-fokken-new second-hand car! Overhauled and resprayed. New alloy mags. State-of-the-art sound system, on which he'd blown his entire Christmas bonus.

His heart started pounding. He could swear he was going to have a coronary. Right there.

"Hey, my bro," he heard his cousin's cheerful voice behind him. Nonchalantly, Charlie was standing on the bottom step of the building's metal staircase, one hand on the railing and the other pulling a cigarette from behind his ear. He was emaciated, like a stray dog. But cool beyond cool – hair shaved in patterns like a gangsta rapper, red gemstones in his earlobes, and cheap, crude tattoos snaking into his scrawny neck. Everything about him enraged Ghaap.

"Which one of the fuckers you tikked and zolled with last night took my car? *Who*?"

"Hey, my bro, chew some ice, ek sê … chillax. You caused me a lot of damage last ni—"

"I'm not your fokken bro, you rubbish! Where's my car, hey?"

Charlie took a cautious step backwards, up the stairs. "No, man, I really can't say I know. But you sure buggered up my sound system."

Ghaap charged at him.

Charlie fell back against the stairs and tried to make himself as small as possible. But there was no stopping Ghaap. He grabbed his cousin by his oversized t-shirt and yanked him from the stairs. Charlie moaned, his scrawny arms folded protectively over his head.

"I'm going to have the whole fokken lot of you locked up!" Ghaap yelled. He was struggling to get Charlie to stand up so that he could donner him. He let go of the t-shirt and the bastard tried to scramble up the stairs again. But Ghaap jerked him from the staircase and threw him down on the wet grass.

"What are the names of those scumbags that booze and ganja with you?" Ghaap shouted, gasping for breath. He aimed a kick at Charlie, who had curled himself up like a hedgehog, pleading.

"Answer me, you bliksem! Stop whining, and talk!" Ghaap barked. Which only prompted Charlie to moan louder. Ghaap took him by the feet and dragged him to where the tracks of the car were still visible in the grass.

"This is where my car stood, bliksem! And this is where I'm going to moer you until you tell me who stole my car. Do you hear me? Do you, fucker!"

"Okay, okay, okay, Jansie! Don't moer me."

"Get up, bliksem!" Ghaap aimed another kick at the yelling man.

"Wait! Wait, my bro! *Wait!*" By now Charlie was really sobbing, and Ghaap bent down to help him to his feet. Expecting a slap, Charlie scrambled away on all fours.

Ghaap let him go and tried to get his heartbeat under control. He swore again and cracked his knuckles. "You'd better listen properly," he said in a calmer tone. "I want the names and addresses, okay? Every last one of them!"

Charlie inched warily up the stairs on his bottom. "Jansie, my bro," he said.

"I'm not your fokken bro. And my name is *Johannes*. You hear me, bliksem? *Johannes*! And I'm not related to you, and I'm no longer your fokken tenant either. Plus, you owe me fifteen thousand rand! For my car! You told me my car was safe here, but you fokken lied! You *and* your mother. You people took me for a mampara, nè? But this mampara will show you! If my car isn't back here in this exact spot at lunchtime, Charlie, I'm locking you up. Did you hear me?"

"No, man, they're always taking cars here! It's not me! Not my tjommies either! But what about my speakers?"

"Fuck your speakers, man. You just get my car back."

Ghaap aimed another blow at Charlie, who quickly moved up the stairs.

"I'll be back at lunchtime," he said. "To fetch my car."

Then he turned around and strode off blindly – he had no idea where he was going. All he knew was that he had to get away from this place. Otherwise he'd commit murder.

13

Gerda Matthee rubbed a hand absent-mindedly over her belly. This baby was impatient, the kicks making her bump bulge at times. A girl. And one thing was certain: she'd be big. Must be the father …

A shadow slid across her mind.

Albertus: his heavy, black eyebrows. The permanent frown. His eyes hiding under all the gruffness. Dark green eyes, with gold flecks that sometimes danced. And his body – like a rock, yet somehow soft when he was with her.

He didn't know about her pregnancy. She hadn't had the strength to tell him. And now the baby was almost due.

She forced her thoughts onto a different track. Today was her last day at work before the start of her maternity leave. She and her colleagues were going to celebrate with a brunch at the Lucky Bean in Melville.

The gridlocked traffic suddenly began to move. She took her foot from the brake. Someone hooted behind her. A greeting. She saw in her rear-view mirror that it was her boss, Hennie Jordaan. In some ways the giant city of Johannesburg was still a village, she thought, and waved back. Hennie had been good to her. Concerned about her welfare. He'd arranged for a cake to be bought when she broke the news that she was pregnant again. Had flowers delivered, out of his own pocket.

Most important of all, his job offer had been a godsend.

They'd been at school together, but had lost contact. Until he'd turned up at the funeral. She hadn't even realised he was there. Everything had passed in a haze because she'd been given an injection just before the church service.

She took a deep breath as the pain reasserted itself. It was there deep inside her, as always. When would it let up?

She switched on the radio. Gareth Cliff was talking about cool ouballies like Willie Nelson and Clint Eastwood. She smiled as she wondered whether he even knew the literal meaning of "ouballie". Would he refer to someone in English as an "old scrotum"?

She spotted a gap in the traffic and shot out of her lane, past the traffic light that had turned orange. A hawker with a huge pile of stuff in his hands jumped nimbly out her way.

The chilly autumn-morning air blew in through the car windows, which she kept slightly open. It made the glass more resistant to shattering in case of a smash-and-grab, she was told. It had already happened to her twice, with the loss of her handbag plus its contents. Cellphone, make-up, ID book, driver's licence, Kleinpiet's day-mother money. Credit cards.

It was better to stow one's handbag in the boot, out of sight. But her mornings were hectic, and she tended to forget.

Kleinpiet wasn't a morning child. It was as if he were scared of starting the day. He didn't want to eat, just wanted to be held all the time. Of course she knew why this was the case. She'd been pregnant with him when it all happened. And there was no way it wouldn't have affected him too, in her belly. And when the time came he hadn't wanted to be born. It had taken an induction to get him out.

And in the mornings there was also her father who had to be sorted out for the day. Pa, who was slowly turning into a child again, right before her eyes. She didn't know how long she'd still be able to care for him at home.

An irritable hooter jolted her, and she saw that the traffic had started moving once more. She released the brake, but soon had to apply it again.

Baz wanted to get married. But she wasn't sure. There were too many issues right then. Things were too fluid, too complicated.

That was exactly his point: "Just stop working, Maggie." He called her that, like in the old Rod Stewart song, "Maggie May". Because he was a year or two younger than her.

But she enjoyed her work. The fact that she was building a new life for herself. The salary was pathetic, admittedly, but she was okay as far as money was concerned. Ma had provided for her from the huge sum that the sale of Oupa's farm had realised way back when. Over the years, Ma hadn't touched any of the money. Instead, she'd invested it for a retirement she'd never been able to enjoy.

There was a defective traffic light up ahead. It was the same story every morning: traffic lights that were out of order, or repairs on the new Rea Vaya bus lane between the city and Soweto.

At first she'd been pleased with the short distances between Kleinpiet's daycare, her workplace and the house. But no matter how close it all was, the traffic was still terrible. The small private school in Parktown where she worked was only a stone's throw away. On the map, that is. The house was in Seventh Avenue, at the foot of the Melville Koppies. The day mother's house was just behind the koppies. But that meant going around them: north in the mornings on Beyers Naudé, then right into Judith. She enjoyed the scenic part of the route running through the municipal sports grounds into the leafy suburb of Emmarentia, where she dropped Kleinpiet off.

Then she had to go southwards again, via a jam-packed Empire Road. And there was no other option: she had to get past Wits University to get to Parktown's quiet, tree-lined streets and her school. The job wasn't exactly rocket science, but it wasn't boring either. And the people were nice. She enjoyed being among normal people. No cops. People who had nothing to do with death.

But there was no escaping death. It always managed to track you down. Like in Ma's case. A stroke, and Ma was gone in the blink of an eye.

Yet somehow her mother's death had convinced her to move from Germiston on the East Rand to the city. And she'd needed a bigger house in any case to look after her dad. In a better environment, though. More civilised. Away from the mine dumps. Too many ghosts around there.

She could start afresh. Maybe. With a new man in her life, Baz, a glimmer of hope.

Bazhunaishvili Rezart, with the melancholy appearance of people who came from the Balkans. Old nations. Ancient histories – of which she was completely ignorant. Though Baz himself didn't know very much about his ancestors either. His grandfather had come to South Africa during the forties to work on the goldmines, but he soon found out his complexion had been a shade too dark in an era of white Afrikaner affirmative action.

He'd ended up running a shop with mostly black customers. Baz's dad was supposed to take over the business, but he died in the border war. In Angola. A landmine or something.

Then after 1999, following the ethnic cleansing in Kosovo, a sizeable Albanian community had established itself in the City of Gold. The shop started specialising in imported Albanian food products. A restaurant was added – Greek and Albanian cuisine, which are very similar.

Baz had virtually grown up in the shop, according to his mother. Ma Bet, as he called her.

He'd been everyone's darling, with his huge cinnamon-brown eyes and his pitch-black curls. He now wore his luxuriant shoulder-length hair either loose or tied back in a ponytail. Large, sensitive mouth, a strong, straight nose, and heavy eyebrows. She had a weakness for dark men, there was no getting away from it. When Gerda saw him the first time, he'd taken her breath away. He'd looked like a GQ model, though not at all gay. With a delightful predilection for older women. Especially older, red-haired women.

The traffic crept forward again and Gerda pulled away. Noticing a gap to her right she pushed in, only to be rewarded by a blaring hooter. Pigs. They'd rather die than give someone else a chance. She turned off into the school road and accelerated.

The baby moved in her belly and her heart melted. She could feel the endorphins rushing through her brain, right down to her extremities. Her cheeks glowed and there was a tingling sensation in her nipples.

A little girl. Who would love fairies and everything pink and be a playmate for Kleinpiet. Who'd kiss him, take his hand, try to console the sadness he carried with him.

The tears came before she could stop herself. She blinked and opened the window for some air.

This pain would never leave her. It held her in its merciless grip. A searing white flame, flaring up unexpectedly, especially on certain days. Like today …

Today it was as if the world had tilted just a little bit, casting long shadows. Pa, who seemed just a bit wilder than yesterday. Baz – who was just a tad … what? Maybe it was just the autumn – Johannesburg, with its millions of trees, was turning brown and rusty-red underneath a high, bleached sky.

She turned in at the school gates and parked under a plane tree. It hadn't yet shed all its leaves, thank God. The sun was still sharp, though the nights were getting colder.

She took a last look in the mirror and fixed her tear-smudged eye make-up.

Okay, deep breath, chin up, face the day.

Climbing out of the car, she noticed a white Honda Ballade drive slowly past the school gate. Inside were two young men, sunk low in their seats. The driver's head was covered by a hoodie. She couldn't see his face at all. The other guy looked straight at her, a black cap pulled low over his forehead, his eyes hidden behind dark glasses. As soon as they had passed the gate, they sped off, tyres screeching.

And suddenly the shadow was back in her mind.

14

Beeslaar felt like a child who'd found a broken toy in his Christmas stocking: excitement giving way to disappointment.

He was fighting the feeling of excitement. Hard. Because he knew it spelt trouble. If he knew what was good for him, he'd bugger off home.

Back to the garden he was laying out in the red soil of his backyard. And to the comfortable small-town rhythm of his life in the Northern Cape.

The unusual policewoman opposite him was steadily working her way through her breakfast, and he followed suit.

Captain Qhubeka finished first. She belched politely behind her hand and reached for the toothpicks. Then sat back and drank her cappuccino in silence as she waited for him to finish eating.

"Is the Panado working yet?" she asked.

"The food's working."

"What do you make of yesterday?"

"Do you know what's been stolen?"

"Cash from the safe – about ten thousand rand. It beats me why anyone would want to keep so much cash. And her wedding ring, apparently a rock of a diamond."

"There's enough security in and around the house, but no broken window panes or anything—"

"And it turns out that she was shot too." She dropped the news like a stone.

"Jeez."

"According to forensics. But that's all. The rest is useless."

"Fingerprints?"

She shook her head, clicking her tongue in mild irritation. She was holding her head high, chin slightly tucked in, as she contemplated him. There was definitely an air about her, Beeslaar realised again. Arrogance? Maybe it was just the way she seemed comfortable in her own skin. Not putting on a front. Yet there was nothing personal in her manner. And despite the expressive eyes and mouth, she was a master of the stony-eyed stare.

"So, the daughter discovered the body?"

"Yes, apparently she was the first to arrive home. She just wanted to flop down in front of the TV, but found her mother there, literally and figuratively spread out across the room."

"And then?"

"I'm not sure. The girl herself can't remember anything else, according to the dad. She'd locked herself in her room. Maybe she thought the perpetrator was still in the house. That's the dad's speculation. It was the boy that phoned him with the news."

"So both kids were at the scene?"

"Yes. But the boy said he'd only seen the blood in the dining room – the streaks along the wall and the footprints and so on. He'd realised something was wrong, ran outside and phoned his dad."

The waiter collected their plates and Qhubeka ordered more coffee for both of them.

He let her have her way, his mind on the red-headed woman, Elmana du Toit, and the Australia-shaped pool of blood next to the coffee table.

"Most of the blood was on the floor in front of the couch. Presumably that's where she died. So, who would have moved her corpse? And how did all three of them get blood on themselves?"

She didn't respond, just gave him a fixed stare. Her face was open, all senses alert to him. Like a cat sizing up a mouse.

"I don't have all the facts in front of me, Captain. But to my mind it doesn't look like a house robbery. There's far too much anger. I, well, I would look around closer to home. Don't you think?"

She blinked.

He felt as if he were squirming under her gaze. But he knew the trick – the old elevator method. People don't like silences. They need to fill them compulsively, with actions or words.

"The victim's husband, Malan du Toit, how did he make his money?" he asked.

"Old Cape royalty, the Du Toits. French descent, they say."

"Huguenots."

She gave him a blank look.

"A bunch of Protestant refugees who fled France in the late 1600s when their Catholic king started giving them a hard time."

"A bit before my time," she remarked drily. "But you might have heard about the famous pecking order among the monied whites here in the Boland? The Du Plessis lot would only speak to the grander Le Rouxs, and they speak only to the much grander Du Toits. And the Du Toits speak only to God." Her eyes twinkled mischievously. "Our Mr du Toit seems to be one of them, inherited his money. But he's also good at what he does. Has a real Midas touch when it comes to property and apparently made his millions from property all over the Cape. During the boom, of course."

"And nowadays? Aren't most people in the property industry going through hard times?"

"Not all of them. Du Toit appears to be a survivor."

"Do we know what time it happened?"

She shook her head.

"Yesterday was a hot day. But the blood there – it wasn't exactly hours old. What did her family members say?"

"The children were home by about half past three. School comes out at half past one, but the boy, Pieter-something ..."

"Dawid-Pieter, if I remember correctly."

"He was at some or other youth movement meeting, and apparently his sister had a piano lesson."

Beeslaar chewed his lip. "So, she was still warm. The kids must have touched the body."

"Indeed. The smear marks on the wall were caused by Ellie, the daughter. The tracks going up the stairs are hers and the dad's."

"I saw her tackies yesterday," said Beeslaar. "Covered in blood. But less of it on Dawid-Pieter. He was barefoot, but there was no blood on his feet. Might the blood on his body have come from his sister?"

She wiggled her head, weighing up the possibility.

"And the father also had a lot of blood on him. Did *he* move the body?"

Qhubeka shook her head. "He denies it."

"What time did you arrive there?"

"Within minutes. I was in the neighbourhood."

"Okay. So what would *I* concentrate on now – hypothetically speaking, that is?"

She lifted an eyebrow but said nothing. With her long, elegant neck, she gazed at him from queenly heights. It was a patronising look, making him feel like some kind of minion. Or maybe it was just the hangover.

Their second round of coffee arrived. Ordinary coffee, this time. She emptied three sachets of sugar into hers. He stopped her as she lifted the milk jug to his cup.

She smiled, a lovely, warm smile, wiping any traces of arrogance from her face.

"Well," he said, stirring his coffee, "I'd be inclined to do it by the book. All the routine stuff. Usual suspects, burglars who've been released from jail recently. The obvious things, neighbours, domestic workers, gardener, and so on. Strangers in the neighbourhood, to eliminate them as suspects. Then I would focus on the father—"

"Who's already told the media in no uncertain terms that I'll make *him* the black sheep. That there'll be another fuck-up with forensics. We'll be fabricating fingerprints, like in the case of that student. And again be sued for forty-six million rand. Was it by any chance you who told him what to say?"

"What? Look, Captain. You can call me a racist, a sexist, a boer or whatever you like. But there's one thing you sure as hell can't accuse me of. And that's fucking with a colleague's case. Pardon my language. But really, buggering up another cop's case in order to brown-nose some rich guy. White or black or whatever."

She didn't reply, just gave him the sphinx treatment.

He took a sip of coffee and changed tack: "You said Malan du Toit is in the property market?"

"A developer."

"And the wife?"

"Don't know yet. But Charmaine, my colleague, is investigating the money angle. She works with the gang unit and knows her stuff, constantly digging into people's finances. Poor thing worked right through the night. Maybe she'll have something by the time I get back to the office."

"Right. So, how has the credit crunch affected him? Is he sinking? Or is he swimming? And what was the state of the marriage? I'd also check out the friends, if I were you. Family members. Have you spoken to the grandmother?"

She smiled. "Ja, tough old nut, with an attitude. But old Prammie buttered her up. After the TV people left, he had a long chat with her."

"Prammie?"

"That's we call the SC. Because of his high-pitched voice. Like a hungry baby mewling for its mother's pram. And his name, of course. Prometius Baadjies."

"What's he like?"

"Could be worse."

"And you get along?"

"We're both Bolanders, so we understand each other, we speak the same Capey taal."

Rather unusually, her English had a "Capey" accent too, he noted.

As if she were reading his thoughts, she said: "Is it so strange for a Xhosa to speak the language of the settlers?"

He looked down sheepishly, and she laughed at his embarrassment. Next thing he knew, he was laughing too.

"I grew up in Wellington," she explained, "and the best school in town was the Hoërskool. All my mates were Afrikaners."

"How many languages do you speak?" he asked.

"Xhosa, Afrikaans, English, Sotho, enough Zulu not to sound like a moegoe. But I didn't invite you to breakfast to show off my language skills. We're here to talk business, okay?"

When the bill came, she refused to let him pay. "This is my town, so I'm paying," she said with a smile. "But you can pay next time, if you'd like to."

"Captain Kewbeka ... Chewbeka ..." Abandoning all attempts to pronounce the click in her name, he said: "I doubt that there'll be a next time."

She said nothing, but her eyes twinkled. They both knew what had transpired here this morning: she'd dangled the bait in front of him. And he'd taken it.

"Let me put it this way," he said, hoping that he looked as resolute as he felt. "Oom Blikkies's daughter asked me to stay till Sunday. For the scattering of his ashes. And ... er—"

His phone interrupted him and he grabbed it gratefully.

"Sergeant Ghaap! How's life treating you in Soweto?" he exclaimed cheerfully and slipped out from under her eyes.

15

"My car's been stolen!"

He had to say it twice before Beeslaar got it.

Ghaap had started walking in what he reckoned was the general direction of Soweto. He had to do *something*.

What was up with Beeslaar? He sounded far too jolly on the phone. The big man was probably enjoying himself in a restaurant, judging by the background noise. Then the line became clearer. Beeslaar must have stepped outside.

"What do you mean, your car's been stolen?" he asked. "Are you sure? You haven't perhaps mislaid it? When last did you drive it?"

Beeslaar didn't seem to grasp the gravity of his news. "Last night!" Ghaap shouted angrily. "But that's not the issue. The car's gone! It was still in the same spot last night. And this morning it's gone. Vanished! As in missing! Disappeared! As in *not here*. Okay?"

"Okay, Ghaap, calm down. I get it. But what am *I* supposed to do about it?"

Ghaap's irritation level rose another notch. "You can tell me where to start looking. That's what—"

"Hate to break it to you, old Ghaap, but that car's already scrap."

"Excuse me? We're talking about *my car*. The one that got me here without any problems. It wasn't on its fokken last legs. I drove it all the way here! There was nothing wrong with it!"

"It's been stripped, Ghaap! Long time ago. I'd say shortly after it was taken, half an hour, tops. Don't even bother looking for it."

Ghaap stopped walking and gazed at the world around him. An ugly world. Blocks of low-cost flats, graffiti on every wall. The mustard-yellow mine dumps against the drab sky.

"And I bet you'd find the shell somewhere along the Golden Highway. That's if they haven't chopped that up too. A skorokoro like yours – hell, it's almost vintage. Just its parts alone must have rarity value by now. Even its bumpers and—"

Ghaap felt he was about to burst a blood vessel. "What are you talking about, Beeslaar? And what about my new sound system, hey? It cost almost as much as the bladdy car itself!"

"You can whistle for it, Ghaap. Your car's gone, my friend. Sound system and all."

"But – shit, I still owe money on it."

"And you don't have insurance."

Ghaap clicked his tongue. "I'm not asking for a situation update. I'm asking you where I should start looking! You're supposed to know this place. Where do I go?"

There was silence on the other end of the line. He waited.

"Sorry, Ghaap. It's wragtig bad, man, but that car of yours is history."

Ghaap stopped at a busy intersection, trying to spot a street name somewhere, in vain. Then he started walking again.

"The best thing you can do now," he heard Beeslaar say, "is to report the case."

"But I thought you knew all the chop shops here? Can't you give me some pointers? You're supposed to know the place like the back of your hand. That's what you always told me!"

"It was a long time ago. And I'm telling you: your car is already spares. For all you know, you could be seeing parts of it driving around where you're walking right now."

"How do you know where I'm walking?" He looked around, noticed there were suddenly fewer buildings on either side of the road. Up ahead was a big intersection and in the distance he could already see the brightly painted cooling towers of the old Orlando power station. He heard Beeslaar laughing at the other end.

"I'm guessing you're in Commando Road, where your cousin's place is. And you're heading for the police station. So listen, when you get to the big intersection with Main Reef, keep going south. The name of the road changes there. It becomes Canada."

"Jissus, Beeslaar, how the hell do you know where I am?" Ghaap's annoyance abated for a moment.

"I have many hidden talents, my friend. But I know already: you've just discovered your car's gone and now you're trying to walk from Riverlea back to Soweto. And you won't get in a taxi because you're too shit scared it might carry you off to somewhere godforsaken in that massive place. So, here's what you will do now: keep walking and phone me again in about twenty minutes, then I'll direct you the rest of the way to the station. The road you're on now will end in a T, where you'll have to turn right. But after that it gets complicated. But maybe you should just call someone. Mabusela, for instance. Let them come and fetch you. Otherwise, old Ghaap, you'll be walking your arse off today."

Ghaap stopped again. "I want to go find my car."

"Forget the car. Call someone to pick you up, and then report the theft."

"But don't you know anybody around here any more? From the old vehicle theft branch, say. Someone who could show me—"

"Ghaap, I want you to listen carefully. Your car no longer *exists*. Either it already has a new owner, along with a new colour, number plates and new VIN number, or it's been stripped. I'm telling you, man! Phone someone to fetch you. And then go chill a bit. Remember, anger makes you stupid. That's when you make mistakes, and mistakes can get you killed. Just do as old Beeslaar says!"

"What's the matter with you, Beeslaar? Are you drunk or something?"

"No, boet. I think this town of winos likes me. I'm hot shit all of a sudden. Hot shit." He laughed merrily and rang off.

Ghaap put his phone away, started walking again. "Well, thank you very much and fuck you, too," he muttered angrily to himself.

16

Beeslaar slipped the cellphone back into his pocket. He felt funny, as if he'd pushed his fingers into a power plug: pain rippled across his head and made his heart pound. But there was also a feeling of elation. Maybe it was just the hangover. Or maybe it was this town. The gabled piety of the architecture. Even the oak trees looked snobbish, as if they'd been planted here by the good Lord himself. Stately old trees. Some were kept upright by cables and poles. Like the decrepit aristocracy of an old order.

"Right!" Qhubeka interrupted his hangover ruminations. "You can come with me." She walked off without waiting for his response. Her pants fitted tightly. A healthy behind, well-covered bones, he noted approvingly.

Then he came back to the present. "No, no, the Du Toits are expecting me," he called after her. "I promised to go say goodbye."

"So, you're driving with me!"

Her vehicle was parked on a yellow line directly opposite the restaurant. An old police bakkie, he noted with surprise.

"The van's nice and big and the cage at the back comes in handy," she replied, as if reading his thoughts. "You can't buy that kind of intimidation value. Much more effective than a pissy little Golf."

He studied her surreptitiously as they drove off. She wore her hair short, not in the customary cornrows most black women seemed to prefer, but relaxed and cut in a modern Afro style that emphasised the lovely lines of her neck.

He should tread warily, he cautioned himself. This woman was playing him like a fiddle.

At a bustling intersection, Qhubeka turned right, joining the traffic flowing up Merriman Avenue. They were going east, he suspected. His internal compass was dodgy in this town where the surrounding mountains hemmed in the early-morning sun. The mountains themselves all looked the same to him.

On either side of the road students sauntered along in groups. They were passing some old two- and three-storey buildings with terracotta roofs, all painted white – university buildings, he presumed.

After a while, they took a right and drove past schools. He kept his eyes peeled for street names, but realised he'd need a proper map of this confusing town to orient himself.

They entered a tranquil residential neighbourhood. Water sparkled in irrigation furrows alongside the roads, with trees on both sides forming an umbrella overhead, their golden autumn leaves fluttering prettily to the ground. Upmarket houses on spacious properties. Old money, he suspected. Some gardens were unfenced. The neurosis of Johannesburg's affluent class hadn't quite taken hold here yet. But he knew it was only a matter of time. Especially after an event such as yesterday's.

Then they were suddenly at their destination. Beeslaar recognised the quiet cul-de-sac with the mountain in the background. Qhubeka pulled in under an oak tree, got out and started walking towards Malan du Toit's next-door neighbour's house.

The door was opened by a bespectacled beanpole of a man, with thinning blond hair. Once Beeslaar had joined them, Qhubeka introduced him, "Willem Bester, Mr du Toit's lawyer."

"I was expecting Captain Beeslaar only," he said. His eyes skipped uncertainly from Qhubeka to Beeslaar behind her.

"You're very lucky, Mr Willemse. Now you're getting two for the price of one," she said without a trace of humour. She stared the man out of her way.

Beeslaar could swear she'd switched around Bester's names deliberately – just to show both males who was really the boss here.

Willem Bester stepped aside quickly to let her pass, and extended his hand to Beeslaar. He had a bone-crushing handshake, which jerked Beeslaar abruptly out of his hangover daze. What in God's name was he doing here? He had bugger-all to do with this case. He should be going home rather than getting himself dragged along like Qhubeka's sidekick.

But he couldn't turn around now. So he followed them in silence, feeling once again like the tame goose. But one thing was sure: not for long.

Malan du Toit and his two children were seated at the breakfast table in a large dining room. Light poured into the room through two sliding doors that led on to a back stoep. A swimming pool gleamed outside. Shrubs sparkled in the early-morning sun, the leaves still wet from the night's sprinklers.

Willem Bester went through the introduction ritual once more. Du Toit didn't get up. He nodded a greeting, his arms reaching for the children on either side of him. He was dressed in a golf shirt, his hair still damp from his morning ablutions. He seemed to have aged a hundred years overnight. Dark bags under his eyes, a stunned expression.

The daughter, Ellie, wore a baggy long-sleeved T-shirt that was miles too big for her. Beeslaar remembered how light she'd felt in his arms the day before. Her honey-blonde hair, also damp, hung in rats' tails over two bony shoulders. The hand she used to tuck a strand of hair behind her ear was milky-white, like a funeral lily. The thin arm seemed to belong to a porcelain doll. There was a barely visible white bandage on her left wrist. She was at pains to hide it with her sleeve.

While she was the princess, her brother, Dawid-Pieter, was the unlovely frog. He sat with his back hunched, moving his spoon around apathetically in an uneaten bowl of cornflakes.

"I'm glad to see you came to no harm," Qhubeka said to the girl as she took a chair at the table and sat down. "And I'm so sorry about your mother. We're going to do our utmost to catch the perpetrator. Will you help me do that?"

The girl didn't reply. She shifted closer to her father and kept fiddling with a mauve cellphone in her hand, turning it over and over. Conscious of everyone's eyes on her, she enfolded the phone in both hands. The action exposed the bandage and she quickly let go of the phone to pull down her sleeve.

"Ellie isn't strong enough for this yet, Captain," Willem Bester protested on her behalf.

Qhubeka ignored him, her eyes fixed on the girl. "The thing is, Ellie," she said gently, "the sooner we can gather all the possible information, the sooner we—"

"With respect, Captain, my client already made a statement last night." The lenses of the lawyer's spectacles flashed in the bright room.

Qhubeka silenced him with a regal look. The man swallowed.

She turned back to the girl. "Ellie, when you returned from school yesterday, did you see anything, or maybe notice someone?"

Silence.

"Ellie?" Qhubeka held out a hand to the girl, who shrank back further in her chair.

The father's gaze hardened: "Yesterday we as a family – it was very traumatic for us. Even now, talking about it."

"I can understand," said Qhubeka.

"I doubt whether you really understand, Captain. I don't know if you have a family, but to …" His voice trailed off and he took a deep breath. "At this time yesterday morning, we were still together. A family."

Qhubeka caught Beeslaar's eye, signalling that he should take over.

"Which one of you was the last to have had contact with the deceased?" Beeslaar inquired.

"What kind of question is that?" Suddenly there was anger in Du Toit's voice. "The last time we all saw one another was in the morning. I wanted to drive the kids to school because it was chilly but Elmana disagreed. We discussed the matter. In the end the children left on their bikes, and I went to work. No one checked their watch to see who left first or last!"

"Did she have any appointments for yesterday? Do you know what her movements might have been? Meeting friends, perhaps?"

70

Du Toit shot a quick glance at his children. "It was an ordinary day, as far as I know. She'd have been at home. Our domestic is on leave for the week, in the Eastern Cape. A funeral, I believe. And Elmana's very ... private. She would have stayed home. She had no plans, I'm sure."

"Any handymen, a gardener? Female friends?"

"She, er, normally she was busy. I think she attended a Bible study group ..."

The daughter frowned slightly, though her eyes were still cast down. Beeslaar couldn't read her expression.

"Not yesterday, though." Clearly annoyed, Du Toit continued, "But what does that have to do with—"

"You didn't perhaps phone her in the course of the morning? You, or one of the kids?"

"For goodness' sake, none of us spoke to Mana. Really! Captain Qhubeka!" He appealed to her, making it plain to Beeslaar that he knew which of the two wore the pants.

"Did any of you touch the deceased?" Beeslaar forged on.

"*What*?"

"Maybe you wanted to see whether she was still breathing."

There was no reaction, though Beeslaar noticed the twitch in Du Toit's jaw muscles before he whispered something in his daughter's ear and planted a kiss on her damp hair. "Go with her, Boeta," he told his son, and the two kids hurried from the room.

"She can't remember anything in any case," he said. "She's on medication. The doctor wasn't keen on discharging her from hospital last night. We're all very worried about her. And the same goes for my son." He frowned at Beeslaar: "I can't believe that you're terrorising *us*. While the damn robbers are running about! Really!"

Beeslaar kept silent and folded his arms across his chest.

"The kids' school finishes at half past one," Du Toit resumed. "But they usually have activities after school. Yesterday Ellie had her piano lesson. She arrived home a minute or two before Dawid-Pieter. So she must've been the first to discover her mother."

"And where was her mother's body when she saw her?"

The man just stared at Beeslaar.

"On the floor, or on the couch?"

"There on the couch, dammit! My son phoned me. I told him to press the panic alarm at the front door and to wait for me outside. I was close enough, but the afternoon traffic – I drove like a maniac. It must've taken me a good ten minutes from the Volkskombuis. It's on the other side of town." He paused to take a breath. "And when I arrived, the guards from ADT were already here.

71

That's our private security company," he added for Beeslaar's benefit. "And the cops arrived minutes later. That's all! Do you honestly think I'd be sitting here eating bloody breakfast if I knew more? Really!"

Beeslaar stood up. "Mr du Toit, you have our deepest sympathy. But if anything should occur to you, something you remember – no matter how trivial, phone Captain Qhubeka."

"There's nothing," he replied angrily. "I'm under suspicion?" It was more a statement than a question. "I know you always look at the husband first." There was a hint of defiance in his tired blue eyes. "But Wim – Mr Bester – can confirm that I was having lunch with him and two clients yesterday."

"That late in the afternoon?"

"That late, yes."

"Were you drinking?"

"What the hell *is* this? What is your actual position here, Captain Beeslaar? Are you working with this lady? I thought my mom said you're a detective from the Northern Cape. And that you would assist us in your private capacity."

"A policeman has no private capacity, Mr du Toit. Right up to his final day," Beeslaar said.

Du Toit leant forward, his elbows on the table and his fingers intertwined. "We're an incredibly close family. My wife, Mana, was excellent at everything she did. By far a better parent and caregiver than me. I don't even come close to her. As a father, I think that I … I wasn't always there for my family. My work demands a lot of my time."

Beeslaar sighed inwardly. If he had a cent for each time a father tried to sell him this tired old story …

"I work incredibly hard. And Elmana supported me extremely well. We were a good team, each doing our very best on our own terrain. Her …" His chin trembled and Beeslaar could see he was gritting his teeth. The cynic in Beeslaar suspected this was a well-worn speech that was regularly trotted out at events such as anniversaries and birthdays, along with the emotional performance.

"And she was strong, too," Du Toit said after a while. "She took care of our household, the garden, the kids. My mother. The soup kitchen." He shook his head, seemingly amazed at his wife's workload. "So many charities. I wonder if this government of ours really has an inkling of how many millions of rands are raised annually, no, daily, in our country for the underprivileged – by people like Elmana. The finger is so easily pointed at wealthy whites. As if—" He stopped, having run out of steam.

"Besides that, Elmana was involved in the school, on the governing body and the parent-teacher association. She served on the board of my mother's old age home as well as that of a home for the underprivileged. She ran the town's soup kitchen, raised funds for ..." His voice petered out again and he looked out at the garden, where a red-winged starling was cavorting in the birdbath.

"I blame myself," he said. "I wasn't there." A tear rolled down his cheek, hung for a moment from his chin. "It's supposed to be a man's first duty. Above all else. He should be there. To protect his family."

17

It was shortly after ten o'clock when Gerda's cellphone rang.

"Pa?"

She recognised her home number. She heard her father breathing, but he said nothing. Lately he'd become a ghost. Of someone else. He didn't speak any more, just stared with vacant eyes. The doctor reckoned it was time for him to be admitted to an institution. But she couldn't do it. Not yet.

"Hello! Pa! Put down the phone, Pa, and call Becca." It freaked her out when he did this. It was a new thing, this phoning. Maybe there was some part of his brain that hadn't yet been enclosed by the web of the Alzheimer's. That still tried to make contact with her.

She ended the call and straightened herself, stepped away from her colleagues in the office. She phoned the domestic worker, Rebecca, who didn't answer. Frustrated, she returned to her desk and gently massaged an itchy spot on her belly. The itch became a burn, and she rubbed hard at the fabric covering it. Her belly already resembled a hot-air balloon. Given the size of this baby, she thought, she was bound to look like a shrivelled granadilla after its birth.

"How long to go, Gerda?" It was Jordaan, the school principal.

"A week or so," she replied, smiling bravely.

"And your dad? How's he doing?" He stood in front of her desk, dressed in his customary grey suit and pale-blue shirt with white stripes. A maroon bowtie added an unexpected touch of flamboyance to an otherwise colourless appearance. And personality, for that matter. But he had a heart of gold and a passion for education. No wonder his school's waiting list was so long.

"Still okay, for the time being," she said. "It seems the new medication helps to calm him down."

"You're going to have your hands full in the coming months. Tell us if you need any help, d'you hear?"

As soon as he'd left, she phoned home again.

The gardener answered.

"What's going on, Xolani? Where's Rebecca?"

"She's helping Oupa. He's crying."

"Did something happen?"

"No, Mevrou. He's outside by the front gate. And he's crying!"

He sounded panic-stricken. Then she grasped what he meant – "cry" as in "shout".

Her blood ran cold. It was the disease. The doctors had warned her that he could start hallucinating, even become aggressive. Until recently it had seemed he'd be taking the gentler path. Just fade away, like a candle flickering out. But he'd already tried to slap her once, right out of the blue. And pushed Rebecca away.

The shouting was something new.

"Xolani, go fetch Stoffelina, the cat. Take it to them. The cat will calm him down. Give him the cat and help Rebecca bring him inside. Tell Rebecca she must give him one of the blue pills. She knows which ones. And then she must call me. Try not to speak loudly. Be soft. Just be—"

"I know, Mevrou. I will help him. I know the pills." Gerda thanked him and rang off. Pa had better not play up now, not until the baby is born. After that she'd have enough time to focus on him, be with him during her maternity leave.

"Is everything okay, ngwanaka?"

The concerned voice was that of Alison Nthonyane, a grey-haired colleague with a passion for small cacti. There were little pots containing miniature plants on every windowsill in the office, which she tended lovingly with dribbles of water. She'd taken Gerda under her wing since the first day she joined the admin team for the principal, his two deputies and the departmental heads. A warm, sympathetic individual with finely tuned intuition. She would, at times, rub Gerda's swollen feet, or offer traditional herbal remedies and ointments to relieve the discomforts of pregnancy. While she had no children of her own, she had raised many. As her four brothers and a sister had succumbed one by one to the Big Sick, she'd cared for their children.

Gerda hadn't managed to trust anyone here with her life story, not even Alison. Hennie Jordaan knew her history, of course, but he kept it to himself. Because she'd learnt that sympathy had a sting. It kept you chained to your misery. Once people knew, they acted differently. They felt obliged to sympathise, to ask how you could bear it. And each time you were reminded afresh. Only to be left flopping around helplessly while they waltzed on, all pious and virtuous for being so empatico!

"Hai, mangwane." Gerda used the respectful seSotho word for "aunt" – in acknowledgement of Alison's tender "ngwanaka": my daughter. "It's my ntate. I think his condition is a bit worse today."

"Au, sorry-sorry." Alison clicked her tongue sympathetically. "Give me that work of yours. I'll finish it in no time."

"It's okay, Alison, thank you. The work is a welcome distraction." She refreshed her screen and saw she'd received a new email. It was from Baz.

Sorry, doll. Got to shoot thru to Durbs. Strike at the harbour (what's new)! My

merchandise stuck. Planes full – scheme I'll sommer drive down quick. Wanted to
cook lamb stew tonihgt to celebryte your laaast day. Have too wait weekend! Luv
you! Just like that. Hadn't even bothered to phone her from the car. Or correct
the spelling errors. Such a devil-may-care attitude.

The tears came before she could stop herself. Damn! She wiped her eyes as
unobtrusively as possible. But in an office staffed by five women …

Alison was the first to react: "Auwe!" She got up and wrapped her arms
around Gerda. "You should rather go home. Go and look after your ntate. We
can have our brunch another day."

Gerda shook her head and tried in vain to fight back the tears. But her
hormone-charged body had a mind of its own. And right now it wanted to have
a good cry!

The next minute the entire typing pool was gathered around her desk. "It's her
dad," she heard Alison whisper. "He's very ill."

She dabbed under her eyes with a tissue and put on her best smile: "Lord
knows, this pregnancy really isn't fun any more. I think it's brought out the cow
in me!"

The women smiled uncertainly.

"And this cow is hungry," she said bravely. "Constantly. What do you say to
some sparkling wine with the brunch? It's on me, though I won't be imbibing, of
course. So you guys will drink on behalf of the pregnant fairy! Let me just find
out if my dad's okay, then we can go."

18

"I smell a rat," said Qhubeka, tapping her red nails on the steering wheel.

She seemed lost in thought and hadn't yet started the engine.

Beeslaar noticed that someone had switched off the fountain in front of the Du Toit homestead. He looked at the crime-scene tape along the wrought-iron fence. A loose piece fluttered listlessly in the warm autumn air. The wind had died down. He hadn't even noticed its absence. Last night it had raged like a rabid thing, trying to turn everything upside down. But this morning there was mercy in the air.

A respite.

So that you could gather your bones again before the next assault. Enjoy a moment's rest; wasn't that basically what everyone wanted? Before the final Big Sleep. You could say this was his own quest too: mercy and rest. In fact, it was the very reason he was here, in this town.

Maybe that's what Malan du Toit was also looking for. Those parting words of his just now, it wasn't just survivor's guilt. He was wrestling with something greater: apart from the notion that he'd failed to keep his family safe, he'd failed to keep them *whole*. Intact. Wasn't that, essentially, a father's job? To be the guard dog at the gate that keeps danger at bay?

But Du Toit had forsaken his duty, he hadn't been at his post.

That's what he was actually saying.

"Penny for your thoughts?" Qhubeka folded her arms over the steering wheel and turned her face towards him.

"I'm thinking of my homeward journey."

She wasn't put off her stride: "How does he strike you, the husband?"

"Like a guy who's not telling the whole truth, and for the wrong reasons. Because I can't see why a robber would've moved the body. Robbers are in a hurry, they want to get away. It doesn't make sense. And that, Captain, is all I have to offer."

She frowned and smiled all at once. "Oom van Blerk would have been proud."

Beeslaar looked out of the window.

"He came to address us at the CPF," she said after a while. "Community Police Forum. To talk about safety at old age homes. Something along those lines." She paused, her eyes softened by the memory. Then she chuckled: "He didn't like me at first. I had to put in quite an effort to get through to him."

"Yes?"

"The oom was old school, as you know. When he left the service ... I don't think he had much time for us darkies. And then a black female, to boot. " She shook her head and rolled down her window, letting in the soft autumn air.

"He just looked me up and down in that way of his. You know?"

Beeslaar didn't reply. He didn't really want to listen to this. It was too close. *She* was too close. He felt the tightness gathering under his ribs. He opened his window.

"Then, one afternoon, I was in Jan Cats – the bar at the Stellenbosch Hotel," she explained. "And the old man was there. He had his own spot, right at the far end of the bar. You didn't see him when you entered the place. But he saw you."

She smiled, dimples appearing in her nut-brown cheeks. "In the evenings when the other old people took out their crocheting and traded stories about the grandchildren, he would set himself up there. Anyway, I was dealing with a tough case at the time. Murder. One of the employees at the home was a suspect. That was how ..."

She didn't finish the sentence. "I wanted to buy him a drink. He was nursing a whisky – vitamin w, he called it. I offered to buy another round. As a mark of respect, you know? He said he was on his last drink of the day. So I ordered a Coke for myself and he asked if I intended to polish my medals, because that was the only thing Coke was good for. 'Bring the girl a glass of sauvignon,' he told the waiter. 'Not that horse piss from a pig's bladder that you dish out to the tourists. Something decent.' It was a bit awkward, because I don't really drink alcohol. The stuff's a curse here in the Western Cape."

It was getting hot in the van. Beeslaar glanced at his watch. Ten o'clock already.

Qhubeka showed no sign of getting ready to leave.

"I think it was because of the case I was struggling with. Prammie was fast-tracked, you know? Zero experience, but from flat paw to colonel overnight."

"Foot," Beeslaar corrected her. "Flat*foot* to colonel."

Ignoring him, she went on: "This old man, on the other hand – he had the *look*. You could tell he'd put big fish behind bars in his day. But I'm telling you things you know yourself."

When he still didn't react, she sighed and started the van. As they drove back, she made a call. Beeslaar assumed it was to her office, as she asked whether Du Toit's financial statements had been received. Ending the conversation, she said, "Sharp-sharp."

They pulled up at his guesthouse.

"So, Captain Kewbeka." He climbed out and leant into the open window to say goodbye. "I wish you all the best."

"Let me know if you're staying for the scattering of the ashes," she said. "You have my number. We can have a drink or something." She smiled, an impish look in her eyes.

Then she drove off.

The phone vibrated in his shirt pocket.

"Yes!"

"And good morning to you too, Captain Boss Beeslaar! And yes, I'm getting hopelessly lost. And yes, I still see no sign of my bladdy car. And no, I'm not phoning to ask you for help!"

"Jissie, Ghaap. I was busy, man."

"I'm walking along a road that leads nowhere. I don't see a street name, and I don't think the people around here understand my English. I've now been sent in every single wind direction!"

"What do you see around you?"

"I see fokkol, that's what I'm seeing! Car wrecks and garbage and dead donkeys. And ten thousand taxis—"

"Take a taxi. It'll drop you off at the cop shop. Or the driver can at least tell you where you are! Otherwise, keep walking. If you haven't turned off anywhere, you're still in Canada Road. And you should be seeing mine dumps on either side of you, and the railway line should be on your right."

"Okay?"

"Okay, so you're still going in the right direction. But get into a taxi. It's cheap, too."

"I've been in one already. With fifteen other people and a fat mama on my lap! Those vehicles, they're death traps, man!"

"Ghaap, don't believe all the rubbish they tell you at home! Just carry on walking. The road will intersect with the Soweto Highway. And the Noordgesig cops are close by. They'll help you!"

Ghaap mumbled a sour response and the line went dead.

The phone rang again immediately.

"Albertus?" A soft female voice. "It's Tertia. Mynhardt and I are at my dad's flat at the old age home. We're tidying up. We were thinking … if you're still around and there's something of his you'd like to have, you know?"

He collected his car from the secure parking area of the guesthouse. He'd checked out before breakfast and put his suitcase in the boot, still firmly intent on leaving. The new jacket hadn't been packed. He'd try to exchange it before hitting the road.

Mrs Adendorf, the matron at Great Gables, came to meet Beeslaar at the security gate.

"Ah! Captain Beeslaar," she greeted him. She was a tall, broad-shouldered woman with sharp eyes that seemed to size you up first thing, and then assign you to the appropriate box. Beeslaar evidently belonged in the one for scrap. He wondered how Oom Blikkies had got along with such an old dragon.

"Mrs du Toit isn't here at the moment," she said. "She told me you're going to assist her family?" She eyed him appraisingly.

"I was actually looking for Colonel van Blerk's daughter."

"Oh." Disapproving surprise. "Come in, then," she said, and the gate buzzed open.

She led Beeslaar through a garden, along a short path, past the big entrance hall – with a fountain – to a stand-alone unit around the corner. Her living quarters and office, she explained. She was formally dressed in a dark-blue suit and a brown shirt with a pin at the collar. Her thin, grey hair was tightly permed and sprayed into place.

Tertia stood up when Beeslaar entered the office, and greeted him with a kiss on his cheek. He'd had to stoop down because she was a small woman. Mynhardt, the spouse, was not much taller, but he compensated for it with a firm handshake.

"We've almost finished here," Tertia explained. "Admin and so on with regard to my dad's flat. If you don't mind, you can go up in the meantime." She handed him a key. "It's on the second floor, number 208. We'll join you in a minute."

The matron clearly didn't approve of this, but she kept her peace.

He walked back through the garden and up the stairs. He remembered how Blikkies had initially resisted the idea of living in this place. "She's booked me in at a bladdy old age home, Jaap." Blikkies's name for him, dating from their early days together when Beeslaar was a rookie under his supervision. He'd never bothered to learn the blougatte's names, calling them all "japsnoet" – whippersnapper. And, in Beeslaar's case, the name stuck, eventually becoming Jaap.

Oom Blikkies was a hard man on the job, but with Tertia he had been soft. He had much to atone for. Debts to repay. The damage caused by his absence. Especially during Tertia's teenage years – when Blikkies simply couldn't handle her sudden rebelliousness, on top of the divorce from his wife, which he couldn't handle either.

Tertia didn't speak to him for years.

After school she'd gone to a college and became a hairdresser at a salon somewhere in the city. At the time, old Blikkies didn't show the pain. But Beeslaar knew that it gnawed at him.

Things changed with his early retirement. He'd been more or less forced out of the service to make room for an affirmative action appointment. That had really shaken him awake: the fact he'd bargained away his family for nothing.

The loyalty of a lifetime thrown back in his face – along with a painfully modest cheque. The old man had been bitter, but then he'd gone looking for Tertia.

Beeslaar found the flat easily and unlocked the door. He hesitated a moment. This was not the kind of thing a man should do on his own.

He found himself incapable of entering the flat. It was as if an invisible wall had been erected in the doorway of *Number 208, B v Blerk*.

He pulled the door closed and went and stood at the corridor windows, suddenly short of breath.

It was a beautiful view, he realised once he felt calmer. Blikkies's crustiness about the home issue had been short-lived. "I'm still in my bladdy prime, Jaap," he'd complained over the phone. "Too young to trade pill stories with the aged. Sitting out my days in Avbob's waiting room. Hell, no."

But there hadn't really been much fight in the indignation. He'd have walked through fire for his child.

Beeslaar waited until Tertia and the spouse arrived. Together they walked through the invisible wall.

It wasn't the typical old man's place that Beeslaar had expected. In Johannesburg, Blikkies rented a poky police flat after his divorce. A depressing place with a cheap brown corduroy lounge suite, a TV on a coffee table that hailed from OK Bazaars. Bare walls and a reading lamp next to a La-z-Boy reclining chair. Blikkies hadn't bothered to beautify the place.

But this flat looked as if his rich son-in-law had coughed up. A deep-pile wall-to-wall carpet, a flatscreen TV, and a pot plant. A pot plant! Paintings, framed family photos, a picture of Blikkies at a medal parade. A wine rack, even a book case. This was a different Blikkies, Beeslaar realised. One that seemed to have become a more rounded human being here. In the glow of his daughter's love.

And once again he, Beeslaar, had been too late to witness the old ballie's joy.

Tertia walked to the centre of the lounge and paused. She looked around slowly, like someone staring at a beloved portrait for the last time.

Beeslaar caught a glimpse of the bedroom through an open door. Here, Blikkies had evidently tolerated no interference: a single bed with wooden legs against the wall below a window, a pair of Crocs in front of the bedside cabinet. On top of it, a book, reading glasses, and a tumbler. A functional bedside lamp, a pill holder with compartments, one for every day of the week. The bed was neatly made. No duvet or bedspread, just a plain brown blanket and a single pillow. Above the bed hung an antique .22. Beeslaar wondered what Blikkies had done with the rest of his firearms. He'd had a sizeable collection by the time he retired.

Tertia pulled back the lounge curtains and opened a door leading to a small balcony with yet another view of a mountain. Beeslaar suspected that this one was Simonsberg.

"I'm sorry I couldn't spend more time with you yesterday."

Beeslaar lifted his hand to indicate that he understood.

"He was so fond of going up Table Mountain with us in the cable car," she said, "so we thought of scattering his ashes there." Beeslaar's heart sank at the prospect, but Blikkies's ashes had to be honoured. "He used to joke that it reminded him of Johannesburg's mine dumps." She smiled, her eyes moist. "But I know you don't like heights, so we'll be going up the mountain on foot, from the Kirstenbosch side."

"You said Sunday?" he asked, his cheeks burning.

"If the southeaster isn't playing up. It's supposed to have calmed down by this time of the year. If the wind blows, there's dense fog on the mountain, making it dangerous. But in the meantime," she said, glancing at Mynhardt, "we'll try to clear out the flat."

"Was your dad ill?"

She shook her head. "They say it's typical of a stroke, that it happens so unexpectedly. We thought he'd live to be a hundred. He was incredibly active, even used to go hiking with us in the Jonkershoek mountains. My dad wasn't so keen on this place, probably because he thought he was too young for it. But in a town like this housing is scarce, and retirement places even more so. And expensive. Mynhardt – and I – felt he had to stay in the best possible place, also with a view to frail care later."

She paused briefly, her eyes fixed on what had clearly been Blikkies's TV chair. "He was the only family I had left. My mom's been dead for a while now, as you may know."

He remembered Blikkies phoning to tell him this. Also that he would never be a grandfather. Tertia and Mynhardt's decision, apparently.

"Would you be able to stay a bit longer?"

He kept his eyes on the mountain, trying to think of the right answer.

"You're very welcome to stay with us. We have a big house, not far from here. It's at the foot of the mountain, and the views are really beautiful."

Beeslaar raised his palm again. "I'm okay. But thanks anyway."

She smiled. He suspected he'd done something that reminded her of her dad. A silence descended on them, but it wasn't uncomfortable.

Then the spouse spoke for the first time: "Darling, what about Maaike?"

Tertia became animated: "Yes! Albertus, she was there yesterday. Did you meet her? The Dutch lady. She has a student flat that's vacant at the moment. It's just around the corner, Mynhardt will drive you there."

He shook his head.

"At least take a look," she urged.

Beeslaar shifted uncomfortably. How the hell was he going to extricate himself from this?

"Maaike's house is special. You'll like it. It's very private, at the edge of town on the Eerste River. And you can stay for free. Her tenant left suddenly and all she wants is a reliable person who'd at least sleep there at night. And then the three of us can go up the mountain on Sunday and say our final goodbyes to my dad. What do you say?"

He ended up following Mynhardt in his own car, a feeling of discomfort in his chest. They drove east, into a valley. Just before they reached the end of the town, Mynhardt turned off to the right.

Tame goose, Beeslaar thought, angry with himself. That's what he was turning into in this fancy town with its stifling mountains.

But he didn't have time to chicken out. They'd barely stopped when a wooden gate in an overgrown wall opened, and a stocky woman with a mop of grey curls ran out and threw her arms enthusiastically in the air.

For a moment he contemplated stepping on the accelerator and getting the hell out of here. But the road came to a dead end, at the river.

Maaike had the gushing energy of a river in flood, flattening everything in its path. She was the kind of person who fired up all your fight or flight hormones.

The moment Mynhardt stepped out of his car, she enveloped him in a bear hug and planted a kiss on each of his clean-shaven cheeks. As Beeslaar emerged warily from his car, he found himself assailed by an enraged dachshund.

"Rembrandt!" The dog didn't pay the least attention to his owner's loud voice. It stood its ground, barking defiantly at Beeslaar's knees. Mynhardt tried to perform introductions above the yapping. There was a bird, too, Beeslaar saw to his consternation. Some kind of parrot, grey, with a curly crest and an almighty beak, perched on the Dutch woman's shoulder, that squawked incessantly. Its name was Vermeer, Beeslaar was told.

He extended a long arm to shake the woman's hand, and to ward off a possible hug.

She laughed for no obvious reason and her dark eyes glittered, scrutinising him as if he were a juicy morsel.

"Godverdomme, what a hunk of a man, hey!" she called out to Mynhardt. The parrot's squawking distortion sounded like "fucking hunk, yay". She ushered them through the gate, along a garden path overgrown with lavender bushes whose fragrance rubbed off on passersby. She walked fast for such a small woman, and the bird on her shoulder had to cling on for dear life. Beeslaar lengthened his stride to keep up, with Mynhardt and the yapping dog bringing up the rear.

The house was an old Karoo-style farmhouse with a wraparound stoep. They passed through the front door into an entrance hall filled with African art. Pictures and masks and antelope horns. Outside the back door, a slate path led to a cottage that looked as if it came straight off a cheesy greeting card. It must once have been a labourer's cottage, Beeslaar reckoned. But it had been neatly restored, with a blood-red stable-type front door, above it a cheerful yellow canvas awning, and pots with roses under the windows. Tinkling wind-chimes were suspended from one of its struts. That would have to go, he decided before ducking his head to enter the front door.

Inside was a small lounge with a fireplace, and a kitchen-cum-living room with an antique table and chairs, and gleaming yellowwood cupboards against the walls.

"Een gezellige keuken," she remarked of the cosy kitchen. The parrot yodelled something after her. Beeslaar's mother had, at some stage, had a bird like that. At times, Beeslaar was convinced she loved it more than the rest of them. She'd spend hours talking to the thing, which talked back, almost like a human being.

The view from the bedroom was possibly one of the most beautiful he'd ever seen. Towers of rugged grey rock that soared into a deep-blue sky and surrounded a hazy valley. Chocolate box, thought Beeslaar. Actually, everything in this town fitted that category. Picturesque, his mother would have said. With just a hint of condescension in her tone.

"And?" Maaike looked up at him as if she were staring at a giant freak – fascinated and excited at the same time. "Potverdomme!" she exclaimed. "But you are a bull of a man, aren't you!" She laughed merrily and told Mynhardt that "no skelm" would dare enter her yard with Beeslaar in attendance.

They walked back to the main house. "Are you doing the murder investigation?" she asked as she handed him the front-door key.

"No. I'm, er, only staying till Sunday."

"Oh, you'll advise the family, or so? A tragedy, isn't it? Grote God!" The parrot echoed the exclamation with an identical Dutch accent.

Beeslaar shook his head.

Mynhardt finally found his tongue: "It's terrible. The newspapers say it may be the same guy who murdered that Matie student. Do you remember the case, Maaike?"

She nodded, and the parrot followed suit. Then together they both exclaimed: "Terrible!"

"And the cops in this town are useless. With all due respect," he said, shooting a cautious look at Beeslaar. "I'm not saying anything against you, or my father-in-law. But dreadful things are happening in this town. Just the other day, for instance, a guy I knew personally. A father of two young children, Shane Williams from Pniel. I had a lot to do with him at the town council. They arrested him for drunk driving, but then he ended up murdered in the police cells. No, shucks."

Beeslaar cringed inwardly. Shucks ... How long since he'd heard anyone use that tight-arsed word?

His phone rang, saving him from an unseemly remark.

19

It was hot. The white Highveld sun blistered the tarmac and traffic had come to a dead halt.

Gerda wiped perspiration from her face. The brunch had been a jolly affair, the women all equally broody about the baby girl who would soon make her appearance. She had phoned Baz. For no particular reason, merely because she felt happy and wanted to tell him about her day. But Baz hadn't been in the mood to chat. He had cut her short with, "I'm busy, babes."

The morning's shadow was back.

This was probably how it would be for the rest of her life. Pretending to be a normal person. With children and a home and a job, watching *7 de Laan* in the evenings, and the seven o'clock news. But below the surface, the picture was different. Like the story of the duck: apparently calm and unruffled as it glides over the water, but paddling like hell underneath.

Paddling to survive, in spite of oneself. To keep afloat. At times she felt like giving up. Surrendering. Shaking off the lifelines, sinking away into the cool twilight of rest.

On other days, again, she had to fight. When it felt as if the long tentacles of a hungry monster from the underworld were clutching at her. The Black Octopus, she called it. Which would rise up and punish her whenever she had the temerity to forget.

Today was undoubtedly one of those days when the old sea monster was up to its tricks.

It was Baz, more than Pa, she knew. He'd been different lately. She couldn't put her finger on it. As if he'd changed gears. He was more tense, curt. Complained that the economy was entrepreneur-unfriendly. He was usually so dynamic, crazy about cooking and food and people. And risk. "Business, babes, should be one long adrenaline rush." She suspected he was referring to more than just the food business. He was smart, a brilliant blackjack player who could break the bank of most casinos. "We go big or we go home," he'd joke whenever she became anxious.

It was precisely his vitality that attracted her so. His joie de vivre, the charged energy around him – the talking and laughing and playing. Being in his company automatically lifted one's spirits. And those eyes of his, like a playful puppy's.

And then there was the other man in her life: Pa. She knew how he'd look when she got home. Like a zombie. He'd be staring into space, his right hand trembling uncontrollably, his mouth agape and dry. Lost to the world. He might as well be dead. Like Ma. Like … like everything that had been precious to her.

She swallowed the tears that rose in her throat. That was all behind her. It belonged in the past. She'd made a fresh start. She was doing it for them. For the two little boys she had lost by … She still struggled to say it. Lost by their father's hand. She was doing it for them. And for Kleinpiet, their little brother who was still alive. And the new baby sister.

For a new future. Safety. A husband who didn't drink. Who was looking forward to the unborn child, even though it was someone else's.

She shook her head. No, she decided, and took a deep breath. We're definitely not going *there*. She glanced in the rear-view mirror at her son, who was strapped into his car seat in the back, moaning.

Kleinpiet was also no happy chappie today, and his fretful whimpering threatened to break into a bawl at any moment. He surely sensed her unease. The restless bones of the dead. The lurking eye of the Black Octopus.

She switched on the radio and the car was suddenly filled with blaring pop music. A startled Kleinpiet began to cry. She turned it off.

"Oh, my golly!" she called out over her shoulder. "The little baboon was singing the wrong song! Naughty baboon." She babbled on about the silly baboon. "Look, Pietman, there he is! In the tree!" She pushed a CD with children's songs into the slot – always her last resort between the daycare and home.

"Look there, Pietman, see!" She pointed to the colourful wares of street hawkers weaving in and out among the line of impatient cars. "Look at the ooms, Pietie, see how they're laughing. Wave at the ooms! Ta-ta! Wave at the ooms!" He lifted a tentative hand, his bottom lip wet and uncertain. But the moment they'd driven past the "ooms", his crying started up again.

Gerda's finger found the CD button and she began to sing along at the top of her voice: "Six little ducks that I once knew … Sing, my boy. Come on! Quack, quack …" At the next robot a hawker with a bunch of roses bent down at her window, but she shook her head and avoided eye contact. He tapped on the glass and tried to make himself heard over the duck march inside the car.

And then, mercifully, the traffic started flowing and she accelerated up the steep hill of the Melville Koppies. She felt around on the passenger seat for the automatic gate remote. And her cellphone. To ask Rebecca to come down to the gate and help her with the fretful child.

The gate slid open, she turned into the driveway, and switched off the engine. She had to get the child into the house as soon as possible. It had been a mistake to pick him up so early. This was nap time at his day mother's house. But it saved her an extra trip later, in the rush-hour traffic.

She pressed the remote again and scooped up the contents of her handbag from the passenger seat. From the corner of her eye she saw a movement at the gate. Rebecca, thank God.

There was tapping at her window. What the hell?

Then she saw the gun.

"Quiet, bitch," a man hissed through the open slit of the window and wrenched her door open.

20

Ghaap kicked at some stones as he walked. He knew he was buggering up his shoes, but he didn't give a fuck. He hadn't felt so bedonnered in a long time. If only he'd beaten the truth of his car's whereabouts from his scumbag cousin.

His leg ached like crazy. And the traffic that scraped past him on the narrow, potholed road that linked the west of Johannesburg with Soweto didn't help either.

A siren blared behind him and a black Golf GTI swerved off the road, stopping right in front of him in a cloud of dust and gravel. Furious, Ghaap stopped. As the driver got out, he realised it was the short-arse trackie from the night before. Ghalla, or whatever his name was.

"Jeez, bru, what are you doing wandering around here, ek sê? The brothers of this hood will jump you if you're not careful. You'll still be walking like that and they'll come nail you from behind and grab your rollie—"

"They stole my fokken car!" Ghaap retorted. "The bladdy bliksems from the flats. Where I'm staying, in Riverlea. Motherfuckers! It's clean gone … Phhht!"

"Hell, man, that's kak. Was it still there last night?"

"For sure! You guys must go find it. I haven't even finished paying off the damn thing!"

"Ag, shame, man." The man shook his head in sympathy as he stood, one hand on his hip. His shirt had been pressed with military precision. "What kind of car was it?"

"Mazda 323, '88 model. Red."

"Shit, man, that's really bad luck." He pointed in the direction of Soweto, which stretched away into the distance behind him. "This place is the number one fan club of that model. But come," he said, "let me give you a ride," and got back into his car. He gestured to Ghaap to hop in on the other side.

Ghaap tried to remember his name, but last night – he was so sure he was going to die.

"Hey, Mauritz," Ghaap heard him speak into his radio. "I've picked up that oke who took the bullet yesterday. Says his wheels were stolen overnight." Ghaap heard the reply, but couldn't make out what the man was saying. He recognised the high-pitched tones, though. It was the giant with the squeaky voice.

"Ten-four," said Ghaap's saviour. "Let's meet up at head office – and remember I take a small one. Yes."

He signed off, turned the key in the ignition, lit a cigarette and plugged his navigation machine back into the lighter socket. All in one movement. Ghaap opened the passenger window a slit and lit up too. They drove in silence for a while, the trackie steering his car expertly through the Soweto traffic. His speed was way over the limit, but no one gave them a second glance. The locals were obviously used to these cars zipping through, day and night, so easily identifiable by the nest of antennas on their roofs.

"So you obviously don't know your way around this dorpie," the man remarked as he turned left into a big road. Ghaap glanced around, recognised the Orlando soccer stadium ahead on their left. They must be pretty close to his workplace.

"I just want to find my car, my friend. That's all," said Ghaap. He took a drag on his cigarette, felt the tar burning its way down his windpipe.

"Ghalla," the man reminded him. "I suppose you're not on duty now?"

"No. Rest day. But I'm not bladdy resting till I've found my car."

"Ag, sorry, bru. That's too bad. Have you had breakfast?"

Ghaap was looking out of the window, just about staring the paint off each car they passed. Eventually, he shook his head.

"Okay, I'll tell you what. Me and the other guys will try to help. But old Mauritz can't operate without chow. So why don't you come with me, and we'll grab a fried egg or two. And then we'll search for your car. What d'you say?"

"No! You'd better drop me right here. I can't wait, I'll look for the car myself."

"But that's exactly the problem. Don't you get it? That car of yours has been liquidised, boet. As in chicken soup. Stripped for spares. If not, the most you can hope for is that it'll be used in a robbery somewhere and then dumped. That's the only way you'll find it. Otherwise it's history, my—"

"My name is Ghaap! Johannes Ghaap! And with such a slapgat attitude, I'm surprised you people ever track down a single car!"

"Hey, hey, hey. Don't you go and get angry now. That's now fokkol use." He veered off the road and came to a swift halt, spraying dust on a group of roadside vegetable hawkers, who angrily started fanning it away with pieces of cardboard. "Look, Ghaap. Jannes. You need to calm down, man. I know it's a bladdy gemors when you've lost your wheels." He tapped a finger against his temple: "But now you have to use your kop. Let's first get all your info while we're chowing, and then we'll figure out what to do. We work according to a plan. Okay? I don't want to force you, but if you go to the cop shop and open a case, it gets buried right there. That docket goes straight to the storeroom. I don't need to tell you that."

Ghaap let go of the door handle. He'd been about to climb out. But this guy seemed to know his stuff.

He'd give it a go. After all, if the bladdy trackies couldn't find a car, then it *must* be dead and gone.

21

His thumbs hooked into his belt, Beeslaar stood studying the murder scene. He was there at the request of Qhubeka, a "last little favour" on behalf of Oom Blikkies.

Only now, from where he was standing – in the doorway leading from the dining room – was he able to survey his surroundings at leisure. The dragonflies would have examined the scene really carefully yesterday, he reckoned. The forensic blunders of the Matie student's murder were still fresh in everyone's minds.

"If the sc finds out you're here, both you and I will be out of a job tomorrow. So you keep your head down." Qhubeka pulled on her rubber gloves. She seemed hot, fine beads of perspiration dotted her upper lip.

Beeslaar didn't reply.

He walked around the couch and examined the scene. There was blood everywhere. The broken glass of the coffee table lay in pieces under the chrome frame. It would have taken a helluva force to shatter it; the glass was really thick.

"Was it the bull?"

"Seems like it. We found brain tissue, blood. But no fingerprints. It's been wiped clean."

He squatted down at the table and inspected the corners of the chrome frame. They still bore traces of the dragonflies' activities.

"But she wasn't only hit with the bull, was she?"

"Correct," she said with a smile. "There was hair as well as blood on the right front corner of the table too. As if her head had also made contact there, though apparently *before* she was shot."

Beeslaar stood up and proceeded to view the scene from each corner of the room. He flipped the cushions on the lounge suite, felt inside each groove with his fingers, found a few sweet wrappers, which he carefully put aside. From the couch on which Elmana du Toit's corpse had been found sitting, he retrieved a craft knife, the type used for newspaper clippings.

Qhubeka clicked her tongue at the negligence, held out a plastic bag into which he deposited the knife.

Then he walked to the open space between the back of the murder couch and the bar and dining nook. This was probably where the family had their evening meals, he decided. Close to the TV, the kitchen, the two full-sized fridges, and also to the liquor cabinet. Row upon row of wine bottles were visible through glass doors.

The day before, the floor in this area was strewn with pieces of porcelain.

"Have you been able to get anything from the footprints yet?"

Qhubeka nodded. "The daughter's, the dad's. But even if there'd been someone's else prints, the scene was wrecked by the time we arrived."

"Yes?"

"Yes."

"Do we know where the Brahman usually stood?"

"The statuette?"

"The statuette, yes. Are you not familiar with a Brahman bull?"

"My kraal origins are not very recent, Captain Beeslaar. I'm not one of the new settlers in the Cape. My family have been here a long time." She smiled. "But the statuette stood on the coffee table, yes."

"The autopsy?"

"Late last night."

"And?"

"It was definitely the bullet, nine mil, in the back of the head."

"And the gun?"

She shrugged.

"I take it that it's not Du Toit's."

"He doesn't own any firearms," she replied. "Or none that are legal, anyway."

"Something doesn't make sense here."

"Damn right. Plus she was as high as a kite. At the time of," she added.

"On what?"

"The lady seems to have been something of a druggy. She had enough methamphetamine in her system to give that cow of yours palpitations!"

"Bull."

She rewarded him with an irritated glance. "Anyway. The doc reckons she wasn't a novice at meth. He also found the remains of pseudoephedrine, benzos, alcohol, and a few other chemical concoctions."

"Pseudoephedrine?"

"It used to be an ingredient in diet pills – Nobese, Thinz, things like that. Fat ladies had fun tripping on it, as the chemical composition is much the same as that of methamphetamine. They say it's only a small step from pseudoephedrine to crystal meth. Better known as tik here in the Cape – because of the tik-tik sound the crystals make when you light them. Doc believes she went for variety, alternating between uppers and downers. She kept a stash of prescription sleeping pills, lots of them, in her bathroom cupboard, at the top. Along with several kinds of tranqs, newer versions of Valium."

Beeslaar walked over to the dining-room table, leaning his backside against it. It was a massive, solid piece of wood, finely finished, which rested on sturdy wooden legs. Would have cost an arm and a leg. He reflected on the information he'd been given.

"The mother's-little-helper syndrome," he said, shaking his head. "Who supplied her with all the pills?"

"The doctor, the shrink, the neurologist – whoever. You name the doctor, and I'll tell you the drug of choice. Charmainetjie says that, in cases like this, three-quarters of the time the doctor is the pusher. But the tik, on the other hand, comes from the streets."

"How hooked was she?"

"Hooked enough; her blood count for benzos and meth was sky high. Doc says her liver was that of a user."

"And the violence here? The tik-heads can go berserk, not so?"

"Yes, we see a lot of that. It's probably our biggest problem here in the Cape. The drug affects your brain, liver, kidneys. It makes you stupid, and your teeth fall out. And on top of that, you become paranoid and extremely violent. If a tik-head breaks into your house he comes with an axe, makes mincemeat of you. Some of the single moms on the Flats who are terrorised by their tik-head kids become so desperate that they kill them. Their own children!"

"How often does it happen here?"

"Too often. The other day a young schoolgirl from the town was assaulted with battery acid. She lost an eye. The mother didn't want to lay a charge, blamed it on a "nasty element" at the kid's school. But we suspect the attack was a message from her pushers. You should know that there are many bored women in this town who don't have to work. When the kid's at school and the hubby's away, they're like ripe figs begging to be picked."

"But the violence here? She wouldn't have buggered up her own plants like that." He pointed to a plastic bucket at the sliding door. Someone had gathered the plants that had been in the broken containers and put them in the bucket. Maybe a dragonfly with a soft spot for green things. The day before, they'd been strewn all over the floor. And they weren't just plants, they were trees. Miniature trees, bonsais. He walked up to the bucket and lifted them out, one by one. Some looked a hundred years old. But they'd been badly damaged – they seem to have been stomped on deliberately. The small twisted trunks were crushed and torn.

Whatever had taken place here the day before, much emotion had been vented. On both the woman and her poor plants. But why the plants too?

They were only plants, after all.

He'd never been able to make sense of this kind of gardening, if one could call it that. Torturing a plant like that: trimming its roots, pruning the branches so severely. For the sake of keeping a hundred-year-old tree as small as a shoe box. No. It wasn't right.

He left the bonsais and walked back to the dining-room table, where Qhubeka had pulled out a chair and sat watching him.

"The plants were demolished, but not really anything else. That's strange in itself, isn't it? Or is there more?"

"Yes, there is. I'll show you." She gestured towards the second floor. "A bit of a mess, isn't it?" she said, looking around the room. "We haven't been able to identify all the fingerprints. The family's, yes. The ones against the walls of the dining room are the daughter's. But there are others too."

"Staff?"

"We haven't managed to track down the domestic worker yet. And there's no gardener – they use a gardening service. They come once a week, but never enter the house."

"Fine. So the father and the daughter were definitely at the scene. She arrives home, discovers the chaos here. Sees her mother lying in a pool of blood on the floor, tries to shake her, checks whether she's still alive. Maybe the father does the same when he gets home. But …"

He looked at the bonsai trees. "The father keeps saying it's a house robbery. But who moved the body? And why shoot her first? And the bull … Why pulp her head like that?"

Her eyes were fixed on him. Hungry eyes. He looked away.

"Show me the bedrooms," he said.

They walked through the formal dining room. The forensic team's plastic runner crackled underfoot, the sound suddenly loud in the silence of the house.

It wasn't an ordinary silence. It was the type you only encountered in a house where a murder had taken place. It was as if every object had contracted, shrinking into itself in shock, holding its breath. The carpets, the furniture, even the pictures on the walls. Everything was quiet.

He marvelled again at the modern lights – tiny stars twinkling in a cloud of crystals over the fourteen-seater table. That too was impressive: smooth blond wood that begged to be touched.

A matching buffet table stood along the far wall, its smooth surface scarred. The culprits lay on the floor: more bonsai trees, their green containers in shards. Someone had clearly been pissed off with the bonsais.

"Are there any more of these trees elsewhere?" he asked.

"You'll see," was all that Qhubeka said.

They walked through a short passage, then up a wooden staircase that made a u-turn to the second floor. There was a safety gate at the top of the landing, which had been crudely cut open during the previous day's attempts to get the daughter out of her room.

The gate opened on to a spacious lounge with a TV and bookshelves. Here, too, the bonsai-hater had been busy.

The boy's bedroom was spartan. A crucifix above a made-up bed, a huge poster of a sweaty man with a microphone in his hand and a crowd below: not rock fans, but people praying with eyes closed and arms outstretched, palms up. They seemed to be in some sort of trance.

Qhubeka looked at the poster and rolled her eyes, pointed to the pocket Bible next to the computer.

The girl's room looked as if a clothes-bomb had exploded inside. Definitely no crucifix above the bed. On the walls, which were painted black, strange images had been drawn with white chalk: an angel with vampire teeth. Various symbols.

"A heptagram, one of the dragonflies told me," commented Qhubeka. "Apparently the devil's trap. It's supposed to ensnare all your demons."

There was a self-portrait that depicted Ellie as a wraith-like figure with big, mournful eyes. Teenage angst at its most obvious, Beeslaar decided.

He went to the window that overlooked the street and saw Qhubeka's police van under the tree in front of the gate. It was a long way down to the ground from here. Either the girl had wanted to make a helluva statement yesterday afternoon, or she'd been in a frenzy of fear.

"The wound on her left wrist?" he asked.

"Look in her bathroom."

He pushed the door open to an en suite bathroom. "Bloody hell, man." The basin looked as if a pig had been slaughtered in it. There was blood on the towels, the mirror, the toilet.

"Fingerprints?" he asked over his shoulder.

"Only hers, for now. I also don't know about the blood yet. Whether it's only her own. Nor at what stage she tackled her wrist."

"But she definitely did it herself?"

Qhubeka nodded.

The main bedroom was almost clinical. A bed the size of a ship. But only one person slept here. There was a water carafe and an open book on a bedside cabinet. The other side looked unoccupied.

"So where does *he* sleep?"

Qhubeka stood at the window, gazing out over the river towards the mountain. She turned around. "One can feel it here, in this room, don't you think?" He wasn't sure he knew what she was talking about.

"That the Du Toits don't qualify for the ABC?" Another of Blikkies's coinages: average buggered-up couple.

She smiled. "Du Toit has his own private den below – next to his office. Bathroom, shower, the works."

She led Beeslaar from the bedroom into a big dressing room. Another chandelier. Wardrobe doors doubling as mirrors. Beeslaar opened one. They were hers, the clothes arranged on the hangers according to colour – from white, through to blue, pink, red. Ending in black. The shoes seemed to be classified according to another system. Like the soldiers of different regiments: all the flip-flops together, followed by informal sandals. Next, informal shoes. Then the expensive trainers. And from there to more dressy, formal shoes, and then boots. There was also a safe, its door open, but nothing inside.

In a mirror he saw Qhubeka walking to the bathroom.

"Come," she said.

The bathroom was large, a symphony in smoked glass, blue-grey marble and snow-white towels. And yet another chandelier, over an oval-shaped bath the size of Vaal Dam.

"Here," said Qhubeka, indicating the space between the bath and the smoky glass of the toilet wall. There was a concealed cupboard with a mirrored door – from floor to ceiling in size. Inside were towels, toilet rolls and other bathroom stuff. Plus a jewellery box whose lid had been forced open. There were no trinkets inside, but instead a few fingers of dagga, a disposable lighter, foil, and a broken glass pipe.

"There you have it," said Qhubeka. "But it's not the main stash. We still need to find that."

Beeslaar inspected the rest of the bathroom. Heated rails, embroidered towels. Just one set. Soft as down. And warm.

Qhubeka was in a hurry as they walked down to the lower level. "Prammie's catching a lot of heat about this thing," she explained. "As if we need that right now."

Recalling Mynhardt's remarks, Beeslaar said: "I've heard someone recently died in the police cells?"

She came to a halt, gave him a long-suffering look. "Don't even talk about it, my friend. The newspapers were hysterical."

"Was it on your watch?"

"Dear God, fortunately not. He was picked up in a drunken stupor, brought in and locked up. There were three other guys in the cell with him. My bright-spark colleagues reckoned the fright would sober him up. But then he ended up being frightened to death. One of the other three strangled him."

"Tough," said Beeslaar. "Tough. But the procedure was somewhat irregular, wasn't it?"

"Damn right, you are. Worst of all: he wasn't even tested properly. Stellenbosch Watch phoned us to say that a man was driving erratically. The constables on duty went to collect him and locked him up, end of story. His three cell mates said he'd spent the whole night crying, talking and praying, wouldn't shut up.

Booze blues. He was a minor municipal official, probably his first time in a jail cell, and he'd disturbed the sleep of the three fine upstanding gents with him. So, you see? We have shitloads of trouble of our own. The Police Commissioner wants Prammie to give the Du Toit case to a more senior guy at Crime Intelligence. I'm not white and Afrikaans enough for 'the community'. But old Prammie's digging in his heels. He's in a state about this thing, so I'd better move my arse. Can I drop you somewhere?"

He declined the offer, said he needed a walk. She locked the house and got into the van.

"You feel like catching a thief at Jan Cats later on?" she asked. Another of Blikkies's sayings.

"Six o'clock," he said, and started walking.

22

A hand clasped her mouth, suffocating her. Gerda bit into it and, for a moment, the hand let go, but then moved down to her throat, pinned her against the headrest.

"If you scream, bitch, the baby dies." The muzzle of the gun was at her right temple.

She felt his breath against her ear, smelt the sweet stench of dagga. She tried to speak, to plead for her child. But there was no air in her lungs.

"Move over," he hissed.

Slowly, she lifted her hands from the steering wheel. No sudden movements: the warning flashed through her head. Carjackers are nervous creatures, which makes them unpredictable. And incredibly dangerous. They shoot on reflex. She kept her eyes down, battling the impulse to look at him.

"My baby—"

The muzzle moved to her mouth, shoved hard through her lips. She could feel the vibration of his body through the metal. It rattled against her teeth. Forced her jaws wider.

"Hhhnnnnlllooo …" She tried to protest, but he yanked the muzzle against the roof of her mouth. She registered pain, tasted blood.

"Move over. Or baby will die."

But the gun that was rammed down her throat was pinning her down against the seat.

"Move!"

He bent right down to face her. It was a teenager, she saw! She smelt his sweat. Lust and fear and excitement glittered in his eyes. He was enjoying this: the brutal penetration of her mouth.

"Move, bitch!"

She groped for the handbrake with her left hand. How was she going to heave her body up and out of her seat?

"Leave the brake alone," he threatened and took the gun from her mouth, trailing it over her chin, her neck, her breasts. He pressed it down painfully on the mound of her belly. She felt something wet on her cheek, his breath hot against her temple. It was when the wetness reached her ear that she realised it was his tongue. He stuck his tongue into her ear, his breath quickening.

She tried to get away from the tongue, shut her eyes tightly – to focus, to remember to breathe – and scooted over to the passenger seat.

"Oh-wee," Kleinpiet declared from the back of the car.

Gerda looked over her shoulder, straight into the muzzle of another gun. There was someone on the back seat next to Kleinpiet! A thin boy in a brown tracksuit top, a Melville Primary School cap pulled down over his greyish-black face.

He grinned at her, revealing blackened teeth. He was sitting nonchalantly next to the toddler, waving his gun at him. "Cooee," said the child, grabbing at it with his fat little hands.

She swallowed. The guy with bad breath had, in the meantime, taken her place behind the wheel and switched on the engine.

"The gate," he said calmly. "You open it. Now!" His eyes betrayed his anxiety. They kept darting between the rear-view mirror and the passageway that led from the open carport directly to the front door. If only Rebecca or Xolani had heard the car.

"The gate," hissed Bad Breath.

She fished around in the footwell, where the remote had dropped from her hand. Found it, pressed the button.

"Please, sir. Take the car. There's money in my bag, more in the house. I'll give you everything. You take the car. Plea—"

"No talking, or I hurt the baby. You understand?"

She gulped, still tasting blood.

"Nod your head, bitch."

She nodded furiously.

Then she remembered the alarm button on her remote control. She pressed it surreptitiously. Waited.

Nothing. No siren, not a sound. It was probably defective; she'd never used it before.

The only thing that happened was that the gate behind them slid open, squeaking, and Bad Breath quickly reversed into the glare of the afternoon sun.

"We going to drive nice. Understand? Nod!"

"I ... please!"

"No talk! You understand? Vrostana?"

She nodded.

"That's better. We are going on a niiiiiice driiiiive. Hey, bébé?" Unhurriedly, he adjusted the rear-view mirror, then drove down the steep hill to the first set of traffic lights. The gun was clutched in his right hand, but he kept it out of sight under his jacket.

She glanced around in the hope of spotting someone she recognised. If she could just catch someone's eye ... anyone's. But the only people at the traffic lights were the hawkers. The one who'd waved the bunch of roses at her a few minutes earlier bent down to look inside the car. "For the lady!" she heard him calling through the closed windows. He didn't recognise her, smiled broadly at Bad Breath. "C'mon daddy! Nice for the house!"

Bad Breath smiled back.

23

"Mauritius! How's tricks?" Ghalla and Mo exchanged fist bumps. "Kwaailappies," Mo squeaked.

He was sitting with a jumbo Wimpy coffee in front of him, slowly stirred in four sachets of brown sugar, looked at Ghaap with faraway eyes. "You know where your car is, of course."

"Where?" Ghaap sat down eagerly opposite him. In the daylight, Mo was even bigger than he recalled. About Beeslaar's height, but considerably bulkier. He wore his thinning black hair in a neat box-cut, the top gelled into spikes. Dark eyes, fleshy jowls that dwarfed a fine, straight nose. A straggly beard around his mouth and on his chins.

"Look, your car was ancient, right?"

Ghaap nodded, the flower of hope starting to wilt.

"So, why would a meerkat want such an old skoroskoro? Only for the parts, or to use as a getaway for a robbery or something. If he needs new wheels, he nabs a more recent model, a less conspicuous car."

"Kentucky Rounder," said Ghalla, who had squeezed in beside Mo. He looked like a schoolboy next to the big man. They didn't wear a formal uniform, Ghaap noticed. But they may just as well, because they looked virtually identical: tight-fitting jeans tucked into soft-sole boots. Merrell, no less. Bladdy expensive for an everyday shoe. But on the other hand: these guys didn't do everyday work. The shirts, in camouflage colours, were tightly tucked into the jeans. Black belts, from which hung holsters and extra magazines.

"He means Toyota Corollas," Mo explained, referring to Ghalla's remark. "That's what they're called here in the district." He gestured vaguely. Ghaap surmised that he meant Soweto.

"A guy that's looking for new tackies doesn't want to be noticed. So he steals a smallish sedan. Preferably white, since there's millions of them on the road. And then he changes it chop-chop: new paint job, number plate, chassis number, VIN number. The full Monty. What kind of car do you have?"

"Mazda 323, '88 model. Resprayed, new alloy mags. And a new surround-sound system! It doesn't bladdy well look like any other car, for sure. I scheme if you guys could help me, we'd track it down before the end of the day. I'll pay!"

Mo lifted a hand the size of a bunch of carrots. "Look, Ghaap, if you were a client of ours and there was a tracking device in the car, we'd find it in no time."

"I'll recognise my car from a mile off! I even helped respray it. And it's my first car, man. How hard can it be?" Ghaap refused to give up.

Mo shook his big head mournfully.

"I thought you guys are supposed to be so good!"

"That's only our technology, my friend. You see, we fit the car with two tracers. Under the dash, so that they're hidden. One's a decoy, a dummy that doesn't do anything, and we hope the meerkatte find it first and think that's that. But then there's a second one – fitted deep under the dash. And that's the live one that sends out the signals. We programme it – as soon as it enters a certain zone, somewhere the owner would never go. Like this district, say," he gestured with a beefy arm, "it starts chatting to our machines at the office. We phone, ask if you know you're driving around in Soweto. If you say no, we know your car's been nabbed."

"My car wasn't even insured, and I still owe ten thousand bladdy rand on it."

The two trackies looked at him sympathetically, nodding sadly.

"That's a problem, " said Ghalla. "Today, in a place like this, there's no way a vehicle is safe without tracking. That's just how it is, boet." He signalled something to a waitress before continuing. "Our system's the best fokken thing they've ever invented. Because we *find* that vehicle. And in the process we sweep up a lot of other crimes as well. You won't bladdy believe it! Missing persons, house robbery, rape, you name it. Stuff that has sweet blow-all to do with tracking. And fraud! Hell, boet. Every oke who's in financial shit finds a way. For instance, he'd tell one of the brothers from the district to take his car for a drive and sell it. Next day, the oke rocks up at our offices in tears, his car's gone. Spins us a story it was hijacked. Somewhere in Gordon Road, say. Then we do a playback on the system. But what do you know: at four o'clock the previous afternoon, when the car was supposedly being hijacked, it was in the client's own yard. That's how we catch him out. Man, I get such a kick out of this new shit. Us okes track down the most cars. Hands down, much more than any of the others!"

"Look," Ghaap tried to maintain a polite expression. "Ghalla. It's all very nice – that you guys are such rock stars and so on. But it doesn't solve my problem. Thank you. So, if it's all the same to you, I'll wait till you've finished here. Then you can please drop me off somewhere. I'm going to look for my car. I have fokkol else to do, in any case. Except to find new accommodation. I'm not going back to that place where my car got stolen."

"You can crash at my place!" Duif had made his appearance. He threw his tog bag down on an empty chair nearby and slid in next to Ghaap. "Howzit, boet. Are you still walking with that leg of yours?"

"He jols all over the place, I tell you!" Ghalla welcomed Duif with a knuckle bump. "I picked him up near New Canada station this morning. Walking like an ostrich, but could he *walk*, this big ou!"

Ghaap didn't allow himself to be sidetracked. "But you guys know where the chop shops are. You can take me there, can't you? To look for my car."

Ghalla smiled and touched Ghaap's shoulder. "Seems to me you still don't get the picture. If your car's been chopped, it's a goner. Gone with the wind, goodbye and so long. It's already sneaked out of that chop shop in a thousand and ten pieces. All that's left is the carcase, and by now they've dumped it somewhere for the donkey-cart okes to scavenge for scrap. But how about you ride with us? What do you say, Mo?"

Mo's jumbo mug was empty. He pushed it aside to make room for the plate of food the waitress was depositing in front of him. Along with a basket of white toast. Ghaap's eyes nearly popped out of his head. Pork sausages, two fried eggs, bacon rashers, baked beans in tomato sauce, fried tomatoes, braised mushrooms and hash browns. All under a thick layer of melted cheese.

To his absolute horror, a similar plate was put down in front of him.

"Yoh," Ghaap protested feebly. "It's a bit too much."

"It's hectic food, my bru," said Ghalla, his mouth full. "Lekker greasy bacon and arsehole fruit. Cures any ailment."

"Arsehole fruit?"

"Eggs, man! Like in the fruit from a chicken's backside. Seems you're still a bit dof, boet?"

The others smiled and tucked in, with Mo first bowing his head solemnly in silent prayer, his knife and fork poised in his hands.

Ghaap buttered some toast, spread it with jam. He'd lost his appetite for eggs. Wondered what his mom would say if she heard these guys.

Once everyone had finished eating, Mo took out his wallet and indicated to Ghaap that he could relax: today he was the trackies' guest.

Mo had just taken some notes from his wallet when the three men's cellphones all chirped simultaneously. They dropped everything and looked at their messages, then jumped up wordlessly and started running. Mo had left the notes next to his plate and signalled to the waitress. She nodded, evidently familiar with this procedure.

Ghaap grabbed his jacket and ran after them. Mo motioned that Ghaap should drive with him. His car was a Mitsubishi Lancer, a brand-new model with a swanky fin on its short-arse boot. The distinctive antennas were mounted on the roof. Mo took two bulletproof vests out of the boot and threw one to Ghaap, talking on his cellphone all the while.

"We're in Lens," Ghaap heard him say. "Where's the signal?" While listening, he waved to Duif and Ghalla in the Golf GTI, telling them to take off so long.

"Head for the Golden Highway!" he called to them. Then into his phone: "Two guys on their way to the Golden Highway. I'm taking Old Potch Road. Keep feeding us those signals! All the way!"

With that, he yanked open his car door; a second later, the engine roared into life.

Ghaap's door had barely closed when they pulled off with screaming tyres. Petrol attendants and people coming from the toilets scrambled out of the way. Anxiously, Ghaap fumbled for his seatbelt.

24

Beeslaar strolled back to town at a leisurely pace, his thoughts on the riddle of Elmana du Toit. He dropped into a chair at a sidewalk café and ordered coffee, shocked at the price. He requested water too – tap water. His cellphone rang as his coffee arrived.

"Albertus, it's Reana du Toit. I'm glad I got hold of you."

He waited in silence to hear what she wanted this time.

"Would it be possible for you to come and see us? Alone."

"Where, Mrs du Toit?"

"We're at Willem's house, my son's neighbour. Malan has just collected me. I thought maybe you should talk to us on your own. So we can … You know?"

He sighed. These people wanted something from him that he was unable to give them. He promised to be there in half an hour, and pulled his cup towards him.

It was Rea du Toit herself who opened the neighbour's front door for him.

"Come through," she said in a worried voice. "You join Malan, I'll get you some coffee." She pointed to a door leading off to the right from the entrance hall.

It was a TV room, he saw as he entered. Malan du Toit was watching a sports channel, the sound muted.

He jumped up when he spotted Beeslaar and switched off the TV.

"Er, thanks for coming. Sit down, please," he gestured. Beeslaar perched on the edge of a recliner, designed for lounging in front of a TV. He detested chairs like these because his legs were so long and he never knew where to put them.

They sat in silence for a while. Beeslaar inspected his surroundings. Willem Bester and his wife seemed to have a predilection for hippopotamuses. Hippos of various sizes were on display throughout the room. The coffee table itself had a base in the shape of a giant hippo, with a glass top mounted on its back.

"You wanted to see me," Beeslaar said.

"Look, Captain Beeslaar. My mother says you're reliable, one of the few experienced people still left in the police."

"Try to give the local police a chance. There really are good people in the police, Mr du Toit. Regardless of whether they're black or white. You should just give them a chance."

"Look, man, if this had been about a stolen bicycle, maybe. But I need to

protect my family. There's been a massive assault on our safety. And Ellie is …
She's fragile. I can't risk her becoming more traumatised. Please. You saw the
state she's in, this morning." The man fought back the tears.

"What does the doctor say?"

"He says exactly that. That's why she's been put onto medication. Any rough
handling at this stage …" Du Toit blew his nose, regained his composure. "Man,
even the fact that it's a black lady leading the investigation … God knows, I'm
not a racist. But we live in a country where white people's lives are no longer
worth anything. Just your skin colour alone makes you a target, makes you
guilty. You're guilty of having being born at all. In Africa, that is. You're fair
game, you're redundant and unwelcome. You're welcome to open your purse,
thank you very much. For the rest, it's shut up and keep quiet!"

He fell silent, his jaw muscles working.

"The mere fact that this investigation is now focusing on *us*," he said slowly.
"I don't know. My daughter can't cope with it right now. She comes home, her
mother's been attacked in broad daylight in her own house, forced to open the
safe, then killed in the cruellest possible way. Surely that can't be normal in a
civilised society, Captain Beeslaar? And then a black policewoman barges in
here and wants to subject the child to interrogation. Really!" He wiped his shiny
bald pate with the flat of his hand. "No, man! Look, I've got nothing against
black people. But how much experience does someone like her have … the lady
you came with this morning? I forget her name."

"Qhubeka," Beeslaar suggested.

He nodded, looked at his hands folded in his lap. They were soft and pudgy,
and a wedding ring cut into a finger.

"I have a good mind to take the children out of the country. That's what I feel
like doing. Switzerland, New Zealand, any place where they can forget this
terrible …" His voice petered out.

"I hear what you're saying, sir." Beeslaar put on his best funeral voice, hoping
to mask the irritation that had welled up in him. "You are quite correct. This was
the worst thing that could happen to a family. I understand that you feel like
fleeing, that you want to protect your children. But one thing I can promise you:
all of us want to find the perpetrator as soon as possible and make him pay."

"So you all say," said Du Toit sceptically.

"Did *you* perhaps move your wife's body yesterday afternoon?"

"What are you talking about, man? For God's sake, I really don't understand
why the family is now being cross-examined!" His eyelids twitched.

"Mr du Toit, your wife's body was moved after she'd died. That is beyond
doubt, but we also have to try and establish what and who we can eliminate
from the investigation. So, please try to remember exactly what the scene looked

like when you got home. What your son said to you. As faithfully as possible. Your daughter, too."

Du Toit didn't reply at once. Both eyelids twitched wildly. "I've probably told my story fourteen times already, Captain Beeslaar. But if you insist." He fell quiet again, searching for words.

"Could you see immediately that your wife ... that she was deceased? You didn't try to, er, help her?"

Du Toit wiped his sweaty pate again, this time with a handkerchief.

"I did ... nothing. When I got there yesterday ..." He closed his eyes, as if he didn't want to relive the scene. "Dawid-Pieter was outside. He was crying. There was blood on him. My first thought was that he'd been hurt too. He was standing in the garage doorway. Someone from ADT, our security company, was with him. The guy wanted to stop me from entering the house, said the police were on their way. But Ellie's bicycle was there. In the garage, so I knew she was still inside. I ordered the security guard to stay with Dawid-Pieter while I went looking for Ellie. And inside ... Well, what I found was what you've probably seen yourself. I could see at once that Elmana ... God ... I heard Ellie calling, found her on the stairs ..." He gulped to get his voice under control.

"Did she have anything in her hands?"

Du Toit shook his head violently.

"The statuette, Mr du Toit. The Brahman bull. Did you see it?"

He said nothing, but Beeslaar could see a shift in the expression of his eyes.

"Whose side are you really on, Captain Beeslaar?" he asked after a while.

"I'm on your wife's side, Mr du Toit. I believe all of us are on her side."

The silence between them lengthened, Du Toit struggling to contain his emotions while Beeslaar sat studying him.

Rea du Toit entered with a tray holding a coffee plunger and three mugs. A plate of ginger biscuits, Beeslaar's favourite. He immediately took two, popping them into his mouth as he depressed the plunger. Du Toit shook his head when Beeslaar offered him coffee. Instead, he got up and poured himself a drink from a crystal carafe on the coffee table in front of them. Beeslaar caught the smell of whisky. He shuddered, his liver still queasy after the binge of the night before.

Silently, Rea du Toit sat down to one side with a mug of coffee, casting a disapproving look at the son's glass.

"I want to appoint my own investigation team," Malan du Toit announced abruptly. "I'm as sure as hell not going to put my family through the trauma of ... of the incompetence of our local police. Do you understand?" The question was directed at Beeslaar.

"You are fully entitled within the law to do that, Mr du Toit."

"And you must lead it." He looked at Beeslaar over the rim of his glass. "You can name your price, bring in international forensic experts, the works. Money is not an issue. I'm prepared to bankrupt myself, but I'm not going to let my family be subjected to the flagrant … the incompetence and dysfunctionality … Not like what happened in the case of that student. Listen, don't get me wrong: I've got nothing against Captain Qhubeka."

Beeslaar couldn't help noticing the pronunciation: "Kewbeka".

"All I'm asking of you, Captain Beeslaar, is that you lead the investigation. Even if it has to be unofficially."

Beeslaar shook his head. "It's out of the question, Mr du Toit. Captain Qhubeka and I work for the same boss – the Commissioner of Police. And, trust me, a private investigator will ask the same questions: for instance, at what stage did Ellie lock herself in upstairs? And why did she try climbing out the window instead of unlocking the security door? And why the cut on her wrist? And why was she not in her school uniform? Things like that. A private investigator needs the same answers to get an idea of what happened, and of what to look out for, in order to eliminate the family from his investigation. That's why he'd want to know whether Ellie had anything in her hands when you found her on the stairs. Where the Brahman statuette was when you arrived."

Du Toit's face started reddening, exasperation in his eyes. "Ellie had *nothing* with her. She was completely beside herself, covered in blood. I think she'd tried to wake up my wife. And what on earth does her uniform have to do with anything?"

Beeslaar didn't reply, just sipped gingerly at his coffee. A bit short on sugar, he decided, but it was good coffee. Then he asked: "And your son, you say he hadn't been *inside* the house?"

"For the umpteenth time, Captain, no!"

"The TV was still on; the robbers wouldn't have tried to take it along with them?"

"I don't know. Things were in a mess. There was so much destruction, such chaos. I couldn't get anything out of Ellie … She was trembling, sat rocking back and forth like a zombie. When I phoned for an ambulance, she became hysterical. I wanted to pick her up, get her out of the house. But she slipped out of my arms and fled up the stairs. I followed her, fearing there might still be a thug somewhere. She slammed the security gate shut behind her, ran to her room. I think she was in such a panic, she didn't realise she'd locked me out. I couldn't get the gate open. It locks from the inside – for security reasons. And then the police arrived."

"And Dawid-Pieter was outside the whole time," Beeslaar said interrogatively.

"Why the hell do you keep harping on that? I've already told you—"

"But he was inside earlier, before he phoned you?"

Du Toit looked heavenwards in what seemed utter exasperation. "He never reached the sitting room. So, no!"

"Did your wife have enemies?"

"*What*? It was a *robbery*, Captain Beeslaar. A house robbery. My safe has been emptied, my wife's too. I thought a man with your level of experience … You of all people ought to know! People invaded my house in broad daylight, tortured my wife, killed her and bashed in … Dear God, what is it that you don't want to see?"

"Your daughter, Ellie. In your view, why did she try to cut her wrists?"

Du Toit stared at him, clearly incredulous. There were black rings around the deep-blue eyes. His cheeks were pale, the skin taut and red. Specks that looked like the dried remains of shaving soap were visible near his nostrils.

"It must be the shock. God knows, she's at a complicated age."

"How was her relationship with her mother?"

"What do you mean? What does *that* have to do with all of this?"

"I would just like to know, Mr du Toit. If they were very close, it may explain your daughter's behaviour yesterday. Have you asked her why she did it?"

"Of course I asked her. A psychologist came to see her last night – the wife of one of my business partners. But Ellie …"

"Yes?"

"She doesn't speak. She remembers nothing, she says. The doctor says it's the shock."

"And are you sure your son wasn't near your wife's body?"

"Absolutely! I instructed the ADT guard to stay with him outside."

"Why didn't you let the ADT guard enter first and secure the house?"

"What do you mean? Elmana was in any case already … I was concerned about my son. And then I saw Ellie's bike standing there. I knew she had to be inside. I almost went crazy with fear that something might have happened to her as well."

"But your son, was he or wasn't he near your wife's body?"

"No! How many times do I have to tell you? He was *not*. It was only me. And Ellie. Just the two of us."

"But the ADT guard was armed, wasn't he? If you feared for your daughter's life, why didn't you let him go in first?"

"Captain Beeslaar. I've answered all the questions. Can't we move on to something constructive now? We're wasting time, for God's sake, sitting here rehashing the same information over and over."

"Just answer the question, Mr du Toit."

"I didn't think. The guard and I arrived at more or less the same time. When I saw the state my son was in … He was crying, there was blood on his hands, on his school uniform."

"If he didn't touch your wife's body, how did the blood get on him?"

Du Toit took a sip of whisky. "He ... Ellie touched her mother and got a lot of blood on her. It was transferred onto us! But neither of them moved her body. Why would they? They were confused and terrified!"

"The statuette? Maybe he picked it up?"

"Then his fingerprints would be on it, surely?" There was defiance in his voice.

Beeslaar put down his coffee mug and was about to get up.

"So you're not going to help us, Albertus?" Rea du Toit said anxiously.

"No, I'm sorry. Even if I'd wanted to, Tannie Rea, but then I'd have to be told the truth. My advice to you is to work with the police. And get hold of a professional, if you like. And to be completely frank with him. In my case, I can't do private work *and* serve in the police at the same time. But I'm still here until Sunday. You can call on me at any time if you have questions. In the meantime, I suggest you work with Captain Qhubeka, give her all the information you can. Time is of the essence. Believe me, the more days that pass, the harder it is to track down the culprits."

He started hoisting himself from the recliner, but Du Toit gestured that he should sit down again. "Wait," he said as he held out the coffee plunger to Beeslaar, who sat down resignedly and offered his mug. There was a tremor in Du Toit's hand as he poured the coffee.

"Mana was a busy woman," he continued. "Not your average housewife. She was very involved in the community. Beauty, our housekeeper, has been with us for years. She and Elmana understood each other well. Because Mana was ..." He looked at his mother, his glance unfathomable. "She was very ... strict. Often too strict. She didn't take any nonsense. Mistakes, miscommunication, things like that. Not every domestic could get on with her. Those ones before Beauty resigned one after the other. Our entire household was ... How can I put it. Elmana didn't tolerate mistakes. There were never any hiccups. Each of us knew our place and pulled our weight. Mana managed it all like a well-oiled machine. She could ..." His voice broke, and he looked at his mother.

Then he inhaled deeply, regaining control of his emotions.

"She was an excellent mother. And she excelled at everything she undertook. A perfectionist, strict, disciplined." He lapsed into silence, frowned at the ice cubes in his glass.

Rea du Toit took the gap: "She was always immaculately dressed. For many years she was chair of our Connoisseurs Club, a ladies' organisation."

"And," Du Toit added, "she demanded the same from others. I'll admit, we argued about that occasionally, especially when the children were younger.

But what did I know? I was always away working. She, on the other hand, was heavily involved in the community."

"And socially?"

"She wanted to keep busy, didn't want to end up in the tea-and-gossip clubs," said Rea du Toit. "Often complained about the town's snobbery. That people looked down on her because of her background. If you ask me, it was just low self-esteem on her part. Though I suppose that's not relevant now."

"I thought you said she excelled in everything?"

Du Toit cleared his throat, said, "You have to understand what kind of person she was. She was an athlete. In her youth, people had great expectations of her. Her coach spoke of the new Zola Budd. But her circumstances didn't allow this. She came from a very poor background. She lived her life with the discipline of an athlete. Every morning at six o'clock she was at the gym – first a spinning class, then the circuit and weights. That's how we met. I was at university at the time. I played rugby, and she played hockey. We were both mad about sport. She wasn't able to study, though. There was no money. But as an athlete, she commanded respect."

"Had her behaviour perhaps changed lately? More tense, unable to sleep, lethargic, maybe?"

Du Toit and his mother exchanged glances, shook their heads in unison.

"If anything, she was incredibly busy," Du Toit said. "You have no idea how many hungry people we have in this town. People who've simply slipped through the cracks, become homeless. Street children. To my mind, people like Mana are the ones who keep this country from burning. That's why her death is such a crying shame; it's Amy Biehl all over again.

"That damn soup kitchen took up so much of her time. And she wasn't always well, especially in the last few months. She suffered from terrible migraines, every now and then."

"And besides," his mother added, "her bad knee was giving her a lot of trouble, wasn't it, my boy? She'd started thinking about a knee replacement."

Du Toit nodded, but his eyes told the truth: he wasn't really familiar with the minutiae of his wife's life. He'd been drifting in a safe haze of denial. "The soup kitchen," he said, "she ran it expertly, you could almost say with military precision. She found sponsors among the town's businesspeople. Begged a minibus from a Hyundai dealer, to collect day-old food from shops like Woolworths and Pick n Pay." He reflected for a moment. "I can't imagine she'd have had any enemies. She didn't have time for nonsense like that." He dropped his head, sat musing for a while.

"Vincent," he said suddenly. First softly, as if he were testing the waters, then with greater conviction: "The soup kitchen's minibus driver. His surname escapes me but his name is Vincent. I don't want to point fingers, but he's the only person I can think of. They had a rocky relationship from the start. The guy's got a massive chip on his shoulder. If the press came to take photos at a function or something, he'd pretend the whole thing was his initiative. Just the other day, for instance, after a fire in Kayamandi, our local black township. Mana had organised food and accommodation for the victims. And when a reporter arrived on the scene – Mana was in any case not a publicity seeker – Vincent stole the limelight. He's the only full-time employee of the feeding scheme and he takes a lot of liberties, especially when it comes to the vehicle. At one stage he even threatened to take Mana to the labour court for harassment or something because she'd supposedly been too strict."

"Do you have Vincent's address, his phone number?"

"It'd be on her phone, which is with the cops. It strikes me now that the friction between them had actually been coming for a while." He looked at his mother, who nodded in agreement. "Vincent often didn't turn up in time to collect the food. Then everyone would phone Mana, complaining about the food going off. I don't know the whole story. I offered to go and talk to him at one stage, but Mana wouldn't have it, said I had enough problems of my own."

"But it's *more* than just the work, isn't it?"

Du Toit glanced at his mother before replying. "I was very busy. The construction industry's going through a bad time."

"Why do you sleep in your office?"

He clucked, clearly annoyed. "I often have to work at night, make calls to America or China or elsewhere. That's really all there is to it."

They sat in silence for a while.

"And your wife's mental health?" Beeslaar prodded.

"*What?* That's got *nothing* to do with any of this."

Rea du Toit cleared her throat discreetly and said: "Lately, Mana was indeed … a little tense. She just had too much on her plate."

"With respect, Mrs du Toit, she used very heavy medication and stimulants. Metamphetamine and diet pills, far beyond a healthy limit."

"Diet pills! You people must be demented," exclaimed Du Toit. "There was one thing Mana didn't have, and that's weight problems. What are you talking about?"

"Metamphetamine. It's a stimulant. Like tik."

"That's darned rubbish, Albertus," Rea du Toit interjected. "It's exactly the kind of thing the police would come up with. Elmana simply took on too much. And her doctor gave her something because she was sleeping so badly."

"And stress," Malan du Toit added, "she struggled with that. She could get very upset. Then she'd take something to calm her down. It's true she was a tense person. As I've said, her nerves were often a bit on edge. Especially after the children were born."

Rea du Toit took over again: "She wanted to give the children one hundred per cent of her attention, didn't believe in nannies bringing them up. She wasn't one for letting them watch TV or play video games. Not like most parents today. The children had educational games. And she was always there for them."

Beeslaar said nothing. To him, this didn't sound like such an idyllic childhood. On the other hand, maybe anything was preferable to the boxing ring in which he'd been raised.

But Malan du Toit hadn't finished singing his wife's praises. "Once the children started going to school, she became involved in the community, took on more and more responsibilities. And along with that came the migraines. Headaches that often lasted for days, and naturally she had to use strong medication."

Beeslaar stood up. He'd had enough. These two were either in extreme denial, or trying to fool him with their dog-and-pony show about the virtuous wife.

And, after all, this wasn't *his* headache.

"I'll say goodbye for now," he said, putting his mug down on the tray. "But I should warn you: don't underestimate Captain Qhubeka. She knows exactly what a heavy user Mrs du Toit was. So, don't think she's going to fall for this story of yours. She'll put hard questions to you, such as where Mrs du Toit obtained her drugs."

"But she didn't use drugs!"

"Wake up, Mr du Toit. Apart from the doctor's prescriptions, she also used heavy stimulants. Tik. And that's something the police definitely won't ignore."

Du Toit put down his glass and also stood up. He exhaled, lengthily. "So you're telling me I'm lying, is that it?"

"Frankly, yes!"

"Then we have nothing more to say to each other. You've already shown your colours. You're on the side of the incompetents, and I bet they'll make sure that my name and that of my family are dragged through the mud. While a gang of house robbers and murderers run around freely!"

Beeslaar waited for the man's anger to abate. "One last question," he said. "Do *you* have any enemies, people who may wish to harm you or your family? Have you maybe had threats of any kind?"

"What are you insinuating by this? *Really!*"

"You're in the business world, the construction industry. And as you've said yourself, there's been a recession after the 2008 credit crunch. The police might want to know about your finances, if you have any debts or owe specific people money."

"Look, Captain Beeslaar. My business is of no concern to the police. I manage my affairs properly, you understand? And I think it's best if you leave now."

Beeslaar shook his head and walked out wordlessly.

This man, he thought, had better start praying.

25

It was dead quiet in the car.

Gerda clenched her teeth, but the hysteria felt like a fist in her throat. Choking her. She kept her hands visible, forced herself not to look at her kidnapper. *Never make eye contact. It rattles the hijacker. Do whatever he says, no unnecessary talk, keep your hands where the hijacker can see them, put him at ease, no sudden movements, don't argue, do as he says, above all, don't make eye contact.*

She'd lost count of the number of times she'd rehearsed this.

The young man turned left into Main Road, controlling the steering wheel deftly with one hand. "Get ready," he said.

"Wha—?"

"Not you, bitch. I'm talking to the boy in the back." He spoke softly, his lips pulled into a flat line. "Don't look. He's got a gun, it's pointed at the baby. If you want your child to live, you must do what I tell you. Understand?"

Gerda shut her eyes tightly. There was a wildness in her body, something that refused to believe what was happening. That wanted to scream, to vomit, to smash, all at the same time. Wanted to tear this man apart with her bare hands. *Breathe, breathe slowly, slow-ly. One-crocodile, two-crocodile. Don't make eye contact, don't speak, do as he says, breathe deeply, no sudden movements. Concentrate. Fill your lungs. Stay rational, calm. That's what you need now. Hysteria will make everything worse, your son … No, your daughter too.* She spread her hands instinctively over her bulge, risked a quick glance over her shoulder. And her heart almost stopped.

The boy with the school cap lifted his jacket, showing her the pistol trained on Kleinpiet. He gave her an innocent smile. The toddler's mouth puckered, about to cry, as he caught her gaze.

"Please," she moaned. "Please, just let him go. You can drop him anywhere. He … he can already walk. Someone will find him. Just let him go. Please!" She was crying now, trying to turn her heavy body so that she could put a consoling hand on her child.

"Don't move, bitch! Mpho, shoot the child!"

"Noooo! Please, I'll—"

The car swerved abruptly to the right, throwing her off balance. She heard cars hooting, tyres squealing. The engine roared up a steep hill. She tried to see where they were, but her mind had stalled. Everything was familiar, yet strange.

Suddenly they reached the top of the hill between Melville and Westdene, and the landscape fell into place again. They were in Fourth Avenue. At First Street they turned right, then left into Ararat Street, sharply right into Warwick, left again into Motor. At every turn the driver checked the rear-view as well as the side mirrors. Evidently on the lookout for pursuers. Then he turned once more: Ararat.

"Wheeeee!" the boy at the back shouted with each wild swerve, a happier Kleinpiet echoing him. Gerda held on to the seat with both hands to avoid being thrown about.

The driver slowed down, cruising down Ararat, and coming to a halt at the Westdene Dam. The streets were quiet. It was still some time before the afternoon traffic would pick up. A truck rumbled past in front of them.

"Wipe your face. You look like an animal."

"I need my handbag." She bent down. The handbag was under her legs in the footwell.

"Don't you move! And don't talk! Just clean yourself up," he hissed.

"I need …" She battled her tears, gulped. "Tissues. My handbag." She found herself talking in a near whisper.

"Use your fuckin' hands!" He was calmly looking left and right, watching for approaching traffic.

Then he quickly leant across, whipped the bag out from under her legs.

With one hand, he rifled through the contents and took out the cellphone. He passed the bag to the boy behind him. "Get the house keys and alarm remote," he ordered.

"I've got money in the house. Let me go get it. And a laptop and—"

"Quiet!"

He put the car into gear and turned right into Lewes, her phone on the seat between his legs.

As they drove over the dam wall, a bus approached.

She made a fast grab for the cellphone.

"Bitch!"

Kleinpiet started crying. "You see what you make us do! Gimme that phone!"

With trembling fingers she was already dialling 10111. But there were renewed screams from her son.

She threw the phone back at the man as if it were snake. Turned to the back, strained to touch her child who was crying loudly by now, stretching out his arms to her. She saw the pistol against her child's ribs, the icy viciousness on the boy's face. Good God, he was a primary-school kid, couldn't be older than twelve! She turned slowly to the front, saw that they had passed the dam and were now turning up into Thornton.

The driver held his pistol and her phone between his legs, partially hidden under his shirt. For the first time she became aware of his odd clothing: torn tracksuit pants and tackies – and a gleaming white office shirt, tie and jacket. Once again she felt a chill down her spine. This wasn't a random hijacking. It had been planned! *Stay calm, for God's sake, breathe deeply, stay calm, stay calm. Concentrate. For the sake of your child ... your children!*

The man suddenly turned left, into Dover Street.

Hope flared inside her. She knew people there. The Claassens couple, Fred and Marita. If she could just catch someone's eye. The street was deserted, not even a beggar or a mealie seller in sight.

Gerda wiped her face again with her hand. She wanted to see.

Houses crouched behind high walls topped with razor wire, rows of spikes, electrified fencing. On the right was a large playing field, but it was deserted. Where was everybody? She looked at 7C, where the Claassens family lived. They took great pride in the sidewalk garden they'd established outside their high wall. A lawn, the works. Fred watered it in the afternoons. As soon as he came home after work. His "gear-switching" activity, he called it.

Dear Lord, please let Fred ... If only she could spot *someone* who knew her. Someone who'd instantly smell a rat and phone the police, or the tracking company.

But there was no sign of life at 7C. It was too early, no one was home yet.

They drove slowly as the driver started groping around under the dashboard, yanking out some electrical wires.

Please God, let him pull out the wires of the starter motor! Cause a short circuit.

He was muttering to himself. She couldn't make out the language. He slowed down even more, constantly checking the rear-view mirror. They drove around the block. Now he was digging at the panelling, chipping away purposefully with a screwdriver he'd suddenly produced. His fingers worked deftly. Whatever he was doing, he was clearly not a novice.

She heard the muffled ring of a cellphone.

Still cruising, the man dropped the screwdriver and took a phone out of his jacket pocket.

"Ja," he answered. "Parcels are fine. We're on time."

Gerda heard a male voice on the other end. Good God, what could the "parcels" be? She and her son?

"Westdene, ja. No. We're on time. I'm just doubling back. Soon now I'll drop the tracking. Then we can move." He listened a moment. "No, I'm nearly there. Easy, I told you. Ja, found the dummy already. I'll park by the dam for the real one."

The voice became more urgent.

Gerda itched to do something – open the door and scream for help. Jump out of the car. They were driving slowly enough, dammit. But her son, buckled up in his child seat ...

"Help us, we've been hijacked!" She yelled at the top of her voice.

"Shut the fuck up, bitch!" He hit her on the belly, the cellphone still in his hand. The blow felt like an explosion in her gut. For a moment, she blacked out. Then she got her breath back.

"You monster!" she screamed and hit out wildly at him. "Monster! Monster!"

She tugged at the steering wheel, catching the man off guard. The car swerved sharply, and Kleinpiet began to scream.

"Kill the fuckin' child, Mpho. Kill it! Make it shut up," the driver yelled over his shoulder as he pushed Gerda away. He grabbed the wheel in both hands, his foot flat on the accelerator. The car jerked forward, throwing Gerda back against the seat.

But she came back at him. "You fucker, you FUCKER!" Fear and shock changed into raw fury. She would kill this scumbag. Drawing energy from deep inside her belly, she heaved sideways. Lashed into him with both fists. He swore loudly as he ducked and warded her off with his left arm.

Summoning all her strength, Gerda hit at him blindly. But he fended off her blows with ease, drove even faster.

Then she yanked on the handbrake.

The car slid, zigzagged.

"Lucky!" the boy in the back yelled. "Lucky, hey, watch out!"

For a moment she grappled with the driver for control of the handbrake. Triumphant, he slammed his foot on the accelerator, but the car had already drifted too far and was heading straight for a plane tree.

Gerda screamed, the heel of her hand about to hit the hooter when she saw the glint of a pistol.

She felt a sharp pain in her temple, and a black curtain descended on her.

Faintly, from far away, she could hear her son's high-pitched scream.

26

Holding his cellphone to his ear, Mo changed gears with the other hand. He'd reached sixty kilometres an hour even before they were past the petrol pumps.

He swerved onto the N12 underpass south of Soweto to join the thick stream of traffic on the N1, the road linking Cape Town with Beit Bridge and Zimbabwe.

Ghaap didn't have time to properly fasten his bulletproof. His priority was to get the seatbelt buckled. If they collided with anything at this speed, he'd be a human projectile. Shoot through the windscreen like Rocket Man and land in Potchefstroom. Or in his mother's backyard in the Northern Cape.

Mo kept talking on the phone, controlling the wheel by turns with his elbow, a knee and his left hand. The dashboard resembled a Boeing instrument panel – crammed with gadgets that beeped and croaked and farted. To Ghaap's surprise, one of them was a police radio. He hadn't realised that the trackers were on the network. Two GPS systems – one below the rear-view mirror, the other directly in front of Ghaap, on the passenger side. There was also a green LCD panel displaying a compass, which chirped and beeped continually.

Mo yelled into the phone, telling the person to stand by as he placed it on the hands-free holder on the dash.

Ghaap couldn't make head or tail of what was happening, but he didn't care. He clung for dear life to his seat, convinced that he might soon see his mother. But first he hoped to see his car. Maybe this was *his* car they were chasing now, he told himself optimistically.

And then the instrument panel said in a posh English voice: "Polo Vivo, hatchback, white. Licence plate Yankee Foxtrot Bravo Zero Zero Five Golf."

Mo's phone rang, and Ghalla's voice filled the car: "We're heading for the Golden Highway! That car's going to Eldo's!"

"Sharp!"

The connection went dead, and Mo again hit the accelerator. Ghaap was dead sure he'd prayed more often than the Pope over the past two days. And each time they rounded a corner he automatically kicked at non-existent brakes in the footwell. The surroundings flashed past his window in one long blur. He was aware they were flying through a poor section, past shacks with old tyres, rusted wheelbarrows and broken furniture on the roof – the poor man's answer to roof nails. Yet poor as they were, most properties were burglar-proofed with an assortment of materials – mattress innersprings, chicken wire, bits of wood, corrugated iron, hubcaps. Long-legged chickens all over the place. And children, goats and mangy dogs. Man and beast made way for the thundering Lancer.

The peeping sound on the dashboard was suddenly more insistent.

Mo phoned again.

"It's not far from me! Klipspruit. Where are you guys? The signal is east of me. In the direction of Eldo's. We'll check out Tros's place first!"

Then the line went dead.

Mo straightened up in his seat and typed something into his GPS. Ghaap noticed that the two devices were synchronised. The passenger would normally do the phoning and typing. Where was Mo's driving partner, he wondered. But there was no time for questions – next moment the car swerved to avoid two scrap-filled supermarket trolleys being pulled along by two old souls in rags. They nearly hit an approaching minibus taxi, which swung out obligingly, giving way to the trackie car. Ghaap was surprised at the taxi's tolerance, but then realised it was more a matter of helping these boys do their job. Everyone equally gatvol with crime.

"How do you know where that car is?" Ghaap called out above the noise.

"It's a Golf Vivo," Mo shouted in turn, "the Bushies really love that car!"

Ghaap grabbed at the armrest as they shot round a corner, the car skidding dangerously. He barely registered the racist term Mo had used for people from his community.

"Happens time and again!" Mo continued. "We get called out for a Golf, we already know it's heading for Eldorado Park or thereabouts. We go wait for them. In Eldo's! Lots! There's an oke there who …" His words were drowned out by a new flurry of radio static. It seemed that the cops had now also got wind of the hijacking.

Mo struggled to keep his voice up, Ghaap noticed. He sounded like a strangled turkey.

"So, what about *my* car?" Ghaap ventured.

Mo's banana-fingers entered new coordinates into the tracking compass as he croaked, "History, my friend," and changed gears – sending the rev counter right into the red zone. The beeping became louder and more urgent and Mo slowed down, glanced around. He picked up his phone: "So where are you guys? The bladdy cops will be here sooner than you!"

"We're close by! Mandela View!" Ghaap recognised Ghalla's voice.

Mo swore and made a U-turn. Approaching cars and taxis had to brake sharply to give him space, then waited for him to finish his move before carrying on, no one batting an eyelid.

"Hang ten!" Mo called out to Ghalla over the phone. The engine gave a high-pitched whine, and Ghaap caught a glimpse of a torn-off street sign. Everything in this place, he thought, every last thing here had scrap value. And what couldn't be sold was put to use – plugged a hole in a wall or a roof or a fence. Madiba Drive, he read on a kerbstone as they sped past.

Mo slammed on the brakes. In front of them stood Ghalla's black Golf. And in front of them the white Vivo hatchback, standing sideways across the road, all four doors flung open and the occupants gone.

Ghalla and Duif sat scanning the area. Then Duif pointed at something.

Ghaap craned his neck but couldn't see anything suspicious. The road was dead quiet. It was a poor neighbourhood, but not wretchedly so. Vibracrete walls, iron gates, breeze-block houses set back from the road. Here and there, an obligatory car wreck on bricks, and clothes lines with rows of baby nappies waving in the sun.

The green-eyed tracking monitor on Mo's dashboard was beeping insistently by now, just like the final scene in a TV drama moments before the patient's heart attack.

Ghaap sank down into his seat. The heavy shell of the bulletproof didn't sink along with him, and he disappeared into it up to his nose. But he couldn't be bothered. Rather mouse than macho, he decided. The tension in the air was palpable. He wished the goddamn beeping would stop. Wished he was somewhere else. At home. His mom baking him vetkoek, spreading them with her home-made peach jam, putting a few extra ones in his lunchbox for his colleagues to enjoy. Maybe he shouldn't have come here after all. He'd been under the illusion that he'd gain experience. Prove himself to Beeslaar. But look at him now. Minus his car. Likely to be shot to pieces at any moment. He'd been told often enough how fucked-up this place's bad guys are – shooting with AKs. Especially at cops. And all for the sake of some or other rich bliksem's car. Jissis.

He gulped, glanced nervously at Mo, but the trackie sat motionless. A solid hunk of brawn and concentration.

Ghaap sank down even lower. He couldn't care less if he looked like a coward trying to crawl down his own arse.

In the car in front, Ghalla had just pulled out a long gun from behind Duif's seat.

Ghaap gulped again.

Then it started. He heard the whizz. Saw the plaster splinter off a garden wall to his left. It sounded like a carbine, automatic. Maybe an R5.

Mo shouted something inaudible, cocked his pistol and slid silently out of the car.

Ghaap was battling to undo his seatbelt. It was stuck. He pulled his head right down into the bulletproof vest, heard more shots being fired.

The shooting died down and he heard feet running, someone shouting, screeching tyres. He lifted himself, saw Ghalla driving off. Where was Duif? He must have disappeared in among the houses packed together on either side of the road. Ghaap strained at the seatbelt, trying to dig his pistol out from under his seat and cursing himself for putting it there. The trackers were pursuing a bunch of hijackers armed with automatic weapons. And here he was, stuck in his seat like a turd in a woollen blanket.

The seatbelt popped open at last and Ghaap gently opened the door, groping for the pistol with his right hand. He felt the warm steel and rolled off the seat, outside. Peered at his surroundings from under the chassis. Someone whistled softly. From behind him somewhere, another whistle, seemingly in response. There was a movement in front of Ghaap, to his right. A youngster wearing a beanie was peeking over a wall. He whistled again, glanced around, listened for the reply. Next moment he was on top of the wall. Jumped down soundlessly, pistol in hand. Then he beckoned to someone.

Ghaap tried shifting his body to take aim, but the heavy vest anchored him. He crawled backwards, slipping out of it like a cat from a paper bag. Crawled forward, using the wheel to hide behind. He released the safety catch. He'd never shot a human being. He closed his eyes for a second, the image of the hijacker against the wall etched on his eyelids. Then he inched forward again, peered at the target. But there was no one there. The fellow had either jumped back over the wall or headed in a direction beyond his field of vision.

Awkwardly, Ghaap edged backwards again, wondered where the trackies were. There's no way Mo with his bulk could have scaled such a high wall.

A shadow fell over Ghaap, and before he could jump up, he'd been pinned down. From behind, someone had landed on him with his full weight, a knee between his shoulder blades.

"Uggh," said his lungs as the wind was knocked out of him. He tried to struggle, but felt the red-hot barrel of a gun behind his ear.

27

As soon as he'd left the Du Toits, Beeslaar called Qhubeka to tell her about Vincent, the driver.

"I'll come pick you up," she said. "Tell me where."

"Do you know the Dutch lady?"

"Maaike?"

"I'm staying at her place till Sunday."

It was only a few blocks from the Du Toits to his new abode. And the walk was pleasant. Old jacarandas, oaks, wild olive trees. Willows trailing leafy strings in babbling irrigation furrows. There was a sedateness in the air. Rather than the exuberance of Africa, something discreetly European breathed here.

Qhubeka was already waiting when he arrived at his new quarters. They drove in a north-westerly direction, out of the town. The black township sprawled along the low hill of Papegaaiberg, mkukus and matchbox houses spreading up the slopes like mielies.

She drove up a steep rise, the road narrowing amidst corrugated-iron shacks that fronted directly onto a sewage-polluted path. At the top they turned west, into an area with rows of small brick houses. It was in front of one of these that she stopped.

Vincent Ndlovu came out to meet them and invited them in. He seemed friendly yet cautious.

The house was dark inside, the small living-room window set high on the wall. The furniture, though simple, was neat. He lived on his own, Ndlovu explained. The house actually belonged to his father, who had moved back to the "land" after his retirement. The rural areas of the Eastern Cape, in other words, where his father's family and his kraal were, where he kept his cattle.

Qhubeka made no attempt to explain Beeslaar's presence and simply introduced him as "Captain Beeslaar". He positioned himself apart from them, leaning against a wall.

Ndlovu shot a quick glance at Beeslaar. He was clutching a handkerchief, which he used to wipe at his nose and eyes every so often. He was still young, barely thirty, Beeslaar guessed.

"When was the last time you saw the deceased?" Qhubeka began.

Ndlovu licked his lips, looked again at Beeslaar, then started babbling enthusiastically in Xhosa.

"Talk properly, man," Qhubeka cut him short. "The Captain here doesn't speak isiXhosa!"

Ndlovu shook his head. "No, man," he said sullenly.

"I'm waiting, Mr Ndlovu," Qhubeka prompted.

"My English is not so good."

"When?"

"Nooo, man. What must I say now? She phones me yesterday, in the morning. She shouts at me, very cross." He wiped the back of his neck. "I was a bit sick yesterday. She says I must work. Doesn't matter if I'm sick."

"What time was that?"

Ndlovu gave a shrug. He repeated the gesture for Beeslaar – as if he had to translate gestures for the whitey too.

Beeslaar glanced at the stack of takeaway boxes in a corner of the tiny kitchen. One bore the name of Nando's. It reminded him of one of their naughty adverts: *The second-best way to cover your fingers in a hot chick's juices.*

"But you see, Captain, I couldn't go. 'Cos, eish, I was very sick. Terrible." He looked up at Beeslaar with wide eyes to make sure he understood.

"It's my stomach. I have a lot of pain. I must go to the doctor."

"What doctor? Where?"

"First, I go to the sangoma. He says I'm bewitched. Maybe someone is trying to make me sick. He gives me muti, but the stomach doesn't get right. Then I go to another sangoma and he says I must go to the surgery."

"What surgery?"

"No, it's the one there in Bird Street. Yes."

Evidently familiar with the doctor in question and the location of his rooms, Qhubeka continued, "Why did Mrs du Toit fight with you?"

"No! She talks a lot of stuff, she says I'm late for work. And ... many other problems."

"Like *what*, Vincent? Like *what*?"

"No! How must I say?"

"*Why* was Mrs du Toit cross with you? What did you do?"

"No! Fokkol. I did fokkol to her, nothing. But that woman ..." He shook his head as he sat crumpling the handkerchief. There was fear in his expression, Beeslaar thought, but nothing wild. He was well dressed. Expensive shoes, chinos with pressed seams, office shirt and tie. On his left wrist he wore a chunky watch, and on the right a leather thong, probably from a goat, the long white hairs of the pelt curling over his slim wrist.

"Look," Ndlovu tried to explain to Qhubeka. He leant forward confidentially, as if he was telling her a secret. "Mrs du Toit, once or twice, she doesn't want me to give someone a lift. She doesn't want me to pick up a granny or a grandpa when I drive the work's car. She likes it fokkol."

"But you give lifts to the cherries, don't you?"

"Aikona!"

"Go on, Ndlovu."

"So," he gesticulated with the handkerchief, "Monday, I drive to Somerset Mall. I go to fetch the Woolies rejects. I bring it back here to the soup kitchen. I pick up, I drop off. The whole day."

Qhubeka was studying her red-painted nails. Then she asked: "And yesterday?"

"No, she phoned me early-early. I must come to her house. I must pick up someone at her house, take him somewhere. But I'm sick. She says no, I'm lying. Yoh!" Indignation flashed from his eyes.

"And then?"

"No! I first went to the doctor. About ten o'clock. You can ask him. Doctor Han Erasmus. Phone him! Here, I'll phone him." He grabbed at a cellphone in his trouser pocket.

"Relax, Vincent. You're talking about Dr Johan Erasmus. Near the Du Toit station?"

The young man nodded vigorously.

"What time did you leave there?"

"No! I …"

"Just the time, Vincent. I only want to know the time."

He looked down, worked at the handkerchief with renewed energy. Then he shook his head, shrugged his thin shoulders. "I was sick," he mumbled. "But the queue was long at Doctor Han. I only finished late."

"If you were still so terribly sick yesterday, how come you're looking so well today?"

"No! Look here. It's my stomach. The doctor gives me medicine, the stomach gets right. It's always like that. Then I go on, I go on, everything's fine. But then it comes again, same thing! The stomach gives me a lot of trouble!"

"So you often have stomach problems?"

Ndlovu nodded.

"And you often visit Dr Erasmus?"

Another nod.

"And the sangoma?"

"No, his stuff helps me fokkol."

"How did you get on with Mrs du Toit?"

Vincent's face grew ashen. He shot a fearful glance at Beeslaar, as if he were a snake in the corner of the room.

"She's very strict, that woman. She doesn't want to hear stories. She gets very angry!"

Qhubeka leant forward, her elbows on her knees. Then she unleashed a torrent in Xhosa, her voice loud and impatient, clicks flying like nails through the air. From Ndlovu's facial expressions, Beeslaar inferred that she was trying to pin him down about the exact nature of the relationship with his boss. He could make out repeated instances of "fokkol" and "eish" amid vigorous head-shaking and apparent denials.

Suddenly the interview was over. Qhubeka stood up and walked to the door, motioning to Beeslaar to follow. Ndlovu remained seated, his eyes round and anxious.

As they climbed back into the van, Qhubeka said: "The bastard's lying about something, perhaps about his so-called sickness. But murder?" She looked questioningly at Beeslaar.

He shrugged.

"Fat lot of help you are, Captain Beeslaar," she said with a sigh as she started the engine.

They drove in silence to the town centre, where she dropped him off at the corner of Merriman Avenue and Bird Street.

"If you happen to have any bright new ideas," she said as he got out, "old Prammie's breathing down my neck."

"See you later in Jan Cats," he said, then turned away and started walking. This side of the town was not pretty in the least, he decided. No trace here of whitewashed buildings or chic coffee shops under the oaks. Merriman Avenue seemed to represent an invisible boundary: cheap shops, a Pep Store, fish-and-chips cafés, bottle stores. The part of town where the poor residents, predominantly black, did their shopping.

Across the road was a massive taxi rank, fringed with hawkers' booths selling cheap imported Chinese goods. The hawkers themselves looked like foreigners: slender, with blue-black skin tones, talking in French, Portuguese and languages from other African countries. Amakwerekwere, as they were derogatorily called. Foreigners.

Beeslaar crossed the street and sat down on a low wall, studying the hawkers. One or two made to approach him but changed their minds. They obviously smelt the law on him.

He sat there for a long time, musing on the schizophrenia of a town like this. The two faces, the separate worlds.

His cellphone chirped: Rea du Toit.

He groaned inwardly, answered.

Could he come by again?

He hesitated. "I'm quite far from you at the moment. Downtown, in Bird Street. Is anything wrong?"

"I feel a bit, let's say, uneasy about our earlier conversation. Malan isn't himself at the moment. And if Balthie was still here …"

Beeslaar took a deep breath. If anyone played that card one more time, he'd lose it.

But he promised to come, nonetheless.

"I'm back at my own flat, at Great Gables," she said.

28

Ghaap heard a shot ring out. But it came from far away. Right now, he was painfully aware of the gun barrel burning against the back of his head.

He tried to breathe, but his attacker pushed him flat against the ground, his knee between Ghaap's shoulder blades. His face hurt where it pressed into the pebbles and gravel of the road, and he battled to avoid breathing in dust.

God knows, his mom would never forgive him if this meerkat shot him dead here. Like a dog in the street, in the middle of some godforsaken coloured squatter joint in Soweto! With the smell of sewage up his nose and the taste of toxic mine dust in his mouth.

The knee was suddenly lifted from his back and his lungs automatically filled; he coughed as he breathed in dust. The shadow over him moved. He felt the man grabbing his pistol. Heard him running off. He tried to lift himself off the ground, to give chase, but his muscles had turned to jelly and he couldn't breathe.

His pistol. The fucker had stolen his pistol!

There was the sound of more shots being fired somewhere, but he couldn't move, he was coughing too much. It felt as if he'd inhaled an entire mine dump. His throat burnt and the coughs wracked his body. He tried to heave himself upright, but all of a sudden his breakfast was in his throat. The next moment he tasted a mix of white toast and coffee with a strong aftertaste of sewage.

"Hey, boet!" Someone was right next to him. It was Ghalla, he saw when the fellow squatted down. He held out his left hand to Ghaap, revealing an elaborate tattoo that ran up his biceps. A naked woman holding a dagger, a monstrous snake curled around her body.

Ghaap wiped his mouth on his sleeve and forced himself up to get away from the vomit congealing in the dust.

"Whoa, careful," he heard Ghalla whisper. "Lie flat and don't move."

"Where are the others?" Ghaap rasped, his throat sore and raw.

"They're okay, man. We potted the one meerkat. Just the other side of that antie's place." He pointed to a small house on their right.

"Is he dead?"

"Don't think so. But he sure needs a doctor. Bleeding like a pig." He chuckled.

Ghaap screwed his eyes shut and tried to lift his buttocks, but he was paralysed. He'd never had a gun pointed at his head. A knife, yes, he'd often come up against a knife. Especially in his younger days, before he joined the cops. But a pistol! He tried to regulate his breathing, to breathe through his mouth. His nose was clogged with dust.

More shots, and Ghaap heard a bloodcurdling scream.

Silence. Ghalla pushed Ghaap's head down with his tattooed hand. "Don't move, man."

They stayed still for a while. Then Ghalla's phone rang. He listened to an animated voice on the other end. "Nice one, Davey," he remarked every so often. "Sharp-sharp," he said at last, ending the call, and helped Ghaap to his feet.

"It's over, boet. Finish en klaar. Sounds like the second meerkat has had it. Old Duif potted him with the long gun. The meerkat's AK had jammed. Damn rubbish the skelms use these days …"

Ghalla left and walked around the car. Ghaap felt so pooped that he sagged down on the passenger seat.

His pistol!

Oh jissus, he was in big shit. That meerkat was moer and gone with his gun. He may as well just hand in his papers. The SC had warned them – there'd been a memo from the top: close to twenty-one thousand firearms had gone missing from the police the year before. The next idiot that "mislaid" his firearm could expect no mercy. He'd be out on his ear. With neither pension nor package.

Ghaap's station commander was apparently new in his post. An unpopular appointment, suffering from new-broom syndrome. At the morning meetings he'd lectured them about this "habit" of losing firearms and how he was going to put a stop to it. His message applied to the blougatte in particular.

And what about his mother? How was Ghaap going to break it to his mom and the others? They thought he was the best thing since sliced bread. On his way to becoming a *real* detective!

Detective, my arse, Ghaap thought bitterly, dropping his head into his hands. When he looked up again, he saw Mo leaping over the wall across the street. He had to be incredibly strong to hoist that huge body so lightly over a high garden wall. Almost like an eland: the size of a cow, it could hop a game fence as nimbly as a bird.

Ghalla walked up to Mo. The two of them stood talking and gesturing for a moment, cigarettes already lit. They returned to the car, still talking animatedly.

Ghaap manoeuvred himself laboriously out of the car. His leg almost gave way as a sharp pain shot through his shin. He'd clean forgotten about last night's "bullet wound". It seemed like years ago, in any case.

"Are you okay?"

Mo was leaning on the roof of the car with his huge forearms. His eyes were narrowed against the smoke of the cigarette dangling from a corner of his mouth.

"I'm okay," Ghaap mumbled, avoiding the tracker's eyes.

"What the hell happened? Look at the state you're in, man."

"It must've been one of the robbers. You guys were already gone, I couldn't see you any more. Next thing I saw a guy came over that fence there, back into the street. I took aim, but I couldn't see him clearly. I was here on the ground, next to the car, and before I knew it he'd jumped me from behind."

Mo shook his head – disbelief and empathy on his big face.

"I tried to follow you guys. 'Strue's Bob. But the bladdy safety belt was stuck. Fokken thing – you should get it fixed. I could've been dead, man, trapped there like a frog on a stick. But that's when I saw that skollie. I hope you shot the shit out of him."

Mo smiled wryly. "Nah. He's lucky, but my hands were itching for him." Mo lit a cigarette and passed it to Ghaap. "But we zapped his one pal nice and good!"

Ghaap took the cigarette. Anything to get the shit taste out of his mouth.

Mo lit up again, blew out a long plume of smoke. "He still thought he was getting away, when Duif came up from the other side. Zapped! In the leg! He dropped like a rag, finished! Sat there puffing like a camel, glaring at us. The oke can thank his lucky stars that the cops pitched up. I would've let him bleed to death right there." He blew out a smoke ring, a happy gleam in his eye.

The cops.

Ghaap gulped. Today he'd see his arse. Well and truly. "Are the cops still here?" he asked.

"Uh-huh. Just on the other side of the houses, round the corner. They're writing up the scene. Two of them. That detective you drove with yesterday, Mthethwa, he's there. But I don't know the other guy. They're waiting for the ambulance. Duif's keeping them company."

"And the car?"

Mo looked at the white Vivo a few metres away. "Ag, it's there all right, but it's buggered, bru, they've already done a lot of damage. The dashboard's been hacked to pieces, the speedometer's glass is broken, and so on. It's a sorry sight. Almost like you," he said with a smile. "Did they hurt you?"

Ghaap shook his head and took a drag on the cigarette. He saw that his fingers were trembling. Gritted his teeth. "I genuinely didn't see that laaitie coming. Wragtig. He was just suddenly – he'd pinned me to the ground, I couldn't move. And then he took my ..." Ghaap's voice trailed away.

"What are you saying? He took your *gun*? Jissie, ou, you're in it up to here." Mo put his hand under his chin.

Behind him, Ghalla flicked away his cigarette and lit up again. He kept shifting from one foot to another, scanning his surroundings. Clearly still full of adrenaline.

All around them, the street was coming to life. People started coming out of the houses again. A woman holding an umbrella walked by, grocery bags in her free hand, a child strapped to her back. Somewhere, a dog had begun to bark, and in the distance Ghaap heard an ambulance siren.

"I suppose we should get a move on," Mo said and climbed into the car. "Face the music. And you'd better get back into that bulletproof, my friend, otherwise you'll be in even deeper kak."

29

"Albertus!"

Rea du Toit had come down to the security gate at Great Gables to open for him. Leading the way to her flat, she seemed smaller today. Her hair, almost certainly done for the funeral, was pressed flat against the back of her head from lying down, the pink scalp showing.

"Sit down, my boy," she said, once they were inside. She hung her keys on a hook behind the front door and waved him towards an old riempie bench with ball-and-claw feet.

"You'll have to excuse me, the place is a bit untidy at the moment," she said, seating herself in an easy chair. Her flat was well furnished, full of artificial flower arrangements, paintings. With a pang, Beeslaar realised he hadn't taken anything from Blikkies's flat the previous day – with the new accommodation arrangements, it had completely slipped his mind.

"I've just got back from Wim's house. Malan brought me. I wanted to stay there with the children, but he says no. There's not enough room in Willem's house. But that's not why I phoned you. My son ..." She looked away for a moment, tears in her eyes. "Right now, those two children can't afford to have their father locked up if he's not even guilty. They're so terribly—"

"Hold on, Mrs du Toit," Beeslaar interjected. "He's only been questioned. That's just routine, the way all investigations like this begin. The police need to gather as much information as possible. So that they can do their work properly. That's all there is to it."

"No one has spoken to *me*."

The accusation hung in the air between them for a while. Beeslaar cast around in his mind for something to say, but she didn't give him a chance.

"You know, you ... I mean, younger people. They think that old people ..." She bit her lip. "We become invisible, you know? People look right through us. Talk as if we don't exist. As if we're no longer part of the ... Ag, well." She looked out of the window, stared at the mountains standing unmoved in the afternoon sun.

"Someone will definitely still come and talk to you, Mrs du Toit. I'm sure of that."

"I'd like you to use your influence ... Please. I don't trust the local police. Take what happened when there was the break-in at old Arnold Sebens's flat – he lives just down the corridor from me. A so-called detective came, a youngster who made a big show of addressing all the residents and telling us to be alert and security conscious. But he didn't lift a finger to find Arnold's possessions. Nothing! Arnold phoned him a few times. He never even bothered to return his calls. So, I have no illusions about how they'll handle this terrible thing that happened to my son ..." She gave a barely audible sob.

Beeslaar waited for her to compose herself. Her flat was small, just like Blikkies's: a tiny lounge that led onto a balcony, and a garden the size of a postage stamp. It didn't look as if she cared much for the garden, it was overgrown with swordferns and delicious monsters – plants that required little attention.

"Those children, Albertus. Those two children ... God knows. Two swallows in a storm. Especially my little Ellie."

"Why did she try to jump out of the window yesterday?" Beeslaar gently probed. "Has she told you yet?"

"Oh, that child." She shook her head and reflected for a moment. "She was so terrified. It sounds to me as if she was simply panicked and scared. She just wanted to get away from all the blood, the awfulness. The child's got problems. She's, well, fragile. Highly intelligent. She does incredibly well at school. Too well, in fact. Until recently. She's always been first in her class, straight As for everything. But lately ..." She sighed, gave him a meaningful look.

"Boys?"

"No, it's not that. She's become a bit rebellious. Wild. Malan and Elmana tried everything. Had her tested. And she was away for a while."

"Away?"

"In some place ... an institution." She spoke in a near whisper. Beeslaar guessed at once: an eating disorder. The girl was as thin as a rake. He'd immediately assumed that her pallor and lethargy were due to shock, but the dark rings under her eyes, the emaciated body indicated something else.

"And that she, of all people, had to be the one to find her mother like that ..."

"Mrs du Toit, did your daughter-in-law, er, did she have many friends? Was she popular?"

"Yes, of course. She was a Du Toit, after all. A real go-getter."

"She didn't perhaps rub others up the wrong way in the process?"

"I don't think so." She gazed for a moment at a spot of sunlight on the Persian carpet between them. "I guess few people *really* knew her, Albertus. Few people."

"What do you mean?"

"She had a deprived childhood. Life hadn't always been easy for her. But I don't suppose that's of any relevance."

"Did you ever notice that she was abusing ... medication?"

She shook her head, but her eyes seemed less certain.

"You won't be able to hide it from me for ever, Mrs du Toit."

"For goodness' sake, what's this nonsense? Her body's not even cold and the rumour mill is already working overtime. Really, people are so … And I suppose the stories are all over town by now. Malan du Toit's wife was addicted to pills, that's why she was murdered. Is that what the police think too?"

"I don't believe the police have come to any conclusions yet. And Captain Qhubeka is competent. We should give her the opportunity to do her job."

"You *have* to help us, Albertus. We don't know what to do. Malan is my only child. He didn't have much of a childhood either. My husband, Malan Senior, died at a very young age. Malan Junior was still small; he grew up fatherless, so to speak. He's always had to fend for himself."

A tear rolled down her nose and fell onto her hands. She didn't bother to wipe it away. Kept staring at her hands, the fingers and knuckles deformed by arthritis. This probably accounted for the gloves she'd worn at the funeral service.

"He's always been such a high achiever. Victor ludorum, at both primary and high school. Distinctions at university. I know the people around here say horrible things about him. But it's pure jealousy. He always tells me: 'Ma, the Lord knows my heart. And that's all that counts.' He's a deep man, Albertus. Deep."

"And your daughter-in-law?"

She gave a quick wipe under her eyes.

"An efficient woman. Malan Junior certainly couldn't have done any better."

Beeslaar waited. But this seemed to be the sum total of Rea du Toit's opinion of her daughter-in-law.

"Did the two of you get on well?"

She avoided his eyes. "She was too strict with the children for my liking. Both of them. And, how shall I put it, she made heavy demands."

"Did you argue about that, Tannie Rea?"

"I know my place," she replied with a shake of her head. "Mind you, it wasn't always easy. Those two children could barely walk when they were already potty trained. And she didn't put up with any naughtiness. But they never lacked for anything. Unlike herself. Her father had been a woodwork teacher. Fond of the bottle, and fond of the cane. As for her mother: shame, poor thing. She was a resident at Great Gables, did you know? But she's gone home, as we say here among ourselves. Recently, about three months ago."

Beeslaar read this tante like a book. She was skilfully herding her Du Toit relatives, steering them away from the precipice to which Elmana du Toit had been leading the whole lot of them.

30

Gerda heard a phone ringing. From afar. The sound came closer. Far too close. It was buzzing in her face. She slapped at it wildly … and woke with a start.

Where's my child, was her first thought. She tried to move, but the pain at her right temple immobilised her.

She glanced around surreptitiously. Where were they? The surroundings didn't look familiar. Dense shrubs and trees.

It was the hijacker's phone that was ringing. He ignored it.

What had happened? she wondered.

Then she remembered. The plane tree they'd hurtled towards when she pulled up the handbrake. They must have hit it, because the bonnet seemed to be dented on the left. Kleinpiet was crying. And next to her the hijacker was still occupied with the dashboard. "Shit! Shit-fuck-shit," he said.

His name was Lucky, she recalled. He was hacking at the panel around the radio with a screwdriver. The phone was still ringing.

And as if the devil himself wanted to complicate things, Gerda's own phone started ringing. Maybe it was Rebecca, wondering where she was. Or Baz, sorry about having been so curt. Rebecca wouldn't leave before Gerda was home. Especially not on a day Pa had had a bad turn. Oh God, Pa – what would become of him if she were no longer …

"Sir, please." She didn't recognise her own voice. It was high-pitched and hoarse. "Take the car. It's old, but it's a good car. Take it. I won't say anything. If you just drop us here—"

"Shut up!"

"I won't talk to the po—"

"Shut *up*!" He raised his screwdriver hand threateningly. "I don't need you, you hear? I will kill you like a dog."

"But why—"

His reply was a punch to her face. She dodged, and though the blow just grazed her cheek, it was hard enough to make her head spin.

"Make that fuckin' baby shut up. Mpho, give him the medicine!"

"Leave him—"

Another blow to her head. Then Kleinpiet's crying abruptly stopped. He was making slurping sounds. She took a peek and saw Mpho holding a bottle to his mouth, filled with some kind of juice. Kleinpiet drank greedily. She had no idea how long they'd been sitting there. A quarter of an hour? An hour? One thing was certain: Lucky was fast losing his cool. He swore continuously as he hacked away at the dashboard.

His cellphone rang again.

"I can't fuckin' finish if you phone all the time!" he hissed into it. He held the phone in his left hand while he groped around under the steering wheel. The car's bonnet popped open – he cursed, he'd accidentally pulled the lever.

Now she could clearly see the dent.

"No! I told you! I'm looking for the second one. Time's running! Sooner you stop calling, sooner … Yes!"

He turned to Gerda: "You keep your fuckin' trap shut. I kill you! I kick your fuckin' baby's fuckin' head, squash it like a fruit, fuckin' bitch." With that, he jumped out of the car and slammed the bonnet shut, stood scanning the surroundings for a moment. In the side mirror, Gerda saw a figure walking in their direction. A man with two dogs, each on a leash. Suddenly she knew where they were. At the bottom entrance to the Westdene Dam. An old man and his dogs, obviously on their daily walk.

Now was her chance! She pulled on her door handle but froze as Lucky walked straight towards to her. She expected him to yank the door open, but he strode past. The back door opened and she heard him unbuckling Kleinpiet from his car seat. "In front," he ordered Mpho.

Pleading with him to leave the child alone, she tried to open her door. But he was leaning hard against it, with Kleinpiet in his arms. Meanwhile, Mpho had clambered into the driver's seat, agile as an acrobat. He kept his pistol trained on her.

The old man drew closer and Lucky rocked Kleinpiet in his arms, a concerned young father giving his whimpering baby a bottle. The man walked past, with not so much as a glance. At the entrance gate he bent down to release his dogs, two black Labradors that immediately rushed towards the dam with their owner in tow.

Kleinpiet was strapped into his car seat again. The child was quiet. Gerda risked a backward glance, saw that he was fast asleep. Mpho clambered back into his seat next to Kleinpiet and folded his arms, the barrel of the pistol digging into the child's side. Why wasn't Kleinpiet crying? Had they drugged him?

Gerda felt a fresh wave of tears welling up. She had to do *something*. If she could only get her hands on her child. They wouldn't dare fire a gun here.

"Please," she whispered to Mpho. "I can pay you lots of money. Lots. Much more than the other people will pay you."

Mpho didn't reply, just kept smiling; his eyelids were half-closed. He looked as if he were high. God, what next: a drugged-out primary-school kid with a cocked pistol in his hands!

She heard Lucky talking on his cellphone. He'd walked round the car and was standing with the phone at his ear and his other hand on the door handle, talking agitatedly in an African language. Then he pocketed the phone and pulled open the door. His phone rang again immediately.

"Will you leave me the fuck alone! I've got the stuff. I'm looking for the tracking systems. And the time is nearly up, because your white bitch won't let me finish the job!" He paused for a moment to listen. A male voice, Gerda could hear. Highly agitated. A white man, for sure, with that accent. Again, Lucky ended the call, and switched on the engine. When the phone rang he grabbed it and threw it over his shoulder to the back: "Just switch the fuckin' thing off!"

He turned the car around and started driving. Calmly.

Gerda saw a girl with a puppy on a leash, heading towards the dam, it seemed. She stopped as the car approached, pulled at the collar to get the dog out of the road. Gerda stared at the girl and widened her eyes, tried to signal her panic and helplessness.

But she just frowned. Then stuck out her tongue.

Tears burnt Gerda's eyes. God, was this all she was capable of? She wanted to scream and shout and kick and hit out wildly. Panic knotted her chest, squeezing the breath from her lungs. What did these people want from her? Who was the man that kept phoning?

They turned right at the intersection with Lewes, and drove over the dam wall.

Lucky had taken her cellphone and was dialling a number. "Ja," he said loudly. "I need the wheels. Now!" He listened to a voice on the other end and shouted, "Just be ready! In ten!"

He ended the call and increased their speed.

At the junction with Perth he turned right. They drove past the Helen Joseph Hospital, in the direction of the West Rand, and Soweto.

God, if she could only phone Baz. He knew so many people. Albanians, all kinds of people.

Or Albertus! *He* knew this area. He'd worked here for so many years.

The car picked up speed as the traffic started opening up. Through a coloured neighbourhood, past Coronationville Hospital. She noticed the Muslim cemetery on their right.

They were almost in Soweto, she realised. The name of the road changed. Commando, she saw on a battered road sign. She tried hard to identify landmarks, in case she got an opportunity to call for help. A broken traffic light halted their progress, with motorists treating it as a four-way stop. The traffic edged forward at a snail's pace.

Taking her chance, she yanked at the door and threw her torso out of the car.

Her hands were on the ground and she kicked wildly to escape. But Lucky grabbed a leg, and pulled her back. In a wordless tussle, Gerda tried to kick at him. Then she started screaming. Felt a stinging pain in her thigh. Kept kicking, but her legs were suddenly sluggish, as the lameness spread.

Behind them a minibus taxi was hooting impatiently.

Why was no one helping her? Couldn't they see she was being kidnapped?

Her stomach convulsed and she vomited onto her hands. She heard a car door slam. Thank God, someone was coming to her aid. Then two hands lifted her.

"Thank you," she mumbled groggily. For heaven's sake, what was wrong with her? "Help me, help … we … my son …"

Her eyelids were so heavy that she could barely keep them open. The nausea welled up again. She retched, but there was nothing left to be expelled.

Vaguely she heard a voice: "Are you okay?"

And Lucky: "The baby is coming. I'm taking her to the hospital. Thank you. And sorry!"

"You must hurry, my brother. She looks sick."

Two arms shoved her back into the car. Pushed her door shut.

Please, she mouthed, please, her tongue refusing to utter the word. And then a big black curtain descended as she slipped into a merciful darkness.

31

"Have you found your car?"

Ghaap had to strain to hear Beeslaar's voice. It sounded as if he were standing in a hurricane.

"You have to speak up, I can't hear you."

"I'm saying: Have you found that skedonk of yours ... Hold on!"

Ghaap waited.

"I'm in the shit," he announced as soon as he heard the noise subside. "I've lost my service pistol."

"*Lost*? Jissus, Ghaap."

"I don't want a sermon. I just want to know—"

"You'd better prepare yourself for a lot of sermons. Starting with—"

"Ja-ja!"

"So, tell me."

"It was a hijacker."

"Where?"

"Mandelaville."

"Coloured neighbourhood. Who were you riding with?"

"The trackies."

"Good God, Ghaap!" There was a moment's silence, followed by the sounds of fidgeting.

"You started smoking again?" Ghaap asked, surprised.

"Don't be stupid, man! I'm just trying to get out of the wind. What business did you have with the trackies, of all people? Don't tell me you convinced them to go looking for your skedonk? Or are you moonlighting? If that's the case, you may as well just hand in your papers."

"Nothing like that. One of the okes picked me up at New Canada Station when I was walking to work. And then, er, I ..."

"And then he got a call and you didn't get out of the vehicle?"

"More or less."

"Hell, Ghaap. Where are you now?"

"At the scene. There were four hijackers."

"What did they take?"

"Kentucky Rounder."

He heard Beeslaar give a barking laugh, probably because he'd shown off his familiarity with Soweto slang.

"They ambushed us. Mo and Ghalla chased them, potted one."

"Dead?"

"Unfortunately not."

"And where were *you* the whole time?"

"I was in the car. I …" He faltered, the words drying up.

"So how did you lose it in the *car*?"

"Don't try to be fokken funny. I was already out when I spotted one of the suspects. And I was still thinking I was taking aim, when he jumped me from the back!"

Beeslaar said nothing.

"He had a gun to my head, Beeslaar. I could do fokkol. Then he took it."

"Just like that?"

"Jissis. *Yes*. Just like that! What do you expect? The bliksem had a gun pressed to my head. Should I have sung a fokken song?"

Ghaap heard a gurgling sound down the line. The bastard was laughing. Ghaap was so angry, he felt like breaking the phone. He kicked the car's wheel instead, and almost passed out from the pain. He'd forgotten about his shin.

He stood with his eyes shut tight, heard Beeslaar asking whether he was still there.

"I'm here," he groaned.

"Hell, Ghaap. You're bloody hysterical, you know that?"

"That's why I'm phoning you, for fuck's sake. The Orlando cops are here. One of the guys I ride with, Mthethwa. I want you to give him a call."

"Won't work, Ghaap. He'd have your balls in a vice if your 'white boss' had to speak on your behalf."

"Then *you* must phone the sc!"

"Hello, Ghaap, wakey, wakey! Do you really think—"

"You have to help me!"

"I can't do anything for you. Phone The Moegel." Beeslaar was referring to their regional commissioner in Upington, Leonard Mogale. "That's the only advice I can give you, boet."

"No." Ghaap knew that if he did so, the story would be all over the Kalahari the next day.

He heard Beeslaar chuckling as he ended the call.

"You're bladdy useless, Beeslaar!" he shouted into the dead phone. It was hot, the place stank, and flies kept sticking to his face. Ghaap wiped his forehead with his shirtsleeve and looked at where Mo was talking to Mthethwa a short distance away. They had brought Mo's car around to the other side, where the scene was being written up. There was another cop with them, busily writing. The injured hijacker sat on the ground at their feet. Ghaap looked at him. A youngster, couldn't be older than seventeen. He sat clutching a leg, his jeans soaked with blood above the right knee. It seemed to be a small wound, a superficial one, judging by the amount of blood. An AK-47 and two automatic pistols were lying on the bonnet of the police car.

A swarm of flies buzzed around the injured man. His hands and feet were shackled, forcing him to flick the flies away with an elbow, or his head. His face was screwed up – his expression halfway between frowning and crying. He checked around to see whose attention he could gain. As he caught Ghaap's eye, he signalled to him pleadingly that he wanted a cigarette. To Ghaap, this was the last straw. His anger boiling over, he rushed at the suspect and aimed a kick at him.

A loud cry.

Someone grabbed Ghaap by the shoulder and pulled him away, but he tore himself free. He would kick the fuckhead's face to a pulp!

"Hau, man!" It was Mthethwa. "Leave him alone, man."

The suspect started crying, yelped at the top of his voice. "Please, my bra," he appealed to Ghaap.

"I'm not your fokken bra. Now all of a sudden we're gabbas! Scumbag! Where's your tjommie? Talk, you moerskont!" Ghaap aimed another kick at him.

Mo pushed himself between them: "Ag, just leave the oke, Ghaap. It's tickets with him, man. Six-love, six-love. He's stuffed, big time."

"But it's fuckers like *him*. Stole my car for scrap! Me, struggling like hell. And my gun! My fokken gun, man!" Ghaap tried to step around Mo. There was a rage inside him that itched to break something. He wanted to get his bare hands on the fucker's neck.

"Chillax, boet. This oke's fucked five ways. Leave him to the gattas. You don't want him to get off because he's been donnered. Okay?"

Ghaap stepped back. Mo was right, he'd like to kick the bastard. But how would that bring back his gun? Or his car. The very thought of his car ... The red-carnation duco, his mom's favourite colour. And the mags, they'd nearly bankrupted him! He ducked around Mo, wanting to have another go at the fucker on the ground.

"Sergeant!" Mthethwa gripped Ghaap by his biceps and jerked him aside.

Then he had his handcuffs out and Ghaap felt the metal slipping around his wrists.

Suddenly, the rage was gone from his body.

In its place, a black cloud of doom: now he was *really* in the kak.

32

Poor Ghaap. That this had to happen to him, of all people. But Beeslaar couldn't help thinking that it served him right. For being so damned stubborn. Get some experience in Upington or Kimberley first, he'd told him. But no, Ghaap wanted to be a hero.

Beeslaar gazed at the busyness of Bird Street with its taxis, its hawkers and bustling activity. He was hungry again. The full-house breakfast with Qhubeka had been walked off long ago.

He'd have to find a restaurant. This part of town specialised in fish-and-chips establishments only.

He walked past the pub where he'd boozed the night before, the Mystic Boer. But he gave it a wide berth; right now, his constitution couldn't even cope with the smell of beer that pervaded the place.

An hour later he'd polished off a hamburger and chips. He set off in the direction of Liewe Heksie – that's how he thought of Maaike, his Dutch landlady. She reminded him of the lovable, rather incompetent fairytale witch so beloved of South African children. The sun was setting, and he wanted to collect his car and get to Blikkies's watering hole for his rendezvous with Qhubeka. The wind was back in full force, blowing dust and leaves and street litter in all directions, battering the long-suffering oak trees.

Beeslaar kept his mouth covered against the dust as he walked, his thoughts on Elmana du Toit. She'd been anything but a warm person, it seemed. On the contrary, the picture of her that was emerging was one of a hard-hearted sergeant major. He hadn't heard a single affectionate word uttered about the woman. She was praised, yes. To high heaven. But in practical terms only: "capable" and "neat" and "perfectionistic".

Or was he being subjective because of his own sensitive ear for words like that? His mother used to extol the virtues of Oom Tol, the "very capable" man she contrasted with Beeslaar's father. God, the quarrels that had raged in that house amid the mine dumps of the East Rand. Pa bellowing that it was because of her "bitching" that he spent his evenings in the bar, Ma yelling back that his boozing was dragging them all down into ruin. After Koefie's death, things had changed, the quarrels suddenly at an end. But the hatred was more intense, perhaps too intense for words. They had tried to glare each other to death. Pa lost the contest. He'd been first to go, absconded after a heart attack.

Ma had died of cancer.

Beeslaar came to a stop; suddenly his chest was burning. He filled his lungs with air, expelled it slowly. It was this wind that was getting to him, he convinced himself. It swept the breath from your mouth. Raced down the street like an evil spirit. In its wake, a carpet of twigs and leaves, still green, which had been ripped from the trees. How do you live in a place with so much fury in it, he wondered.

Which brought his thoughts back to Elmana du Toit. The fury that marked the scene of her death. Had the violence taken place before, or after her death? The fatal shot itself had been cool and clinical. A standard bullet, nine mil, soft nosed. Left a small entry wound on the outside, but puréed everything inside. And she'd been shot from the back, so half her face was gone. No, the actual fury was the work of the person who'd wielded the Brahman bull. Whose prints had been wiped so neatly from the statuette. And the bonsai trees. The same person? For what reason, for God's sake? And why all the destruction, when she was dead anyway? What message did they want to convey?

This was not typical of house robbers. Or was it, in fact, the current modus operandi? He didn't know any more. Living in a country like this, you had only one certainty: that the brutality with which people were butchered bewildered you more and more every day.

What had Elmana du Toit done to unleash such fury?

And what about Malan du Toit? He'd been at a restaurant. His lawyer had confirmed this. But on the other hand – that was how lawyers earned their daily bread. By lying like troopers.

Tertia and Mynhardt had invited him to supper, but he'd declined. He didn't know why. Maybe he simply didn't know what to say to them. He had never heard Blikkies talk much about Tertia, especially before, when they'd still been colleagues. She'd simply never been part of the picture. And now the two of them stood facing each other … on either side of a deep ravine.

Rembrandt, the little sausage dog, welcomed him at the front gate, led the way to the house with his tail erect. Beeslaar needed to ask for directions to the hotel bar, where he'd arranged to meet Qhubeka.

"I thought you're not involved in the investigation?" Maaike asked. Her inquisitive eyes searched his face.

"A collegial courtesy drink. She also knew my ex-colleague, Van Blerk. That's all," he replied.

"I knew him too, you know? Do you want to know how we met?"

Beeslaar's half-smile was all the encouragement she needed.

"It was one of their staff members. Over there," she vaguely indicated. Beeslaar assumed she meant the old age home. "She was convinced she'd been … what do you call it again? Betoverd."

"Bewitched," Beeslaar suggested.

"Potverdomme, ja," she cursed again. "And that woman believed it, very strongly, and became very ill. So Mr van Blerk paid me a visit and asked if I could do anything for the woman. I went to see her, but she was already far gone. Next I heard, she was dead." She exhaled, loudly and long. "Shows you how powerful the grey matter is, doesn't it?" She tapped her temple with her index finger.

"Er, yes," was all Beeslaar managed, but he suspected that his face betrayed his scepticism.

"Look," she said, "I've often come across this witchcraft. I studied it, you know? That's why I came to South Africa. I wanted to – but that's a very long story. Balthie told me it was the only thing he was scared of – as a cop. He'd seen with his own eyes how strong this was in some communities. You know, when someone believed they were bewitched." She shook her head and shot him a meaningful look. "Among white people too, did you know? In a town like this!"

"Er, sorry, Maaike, the hotel?" he reminded her, itching to leave.

"Ja, of course! I talk too much," she said and disappeared into the house, quickly returning with a tourism brochure. She showed him the map inside and the location of the hotel. "I'll have something ready for you to eat when you get back, okay?"

He declined the offer, said he'd grab a bite in town.

"Don't underestimate Maaike," Qhubeka said later. "She may come across as a bit airy-fairy, but it'll be worth your while listening when she has something to say." They were sitting in Jan Cats, at the bar. Outside on the stoep, the wind was far too gusty.

"Seems to me that you all know each other in this dorp?" He had an ice-cold Windhoek Lager in front of him, she a glass of Ken Forrester white wine. And a Coke.

"It may look that way to you. But it's same old, same old. The same old divisions, three worlds. The whites in the town proper, behind lock and key. The coloureds in their place, among the gangsters. And the blacks in the location on the other side of the iron curtain."

"Iron curtain?"

"The railway line and industrial area. Squashed up against Papegaaiberg. Location, location, location."

She chuckled at her own joke.

"For the rest, everything's the same."

"And where's the money?"

"Where it usually is – passed along under the table."

They clinked their glasses in a toast to another of Blikkies's sayings, sat sipping their drinks in silence for a while.

"The Du Toit girl," Qhubeka said. "Something's not right with her."

"Could you get anything out of her?"

"The Nappy Squad spoke to her. No luck." She took a sip of Coke. "I had the wounds on her arm looked at. Seems she's an old hand at cutting."

"Self-harm?"

"Yes. Especially on the thighs, where no one can see it."

"Shit. That's the one craze I can't get my head around. I saw a lot of it in Johannesburg. The young prostitutes, and rich young girls in clubs at night. High on speed and ecstasy, and they lay into themselves with blades. Inflicting physical pain to relieve emotional pain."

"Yes, but what pain can a girl like that possibly have? She's got *everything*. Look at that house. And shoes! Did you see how many pairs are in her wardrobe?"

Beeslaar shook his head, took a long drink of his beer. "But money can't buy you love," he said, and was rewarded with the flash of a smile.

They nursed their drinks, both conscious of the empty chair between them.

"How long have you been here?" Beeslaar asked after a while.

"Twelve years. Started here as a blougat, with many of the larneys from the old days still in their posts. Those were tough times."

"And today?"

"Ag, we get by. Same problem as elsewhere: everyone covers his own arse. Prammie's okay, though. Not very popular, but I like him. He zoomed up through the ranks, on speed dial. I don't think he's ever had to break up a drunken brawl. But he's okay. Doesn't let himself get pushed around."

"Was he here when the student was murdered?"

Qhubeka sighed wearily. "It seems we'll be dogged by that fuckin' case till kingdom come. And do you know what the irony is? The investigation team was lily-white. All whiteys. The lot of them."

"Were you involved?"

"No, thank heavens. But now Prammie's put *me* in the hot seat. And I can have my own team. Any extras I need, too."

"Well, congratulations then."

She pushed the wine glass aside, ordered another Coke Zero. "Congratulations, my foot. You know as well as I do: if I mess up, it's easy for them to wash their hands of me. Inexperienced, a woman, a darkie – flat nose and frizzy hair to prove it." She smiled, her cheeks dimpling. Beeslaar smiled back. They clinked glasses. Beer and Coke Zero.

"But if *you'd* been the last bliksem in the box, drawing the short straw?" They immediately clinked again in honour of Blikkies's regular saying.

145

"Well, I'd start by looking at other break-ins in the area. My landlady tells me that the Karindal-Uniepark neighbourhood has been plagued by a man who can apparently jump any wall. The last time, he stole two German tourists' stuff—"

"That guy, yes. He's already been locked up. But he was sly. Unfazed. Used to walk around in full view of the security cameras, always with a cap or a hoodie hiding his face. And there are plenty more where he came from. It's this town; draws them like a magnet. Because there's money here, lots of it. Neighbourhoods like the Du Toits' are rolling in it."

"But house robbery ... You don't have so many here, do you?"

"Not yet, but they're bound to come, along with all the rich migrating down here from the fleshpots of Joburg."

She ran a finger along the condensation on her glass. "You know," she said, "actually, there wasn't much stolen from the house. Her diamond ring is missing, but Du Toit says she tended to take it off and forget where she put it. He can't recall when he last saw it. And the money's gone from the safe. But that's all. The kids' laptops, Du Toit's computer in his office, they're all still there. There are lots of TV sets in the house: in the home theatre in the basement, each of the three lounges, Du Toit's office, the bedrooms. Not even her cellphone was taken. Her handbag lay untouched on a chair in the kitchen, her purse and everything else still inside."

"She knew her attacker, then."

"There's no doubt about that. It could have been her dealer." She took a hearty sip of her Coke, the ice tinkling as she did so.

"Yello man—"

"Sugar man, grandpa. Sugar man, won't you bring back the colours to my dreams ... Remember?"

The Rodriguez song that was a hit in his schooldays. When drugs were still a foreign thing in the country, Beeslaar mused.

"So, my Charmainetjie has done her rounds."

"Hold on. Who's Charmaine again?"

"My colleague. She's a sharp lady, good head for figures. I'm fighting hard to keep her, but the task-force guys, organised crime, are trying to poach her. Apparently they're in the process of building a case for the Public Protector's office against a big fish in the ranks of the Cape gangsters."

"Maybe it's a better career move for her?"

"You're probably right. But, quite frankly, I hope she stays. She knows the Cape gangs. You could say she grew up among them. So she has a nose for them. She's broken many cases for us. But getting back to our case: she had rumbled every last dealer in this town. We haven't yet found the Du Toit woman's specific dream merchant, but we keep looking among them."

"And the money?"

"That's going to be more complicated. Du Toit has been hard hit by the recession, according to Charmaine's financial tjommies. But he's still floating. He has a finger in just about every pie. There's a wine farm, which he owns jointly with a company. Then he has a partnership with a guy who has factories in China. And then building projects in Argentina, in Australia and in several African countries too. High-risk businesses, all of them. But his affairs are now Charmaine's baby. She'll sort it all out for us. Apparently much of it is in the wife's name. He was playing it safe in case he was bankrupted. But it's still early days. Methinks he's a fixing cat with many …"

"… tricks," Beeslaar completed Blikkies's expression. They remained mute for a moment, let the memories wash over them.

Beeslaar ordered another beer. "The Du Toits are still on my back," he remarked as the barman put down a bottle. "They want me to be their man in the investigation."

She didn't react, just blinked slowly. Took a sip of Coke.

"I said no. Because they keep lying. I think *he* was the one who moved his wife's body. "

"Why would he do that?" she asked sceptically.

"That I don't know. But there's no way a robber would shoot her, then smash her skull, and then arrange her body neatly in a seated position on the couch. Oh, and then still rush around damaging all the plants in the house. Makes no sense. He'd just take the ten thousand bucks and run."

"So you think Malan du Toit … is he protecting his wife's reputation, or what?"

"I think it's more than that. His lying is too complicated. The whole family's lying, including the grandmother. And the victim seems to have had a lot of issues."

"So, do you think they all know who killed the woman?"

"Not necessarily. But they're trying their utmost to convince *you* that it was a house robbery."

"We've had a few of those, make no mistake. Ugly, very ugly. But it hasn't yet become an epidemic like in Johannesburg. And the rich people keep flocking here, to Stellenbosch in particular. I reckon this place has more billionaires per square metre than there are fleas on a dog's back. Boer types, in particular. They make their money in Johannesburg, and then they return to their roots in the Cape. It's wine farms and horse farms, golf estates and hotels and spas – everyone's pursuing their own little hobby. Most come from Gauteng. In fact, from all over, foreigners too. At Eastertime, like now, you should check out the streets of the town. The place looks like a Rolex convention."

Beeslaar didn't respond at once, allowed the information to flow over the details of the murder scene in the Du Toit home. "You know," he said at last, "I'd still buy the burglar theory if it wasn't for those bonsais." The beer was ice cold against his palate as he took his first mouthful. "I've had to deal with many home invasions in Johannesburg. I know what they look like. Chaos. They're terrorists, those guys. Clever, too. Well drilled, each man deployed with one specific task. In and out within minutes. Empty the safe, get the firearm. Then the electronics. The people in the house are tortured if they don't cooperate quickly enough. I've seen some cases where the children were burnt with hot irons, the mother dragged to the bedroom. They know their stuff. Know exactly what time the father comes home at night, what time he goes to sleep. And that's when they strike, when he's mellow and relaxed, ready for bed. Reckless. Kick in the front door, shoot the dogs, grab the children and the wife … The father's like putty in their hands."

"Okay, but the Du Toits have got good security. And there's no sign of a gate or a door that was forced open. So, how did they gain entry?"

"Guys like that are as cool as cucumbers, do recces beforehand, gather information, watch the house, milk the household staff. I remember a house in Johannesburg, it had just been repainted. The thugs painted the housewife green. In other cases they left excrement. Everywhere you looked. And pee on the beds. Things like that."

"So you think it might have been robbers? Maybe they were young, nervous, which could account for the overkill. First shooting the victim and then crushing her head."

Beeslaar shook his head. "There's too much … hysteria there." He looked at Qhubeka. "This seems somehow more personal. And the whole family is lying. About what, I don't know. Not yet."

She stood up. "Do you need a lift?"

"No, thanks, I came in my car. And I think I'm going to hang around here a bit longer. Have something to eat, maybe. You don't feel like—"

She raised her eyebrows. "I thought your landlady was preparing food. Sounds to me like she's really excited having the Kalahari boer on her premises."

Beeslaar picked at the beer label, aware of her teasing tone as she said goodbye and walked off.

He stayed a while longer. Until the label had come off completely.

His body was still suffering from the previous night's overindulgence. Ordering a hamburger, he finished his beer and ate in silence. One image remained with him: Malan du Toit's face when he'd confessed that he hadn't "been there" for his family.

The town was quiet by the time he drove back. He was exhausted. The terrible hangover and the lack of sleep the night before were starting to take their toll.

All was quiet and dark at his new abode. He tried his best to tiptoe past Liewe Heksie's house. She and her menagerie were the last things he felt up to right now.

Then Rembrandt tipped her off.

A light went on in the entrance hall and a head peered around the front door. The dachshund barked excitedly as it stood at its mistress's feet.

She switched on the stoep light and stepped outside. Beeslaar noted to his surprise that she was still fully dressed. Yet the house had been pitch dark when he arrived. He had a sneaking suspicion she'd sat waiting for him in the dark.

She greeted him in Dutch, calling out over the noise of the barking dog. "I still wanted to tell you …" She picked up the dog to quieten him down. "My neighbour on this side," she gestured to the right, "she served with Elmana du Toit on the soup kitchen committee. And she was a member of Elmana's Bible study group."

Beeslaar shuffled his feet uncomfortably. "Actually," he said, "I'm not involved in the investigation."

"You know Vuvu by now, don't you?"

"Vuvu?"

"Qhubeka!"

"I've, er, yes, I've met her."

"So. Let me tell you something that no one will tell *her*. Vuvu. Do you get me?"

He knew what she was getting at. It was a racial issue. What was it with this town, he wondered. Still stuck in colonial times.

"Mrs van der Wiel," he said firmly, "Captain Qhubeka … Vuvu is the only person you can speak to about this case."

This clearly made no impression on her. She continued, unperturbed: "Maaike. Call me Maaike. But you should speak to the woman next door, to Hanna! She was also at the funeral yesterday. She says the feeding scheme organisation wanted to fire Elmana. They'd had enough of her. But no one wants to speak ill of the dead, do they? Especially to a black policeman, you understand?"

Beeslaar sighed with exasperation. "So, was there more gossip? About Mrs du Toit, I mean."

"Yes, a lot. They called her an arrogant snob. But you know what I think it was?"

Beeslaar shrugged.

"She came from rags to riches, to put it crudely. But on the inside she still felt

149

the same. White trash. Never good enough. I always say, the bigger the snob, the bigger the complex. Understand?" She shook her curls and looked at him meaningfully.

He nodded.

"And her mother, depression all her life, you know? Right until she died recently."

"How long ago, exactly?"

"Ah. Beginning of last month, I think. About six weeks. It was a sort of, what do you call it? A *crisis* for Elmana. Hanna says she wasn't the same afterwards."

Reluctant as he was to admit that this strange little woman with her noisy menagerie was right, it made sense. And isn't this what Rea du Toit had tried, in her own way, to tell him that very afternoon?

He went to bed, but struggled to sleep.

He missed the CD player that stood on his bedside cabinet at home. With Mozart's horn concertos on hand.

Hell, he missed his house. The silence, most of all.

He'd grown used to it in the Kalahari. A silence so overwhelming you could hear your own heartbeat. Especially on hot days. When not even an insect dared move in the broiling sun. Let alone the birds. It was on such days that you'd see a biggish bird – a mousebird, say – literally drop dead if it tried to fly from one fruit tree to another. Overcome by exhaustion, it would tumble soundlessly to the ground. Where the sun would suck the life out of it.

But this place. Here you had the wind. And fountains. And sprinkler irrigation at night. Zik-zik-trrrrrr. Incessant whirring. Water drumming on broad-leafed plants.

And hadedas, their wailing cries filling the air. He'd thought they were unique to the Rand, but the vile squawkers also flew around here. They'd probably migrated along with the wealthy, attracted by all the new golf estates.

Noise was not what was keeping him awake, however.

It was a creature called Mathilda. A giant spider who'd sat waiting for him when he arrived home tonight – on the ceiling of his bedroom, right above the bed. Maaike had informed him of her presence, requested him please not to kill her. Apparently she did "good work" here. Emerged at night and preyed on the mosquitoes. She was a harmless rain spider, Maaike had explained, and he shouldn't be alarmed, even though her appearance might be "a bit off-putting".

But "off-putting" was the understatement of the century. The creature in his bedroom was enormous. As big as the palm of a man's hand, with long, speckled, hairy legs. One thing he knew: it'd be either Mathilda or him sleeping in this bedroom tonight. Certainly not both of them, her "good work" notwithstanding.

He duly fetched a broom from the kitchen, hoping to beat her to death. But she scurried away at the speed of an express train. A flurry of legs … He shuddered in revulsion. Down to his toes. She eventually left through the window. He swiftly shut it behind her, and couldn't help wondering if she was leaving any friends or family behind.

But it wasn't only Mathilda that was keeping him awake.

He thought of Qhubeka. He had a weakness for big women. Their softness and femininity. Skeletal bodies held no attraction for him. Gerda had been at her most beautiful when she was pregnant with Kleinpiet. The full breasts in the low-cut summer dresses she'd worn. The reddish freckles dotting her neck, the skin fine and soft. Pretty legs, too – well formed, with a layer of softness. He recalled the heat of her body, the curve of her hips, her silky thighs. She wasn't so much beautiful as interesting. A mischievous, intelligent face: green cat's eyes. Her skin, milk with a sprinkling of cinnamon. The red hair …

He turned over to face the window. Outside, a light blinked on and off randomly. Possibly a security light activated by the wind. He watched the shadows at the window, his thoughts wandering back to Qhubeka. How she seemed to have won Blikkies's affection. Not everyone could get so close to the old curmudgeon as to remember his unique sayings.

She had a way about her, Qhubeka did. Reeled you in slowly. Yet she revealed nothing about herself. He wondered whether there was a Mr Qhubeka. She didn't wear a wedding ring. And she seemed to take her job very seriously, a tough, no-nonsense cookie who wouldn't stand back for any man.

33

Gerda was woken by a voice.

For a moment, she wondered whether it was human. An eerie crooning. Someone praying, plaintive. A man, elderly. He spoke in what sounded like Zulu, repeated certain words over and over again, like a monk reciting his daily mantras.

He was here, right next to her. The sound came in waves. Louder. Then fainter, almost fading away, like an old-fashioned radio transmitter. Or was it her? Coming and going, flowing into a deep, soft tunnel. But there it came again, echoing from a different direction.

She felt light, floating, weightless and carefree, a thistle on the lazy, languid surface of a dam. Huge, endless.

Then the dream shattered. She became aware of ... pain? Searing. Somewhere in her body. Flowing in, ebbing away ... Where was the pain coming from? Like waves breaking. She listened closely, tentatively. The pain flowed with the sound, the crooning, praying, muttering. Where was she drifting, then, with all these echoes? The was a soft, dark cloud. It was beckoning to her. She shouldn't succumb, but she wanted to.

She needed to go and fetch her dead children.

She called out their names, kept calling. Boetatjie. So small, just two years old. And Neiltjie. His grandpa's name. And his mamma's carroty red hair ... his head ... the little red child's head ... no-no-no-no not red like that, not that horrible red. Not blown apart by an ugly gun. The red head, such a splattery and squishy red ... no, red like baby carrots from the garden, nice red-red ... her two lambs who were hiding *deep* inside that little cloud. Where the naughty pappa wouldn't find them. They were waiting for Mamma there. Mamma's coming, my lambkins, Mamma's swimming like a big dolphin. Coming to fetch you.

But Mamma was tired. So tired, so tired.

What was going on here? What had happened?

It was Kleinpiet, the little rascal. He didn't want to go to sleep, he was scared his mamma would leave ... run after his dead little brothers ... shush, don't cry, dearest child. Shhh. Hush-a-bye, baby, don't you cry, go to sleep, mamma's gonna watch ...

She wanted to touch him, lying here, right next to her on the bed. She wanted to look at him lying beside her. For hours on end. The blond halo of curls around his head. The little eyes half-open.

What would he be dreaming about? Tadpoles. And a puppy, perhaps?

Somewhere, a cellphone rang.

The muttering stopped.

"Yebo."

It dawned on her: she wasn't at home. Where, then?

She wanted to float away again, but the question followed her. Along with a smell. Something was burning, hair and paper. There was something hot near her face. The smell assailed her, through her nose and mouth. An overwhelming smell.

"One thousand," a voice echoed from far away. "No. That is only your deposit."

She slipped away again …

A fish. She was a fish. She hung weightlessly in the water, the deep green shadow where she was sheltering. Sheltering? She was waiting … for the danger to go away. A big danger.

A bird came swimming towards her. No, a cat. A wild thing: spots and feathers, eyes that burnt blood red. A burning cloud. Closer. It was the cloud that was suffocating her.

"Yebo," she heard from inside the cloud. "You want the unborn, you pay the price. Fifty thousand. The other little one is more. 'Cause why, it's a boy."

34

Duif Vermeulen bred pigeons in his backyard.

Pigeons that suffered from insomnia.

Ghaap lay listening irately to the fluttering and cooing outside his bedroom window. He could swear he was developing an allergy to all things feathered. He'd already been put off eating chicken.

His throat burnt, and he was coughing. Could only be from the pigeons.

Or perhaps the pack of cigarettes he'd puffed his way through in the course of the afternoon. It had been touch and go; Mthethwa was on the point of throwing him in the back of the van – along with the hijacker. Mo had to cajole and plead before Mthethwa removed the cuffs, even. He was furious, saying it was cops like Ghaap that gave the SAPS a bad name.

And they were hardly back at the station, when Mthethwa made a beeline for the SC. Unceremoniously strode into his office, Ghaap in tow. Demanded that the SC reported Ghaap to IPID in Pretoria. That an example be made of Ghaap.

But the SC wasn't in the mood to be ordered around. "Uncle Solly", they called him. Colonel Suleiman "Solly" Kajee, station commander of Orlando East, the new broom who still had to gain trust. Especially among guys like Mthethwa, chip-on-the-shoulder types. Uncle Solly came from outside, Ghaap had heard Mthethwa grumbling. One of Laudium-Pretoria's prominent Indian families, who donated generously to ANC coffers.

There were three charges, Mthethwa had said. And the last one was probably the most serious: Ghaap pretended to be off sick because of his "so-called" bullet wound, but meantime he was moonlighting for the trackers.

The uncle, however, hadn't been receptive. He'd sighed wearily: "But why are you standing here, man? You should be out there catching the man who stole Sergeant Ghaap's service pistol! You're standing around fiddling with horseshit while this place is burning, man!" His voice was pleasant and melodious. Calm. A strong Afrikaans accent.

At some point Ghaap had sat down uninvited. His battered shin was complaining. Not to mention his nerves.

"What are you going to do about this?" Mthethwa had insisted.

Uncle Solly then shot him an impatient look, ordered tea. One cup. And sent Mthethwa out of the room.

He'd focused his weary gaze on Ghaap, scrutinised him with his Hush Puppy eyes, his cheeks bulging like saddlebags on either side of a small, purplish-blue mouth.

"You know, of course, that I don't have a choice, Sergeant," he'd said.

"With respect, Colonel, I haven't been moonlighting. Honestly. My car was stolen last night. And when I was walking to work this morning to report the theft, one of the trackies gave me a lift. And then he bought me coffee and explained that I shouldn't bother trying to find the car. It'd be scrap by now, seeing that it was such an old car and everything. And the coffee place was far along the N12, between Lenasia and Soweto. At least I think so. So they had to take me with them when the call came."

His mom would skin him alive, he'd pleaded with the uncle, if he had to be sent home with a suspension. And he'd rather die, because there was no other job he wanted to do. He just wanted to be a cop. Until the day he died.

Then the tea had arrived. And the uncle had signalled to his secretary that she should give it to Ghaap. "Lots of sugar," he'd said.

Ghaap had been speechless, this was unheard-of behaviour for a station commander. This Indian man truly had a Christian heart, his mom would've said. *And* he was Afrikaans.

"My problem, Sergeant, is this. I'm sitting here with a corps who are not very cooperative. They don't like us makulas, you know." Ghaap had gulped when the man used the derogatory term for Indians.

"Let me teach you one thing from the outset, Sergeant. Diplomacy constitutes about ninety per cent of a commander's daily duties. And that's why I'm sending you home."

Ghaap had been gobsmacked. He'd hung his head and screwed his eyes shut. It had been a mortal blow.

"Look at me, Sergeant. Let us understand each other clearly."

Ghaap had looked at him.

"You know the rules. And Mthethwa has a good point. I feel like throwing your arse to the Prov Com, to make an example of you. But, we're short-staffed. So you're going home for three days. You have to take rest days in any case."

"With respect, Colonel—"

"That'll be all, Sergeant." The uncle's weary eyes told Ghaap he'd better not talk back. He'd got off lightly enough, after all.

Ghaap then jumped up and saluted.

"And leave the cup with Pinky on your way out," the uncle had muttered, his attention already on something else: a half-eaten box of Turkish delight. Daintily, he selected one with his podgy fingers, gave it a shake, and popped it into his mouth. As he did so, the red garnet in his pinky ring seemed to draw a thick line under Ghaap's dreadful day.

35

Beeslaar was woken by a sudden weight on his chest and a purring in his ears. He sat up abruptly, and two protesting cats leapt to the floor.

It was still dark outside, though his watch said it was half past five. Maybe it was the mountains and the many trees that held back the dawn. Or the blustering southeaster. Hell, if he'd been the sun, he'd also have had second thoughts about rising in such a wind. He threw the duvet aside and put on his trainers. And a fleece jacket against the autumn bite.

As he walked past Maaike's house, he heard Rembrandt barking inside. There was a faint glow in one of the rooms. It flickered, like a burning candle. He became aware of a low murmuring, a male voice. He halted and strained his ears, but the wind was making such a racket that he could barely hear. Didn't sound like trouble, in any case. And then the sound stopped and the light faded. He smelt something – dagga?

He was on the point of walking off when Rembrandt unexpectedly yapped behind him. He bit his lip to stop himself from exclaiming in fright. The dachshund stood up against his leg, the thin tail upright, like an antenna, vibrating. "Shush," he reprimanded.

As Beeslaar closed the outside gate behind him, the dog slipped out too. He tried to stop the animal, called him back, but the wind scattered his words.

He strode off in a northerly direction and soon arrived at a T-junction. To his left the road led into town. To the right, he noticed the gleam of dawn behind the high rocky peaks. He set course for the mountains, east. Straight into the maw of the wind. Ahead he could see the distinctive southeaster cloud that churned angrily all along the mountain tops. There'd be no end to this wind, he was told. It forced you into submission, made you walk like an old man, battling the downward pressure of an invisible hand.

The road ran up a gentle slope. Vineyards to his left and right and, further along, the mountains encircled a green valley. It had to be the Jonkershoek Valley, he decided, and accelerated his pace. He kept to the cement path for pedestrians on the right side of the road. Behind him he heard the patter of Rembrandt's paws. The dog kept up with him, despite being so small.

As he walked, his body fell into an automatic rhythm, with muscles and joints working in unison like a well-oiled engine. His thoughts began to ramble. It had been a turbulent night. In the first place, he always slept badly in strange places. And last night the window had to be kept closed, which made for a stuffy room. He made a mental note to buy a can of Doom. Bugger Mathilda.

And secondly … What? He had a "feeling", as Blikkies would have said. Impending doom. And he wasn't even hung over. Maybe it was just depression. Because, yes, he was fuckin' depressed that Blikkies had chosen to check out now, of all times. He'd miss him. Actually, he hadn't had a chance to come to grips with his death. Things had been happening so damn fast.

He and the old guy had been planning this visit for so long. Blikkies, who had cautioned each time Beeslaar postponed it on account of some or other investigation: "One day you'll arrive here, only to be in time for the funeral!"

Beeslaar halted and fumbled in his pocket for a handkerchief. There was a wetness in his eyes. Feeling only the keys and his phone, he used the sleeve of his jacket to wipe his nose and cheeks.

Suddenly it overcame him. The urge to cry. Tears running down his cheeks, and him gritting his teeth to hold back the grief. How was it possible that things had worked out so badly?

He sniffed angrily and wiped his eyes with his hands. Blew his nose into the hem of his T-shirt. Just water, after all.

The dog stood looking up at him, both front paws against his leg.

"Go home!" Beeslaar said. The dog didn't budge, just balanced on its hind legs, its small elongated body standing upright. "Buzz off!" Beeslaar bellowed. But Rembrandt was adamant as he stood there, his two ears like floppy bows on either side of his pointed face. He made whimpering sounds, gazed pleadingly at the giant before him.

Beeslaar sighed. "This is *exactly* what I knew would happen!" he scolded as he bent down and scooped the dog up with one hand. "You're fokken cocky when you run out of the gate, but now that you're tired, *I* have to fokken carry you." The dog looked up at him expectantly and gave a loud, commanding bark: Hit the road, Jack.

Beeslaar shook his head, started walking. He was losing his bladdy marbles. Standing here at the crack of dawn, in the wind, conversing with a damn dog. He wiped his nose once more.

This morning he had that solitary feeling again. As if he were alone in the world, on an unfamiliar road in an unfamiliar place. With a ridiculous dog in his arms and a wind that was raging as if it held a personal grudge against him. Hell-bent on flattening him, rolling him into a ditch.

You've lost, brother, the wind hissed at him. Six-love. You have nothing. You *are* nothing. Devoted a lifetime to being so alone. First Koefie left you, then Pa. Followed by Ma. Who'd wilted like a flower. She had hated Pa, blamed him for all the bad things in their lives. It was if her hatred had anchored her. She'd turned into a ghost overnight, after his death. Vague and insubstantial, cancer eating away at her. Her eyes had no longer focused. It's the morphine, the doctor had said. But no, she'd said, she was seeing Koefie: "He's coming to fetch me, Albertus. Koefie says he's alone. We must go to him …"

Koefie had been *her* child. Skinny like her. A greyhound. The Forrest Gump of Germiston. Indefatigable. Good-looking, like Ma. Well-built, the perfect athlete. But gentle. And full of laughter. With his violet-blue eyes. Who one fine day …

Beeslaar came to a stop, took a deep breath. Dear God. What was he doing? How many more old wounds did he want to open this morning?

He remembered Ma's memorial service. How few mourners there'd been. One or two acquaintances from the old mineworkers' neighbourhood in Germiston. Where the women had gone around with curlers in their hair during the day. Dropped in at each other's houses to share a cigarette. Or to bum one. And to cry on each other's shoulders, or nurse the ones whose husbands beat them up. His own dad had stopped after Koefie's death. And then he'd taken the coward's way out: booze. Ma always reproaching him. Like a rusty windmill that needs grease, Pa would yell, before fleeing to the bar.

Blikkies had accompanied him to Ma's funeral. And afterwards, shepherded him to the bar at the Turffontein race track. Where he'd made sure that Beeslaar got properly drunk and unburdened his heart.

But he hadn't talked about his mother. Mostly, he'd complained. Because he'd been overlooked for promotion again, as the rest of the youngsters were notching one rank after another. While he was being left to drift around with the dead wood, the old ballies waiting around for their pensions.

Blikkies had allowed him to vent his anger. Until he'd been emptied out. And had vomited from all the brandy.

He hadn't said anything in response.

And then, a while later, Blikkies casually said one day that there was no such thing as an ideal job, an ideal boss or ideal conditions. If that's what you wanted, you'd better hand in your papers. Because life was tough. And unfair. And it ground sissies into the dust. If you wanted to be a man, you had to learn to deal with reality, accept things as they are. The same went for change. You had to model yourself on the karate guys; you give way, stay supple, roll with the punches. You didn't waste your energy on stuff like self-pity and discontent and envy.

You did your best. That's all you worked on. The rest was God's business.

Yes, old Blikkies. God's business.

Was it God's business that had caused the woman you loved … That your love had destroyed her life? He wouldn't let her go, even though he *knew* it was over. She'd told him repeatedly: "I can't do this any more, Albertus. It's too traumatic for me. I need to hang on now, for my child's sake. That's all I have left. Do you understand? That's all."

"You also have *me*, Gerda."

"You carry too much grief inside you, Albertus." It had been late that Saturday evening, in his hotel room after her mother's funeral. He'd flown from Upington to attend the service.

But she hadn't been pleased to see him. Had clung to the long-haired foreigner. A gorilla with a gold chain in his chest hairs. Sly eyes like a jackal, the mouth of a weakling. He'd wanted to tear the guy limb from limb, right through the ceremony, it was all he could think of. He hadn't stayed for refreshments afterwards. Just fled.

But then she'd come looking for him that evening, in his hotel room. And they'd surrendered. As they always did when they were alone. When the grief and the guilt and the black loneliness paralysed them, swept them together. She'd lain in his arms. And he'd kissed her. On her forehead. Her closed eyelids. On her cheeks, where he'd tasted the salt of her tears. Down her neck, in her soft, pulsing throat dimple. All over her slender shoulders, her heaving breasts. The intimate parts of her belly.

They had made love. Like in the old days. Slowly, tenderly, as you'd massage a shared wound.

And when they lay sweatily in each other other's arms afterwards, she'd softly sobbed.

"Stay with me," he'd pleaded.

But she'd left him anyway.

Beeslaar shifted the dog to his other arm. The animal sprang against his chest and licked his cheek. He turned his face away in disgust. He didn't like small dogs. Maybe because his mother hadn't been keen on them. Stoepkak-kertjies, she'd called them, because they shat on the stoep and gave you ring-worm. And scabies. Probably her way of saying no each time he'd begged her for a dog.

But when you were a child … Your parents were gods. The gods who had called you into being. You'd had no say in the matter. They had created you. Created your world for you. They determined how welcome or unwelcome you felt in the world. How far inside or outside the circle of humanity you stood.

They knew more, were better, stronger, cleverer than anyone else. His dad – with the strong forearms. The ease with which he'd loosen a rusty nut, his sinews and muscles bulging. His dad had been the strongest man in the world. Stronger than Superman. Ma had been the best-looking woman. Pa used to say she was the Elizabeth Taylor of Germiston. Of South Africa. Hell, she was more beautiful even than old Liz Taylor herself!

Your mom and your dad … To Beeslaar, there wasn't even a contest in the nature vs nurture debate. When you were a child, your mom and dad were the ones who held your heart. They were the determiners of your fate. From them you learnt not only the practical things like good manners, but also the in-between things. What love looked like. What humour looked like. How to be a man. And how to treat women and children.

His mom had kept him and Koefie apart from the other kids in the neighbourhood. Said they weren't clean. Where would she have picked up that idea? Her affluent background, no doubt. Where there'd been money, servants who'd scrubbed and polished all day long.

It was only later that Beeslaar realised how hard life in that community of coarse mineworkers would have been for her. She'd been too young when she'd married Pa, he'd occasionally hear her say to someone. He had made her pregnant with Koefie. Her parents who'd disinherited her. She had never forgiven Pa for that.

She thought she was too good for him, Pa used to yell. Raised his sons like pansies, and no, there wasn't any money for more children. Albertus was already one too many.

He shifted Rembrandt again. Like a king, the animal was lying along the length of his folded forearms, and barked at anything that dared come their way.

As a group of guinea fowl noisily crossed the road, he jumped from his lofty seat. Fearing he might break his neck, Beeslaar tried to stop him, but the dog was too quick. He charged at the guinea fowl, his crooked little feet becoming a blur as he ran. Once the guinea fowl had screeched over the boundary fence, the dog gave a final bark: *Don't dare let this happen again!* Then he pattered back smugly across the road to where his personal charioteer stood waiting, hand on hip.

The road narrowed ahead, Beeslaar saw, with tall trees lining the tar, plots and small farms on either side. He observed all the interesting name boards, walked past a fancy gate with CCTV cameras and a poor bugger in uniform on guard duty in a cubicle. They nodded to each other.

A group of cyclists came up from behind, chatting to each other. Greeted him as they rode past. Rembrandt returned the greeting on his behalf.

Ahead was a steep rise with a forest of poplar trees on either side, making the road seem a dark tunnel. He struggled as he lugged himself up the hill. His heart was pumping like a steam engine.

When he reached the top, he put the dog down and rested a second or two, then bent over to recover his breath.

It was only when he looked up again that he noticed his surroundings: a giant billboard before him announced the construction of an exclusive security complex. *Jonkers Valley.*

Beeslaar stared at it, nonplussed.

Then he saw the name of the contractor: *Malan du Toit.*

36

He must've fallen asleep after all, was Ghaap's first thought as he opened his eyes. Outside his window he heard a strange kind of cooing. It was Duif Vermeulen.

"Here, my girlie. How are we feeling today? You're going to do a bit of flying? Come now, come, there's a good girl. Oops, the girlie has a temper this morning? Yeeees-yes-yes-yes-yes. There we are, that's it. Not so fast, Frikkels."

Ghaap decided to get up. There was no way he could continue listening to *that*.

He walked to the kitchen, where a mega-box of Coco Pops and some long-life milk were on the table. On either side, a plastic bowl. Jissus, how was he going to get through the day on air? The only breakfast that filled his stomach was stywe mieliepap. His mom's porridge, thick and stiff.

The thought of her brought a lump to his throat. God, he'd had enough of this place.

Then he remembered his car.

He sank down onto a chair, his head in his hands. He'd had so many plans when he bought that car. He'd wanted to become one of the best cops, too. Who wore the uniform like a dominee wore his robe: a man of destiny. Like Leo, the hero of *The Matrix*. With his coat and all. In fact, his mom had made him a coat exactly like that. Not genuine leather, but still … He'd even brought it along with him, but it lay scrunched up in his suitcase, next to a bladdy pidgeon coop. At the home of a man who talked to birds.

"Good morning," this very man's voice floated in. Duif was standing at the back door, a silly grin on his face and a pouter pigeon in his huge right hand. The bird flapped its wings as Ghaap got up.

"Looks to me like you're still fast asleep, my man?"

"Ag, just thinking," Ghaap mumbled, and began to look around for a kettle.

Duif showed him where the coffee things were. "Come and meet my children while you wait for it to boil," he said, and disappeared.

Outside, Duif took a pigeon from the dovecote, and introduced Ghaap to Girly. Then he fetched another one. To Ghaap they looked exactly alike, peas in a pod.

"And this is Kokkedoor, my top sprinter," Duif said proudly. "Do you want to hold him?"

Ghaap shook his head and raised his empty coffee mug. His hands were full, he indicated, noting with relief that his refusal hadn't in the least dented Duif's enthusiasm.

Somewhat disgusted, Ghaap stood to one side as he watched Duif changing his creatures' water bowls. The dovecote stank like wet mealie-meal. Pigeon piss, Ghaap decided. The same smell as in his bedroom. The thought of their cold, wet, stinking claws gave him the bladdy creeps.

Duif whistled as he removed the old water bowls filled with debris and feathers and pigeon shit, and replaced them with clean ones.

They went inside, poured themselves some coffee, and sat down to breakfast. Ghaap noticed that Duif hadn't yet washed his hands. It made every Coco Pop stick in his throat. They were halfway through their meal when Duif's cellphone chirped. He looked at the screen.

"Car theft," he exclaimed and jumped up from the table. "Wait in front, at the car! I'm just going to lock up!"

Ghaap rushed to the bedroom and dived into his jeans. Tackies and socks in his hand, a squeeze of toothpaste in his mouth. Then he sprinted to the front door; he was wide awake, full of adrenaline.

And eagerly looking forward to the hunt.

37

Beeslaar's phone rang.

He unceremoniously dumped the dog, who yapped in protest, but followed the big man nevertheless. They were half a block away from Maaike's house.

Qhubeka.

"Can I pick you up for breakfast?"

"I'll come with my own wheels. I've got some other stuff to do today."

"Oh?"

"I'll tell you over breakfast. In half an hour?"

She agreed and ended the call.

By now Rembrandt had caught the scent of home, and he raced towards the front gate. He jumped up against it and barked excitedly. Little bugger, thought Beeslaar, he was as fresh as a daisy. And the poor arsehole who'd had to carry him most of the way was itching from top to toe, thanks to the dog hairs.

He was about to insert his key when the electric gate buzzed open. A tall, thin figure came walking out, stopped short in apparent surprise when he saw Beeslaar.

Rembrandt evidently knew the fellow, as he yelped cheerfully and stood up against the man's leg. The man was dressed in a scruffy t-shirt and denims, a baggy jacket made of springbok-skin, Jerusalem sandals that looked as if he'd cobbled them together himself with an awl and thongs. He wore his dark-blond hair in dreadlocks that dangled below a broad-brimmed hat with a leopard-skin band.

"Heita, Boss," the man said and extended his hand. "Andries April."

They shook hands and then April bent down and picked up Rembrandt, who started licking his hand. "A little bird told me you's a bush penguin, ek sê?" When a mystified Beeslaar failed to react, he explained: "That's what we Capeys call you people from the inland, mos."

Beeslaar gave a half-smile.

"So, you with the gattas, I hear?"

Beeslaar frowned.

"I just came for a skinner with the Dutch antie, bit of a news exchange. She tuned me lekker."

Beeslaar made to move on, but the man stopped him.

"Ek sê," he called out, "you also working on that larney murder?"

"Why do you want to know?" He couldn't keep the irritation out of his voice.

"No, I scheme you gonna braai your brains with this thing, ek sê."

"Ja?" Beeslaar guessed he was referring to the Du Toit case. He was about to close the gate behind him when he saw that Rembrandt was still perched blissfully in the Rastaman's arms. He reached out to take him.

"That Malan du Toit," said the Rastaman as he passed the dog over, "he's the biggest crook in this place."

"Now, what makes you say that, Mr April. Do you perhaps have an axe to grind with him?"

"For sure, ja. Him and the rest of his kind. Money maniacs, all of them. Raping Mother Earth, with blood on their hands."

"*What*?" Beeslaar stared at the man. His eyes, a strange milky blue, glinted vengefully in a yellowish face, the colour of old parchment. His hands, again, were speckled with pink.

"Him and his larney lot," he ranted over the howl of the wind, "they're sick with greed. Buggering up everything with their so-called march of progress! Rolling like pigs in the dosh, and still scheming every day how to make more. Gobbling up the world like bladdy locusts. Any little patch of virgin soil they grab. One of these days they'll cover everything from here to Cape Town in fancy-schmancy shopping malls and security estates. You'll see!"

Dumbfounded, Beeslaar started closing the gate.

"You better get wise, detective!" Two blotchy hands held the gate open. "There's plenty people who'd want to zaber that fat cat. Any which way, stick a knife in him. And where d'you hit a guy like Du Toit? Touch him on his snoek, where it hurts. You get me?"

"I'll convey your opinion to Captain Qhubeka, Mr April. She's in charge of the investigation. Thank you very much!" Beeslaar tried to pull the gate shut, but the wild man was strong.

"I'm not tuning you kak. I *know*."

"And what exactly is it that you know?"

"His wife. She was planted there on purpose, with a message. That's what I know."

Beeslaar grunted, let go of the gate. "Ja-ja," he said, and then turned around.

"Hey, Beeslaar!"

"*What*?"

"Just ask your landlady. She saw it in the bones. Tell her she must throw the bones for you."

Qhubeka had already been served her cappuccino when he arrived at Julian's outside the Eikestad Mall. He'd told Maaike to keep the promised breakfast on hold as he had to go into town.

165

"Do you know one Andries April?" he asked as he sat down.

Qhubeka rolled her eyes.

"He reckons Elmana du Toit was killed to convey a message. Suggests it was a murder waiting to happen."

She blew on the foam, tore open a sachet of sugar, and poured it through the frothy hole she'd made.

Changing tack, he asked: "Have you seen the new housing development in the Jonkershoek Valley?"

When she looked up, the dimples were already in evidence.

"You see?" was all she said, a satisfied twinkle in her eyes: she knew, and he knew, that he was now well and truly hooked.

He grew uncomfortable under her gaze, felt the heat rise in his neck.

"Look," he said, "if this is a question of property rage, it throws a whole new light on Elmana du Toit's death. Then the bonsai fury begins to make sense. Because it sends a message, doesn't it?"

The twinkle left her eyes and she became serious: "He's a troublemaker, our Mr April. A guy with many irons in the fire. Works for a Wellington NGO that campaigns against evictions of workers from white farms – or something like that. He's a great believer in the idea that the 'first peoples' in the Cape should have their land returned to them – preferably along with the house, the vineyards, the tractors, the works. His big hobbyhorse here in Stellenbosch is the developers. He's constantly quoted in the press, railing against new developments for the wealthy. Particularly if they're built on what used to be agricultural land. Says it's a new kind of colonialism. Whites who haven't yet emigrated to Australia semigrate instead to security complexes – like Jonkers Valley." She took a sip of coffee, wiped the faint line of foam from her upper lip. A languid, sensual movement.

"The guy's very active," she resumed, "but always within the law. He's managed to get a foothold somewhere in the valley. He runs all kinds of activities from there, especially with young people from Cloetesville and Idas Valley, our two so-called coloured townships. He claims he's keeping them out of the clutches of gangsters, but if you ask me, he provides more gangster training than anything else."

Beeslaar reflected for a moment. "The other day at the crime scene, when the girl jumped like that. There was an unsavoury fellow among the bystanders, tattoos on his face and arms. Typical prison tats."

She shook her head. "There are so many of them. I'll ask Charmainetjie. She's more clued up about the gangsters."

Their food arrived. She bowed her head, and Beeslaar waited respectfully for her to finish before wolfing down a mouthful of egg and toast. "What church do you belong to?" he asked as he chewed.

"I was brought up Catholic. But nowadays – I find most religions rather absurd, primitive, even." She took a sip of coffee and cut her fried eggs into squares, stirred the baked beans and mushrooms into the egg with her fork, and loaded the mixture onto a piece of thickly buttered white toast. "I *believe*, don't get me wrong. But I think I'm a bit over the picture of a white man with a beard, Noah and the Ark, and so on. And the concept of a pope. An old omie in a caftan, very likely a paedophile too."

"But you pray, Qhubeka. So, who do you pray to?"

"The man in the moon," she smiled.

"Or are you one of those who keep a back door open, just in case?"

The smiled stiffened, her eyes telling him to back off.

"Do you have any clarity about Malan du Toit's financial affairs yet?" he asked. "I mean, that development of his in the valley – Jonkers Valley. It must be very expensive?"

"It used to be part of a farm, apparently not very suitable for agriculture. Too marshy, or something. Back in the day, the apartheid town council bought it as a whites-only picnic site along the river. But today, every grain of sand there's worth a ton of gold – so there were tenders. Du Toit's people came out tops. The first thing they did was evict the coloured people who'd rented cottages on the land. And that's where Mr April and his group come into the picture, see?"

Taking a big swig of coffee, Beeslaar washed down the last remnants of the fried egg. The beans he left untouched. The fat white beans in the red sauce took away his appetite.

"The rage," he said to distract himself, "I think your focus should be on the rage. It tells another story. Someone who's lost his home. Maybe his job too. How angry is a guy like that?" He spread some jam on his toast. "If you plan a murder like that, it makes sense to me … the bullet. Even the first blow with the Brahman. But the vandalism? To my mind, that's more personal. If you …" He chewed and swallowed. "If you're really pissed off with someone. So angry you could kill them with your bare hands. Maybe you'd just shoot and run, don't you think?"

Qhubeka had put down her knife and fork, her full attention on him as he continued.

"Let's say it was someone like the guy with the tattoos I saw there that day. Why would he move the body? And how did he get in? That house is like Fort Knox. Did the woman let him in herself, or what?"

"Er, yes?"

"Or suppose it was the lord and master of the house."

"Who, according to a witness, was in a restaurant all that time."

"Vra my vriend Frik," said Beeslaar.

"Come again?"

"It's an old Dutch expression: Ask my friend Frik, he lies just like me. Something my ouma used to say, according to my mother. Schoolkids were forced to learn Dutch, back then ... Never mind. What I mean is: Malan du Toit's only got his best buddy the lawyer to confirm his alibi. Did you check with the restaurant?"

Her response was just to blink.

"Right. But in my book he's still a candidate."

"Motive?"

"Two immediately spring to mind. First, the marriage was over, but divorce is expensive. And second, her addiction. I wonder what the children have to say?"

Qhubeka shook her head. "Keeping mum. Not even the Nappy Squad can get anything out of them."

"Okay. What do we know about Malan du Toit? The people he does business with, who his enemies are? And the victim herself: Who was her dealer? Apart, that is, from the doctors in the town."

"We've established that each of her doctors wrote scripts for her. She had repeat prescriptions at three different pharmacies. But the meth came from the street. And the connection may have been our chronically ill Mr Ndlovu."

"You said earlier that she'd visited a neurologist as well. For what ailment?"

"Fibromyalgia."

"Firo-what?"

"Fibromyalgia, a kind of nervous disease."

"Good Lord in heaven."

"Ja. You suffer from pain all over your body, but the pain doesn't have a physical cause – like a slipped disc, or a strained muscle. It's more emotional in nature, apparently a typical stress-related disorder."

"Which makes me ask again, what stress could a woman like her have had? She had everything. Except maybe for stress about where the next hit would come from. What do we *really* know about the woman herself? What had Elmana du Toit done that could have made a person or persons that angry? And what went on in that Du Toit family? The picture I'm starting to get of them is not a happy one, to put it mildly."

She nodded in agreement and pursed her lips.

"Have you spoken to friends and acquaintances on the committees and things she was involved in?"

Again, she inclined her head. "But no one is prepared to say anything negative about her. Seems she was surrounded by love and light."

"Not really. Not if I listen to what the family says."

"Why won't they say anything to me? Because I'm of the darker persuasion?" she said, a dimple appearing in each cheek.

38

"Ghalla, where are you? Are you getting signal?"

Duif was talking "hands free" to Ghalla while simultaneously changing gears and getting the GPS going.

Ghaap's head whirled. He heard Ghalla replying through the loudspeaker. "Hos, my bru. We're looking for a white Dolly Parton. Plates: Bravo, Alfa, Sierra, one, zero, nine, Golf. And it didn't send a signal, we got a call-out. The housekeeper who said the madam didn't come home last night. She and a twenty-month-old boy."

"What do the cops say?" Duif asked.

"They don't know anything yet, but The Trickster is in contact with Melville's cop shop. Maybe it's been officially reported, but they're not looking yet. It hasn't been twenty-four hours. But it's definitely one of ours. Most likely hijacked last night in Melville. And the meerkatte must've parked off somewhere to let things cool off. Somewhere outside the district. But the computer boys are now going to track it from Melville."

"Has the signal been activated?"

"Positive. We picked it up in Lens. But I think that may be where they dropped the unit. Car's long gone. Mo's on his way to Lenasia. I'm still on Ontdekkers Road." He ended the call.

"Dawid," another voice came on, one Ghaap didn't recognise. Perhaps the boss. "I'm sending someone else out too. I want you guys to cruise three spots. You take the north-east. The others will cover south and west. Keep in contact. And keep the peace. That police boykie, is he with you?"

Duif confirmed.

"Remember the rules, nè? He must wear a bulletproof. I'll bring the indemnity form. We don't need extra kak with the law."

Duif again confirmed, and the line went dead. They were on a road that Ghaap recognised. It ran south from Duif's house and linked up with Main Reef Road, a busy two-way running east-west. Duif turned left into the heavy traffic and wove his way hurriedly through trucks, cars and millions of minibus taxis.

Ghaap hadn't made head or tail of the phone conversation, but he decided he'd better not ask now. Old Duif was driving like a bat out of hell. Ghaap was barely capable of uttering a sound, anyway. He sat gulping, like a Christmas turkey listening to "Silent Night".

They soon intersected with Commando Road, which ran from the Johannesburg CBD to Soweto. Duif was undeterred by the stationary traffic. He had his flashlights on and the vehicles edged out of his way – including the taxis. Commando was jam-packed too.

Up ahead in the south-western sky hung the grey-brown haze of Soweto's early-morning fires. Along the road, people were making fires in big petrol drums with slits cut in the sides to help fan the flames. Clumps of workers warmed their hands as they passed by. Here and there, small fires burnt on the pavements in front of taxi ranks, fuelled by scraps of plastic and paper from nearby rubbish bins.

The closer to Soweto, the narrower and more cramped the roads were. And more numerous the fires, and the hawkers selling fruit, packs of pap-en-sous, the *Sowetan* and the *Citizen*. Ghaap even spotted an occasional *Beeld*.

While waiting for the traffic to move, Duif told him to get the bulletproof from the back seat and put it on. "I don't expect trouble. We're going to cover the better parts of the district. But you never know." He spotted a gap and pushed in, leaning on his hooter. Swore when the vehicle in front didn't make way quickly enough. Then he shot through. The light was orange, but he put his foot down. Ghaap didn't want to see how fast they were going – he knew he'd get an instant stomach ache. He struggled with the vest and the safety belt, prayed for another traffic jam so that he could fasten them properly.

A minute later they were free of the blockages and speeding down Canada, past the big New Canada train station. Then they were in Orlando East, near Ghaap's workplace, in Mooki Street. Duif swung into a side street and shifted down a gear. They slowed down, and Duif relaxed into his seat. They were now in cruising mode, Ghaap knew. Scanning the surroundings, on the lookout for the Dolly Parton. With his seatbelt buckled and the oversized vest fastened, Ghaap no longer felt quite so much like a Ninja Turtle.

"What are we looking for?" he ventured. He'd lit a cigarette and handed it to Duif, then lit one for himself. Duif drove with his window down, but Ghaap didn't share his trust in the apparent calm of their surroundings. His window was open just enough to allow the smoke to escape.

"Dolly Parton. That's what they call the old Mercedes SES. The old models."

Ghaap tossed away his half-smoked cigarette. His mouth tasted of shit. "Why's that?" he asked, winding up the window.

"The name's from the cash-in-transit guys. The meerkatte have a thing for those old Mercs. Way back, cash was transported in HiAce vans. Ag, that van was useless against the meerkatte. They'd ram into it with a BMW, a front-heavy car. The van didn't stand a chance. Tipped over easily, on its back sommer so, like a cheap slut. But then the vans got bigger, double wheels at the back, armour-plated too. So the thugs said, no, now we need a *really* strong car. And that's why they got the hots for the old battleships. That's their other name. With the SES, sixty-five per cent of the weight is at the front. A bit top-heavy, see? Just like Dolly."

Duif's eyes were constantly on his rear-view mirror, on the lookout for what was going on behind him. "It works like this," he continued, tipping his ash out of the window. "They plan the move months in advance. Get the right equipment. Cars, AKs, the info, angle-grinders, explosives – the works. And then, one fine day, they strike."

He took a deep pull on his cigarette, settled himself comfortably into position. Ghaap kept quiet.

"Okay, so I've got my Dolly Parton. I'm doing about a hundred and thirty. Just before crashing into the van, what do I do? I brake. Like a rugby move. I come in from the side, because that's the only way you can lift him. You ram it so that it topples over. You need to cut open the underside or the roof. Those parts aren't armour-plated. They say you should armour-plate everything, but you can't. The weight makes the van too slow and increases the body roll. Anyway, I want it on its side. The cops are far away, so I've got time to open it up like a can of sardines."

"Sounds like a helluva lot of work," said Ghaap.

"When last did you hear about a successful bank robbery? You tell me: which of the two operations do you make more money from, and which can you escape from more easily?"

"Still – having to plan so long in advance, and everything."

"Ag, no, it's easy as pie, I'm telling you. I've seen how they go about it. They're clever, the meerkatte. And they approach it like a military operation. You remember Colin Chauke?"

Duif had finished his cigarette, so Ghaap lit another, ready for the story. They were literally crawling up and down each street, waiting and watching. They slowed whenever they saw a white Mercedes in front of a house, but none of them was a Dolly Parton.

"Now that guy, Chauke. He was ex-MK, nè. Knew his AK and knew military strategy. He had a small army of his own. Stole millions in cash-in-transit heists. In one robbery he killed six security guards and took ten million rand. Another time, in Pretoria, he took out two guards, stole – I can't remember exactly, but I think it was seventeen million on that one occasion."

"Shit," said Ghaap, clearly impressed.

Obligingly, Duif continued. "And the ex-MK guys. Yoh, yoh, yoh! Those okes have got weapons, I tell you. When they came back from the bush after '94, there were no jobs for them. Most had hardly finished school. And the politicians just shrugged. It was like, thank you, guys, you were great in the liberation struggle, but now you're on your own. And there are thousands of those guys, bru, suddenly idle. And they're fokken pissed off. And hungry. Sitting with girlfriends and a bunch of kids that want food and Nike tackies."

"But," Ghaap interjected, "d'you think the car we're looking for ... the Dolly Parton."

"No, not necessarily. I'm just educating you a bit. Maybe you'll come and work for us some day. The pay isn't as bad as with the cops, my man."

Duif's phone chirped.

And Ghaap's stomach instantly contracted: please Lord, don't let this be another wild chase.

39

"I'm going to pay Mr Ndlovu a visit. Are you coming along?"

Beeslaar chewed his lip. "I actually feel like going for a walk."

"For a walk." Qhubeka took a note from her purse and put it on the breakfast bill. She popped a peppermint into her mouth, waited for him to elaborate.

"Not going for a walk as in playing tourist. I do my best thinking when I walk. Have you managed to track down the domestic worker yet?"

She shook her head: "Housekeeper. Domestic worker sounds to me more like a slave. I depend on one myself, otherwise my household would come to a standstill."

"You have children?"

"Yes."

He waited for more information, but saw from her expression that it would not be forthcoming. He left it there. "Who are the town's conservation people? Do you know anyone?"

"No, not unless they maul or murder each other, I don't really know the white community. And it's only the whites who have time for things like conservation. Maybe you should start with Kokkewiet, the editor of the local newspaper. And Henkie, an estate agent. She grew up here and knows everybody." She took out her phone and punched in a number. He heard a female voice on the other end, confirming that she was available right then.

Qhubeka put the phone in her pocket and said to him: "Henkie is within walking distance – just down here, in Andringa Street. You'll see the agency building."

They stood up together, and left.

"By the way," said Beeslaar once they were outside in the wind, "how well do you know my landlady?"

"Well enough."

"This April character. Is he a boyfriend or something?"

The devils starting dancing in Qhubeka's eyes again, and Beeslaar felt the annoyance rising in his neck.

"Relax, man," she said soothingly. "And no, they're not lovers. He was her previous tenant. And I think he's probably consulting her."

"*Consulting*?"

"Yes. Maaike possesses wonderful knowledge and skills. She's a counsellor of sorts."

"On what?"

"Ask her yourself, Beeslaar. It won't do you any harm to get better acquainted with your hostess."

"But April said something about 'throwing bones'. Is she like a sangoma or something?"

Qhubeka laughed. "And you're afraid that you're at the mercy of a witch."

He didn't answer, asking instead: "What's the estate agent's name again? Henkie?"

To his dismay, Henkie Cilliers had some coffee ready for him when he walked into her office a few minutes later. The breakfast at Julian's had left him with heartburn.

The agency consisted of a single office with big glass windows facing onto a busy tourist street bustling with camera-laden tourists in expensive walking shoes and khaki outfits, as car guards sat around idly, watching the passing parade. The office windows were almost completely covered with photos of houses and farms for sale: the cheapest house, Beeslaar noticed before entering, cost R4.2 million.

"Undoubtedly among the most expensive properties in the country," Henkie said as she walked up to greet him. She spoke Afrikaans with a Boland burr. Her long blonde hair was streaked with highlights, and she wore heavy make-up. Pants and a matching top with a light jacket completed the picture. "Don't ask me why. But when you have Stellenbosch, Franschhoek or Clifton as your address, you've arrived," she said with a laugh.

She closed the door firmly behind them and hung up the *Closed* sign. "Right," she said. "Now we can talk undisturbed. And have a smoke while we're at it."

She led him to a nook out of sight of the front door.

"Most of the people who work in this town can't afford to live here. They commute from places like Somerset West, Bellville, Kraaifontein. One of the reasons is all the agricultural land surrounding the town – there's very little space for expansion. And that makes every bit of property valuable. But what exactly is your interest? Are you assisting Vuvu with the murder investigation?"

"No, I actually came for a funeral, but I suppose you could say I'm 'consulting'. So, can you perhaps enlighten me about the new development in the valley?"

"What do you want to know?"

"For one thing, how much money is involved?"

"You mean whether it's enough to give a man a reason to kill his wife?"

"Not exactly. But feel free to express your opinion on the matter."

She smiled and frowned simultaneously.

Beeslaar made another attempt: "Er, how well did you know the deceased?

175

Or her husband." He felt uncomfortable. He wasn't a private eye's arse, he realised. Struggled without the authority of the law behind him.

"You see," he said, "I don't know this town or its people or its issues. I'm just looking for some background information, you know? Nothing official – we're just talking. Off the record, okay?" He found he was sweating, cursed himself for having allowed that pretty Xhosa woman to rope him in.

"Okay," said Henkie cautiously. "But it remains between you and me?" She waited for confirmation, then continued: "I think that particular development will probably end up in the high court."

"How come?"

"Because everybody's threatening everybody with lawsuits."

"Who's everybody?" asked Beeslaar.

"From Cosatu to the Ratepayers' Association, the white residents, the DA councillors, the Heritage people, the university. You name it, they're suing!"

"Du Toit only?"

"Well, him for starters. And the so-called Jonkers Valley Trust."

"Trust?"

"Look, I don't know exactly who all have invested in this project – you'll have to ask him that yourself. I also don't know how they managed to get approval for a development on that site."

"What kind of housing does he have in mind?"

"From very expensive to cheaper cluster housing. That's what all the fuss is about. Everyone who's complaining says it'll end up with the entire valley becoming built-up. It's an agricultural area with a rich history, after all."

"But ..." Beeslaar pushed his cup aside. "Who will, or rather, who *can* stop it?"

She reflected for a moment. "Look, you can't just ... Let me put it like this: agricultural land here in the Western Cape is as scarce as hen's teeth, which is why it's so expensive. And in the valley even more so: an unpolluted river running through it, no through road carrying heavy traffic. And it's incredibly beautiful, of course. We're talking about three to five million rand per hectare. So, for every patch of land you want to have approved for development ... You just about have to walk on hot coals before you can swing it. First of all, the land has to be rezoned. And to get *that* done is an Old Testament epic, as far as red tape is concerned – nightmarish. Starting with the Minister of Agriculture, who has to give approval. And then your battle starts with the incompetent officials in that department. And then you need an environmental impact study, and then the development must be approved by the town council. And the province. And Cape Nature, the province's conservation people. Especially if it's land adjacent to a nature reserve – which is indeed the case here. And Jonkers Valley's land … Man, oh man! For many years now there've been rumours of more and more rich people buying land in the valley. Wealthy businessmen from Gauteng, foreigners, people like that. The Jonkers Valley sale happened very quietly, no uproar or outcry, but then the workers were thrown off the land, and suddenly everybody sits up and asks what's happening."

"How much money are we talking about here?"

"Lots, I can tell you, lots. Even if your name was Bill Gates, you'd be hard pressed to cough up that kind of money … It's a helluva lot."

"But what would a ballpark figure be, more or less? Give me an idea."

"Gosh, no, that's asking for a short cut to the moon. You're sure you don't want me to top up your coffee?"

Beeslaar put his hand over his cup. "But if I understand correctly, Malan du Toit does have a lot. And judging by his modest residence in this town …"

She laughed. "I sold him that house, so I know what you mean! But yes, he has a lot. Of everything. Land, in particular. Here, in the Boland. He owns a horse stud in the Hottentots Holland Mountains, a game farm in Namibia, and so on."

"So? What are you really saying, that he's gambling with his own money?"

"He'd have to, wouldn't he? The banks aren't granting any loans because of the recession. So you *have* to sell your units first. And it's only once you've raised the money that the bank will come to the party to finance construction. But by that time you'd have paid for environmental, aesthetic, traffic, and other impact studies, setting you back at least five, six million rand. At *least*. Land surveyors, engineers, soil experts, you name it. And bear in mind: the whole time those guys are doing their thing, you're running against time, because your debt accumulates interest. It's not any fool's game!"

"Right, so he'd need partners and financial backers."

"For sure. But not a bank. These days, you haven't even greeted the bank manager before he slams the door in your face. The credit crunch swept through this part of the world like a smallpox epidemic. Only the big players survived – by the skin of their teeth, I tell you."

"And Du Toit? Where does *his* money come from?"

"Look," she began, a short blue-tipped nail counting her fingers, "at a rough guess, you need at least eighty-five to a hundred million rand. And as we know, it's a difficult time in the construction industry, what with our falling rand and everything. People don't have money, and the banks don't hand out credit. And everywhere, prices have really dropped. Conditions are tough. And for a project like Du Toit's, you need a lot of money. Cash, for starters. Never mind the number of palms that have to be greased in the process. For Du Toit to have pulled it off – he's either a miracle worker, or he's got connections in every conceivable place, you know? Because you just about have to go and pluck a feather from the Angel Gabriel's wings before you'd get agricultural land approved for development!"

"But it seems to me that the construction is going ahead?"

"It appears so, yes. I don't know where he gets the money from, but there's an open tap somewhere that runs directly into his bank account. And besides, I don't believe Du Toit will let the greenies and the objectors get the better of him."

"And you? How do you feel about it?" She had deep lines around her mouth, Beeslaar noticed, and frown lines on her forehead. It must take nerves of steel to keep afloat in a market like this, he thought.

"Look," she said after a while, "it's a thorny issue. Around here, people fight about every centimetre of land. With long knives. I just try to keep a low profile as far as I can. But sometimes it gets rough."

"How rough?"

She pursed her lips. "What I'm going to tell you now stays between the two of us, right?"

Beeslaar signalled agreement, and she went on: "Because God knows, someone like me can't afford to take sides. I earn my daily bread from all sides of the community. And nowadays the politics isn't as clear cut as it used to be. You no longer know who's in bed with whom, whose money is behind which project."

"We're only talking background," Beeslaar assured her.

She sat back, fumbled in a jacket pocket, produced an e-cigarette and took a deep pull. There was no ring on the third finger of her left hand, though she had rings on nearly every other finger. Inexpensive chain-store gold. Several fine gold chains of different lengths and thicknesses hung from her neck in a way that drew attention to her generous cleavage.

"There's a so-called watchdog organisation in the town," she began, exhaling vapour. "Quite a formidable bunch. And they have enough money for court cases. When they feel strongly enough about an issue, you can be sure that a big fight is on the cards. Unless it affects their own pockets, you know?" She drew deeply on the e-cigarette. "This town," she resumed, "has a long history. Three centuries. It's the oldest official town in the country. So we're dealing with three centuries of claims and injustices. And it's been an ugly history at times."

"Ugly enough to kill a developer's wife?"

"That I can't tell you. But not so long ago, in the 1960s, the coloured families were evicted from the town centre because of apartheid. The northern part of the old town, it had its own name, Die Vlakte. It was a mixed area, many people lived and went to school there. The Muslim church is still there today. Mosque, I should say."

Beeslaar shifted in his chair, not too keen on a history lesson.

"Be that as it may," she continued, "there's still a lot of emotion about those forced removals. There were families who'd had businesses in town, who'd given their children a good education, but who were then pauperised to the level of manual labourers within a single generation. I tell you, the whites think it's all in the past, let bygones be bygones. But there's still a lot of hurt and sadness in the community about what happened."

She paused, and Beeslaar looked at her expectantly.

"And now the whites' new thing is conservation. They preach it all the time. My dad used to be in education, at the time they closed down the coloured school where he taught. He'd seen white greed in property dealings in those days. The coloured people had hardly been evicted when what you might call a demolition frenzy swept through this town. It's a miracle that there are still any buildings left today that are older than two years. Historical houses, shops – it was as if the Boere wanted to erase history too. My parents were young at the time, and they saw it all first hand – white nationalism, the way the politicians ranted. The naked racism with which they squeezed out the coloured people and took away their right to vote. My dad is still alive, you know. And you don't want to hear the stories about those days. It was really rough."

"Okay. But what about *now*?"

"Oh, these days we form a laager around conservation, it's one legitimate way of keeping out this new lot of political fat cats." She laughed. "Some rotten snoek heads were dumped in a developer's post box not too long ago. That's the kind of revenge the conservationists go in for. Definitely not murder."

She gave a last pull, then put the e-cigarette back in her pocket.

"Hell no. But the developers keep coming thick and fast. When a spot becomes available, you must just know: tomorrow the bulldozers are there. And *expensive*."

"But who are the buyers?"

"Ag, everybody. You have a rich dad from Gauteng, for instance, who wants Sussie to study at the last Afrikaans university in the country. He's prepared to cough up a million or two for a tiny flat somewhere. And there you go!"

"But Malan du Toit …" Beeslaar reminded her. By now his heartburn had risen to his throat.

"I can't really say. There's a lot of gossip about him. But lately it's been more about her, an odd bod in her own right. I was in a Bible study group with her. That's what the housewives do in this town: Bible study. There are many different religions here, from happy-clappies to the Muslims. But our little group – we go way back. Many of us were at school together. Probably the only reason I've been included, because those women are queen bees. High society. They go on skiing holidays together, that sort of thing."

"And Elmana?" Beeslaar tried to steer her back to the topic.

"Ja, Elmana. Her family comes from around here, but they weren't well off. She worked in the bank when she was young. But with her looks – she was damn beautiful, you know. Perfect body, perfectly groomed. But I think she's the one who wore the pants in that family. A quick temper, and an opinion on everything. I've seen the way the papers are writing about her. But that's not how I knew her, I must tell you."

"So you think she made enemies?"

She chuckled. "Recently, at a town council function, she was involved in an argument. A coloured professor had said that her food action work was aimed at salving her white conscience. Her husband evicted people from his land while she traipsed around like Mother Teresa, handing out food. She told him in no uncertain terms where to get off. No, she wasn't scared of speaking her mind, especially after a drink or two."

She was thoughtful for a moment, then said: "I suppose it isn't always easy being white … especially if you're rich and white. Always waiting for vengeance – because of the sin of apartheid. For the hungry hordes to invade the safe white suburbs with burning tyres and stones and pangas."

"Do you know a man called Andries April?" he asked.

"Who doesn't? All of a sudden he's everywhere. Says Du Toit contravened the Extension of Security of Tenure Act by evicting the coloured people from the Jonkers Valley land. Oh, and that the entire valley actually belongs to them. Apparently the first landowners there were freed slaves. And before them, the Khoi. There've been marches and protests, and vineyards on one of the valley farms were set alight."

"But the construction work is continuing?"

"Of course! There's a helluva lot of money at stake. The town council's sitting with folded arms – because they've already been paid off. And there hasn't been a peep out of the province yet. Apparently still 'studying' the case. But by the time they've finished, it'll be a built-up valley!"

"The march of progress," remarked Beeslaar, and stood up.

"The march of history," she said.

She took leave of him and gave directions to the local newspaper offices. Where he'd find the editor, Kokkewiet Syster.

"Good luck," said Henkie Cilliers as she removed the *Closed* sign from the door. "And you should ask Kokkewiet to tell you more about Elmana du Toit, especially how out of sorts she was in the last few weeks."

40

Gerda was drifting between sleep and wakefulness. She thought she could hear children's voices. No – dogs whining. Something between whining and laughing. She smelt apples. Close by. The smell of a living creature. Agitated, pacing up and down. She could hear it. The thing that was whining so piteously. With each step, a squeaky clanking sound. It was dragging something along with it … a chain?

She woke with a start: Where *was* she? Where was her child? What was going on?

She tried calling out, but there was something in her mouth. Dear God, what had happened?

She was … Pa, crying at the gate …

Then it hit her.

She wanted to jump up, scream. But she wasn't even able to open her eyes, couldn't feel her arms. What had they given her? And where was Kleinpiet? Oh, God. She felt the tears, choked as they ran down her throat. The children … her children. Kleinpiet … Oh God, she prayed. You're not going to take my children from me *again*. I've already paid for my sin: twice, with two healthy little boys. Surely we're even now?

Please just spare my children. Just this *one* time? Or take us all.

"Into damnation," she recalled her father's words from long ago. She'd known he'd be upset. She'd been the apple of his eye. His redhead rebel. Rierie, he'd called her. And he, in turn, had been her hero, with his uniform, the shiny buttons and medals. A full colonel.

But the day they released Nelson Mandela – that day everything changed. Pa became angry – with everything and everybody.

Gerda felt the old familiar pain pricking in her throat, flames of emotion rising in her nose. Was *this* what Pa had meant? Had he been right all the time? With all his authority, including that of his uniform. Colonel Casper Cornelis Matthee. One of the stalwarts of Wachthuis, the old police headquarters in Pretoria. Used to accompany the Minister at parades. And from one day to the next he was out in the cold with a package, discarded like a dog's carcase. Ma had urged him to start his own business. Security. But Pa had withdrawn into a bitter silence. He'd cut everyone off, colleagues, friends. Wanted nothing to do with any of them. Sell-outs, he'd railed at them. He'd battled the terrorists for God knows how many years, seen the blood of how many young recruits flow in the townships. And for what?

She'd been the only one he still talked to. Until she told him she'd met the man she was going to marry. Denzel Fouché.

His daughter with a coloured man. That was the last straw.

"God will spit you and your descendants out of his mouth," he'd raged. After Neiltjie's birth, she'd phoned him. "You have a grandson, you know? With your name."

"He's nothing of mine." He had put down the phone in her ear. Ma told her at the time that he'd joined another church. A group who believed that non-white people were the progeny of Satan. They called them the "mud races", spawned by Eve's adultery with the serpent in paradise. And Ham, who'd had "intercourse with animals".

"Pappa," she'd once tried to plead with him, "we love each other."

"This is what the *Bible* says," he'd coldly replied, rattling off the relevant texts – from Genesis to Deuteronomy.

But it was the one from Leviticus that had stuck in her like a barb. That damning, hateful curse. The one about "unclean people" with "deformities". And those with flat noses. Flat noses!

"Pappa, but God is *love*, not *hate*. Love."

"My child, God is just," he'd said wearily. "He hates only Satan. And the progeny of Satan. You can cry all you want to, it doesn't make it right. And I made a vow to God. I dedicated *you* to Him! And then *you* denied God! Deuteronomy 23 verse two: 'A bastard shall not enter into the congregation of the Lord.' *That* is what's written there."

She'd turned around, walked away. Away from his terrible eyes. And a bitterness that was so strong she could smell it on him.

41

A woman, Beeslaar realised in surprise when he enquired about the editor at the *Akkernuus* office.

Syster – an old Cape surname, Beeslaar guessed. Veronica Syster – aka "Kokkewiet". Caramel-coloured skin, high cheekbones, pretty light-brown eyes. And a birthmark across her left temple that bled into her eyebrow, right up to her lashes. It looked like a hand reaching in from somewhere, grabbing at the eye. Her hair was long, tied back.

Apart from a fringe she used to hide the mark, it didn't seem to bother her much. She listened to him, a quiet confidence in her eyes, as she tried to establish what exactly he wanted from her.

"But you yourself are not from the Stellenbosch police service," she again confirmed when he'd finished.

"In fact, no, I'm really only looking for background, er ..." He hesitated.

"You don't know the community, is that it? And this time the police are treading more warily than arresting the first available suspect and being sued for fifty million two years down the line."

He sighed, not in the mood for arguing. He should have known better than to approach a bladdy journalist for information. He glanced around the room, noted the photos of children on filing cabinets and on a bookshelf behind her desk. She didn't wear a wedding ring, though, he'd noticed.

She followed his eyes to the photos but said nothing.

"So ask me, Captain Beeslaar. And then we'll see how far we get. You realise, of course, that this is a two-way street?"

"I honestly don't have any new information about the case. And you will understand, I'm sure, that we're at an early stage—"

"Ja-ja, I know the story. The cops may use us for their purposes. And in exchange ... oh, in exchange you may use us *again*. Because what you do is in the national interest while we, on the other hand, are only seeking sensation. Am I right?" She took a sip of water from a glass next to her open laptop.

"I don't want to waste your time, Mrs Syster. But I was led to believe that you knew the deceased well?"

She took a deep breath, stared at her computer screen as if it showed something fascinating. Her office faced onto a busy street in the historic town centre. Through the window, Beeslaar could see a big lawn, bordered by old gabled buildings.

"We weren't close friends," she began. "But I came to know her well through the food action scheme in the town."

"Is it a church initiative?"

"No. Our newspaper is the chief sponsor and organiser. And the rest is in the hands of a group of volunteers."

"One of them being Vincent Ndlovu?"

She looked hard at Beeslaar, an invisible radar scanning him for hints of innuendo. "Not a volunteer, no," she said at last. "A salaried employee. Thanks to people like Elmana, we get donations from businesses in the town that make our work possible. We feed the poorest of the poor and look after homeless people and street children. Vincent's job is to collect the food donations on a daily basis and distribute them to the right places."

"But he and Elmana du Toit didn't exactly have a warm relationship?"

"I know of few people who really had a *warm* relationship with her. She, er, look, I don't actually feel comfortable … My newspaper's official position is that this thing is a heavy blow to the community. And that it's a shame that the police are unable to protect the community. Anything else?"

Beeslaar stood up. It was a stupid idea to try and pick a journalist's brain. Qhubeka would just have to ferret out this kind of information on her own.

"Thanks for your time," he said.

She didn't reply and remained seated, already pulling the laptop towards her.

And then she said: "I'm sorry if I sounded abrupt, but I don't know whether I'm the right person to inform you about this town. It's a complicated place. And I can't afford to take sides in the matter. This is a community newspaper, we represent all the residents."

Beeslaar stood with his hand on the doorknob. "I understand," he said, waiting for more, but nothing was forthcoming. She focused on the computer, the mark on her forehead seeming to smoulder.

"Well, goodbye then," he said, "and thanks again for your time."

He turned the knob, but released it again when he heard her voice behind him: "Just remember, Captain Beeslaar, this entire community is traumatised. People drop all kinds of remarks, say things they wouldn't normally say."

"Like what, Mrs Syster?"

She gave him an appraising look. "Everything here is politics," she said, "just keep that in mind when you talk to people, okay?"

"That's nothing new," he muttered as he opened the door. She started speaking again: "Towns like these are still very 'old South Africa', if you get my drift. Things are still very, er, *apart*. And to the white Afrikaner, Stellenbosch is … It's more than just a town. It's an institution, a symbol, maybe of greater significance than any monument. The idea of the 'Afrikaner' was born here.

And for many this town represents the decent face of the Afrikaner. Here they can show that they can't all be tarred with the same brush of apartheid evil – what with the university and the wine culture and the historic architecture." She moved the mouse, her gaze focused on the screen.

As he turned again to leave, she sprang a casual question: "So, have you arrested anyone yet?"

"No."

"Crime has got us all down. And a thing like this, what happened to Mana …"

"Was she behaving differently, the past while?"

"What makes you ask that?" She gave him a hard look.

"Oh, just wondering. Her husband said she'd been very tense."

She fiddled with her computer mouse, then said, "More overwrought, I imagine. After her mom's death. She was often ill, suffered from migraines, and so on. Quarrelled with people – more than usual."

"With Vincent Ndlovu?"

"Poor Vincent. At one photo opportunity … She pushed him to the front – made her charity look politically correct. But behind the scenes she treated him so badly … especially lately."

Her voice grew softer, and Beeslaar had to strain his ears.

"Accused him of selling the food donations for his own gain. And then, at other times, she was … I thought she was losing it. Because sometimes she'd say things like he wanted to get rid of *her*!"

"Oh? Did you believe her?"

She pulled the laptop closer, her eyes still averted.

After a while she said: "I conducted an investigation, of course, on behalf of the soup kitchen board. And I confronted him. I mean, *we* pay his salary. But I couldn't find any proof. Ag, and I could just see, quite often, you know, that she wasn't really herself."

She bit her lip. Beeslaar waited.

"Poor Vincent. At some stage he …" She paused for a moment. "He stopped going to work."

"When was the last time you spoke to her?"

She frowned at the computer. On tenterhooks, Beeslaar sat watching the bustle outside her office window. When she spoke again, her voice was so faint that he could barely hear.

"She phoned me the morning of her death. Wanted me to come her house. She was a bit, er, incoherent. I don't know whether she was … sober. She babbled on about blackmail, people wanting to destroy her. Other people, not Vincent. I can't recall everything she said … I was impatient, told her I was busy." She looked up at him with a worried expression. "But now … Maybe if I listened better, went to see her, she might still have been alive."

"I've heard that you were in any case on the point of relieving her of her duties?"

She dropped her head, eyes closed, waved him from her office with a gesture.

A moment later Beeslaar was back in the busy street, adrenaline buzzing in his head.

42

She was blindfolded. And her hands were bound to her sides. Tightly. She could barely feel them.

She'd been lying awake for some time now, concentrating on listening.

She was somewhere in a township, that much she could tell from the faraway sounds. Someone calling out in Tswana, a voice answering. And every now and again a train rattled past. Somewhere far off. Closer by, all was quiet. Too quiet. As if she were in a cemetery. She smelt sewage. And the strange, intermittent scent of apples.

Her head ached. But there was something else. Something more pressing that demanded her attention. Fear. Hovering at the edges of her consciousness.

She wanted to speak, cry for help, but her mouth was taped shut. She tried moving her head from side to side. Strained to free herself. To not just lie there, so helplessly. Oh God, so this was what her end was like. Horrible. Fear gripped her, and she screamed and struggled with all the strength she could muster. But all she produced was a whimper. A slight wriggling.

Her child! Where was her child? The screams rose in her throat again, broke against the gag on her mouth. She strained at the ropes around her hands and feet. Where *was* she, for God's sake? And Kleinp—

She had to calm down. Right now. Hysteria would get her nowhere. She had to think. If there was the slightest chance that Kleinpiet was still alive ... Oh, God, what might they have done to him?

And the baby ... She felt no movement. She had to calm down. Calm. Calm. Breathe slowly. She snorted to open her nose canal. Concentrate on breathing, she told herself. Think of positive things. Talk to Neiltjie and Boeta. And Kleinpiet. And Lara. Her little girl. She had to do what she did at home every night. Say goodnight to the four of them in turn.

But the fear broke through: how did she end up here? The last thing she remembered ... The wild struggle in the traffic, the stinging pain in her thigh. He must have injected her. Mpho, the young one who'd sat at the back with Kleinpiet. How long had she been here?

And Kleinpiet. Was he even still alive? And her daughter? She listened closely, hoping to hear another little heartbeat. Why didn't she *feel* anything? Had she had a miscarriage? Because of the injection? The shock?

Breathe, breathe more slowly, she scolded herself. Her children were dependent on her. On her alone. Never ever again would anyone hurt her children, leaving her to face the hell of survival. No. When that coward in his drunken stupor … Her boys, little bundles of warmth. And joy, smelling of honey. Pistol to the head. Pulling the trigger … Had he done it quickly? Could they have been aware of what was happening? Boeta. The sensitive one. With his big blue eyes and his ginger curls. Who'd followed her around like a shadow. Clung to his dummy. The nightmares whenever Pappa got drunk. So drunk that he broke everything. Had the first shot woken him up? Had Neiltjie called out, perhaps? He'd been the first …

And she'd heard the shots. She had *heard* but she hadn't been there. She'd been with her lover across the road. She should have been with her children, that evening. So that there was *someone* there for them, to hold them. To stop the bullets with her body.

The old anger flooded her mouth with bile. God, how many times hadn't she damned him with her curses. His own children.

Never again. Never again would anyone do this to her. Or her children.

She had to get out of here. She had to get help. Albertus, where are you? she screamed soundlessly. You child is in danger! Help us! You're the only one who'd know what to do. You, who know every inch of this place!

She took a deep breath. Stay calm, she reminded herself.

Suddenly, a new sound!

A hard, scraping sound. A door, maybe? She felt a change in the air. A cool breeze.

The sound of breathing.

She lay motionless.

Someone seemed to have squatted down next to her. A hand rested on her belly. She heard a rustle, felt a hand on the side of her neck. A gentle touch. Feeling for her pulse.

The hand touched the blindfold over her eyes, explored the wetness of her tears.

"Are you awake?"

It was a woman!

Gerda lay like a statue.

"Your child is being taken care of," whispered the voice.

She couldn't help it. The sob exploded from deep inside her belly.

"Shh-shh. He's doing well. Don't worry. You must rest."

Gerda tried to speak.

"No, no, no! Think of the little one. Be quiet. Rest, just rest. You're doing fine. As long as you—"

Her voice was drowned out by the whining of an animal. Its paws were scratching at something. Close by. Sniffing and scratching. It smelt her, smelt her fear. The animal was aroused by it. It carried on scratching, ever more furiously. She could hear its teeth clattering. And a scraping sound.

"Lie still, lady. Please, you make the Shaka very angry. Be still. It is best for you."

43

This morning the "boss" had joined them for breakfast at "head office".

He was introduced to Ghaap as Patrick van Breda, head of the firm's specialist unit. The guy was super neat. Hair shaven to way above the ears, with a box-cut as manicured as the green on a golf course. His shirt had crisp creases on the sleeves – ten to one he'd learnt to iron in the army. The tight-fitting black jeans looked brand new, and his Merrells were laced to above the ankles.

"What specialist unit?" Ghaap asked.

"You're looking at it," Mo groaned. He was staring at the Wimpy menu with rapt attention. As if, after all these years, there might still be some item that had eluded his gourmet's eye.

"Oh," Ghaap said sheepishly and sat down.

"I handpicked these guys," Patrick explained calmly. Ghaap wondered whether he knew they had several nicknames for him – varying from Patsy and Parras to The Trickster.

"Collectively, they have more experience than there are barbels in Loskop Dam. And they know the district. They command respect. They have respect for the people. And vice versa." He spoke softly, as if he were sharing a secret. Ghaap had to strain his ears to hear him over the Wimpy noise. Earlier on, Patrick had phoned to say they'd lost the signal: there'd been a helicopter, making the hijackers go underground again, and then he'd ordered them to "head office".

Which turned out to be the Wimpy on the N12.

The Trickster leant forward confidentially. "I collected these guys one by one. You haven't met them all yet. They have a success rate second to none. We get into places where you cops – with respect, nè – where you've given up long ago."

He leant back, allowing the waitress to bring him his coffee. Ghaap saw that she'd brought him five sachets of sugar. Clearly not his first cup of coffee at "head office". He thanked her in a local language, and she retorted with, "Pleasure, my baby!" She was a middle-aged woman with shiny smooth skin, bulging hips and thighs, and breasts like watermelons.

"Last week they tracked down a father who'd vanished into thin air. The mother and daughter had reported him missing. He wasn't even a client of ours, but the cops asked us to help with the search. Then these guys found him. In his own car, stone dead, among the mine dumps outside Krugersdorp. He'd gassed himself. But the thing is, when the guys found him, two jackrollers were busy dragging the body out. To steal the car. And they started shooting at us—"

Four simultaneous chirps. The trackies dropped what they were doing and grabbed their phones. The Trickster jabbed at his speed dial and stuck the phone to his ear with an index finger. He listened intently for a moment, all eyes directed at him. He shook his head at them, and everybody relaxed.

Then Ghaap's phone rang. He whipped it out of his shirt pocket and quickly pressed it to his ear, almost dropping the phone as the index-finger trick failed.

"Jaaans." He heard his mom's voice. He jumped up guiltily. He should have phoned her by now, but yesterday—

"Jannes, is it *you*?"

"*Of course*, Mammie," he said, edging away from the trackers. Not a good time for a chat with one's mother.

"So why don't I hear anything from you? I spoke to Antie Ursula, and she told me you'd gone and assaulted Charlie?"

"No, Mammie! I didn't ..." Ghaap saw that all four trackies were watching him, and he stepped further away, lowering his voice as he said, "Ma, I'll explain later. At the moment I'm—"

"Jannes, don't make me come and fetch you—"

"Mammie, please! I'm *working*!"

"What work? They don't even know your name at the police station."

"I'm working undercover, Mammie," he whispered. "Can't talk now. Later, okay? Tonight—"

"Johannes Ghaap, you're *lying* to me again. Remember, you may not have a dad, but I'm not going to—"

"Mammie! I'm on a case! Can't talk now. Life and death situation here!" He ended the call, switching off the phone as he did so. He knew she'd phone again. She couldn't care less about what he was busy with. If there was family trouble, *that* had to be sorted out first.

He returned to the table, and the food had arrived. Mo had obviously said grace already because he was tucking into the fried eggs, bacon, pork sausages, beans, fried potatoes and toast. With brown sauce over everything. Ghaap gulped. They would laugh in his face if he asked for mieliepap. He pulled a side plate towards him and buttered a slice of toast. Luckily the waitress had brought jam and some grated cheese too.

Ghalla was the first to push away his plate. He gulped down a big pink milkshake, ignoring the straw. When his glass was empty, he vigorously wiped away the pink moustache, using a handful of serviettes.

"Looks like you're missing your mom's cooking?" he said to Ghaap.

Ghaap looked away. Not keen on his mom and his origins becoming the topic of conversation.

"*My* mother-in-law," Ghalla continued, "no longer cooks. Says she's retired. The only exception is Christmas. Then it's like a war zone. Even the meid gets involved."

Shocked at the un-PC term, Ghaap glanced at The Trickster. The man didn't strike him as someone who'd tolerate racism. But Patrick said nothing, focused on methodically clearing his plate, from the left.

"Christmas is about the only time my father-in-law can persuade me to go fishing with him," Ghalla went on, unperturbed. "Because Dingaan drives us up the wall. She insists on cooking the traditional roast and yellow rice, followed by tickey pudding. And my wife and the meid fight back. They want to do turkey. And ice cream, because the kids damage their teeth on the two-rand coins in the Christmas pudding. Then Skoonpa sneaks off with a bottle of brandy and a bowl of stywe pap and some worms."

Ghaap drank his coffee, kept his trap shut. But he was starting to have serious doubts about this guy who babbled on about fishing and a mother-in-law he called "Dingaan". He was a bladdy racist.

Ghaap's ears cut out. He folded his arms and gazed in the direction of Soweto. Between the Wimpy and the drab skies above the big black city lay the busy N12. As he watched the trucks and cars flying past in both directions, Ghaap felt the tug of home. It was this very road that had brought him here. And why, of all things, had Mammie found it necessary to mention his "dad" today? There had never been any such a person in his life. He remembered a man who'd pitched up at their house before church one Sunday, with a bag of sweets for him and a headscarf for her. Mammie had sent Ghaap to his room. And he'd heard the two of them talking, until she finally told the man he had to go. "My son and I will be late for church," she'd said.

He recalled how proud he'd felt. She'd referred to him as if he were a grown man. "My son and I!"

Ghaap was jolted from his reverie when the four cellphones began chirping again.

Once again The Trickster jabbed at his speed dial to call the control room. This time he gave a nod. "Stolen vehicle," he barked at the others, who all jumped up.

Ghaap tried to dig out his wallet, but The Trickster pointed him to the door.

The road into Soweto was on the other side of the highway. They took a short cut along a makeshift dirt road alongside until they reached a huge opening beneath the N12. It was a giant stormwater drain that had been converted into a pathway by the locals.

As they emerged on the other side, Soweto lay sprawled in front of them, virtually treeless. Tens of thousands of shacks gleamed in the dull morning sun. Their ramshackle roofs were like scales on a fish.

"We've got a signal," Duif called out when the dashboard monitor began beeping, "moving north-east." He phoned, informing his colleagues that he was in Boundary Road, driving in the direction of Chicken Farm.

In turn, they told him where they were, and Duif ended the call. "If it's Chicken Farm, that vehicle is skedaddling to, it's going to be tough," he told Ghaap.

Ghaap nodded in a comradely fashion, but he didn't have the vaguest idea of what they were chasing or where they were. The police radio started croaking, a voice shouting something unintelligible. The beeping from the green-eyed tracking monitor became more and more insistent as the signal strengthened. A woman from the tracker control room called out the coordinates for the GPS. Meanwhile Duif's phone had started ringing again. He had to yell to make himself heard. "Staan vas!" he shouted into the phone, his eyes fixed on the road and his left hand alternating between the gear shift and the steering wheel. At times he steadied the wheel using his knees only in order to tap at the phone on the dash. "Ghalla is in the shit," he called out to Ghaap.

They crossed a bigger road: Turf Avenue, Ghaap saw.

The phone rang again. "Ghalla, I can't hear what you're saying!" Duif yelled. "Calm down, man. Calm down. I can … Ghalla!"

Duif passed the phone to Ghaap, switched on the strobe lights and hit the accelerator.

"I have …" Ghaap couldn't make out what Ghalla was shouting. But one thing he did know, the guy was stressed.

"*Where* are you, Ghalla? *Where?*"

"They're shooting—"

"Ghalla!"

Duif jerked the phone from his hand, ended the call, and pushed speed dial. As he handed the phone back to Ghaap, he braked sharply for a bulldozer pulling in from a side street.

The phone flew from Ghaap's hand, and he clung desperately to his seat. Duif swerved around the bulldozer, directly into the path of a minibus taxi hurtling towards them. The taxi veered onto the gravel shoulder of the narrow road, the two vehicles missing each other by a hair's breadth. Fleetingly, Ghaap registered the whites of shocked eyes in the taxi, but Duif was already speeding off.

Ghaap felt under his seat for the phone, managed to grab it.

"The fuckers are *shooting* at me," he heard Ghalla yell.

"Where are you?" He heard only noise.

193

"Tell him to SMS his coordinates!" Duif called out.

"Ghalla. *Ghalla*! Send your—"

Duif yanked the phone from his hand again and shouted the instruction. He ended the call and immediately made another. "Ghalla's under fire," he called to the voice at the other end. "I don't know exactly where he is, somewhere in the north, I think. Get me his coordinates. I'm closest!"

They sped down narrow roads. Near a railway line. From what he'd tried to memorise of the map, Ghaap knew that two north-south lines ran through Greater Soweto. This had to be the one separating Dlamini from Pimville. He recognised the dilapidated buildings of Kliptown. Further ahead were the big buildings around Freedom Square, the Soweto Hotel, which seemed wildly out of place here.

They raced past the four-storey hotel – possibly the highest building in the entire area. Duif wove his way his way deftly through hawkers, pedestrians and traffic. The trackies' green-eyed signal was getting fainter; they were driving too far east, Ghaap reckoned.

They crossed the railway line, slipped across the Old Potch Road and past Orlando Power Station's colourful cooling towers. The territory became more familiar to Ghaap. It had to be Orlando East: at one point they sped past the police station where he was supposed to be working. Then they were on the Soweto Highway, going east. And off the highway again, driving among houses. A massive mine dump loomed ahead.

As they rounded a corner, they saw Ghalla's car, its doors wide open.

No sign of the man himself.

44

She seemed to have lost consciousness again, because she woke up to the same scraping sound. It's a door, she guessed. She pricked up her ears. Someone was tiptoeing towards her.

A hand on her cheek. This was a different hand. It picked at something stuck to her skin.

"Don't cry out, lady. Please. I want to—"

She began to struggle and moan. She couldn't help it.

"No! You must be quiet." A boy's voice.

The hand lifted. She heard soft breathing. Fast, anxious.

The hand picked at her cheek again. It wasn't ordinary duct tape, she realised. It was more sturdy stuff, clinging stubbornly to her skin as the boy struggled with it. When he managed to lift a corner she felt her skin being pulled, a sudden jerk, and then sharp burning pain as skin was ripped from her lips.

"Shhh. No noise. I don't want him to hear."

"Who …" She tried to speak, but her tongue was parched and her lips numb.

"Don't talk. I give you water."

She felt the hand over her mouth. "You must be quiet. Otherwise I can't give you water. He will be angry."

Gerda felt something cool against her burning lips. Water flowing into her mouth. She drank greedily, choked momentarily, but kept drinking. Felt the cool water running down her chin into her neck.

"Not too much," he said.

She pleaded: "Please, my eyes. Just for a minute."

"I can't, lady."

"My little boy. Where is he?"

"My mother—" He bit off his sentence, realising he might have said too much. But Gerda had already identified the voice. It was the young boy who'd sat at the back with Kleinpiet during the hijacking. She clearly remembered his name.

"Please, Mpho!"

"No!" He stuck the tape to her mouth again, smothering her cries.

She heard his footsteps retreat. Then silence, followed by a creaking, ticking sound above her head. A corrugated iron roof, she guessed. Though blindfolded, she sensed it was morning from the probable sounds of metal expanding in the morning sun.

And then crunching sounds, bones cracking. It must be a really big dog, she thought. It was to the left of her, on the other side of a thin wall, most likely corrugated iron too.

And the smell of apples? What was that about?

She'd been handed a straw – something to clutch at. Kleinpiet was alive, was okay. She could smell that she'd wet herself. It was a bad omen that they kept her lying here like this. Like a pig about to be slaughtered.

But what did these people want from her?

Then she remembered. There'd been a man in the room with her. Earlier, at some point in her foggy dreams. A phone ringing. *Fifty thousand for the unborn.*

Her heart hammered. The unborn …

Would anyone be looking for her? Rebecca, surely?

Baz … He was preoccupied with his import problems – *Sorry, babes, I'm busy.* She suddenly knew what had been bothering her lately. He wasn't right for her. No one was. Because, ultimately, she was on her own. It was just her, alone. Always battling to hold on to life. Life, which carried on inexorably … like a machine … tack, tack, tack, tack. Going through the motions. Having to vacate the police service house in Fordsburg. *That* was the hardest thing. The twist of the knife. Because they'd still been present in that house. Her two baby boys. When she lay still on Neiltjie's bed, she could feel him. His fat, soft little hands on her cheek. He smelt like warm butter. But she'd had to move out. The housing shortage in the police service …

Albertus, who'd begged her to come to him. Said he'd love her … until she was whole again.

Until *you're* whole again, Albertus. It's your own healing that you're looking for, my love. Your heart lies buried very deep. So deep that you yourself can no longer find it. Reduced to a scrap of tin, a splinter of glass. Withered. Long since, from the time your ouboet Koefie died. You told me, remember? How you'd kept an all-night vigil next to the bloodstain on the street. That's where you left your child's heart behind, my love.

Us two … we have too little left to take care of each other.

She felt her bladder go. As she smelt the urine, a new wave of crying threatened to suffocate her.

"You cry too much … you lose much water."

It was the voice. The one that had spoken on the phone. Earlier, in her dreams. God, was she going crazy on top of everything?

"It will not help, the crying."

The voice was deep, but soft. She wasn't even sure she was hearing it. She held her breath, listened closely. To her left, The Beast had stopped chewing too.

"But I've got good news." A guttural laugh. "Your suffering will not be long. It will go nice and calm …"

The voice died away. She lay, ears straining, every sense in her body alert. She thought she could hear an echo, someone crooning far away. Or muttering. Then it became completely quiet. She waited for the scraping sound, the door? But she heard nothing. Not the slightest rustle. A strange, smoky smell hung in the air. Sweetish, like herbs. But that, too, grew fainter, and after a while she wasn't even sure it had really existed.

The Beast resumed its restless pacing.

A new realisation struck her: she had landed in the clutches of something evil. And for the first time she was afraid.

Truly afraid.

45

"Just look at them … all the greyness here," Trula Momberg said to Beeslaar. She was wearing her long white hair loose today. It fell like a white veil over her shoulders, giving her the look of a marble Madonna. They were standing at a sliding door that opened onto a courtyard at Great Gables, where twenty-odd old folk were having afternoon tea.

The scene seemed quite pleasant to him, but he found it hard to imagine curmudgeonly old Blikkies in this company.

Beeslaar was struck by one old lady in particular. Her walker was parked next to her chair. She used it as a support, to steady the hand in which she held her cup. But still, it trembled so badly that the tea trickled down her chin and wet her blouse.

"That's Miss Aggenbach," Trula said. "A lonely old soul. With neither kith nor kin. Nothing. She was a school principal in her day, with a string of doctoral degrees and stuff. That's also all she can talk about. How important she was and the big shots she knew. Doctor this and Professor that. Probably all dead by now. No one comes to visit the poor woman. She sits here Christmas after Christmas, all by herself. But she's a tough old bird. No one is allowed to help her. She refuses to drink tea from a mug with a spout, or to be assisted when she eats. So, she sits like that, making a mess."

She turned around to walk on, and Beeslaar followed. "This is what happens in places like these, Albertus. We all end up here. And we become nothing. Part of the great greyness. Banished to the margins. Bit by bit, you lose your place among the living. And a different kind of fear settles inside you."

Beeslaar didn't know what to say. He had never really dwelt on the issue of dying of old age. Because his own family, the lot of them, had made an early exit. Koefie, who'd started it all. And Beeslaar knew that he wouldn't make old bones either. Or not like *this*, at least. In his dreams, he's with Gerda, untying her hair. At night …

"… only too glad when a child phones you." He became conscious of Trula's voice again. They were walking up the stairs to her flat. "Even if it's just to say goodbye before going on holiday. It's not all of them. But there are people here, I tell you, who worked their fingers to the bone to give their children a good education. Better opportunities. All they have to show for it are gnarled old fingers. I often find myself looking at the hands here … Some say people's hands are the real windows of the soul, you know. They catch your tears, your joy, show your love, hold your children, your grief. Anger. Everything. Your grip on things. Your sorrow and your regret. It all shows in the hands."

She unlocked the door of her flat, and they walked in.

The layout was the same as that of Blikkies and Tannie Ria, and just as small. Her books were the first thing that caught his attention, the shelves packed full. "It's my weakness in life," she confessed. "Balthie and I were good pals, but my books are my true friends."

"Was *he* happy here?"

"He was, well, how shall I put it? He had a rather difficult relationship with Tertia, as far as I know. But it was a relationship nonetheless. She came here often. I think she loved him more than the other way round." She sat down, took a cigarette from a pack on the arm of her easy chair, and lit it. "Just one a day. Two, at most," she smiled. "Most people here don't even know. Because I don't exactly encourage them to drop in." She smiled. The smoke enveloped her pale face and the silvery whiteness of her long hair.

"She was always trying to drag him along on holiday. He did go once, but swore it would never happen again. He wasn't one for fancy places and putting on airs. His son-in-law is one of those yuppie types who like to play golf with VIPs, and doesn't mind paying two hundred rand or more for the scrap of food they bring you on a restaurant plate. But Balthie – ag, he did his own thing. Went fishing. Often with one or two younger men he'd met in the bar. And Tertia ..." She sighed. "I'm sorry for her, you know? Children like her, they want to put their parents on a pedestal. As if, in that way, they can heal the hurt of their childhood."

She stubbed out her cigarette, even though she'd only smoked half of it. Focusing her eyes, she twisted it in the ashtray. Then she lit up again.

"It's that longing, I think, for a mother or father who never existed. The love or patience or respect that was lacking. Such children keep constructing and restoring that image. I was lucky. My parents were simple people, Namaqualand farmers. Poor, but they treated us lovingly. There was never any violence. Quite unusual, actually, in an era when children were neither visible nor respected." She blew some smoke at the ceiling, looked at him through the blue fumes. "But you're not here for my psychology lessons. Have you decided to assist with the Du Toit investigation?"

Beeslaar shook his head. "No."

"So, what would you like to know from me?"

"I, er, I just wanted to find out how things were going with Oom Blikkies recently. I've been rather busy these past weeks. We used to chat regularly on Sunday mornings, but lately, well, I thought I was coming here in any case."

"Yes." She regarded him with gleaming eyes. They were alert eyes, hidden behind thick-rimmed glasses.

"You've met Vuvu by now, haven't you?"

199

"Captain Qhubeka. Yes, I have," he said.

"She's one of the strangers who used to visit Balthie. At all hours of the night, sometimes." She wiped a hand across her broad, unlined forehead, then slid her fingers over her hair, smoothing it down. She'd probably had those tresses all her life, Beeslaar reckoned, the action seemed so automatic.

"Yes, his death was quite a blow. Especially because it was so sudden. One minute he was still here. The next minute he was gone, poof. Of course, it was better for *him* that way. No drawn-out suffering and senility and so on. Rode out of life still firmly in the saddle." She paused briefly. "And now, with what's happened to Rea's daughter-in-law. It's all everyone's talking about. Balthie has already been forgotten. I suppose it's also because of who Elmana was."

"She probably came here quite often?"

"When her mother was still here, poor thing."

"What kind of person was she?"

"Who, the mother?"

"Mrs du Toit."

She paused a while. "Elmana was a real piece of work," she said, and then touched her tongue lightly, as if lifting a stray bit of tobacco. Another habit of hers, Beeslaar had noticed.

"She was a real shrew, if you want my honest opinion. Downright venomous. The mother, though … A damaged person. It was probably true of both of them. The father had apparently been a tyrant, right up to the day he died. He'd forced the poor old woman to move into a frail-care institution with him because he refused to be fed by strangers. And there she'd stayed, among the demented and dying, until his death. Then she came here. But she was a wreck. She'd cry if you so much as greeted her. The daughter, on the other hand, was a fighter."

She knitted her brow as she reflected.

"When we were children, I had a friend whose father was also a mean old bastard. Punished her for the smallest little thing. I saw it in my friend's case. Children like that remain emotionally hungry. For more, no matter what it is. They keep searching. To fill the hole, I think, to satisfy a greater hunger. And once they're adults and have their own children, that violence returns. The sins of the fathers, visited upon their young."

She frowned. Her ash dropped onto the armrest and she gently blew it away.

"But I suppose all of that is irrelevant now. I didn't know Elmana well, but I could read the signs. And if I understand it all correctly, she became quite unhinged after her mother's death. Rea told my neighbour she was worried about the grandchildren, even considered taking them away from there. Yoh. And this morning's newspapers seem to talk about a serial killing. Do you believe that?"

"No. Newspapers specialise in serial lies. At the best of times."

After saying his goodbyes to Trula, Beeslaar walked over to Tannie Rea du Toit. She opened the door instantly, asking whether there was any news about the investigation. Beeslaar had to disappoint her. "I happened to be in the vicinity," he said, "so I thought I'd drop in."

"Let's sit down," she said and pointed him to an upholstered chair with high legs. "Old Balthie liked sitting on that chair – once a year, on my birthday. He enjoyed the Spanish sherry my son always brings along for me from overseas. My husband was also partial to a glass of sherry before supper. I keep up the tradition." She smiled wearily.

Beeslaar noticed the bonsai tree on a coffee table in front of the window. Its knobbly trunk rose artistically sideways from its pot. The tree looked as if it had cowered before the southeaster all its life, a visual scream of suffering and sadness.

"The bonsai," asked Beeslaar. "Did you get it from your daughter-in-law?"

Rea du Toit's expression hardened as she gazed at the tree.

"That's Elmana for you. She used to waltz in here every second week to swap the trees around. So that she could attend to them herself, see?" He was aware of the reproach in her voice. "Maybe this is the only one that survived the … attack," she said. "I'm not exactly fond of bonsais myself."

She fell silent for a moment, contemplated the tortured tree.

"I'm not crazy about them either," said Beeslaar. "This one looks as if it's been raised by your wind."

She smiled. "Yes, the wind. I like the wind, though. It blows away the smog."

Her eyes were grim again: "But Elmana … You didn't say no to her. And these plants are extremely pricey." She sighed resignedly. "I rather just let her have her way. She wasn't easy. She reminded me a lot of my own younger days. When I could at least … Before I became an oxygen thief." She smiled wryly. "I ask you! That's what a child shouted at me the other day. A youngster on a skateboard. Oxygen thief!"

She shook her head. "It's their world, nowadays. The children. Most of the time I don't understand what they're saying any more, even when they speak Afrikaans."

"Your own grandchildren too?"

She didn't reply, kept scratching at a spot on her skirt with a fingernail. "Balthazar still kept up. His daughter had bought him an eye … eye … Not the phone, the other thing. Bigger."

"iPad," Beeslaar prompted.

"Yes. He used to sit with that thing at the breakfast table. Said he was reading the papers. But he had a computer too. He and old Arnold, the only other person here who has a computer, because he takes photographs."

The name rang a bell, but before Beeslaar could ask, she said: "He was the one whose Krugerrands were stolen."

"Many of them?"

"According to him, yes. Apparently worth thousands. But to tell you the honest truth, I never saw the coins. I don't like going into his flat. He smokes a pipe as well as cigarettes, and the place stinks terribly. But that's not important at the moment. What I wanted to say, um …"

"You were going to tell me about the grandchildren."

"Yes. I'm very bitter about those two children. *Very*. They're gentle children that need a lot of tender care. But that's not what they're getting." She stopped picking at the skirt, placed her hands on her lap. The narrow gold band on her ring finger seemed to have been cemented into position, as if it had become a part of the arthritic hands. It would probably have to go with her to the grave.

"I'm too old now. If I'd been younger, I'd have taken them away from there. But I no longer have a say. Just sitting here, on the rubbish dump of life. No one who needs a single thing from you any more. I *know*, because I've experienced it myself. In your thirties, when your children are small, you're busy. Your husband's career, which you're both building, your community, your need for recognition. In your fifties, you make a final attempt to prove yourself and then, from one day to the next, you find you've become redundant. And by then your lonely parents are dead, and it's too late."

Beeslaar's phone rang.

Qhubeka: "Where are you?"

"Can I phone you back? I'm in a meeting."

"*Meeting*? What—"

But he ended the call, switching the phone off at the same time.

Rea du Toit stared vacantly outside. "Those children are actually lonely," she said suddenly. "That's the main problem, I think. They feel like I do. Redundant. Ellie's been visiting me a lot lately. I'm … In all honesty, I'm very concerned about her. She's not strong enough to cope with this terrible thing. Some people are tethered to life quite flimsily, you know. And Ellie is one of them. What she did the day before yesterday – it wasn't the first time."

"So she's tried to cut her wrists before?"

"Twice." She swallowed hard, sniffing back her tears. "It seems to me we could have prevented this thing. Both of us – Malan and I – we're to blame for Elmana. And the children. Because we didn't try harder."

"Did Malan ever mention divorce?"

"Not to me. But I do think he was desperate. Definitely," she said, her tears flowing freely by now.

Beeslaar felt in his pocket for a handkerchief and offered it to her. She sobbed quietly, and after a while he excused himself, practically tiptoeing to her front door.

Then he let himself out.

46

Gerda started awake from a doze. She heard a child screaming.

"No!" he yelled. "It wasn't me! No, please, please, please, PLEASE!"

She heard the swish of a sjambok, the blow hitting home, another scream.

Next to her, The Beast had stopped pacing. It was the violence in the air. The animal sniffed at it eagerly.

Another blow. And another.

Louder screams, with every blow.

Who in God's name would beat a child like that? The blows didn't stop. Some of them sounded duller, the victim trying to block them, perhaps. Gerda lay as stiff as a poker, too scared to breathe.

And then the boy stopped screaming. She heard a few more blows, but the boy, she realised, had either given up or lost consciousness.

In the deathly silence that followed she heard footsteps shuffling away, as if the attacker had exhausted his strength.

What offence could the child have committed? Was he even still *alive*? The place was as silent as the grave. Even the neighbourhood dogs observed the silence. Or was it fear? The woman who'd been with her ... How could a woman allow something like that?

A new wave of despair washed over her. She knew she couldn't allow herself to capitulate, to leave her children to the evil in this place. The Beast was scratching and sniffing close by, as if it were smelling her thoughts. All the while, it made low yelping sounds. Ever faster, and more frantic.

She tried to shift her body. Away from the evil. A pain erupted from her belly and she moaned out loud. Heard The Beast stop and sniff at the air.

Her dress – it was just that, she decided. A fold that had formed somewhere below her belly was pinching her skin. But then the stabbing pain came again. It wasn't the dress, she realised.

It was the baby. She was going into labour!

47

The bleeping sound from the dashboard had reached fever pitch.

"Bulletproof!" Duif shouted to Ghaap and jumped out of the car. He had his firearm out and ran in a crouching position towards Ghalla's car, while Ghaap grabbed the vest from the back seat and struggled into it. Softly, he opened his door, then suddenly Duif was back.

"Look in the cubbyhole. You'll find a chicken leg there," he whispered.

What the fuck, Ghaap wondered, but now wasn't the time.

"I'm going to look for Ghalla," Duif whispered. "He's not in his car. If he's taken a bullet, he's got to be somewhere close by. Stay put, I'll signal as soon as I need you."

Stooping, he ran in the direction of the mine dump, his cocked weapon clutched in both hands.

Then he was gone, swallowed up by a patch of veld with shoulder-high grass.

Duif had switched off the trackie transmitter when he stopped the car. So the only sounds were those of the police radio, shrieking and spitting codes into the tense silence. Ghaap turned down the volume.

Where was Ghalla? Why didn't he whistle or something? The hijackers must have got away because Ghalla's car was the only one there. Then a shot rang out. And another.

He ducked behind the open car door, but the gunfire was far away.

A child started yelling excitedly.

Slowly, Ghaap straightened up. Saw a bunch of kids in the road about a hundred metres up ahead. Young ones – not yet high-school age. They waved eagerly, gesturing towards the mine dump. Ghaap looked, saw nothing. Not a sign of Duif either!

Oh fuck, what was he going to do if Duif had been shot too? He had to sound the alarm, phone The Trickster. Duif's phone: the number must be on it.

He bent down into the car, looked around for the phone. Felt under the driver's seat.

His clothing caught on the handbrake and he wriggled to free himself. Swearing in exasperation, he managed to detach himself but couldn't find the phone. He cursed the scumbag who'd taken his gun the day before. Now he was stuck here like a parra, no bladdy use to anyone.

Where were the hijackers, he wondered. There was no sign of the Dolly Parton, though the transmitter had been at heart-attack level when they'd arrived.

He ducked instinctively when he heard another shot. An R1 this time. Ghalla's long gun, he guessed. He raised his head, peered out.

Duif was perched on top of a vibracrete wall some distance away. Ghalla next to him, his R1 aimed at the mine dump. Now and then he fired a shot. Ghaap tried to spot the target, saw no movement on the mine dump.

The duo sat on the wall for a while longer, heads moving from side to side as they searched for movement. Then they relaxed and lit up.

The children ran towards them, whooping and shouting. "Where's the bodies, where's the bodies?"

Ghaap slammed the car door shut, adjusted the bulletproof and started walking in their direction. He felt as useless as a bladdy foreskin.

Mo came speeding up, screeched to a halt, two police vans in his wake. Ghaap's heart shrank at the thought that he was in for a new round of shit. Then he saw with relief that these were unfamiliar faces.

Mo swung his huge body out of the car, pistol in one hand and an R5 in the other. The cops remained seated in the vans. Typical, thought Ghaap. He waited for Mo to catch up with him, and walked with him to the wall.

It was high. Ghaap just managed to heave himself up, but Mo remained standing, and rasped: "Give me a hand, Ghalla. Come on, Duif. I'm too fuckin' fat!"

Ghaap guessed that the old eland had lost his spring today.

Ghalla passed his rifle to Ghaap, jumped to the ground, and squatted in front of Mo. Ghalla groaned as Mo put a knee the size of a barrel on his back. But he held his position until Mo had hoisted himself up to take a seat on the wall.

Ghalla straightened up – the cigarette still dangling from his mouth. His face glistened with sweat, but he hopped back onto the wall with the greatest of ease.

"I thought you'd been shot," Mo remarked once he'd lit up too.

"Nine lives, man, I'm telling you. Old Dingaan's keeping count." He cough-chuckled, the cigarette held tightly between his lips, his hands digging a sachet of Grand-Pa headache powder from the back pocket of his jeans. He threw his head back and let the powder run into his mouth. "Aaahhh," he imitated the old radio ad, "*Grandpa*! Nothing perks you up more than a piss or a powder." He swirled the powder around in his mouth and swallowed a few times before taking his rifle from Ghaap.

"But what happened?" Mo nagged in his strangled voice. "Could you spot the antie with the baby?"

Ghalla shook his head. "Looks like they dropped her long ago. Somewhere." He opened another sachet and downed it.

Duif took up the story: "The one guy stayed in the car, and the other two were busy dumping the unit with cables and stuff in the veld when Ghalla rocked up. They shot at him, of course, but when Ghalla whipped out the long gun, the driver scooted. The other two jumped over the wall here and disappeared. Almost took Ghalla out. Show them, Ghal."

Ghalla put the cigarette back in his mouth. He wore a khaki-green camouflage hunting jacket. Pulling the left panel aside, he pointed and said, "Check here! Here's where bullet entered." He indicated a burn mark in his shirt fabric, on the right-hand side of his abdomen. "And there's the exit." Another hole just behind the side seam. The cigarette in his mouth was trembling slightly, Ghaap noticed.

Mo heaved his body sideways and poked podgy fingers through the holes. "Jissus, man."

Ghalla flicked the butt away and immediately lit up again. "But I was only fokken *pap tyres*, 'strue's Bob. And the little fuckers were *fast* ..." He took a deep pull. "I ran my arse off after them. Because now I was really the hell-in, totally befok, but they kept shooting back. By the time Duif joined me, they were gone. Youngsters, man. Young, young, young. School-bladdy-kids. And then it was all over. We've gone through this place with a fine-tooth comb, but there's zilch."

The four of them sat in silence for a while, gazing at the vast mine dump in front of them.

A mine dump wasn't really such an ugly thing, Ghaap mused. Especially now, in the late afternoon. The angle of the sun transformed the fine white sand to rosy gold, so that it looked like a mountain of glowing pink sugar. From how far underground had the sand come, he wondered. He'd heard somewhere that these mines were the deepest on earth. Unless that was sommer a shit story.

Ghaap looked past the mine dump, at the traffic on the N1 highway worming its way south-north. Everything looked so normal, almost pretty, but somewhere in the bowels of that silent pink monster, two youngsters were running around, he knew. Hungry, maybe, with cramps from the heat, from thirst, from exhaustion. With only one thought on their minds: survival.

Until next time.

48

Beeslaar switched on his cellphone, saw he'd missed two calls from Captain Vuyokazi "Vuvu" Qhubeka. And one from Ghaap.

"What's up?" he said when Ghaap answered.

"I'm thinking of handing in my papers."

Beeslaar stared through the window at the scene in the quad below, the elderly taking their tea. He looked for the lady with the doctoral degrees, the ex-principal who drank her tea so messily. She was asleep in her chair. Her jaw hung open, her head leaning back at an angle, and drool dripping into the thick cardigan she wore over a polka-dot blouse. One arm hung down the side of the chair. She slept like a child, Beeslaar thought, defenceless. The grey hair had been cut short. Practical. A pink scalp gleamed through the wispy hair. Suddenly, a deep sadness lodged itself under his ribs. If his mother was still alive—

"Hello? You still there?"

"Yes, Sergeant. I'm here. Talk."

"Mthethwa dropped me in the shit yesterday. Reported me to the station commander!"

"So you're phoning *me* about it?"

"I'm phoning to ... er, Ghalla was almost shot to moer-and-gone just now."

"I'm assuming he's one of the trackies?"

"We were chasing a Dolly Parton. It was hijacked in Melville yesterday. With the—"

"A *what*?" Beeslaar laughed. "Good God, Ghaap. You can't be seriously thinking of joining those guys? There are no trackies in the Kalahari."

"Yes I *know*, but I'm thinking if the cops don't want me anyway ... Seems they're hard up for good people, the trackies. And I get on well with—"

"Ghaap, let me tell you one thing, and it's something those cowboys haven't told you: you need to notch up *many* years of service before they'll offer you a serious job. With your current experience, you'll be making tea, my friend. You certainly won't be given your own little speedster for charging around in the townships. I guarantee you that!"

"But ... but I talked to the boss himself this morning. Patrick, he says he knows you."

"Many people know me. Many. But it doesn't mean anything. My advice to you is to go back to your job. Let the trackies do their own work. You should first learn a bit more about police work in that place. It's the best training you can get, as you've said yourself. Okay?"

"The thing is … I'm sort of suspended. Because I lost my gun."

"Bad luck, man, that's tough. But there's really bugger all I can do for you. They lose lots of weapons in that place. Every day. You won't be the first. Go and speak to the commander. And to Mabusela. Tell him I send my regards. And leave the trackies alone!"

Beeslaar had barely ended the call when the phone rang again.

Kokkewiet Syster greeted him in formal tones.

"Madam editor. To what do I owe this honour?" Beeslaar didn't try to hide his surprise.

"I hear that Vincent Ndlovu was arrested this afternoon, Captain Beeslaar."

"I … er … oh!"

An icy silence. Then she said: "So that's your way of cooperating?"

"Mrs Syster—"

"The first available suspect will do. And so much the better if it's the black guy. Because there's always a darkie in the story, isn't there?"

"Wait a bit. Hold your horses."

"Yes, yes. Wait for another cover-up? You people are all in cahoots."

"With whom?"

"The last guy who dared say anything is now six feet under!"

"What are you talking about?"

She didn't reply, just ended the call.

Beeslaar frowned, returned the phone to his shirt pocket.

Outside, the ex-principal with the walker was still asleep in her chair. A woman seated next to her was knitting. Her eyes were not on her handiwork but on the company, to which she contributed an occasional word or a laugh.

Is *that* what we're all headed for, Beeslaar wondered. So apart, neatly winnowed from society, and cast aside. Swept under the hem of the long shadow. You could see it in their dimming eyes. Suddenly forgetting a name. Next, a grandchild's. The panic when that happened.

And Blikkies? On the phone he'd always sounded so … What? Brave? Probably the only way to deal with it. The change from something … to nothing. A grey apparition with mottled cheeks, your face losing definition. Skin hanging from bones. Bones that had shrunk. Would *he* one day sit and drool like that too?

He started walking. He had to get out of there. While he might not yet be in his dotage, these gloomy thoughts would get him there soon enough.

"The mind is a dangerous neighbourhood," Blikkies used to say. "You don't go there alone."

At the front entrance, a wizened old gentleman with a camera around his neck was struggling to open the front door. He carried a walking stick, and a plastic bag. He held on to both as he battled to slide open the heavy door.

Beeslaar reached over and pushed the door open. The man glanced up at him over his shoulder with a frown, not overly pleased with the unsolicited help.

"Are you Balthie's boy?"

"Yes, Oom."

The man shifted the plastic bag to his walking-stick hand. "Arnold Sebens. He told me about you."

They shook hands.

"He said I should wait until you arrive."

"Oh?" Beeslaar didn't believe for a moment that Blikkies said that.

They walked out, and the older man sagged down onto a garden bench on the little stoep. He put the bag down carefully next to him, as if it contained treasure, and gestured to Beeslaar to sit down.

"So, the other day, they broke into my flat, see? The police were here and supposedly took fingerprints, but that's also the last I saw of them.

"It happened in broad daylight. We were having lunch – over there in the dining room." He pointed to a row of windows. "I returned to my flat earlier than usual. We don't really lock up when we go out. Who can get in here? You've seen the security at this place. But then I *heard* it as I opened my door. The fellow was standing there, at my desk. And then he threw something at me and disappeared. As quick as lightning. Through my stoep door, see?"

"Yes, Oom—"

"Call me Arnold, please. I just look old, but I'm still under eighty."

"Arnold, you know the police are actually best equipped—"

"Pah! There was a young inspector here and a so-called fingerprint specialist. But nothing came of it. I phoned the inspector chappie again the other day. But this lot here! They have the cheek to call me oupa. And even worse: oubie! Can you believe it! I was so disgusted, I just threw down the phone."

"Oom Arnold, you should at least give the police a chance. What items were stolen?"

"Give them a chance! Do you think *I* was given a chance? My flat was turned upside down and all my things were thrown around. *Years* of work, I tell you. My computer case was stolen. All my albums were pulled off the bookshelves. My external hard drives, three of them. They cost a thousand rand apiece. And my Krugerrands!"

"What was on the computer?"

The old man's lip trembled and he gulped a few times. Frowned to get the tears out of his eyes.

"Everything. My entire …" His voice caught and he sniffed. "Honestly, I still can't believe it. All the other stuff is still there. You can take a look if you want to. It's just down the corridor—"

Beeslaar raised his hand. "Arnold, I'm already late for another appointment. I'm sorry the guys dropped you. But I can't promise you anything, except that I'll inquire personally. Most of the thieves who steal coins melt them down to sell the metal. I'll ask whether there's any news yet, but right now I have to run." He felt in his shirt pocket for a business card and held it out.

The old man took the card, but didn't get up from the bench. He just sat there dejectedly, staring at the card in his hand. Beeslaar was convinced that the detective who was there had also given him a card and walked off after making nice promises. And then gone on to open a docket. Which ended up at the bottom of forty others on his desk. Because that's just the way it was.

The wind made its presence felt as soon as he was out of the gate.

He started walking and phoned Qhubeka.

"I hear you've picked up Ndlovu."

She groaned.

"Is that why you were looking for me?" he asked.

"No. Yes. Actually, this whole business smells bad. But I can't talk now. And I have a shitload of paperwork. Seven o'clock. Jan Cats."

The line went dead.

He'd only walked a few steps when a Citi Golf swerved into a parking space ahead of him. A group of young people piled out, along with loud music. Gospel rock, Beeslaar realised with some surprise. Either that, or the rocker was sitting with his arse on a nail; he kept yelling: "Jeeeezas! Loooooooord!"

Walking past them, Beeslaar recognised young Du Toit, Dawid-Pieter, who greeted him self-consciously.

"Hello, young man," Beeslaar said, and stopped.

The rest of the group looked at him curiously.

"He's with the police," the boy mumbled. Two of the boys approached and shook hands with Beeslaar, introduced themselves and the rest of the group. Two girls and two boys, aged between fifteen and eighteen.

"We're going to visit Dawid-Pieter's grandmother," said the open-faced boy who'd introduced himself as Francois. "We've come to pray for her." He had fashionably gelled hair, with a ridiculous little spiky fringe that pointed upwards. Like a tuft of grass he was growing on his forehead.

"She's not a member of our congregation, but she knows us. We often visit the home."

"And what do you do when you come here?" Beeslaar asked. "Is it charity, or is it a recce?"

"Oom?" It was the tufthead.

"I'm asking, what do you do here?"

"We come to pray for the old people. It's our service to the Lord, Oom."

Beeslaar frowned. He'd heard of these churches that addled young people's brains.

"We're all born again, Oom. We've given our hearts to the Lord. And we do His work." The tufthead stepped back. Beeslaar could read the blend of judgement and uncertainty in his eyes. Just before the boy turned to go, however, he extended his hand and offered Beeslaar a card. Taking it, he saw that it contained a Bible verse. Beeslaar felt his irritation rise, but he quelled it.

"Okay, then," he said, and the group walked on. But he headed Dawid-Pieter off. "I'd like to ask you something first," he said.

The boy halted but didn't say anything. He was dressed in tight-fitting jeans and a baggy T-shirt. His unwashed hair hung limp. He didn't look up, stared at the ground, his pimply face expressionless.

"How are you doing?" Beeslaar asked.

The boy didn't reply. He shot a glance at his friends, who were waiting outside the home for someone to open the gate, then looked down again.

"Your sister, Ellie, is she also a member of your church?"

He shook his head.

"And your dad?"

Another shake of the head.

"So you're the only one in your family."

A nod.

"Why is that?"

A long silence. Then the boy spoke: "They're not … ready yet. Haven't yet heard the call …" His voice cracked, and he cleared his throat. "Sin is powerful, Oom. I pray. I prayed for my … for my mom too. All the time …"

Beeslaar's heart went out to the boy, who seemed to believe he could've protected his family in this way. "Ag, my boy, things sometimes get quite complicated, don't they?"

"It's the Enemy … The Enemy is on the loose … We get what we deserve."

"Who?"

"Us, Oom! Sinners! It's been foretold."

"What has been foretold?"

The boy shook his head, shoved his hands into tight pockets and muttered that he had to leave.

Beeslaar allowed him to go.

Liewe Heksie was waiting for him. And Rembrandt too. He rushed up to the garden gate, barking.

Beeslaar picked him up, mainly to shut him up. The dog jumped up against his chest and tried to lick his face. He put the animal down in disgust. Ringworm, was his immediate thought.

"Quiet, Rembrandt!" the Dutch woman admonished from the stoep. She was wearing a kind of caftan, with strings of beads around her neck, and also her arms. Her feet were bare, apart from the rings on her toes. The bird was perched on a table next to her chair.

"Goodness, is something wrong?" she called out as Beeslaar approached.

He halted in surprise. "With me?"

"With you, yes!" As she waved him onto the stoep, the bird hopped onto her shoulder. A bottle of wine and two glasses stood on the table, as if she'd been expecting Beeslaar's arrival.

"I have an appointment," Beeslaar said.

"Yes, I know. Vuvu was looking for you. But in the meantime you can sit down for a minute or two, have a nice glass of wine."

He walked up the steps, though without joining her at the table. He sat down on the top step, his back against a pillar and the dog on his lap. Bugger the ringworm.

"You look a bit dazed," she said as she poured him a glass.

He sniffed at the wine, took a cautious sip, and then sipped again. It was unexpectedly good. He raised his glass to the setting sun. "Proost," she toasted, and did the same. They sat watching the late-afternoon light on the yellowing leaves of the birch trees in front of her house.

"So?" she prodded.

"I called on your neighbour, Hanna, just now – the one you told me about last night. But no one was home. In the meantime, though, maybe *you* can answer another question. What makes a young boy of fifteen – at an age where his hormone-infected mind should be focused on one thing only – what makes a boy like that live like a monk and hang out with Jesus freaks? If he were Muslim, he'd be going around in a suicide vest, without a doubt."

She laughed. "You Afrikaners, well, you're quite … how can I say, you have a hang-up about church and religion."

"What do you mean?"

She took a sip of wine, held it in her mouth before swallowing. "Very serious. About church and religion. As I see it, during apartheid you were quite hung up on so-called morality, not the political kind, but you know what I mean. And then the pillars of political power that propped you up disintegrated, and you were—"

"Okay, Maaike. I was actually just wondering about the child."

"But that's exactly my point. You dropped the apartheid church. And then it became a new kind of religion, didn't it? The feel-good kind of the Americans. Instant gratification."

Beeslaar groaned inwardly, took another sip of wine. He'd be getting out of here as soon as he'd emptied his glass.

"For Dawid-Pieter," she continued, "it's an escape, in my opinion. No, a refuge, in fact!"

"But it's not normal, is it?"

"No, certainly not. But when you're emotionally hungry, when there's an emptiness inside yourself, and you see your world falling apart ..."

"You're talking over my head now." He stood up and seated himself next to her, passed her the card the tufthead had slipped into his hand. She shook her head, said she didn't have her glasses with her, and handed it back.

He read aloud: "Two Chronicles seven, verse fourteen: *If my people, who are called by my name, will humble themselves and pray and seek my face and turn from their wicked ways, then I will hear from heaven, and I will forgive their sin and will heal their land.*"

He flipped the card over, looked at the fish symbol and the cross on the back, a telephone number and a name.

"Ja," she said. "There was a great hunger in that child's home. Emotional hunger, I mean. Elmana wasn't at all a warm person. And very self-absorbed."

Beeslaar turned the image around in his mind. He recalled Dawid-Pieter's spartan bedroom, Ellie's black walls with the occult signs. Both cries for help, in fact, if you looked at it all in a certain light.

"How well did you know her, then? The mother?"

"From the feeding scheme, a couple of years ago. She came in and wanted to take control of the whole set-up."

"And then?"

"Then nothing. I let her have her way. What did it matter to me who was the boss? It was far more important just to feed the poor, I thought." She shrugged. "But I saw it in those days already. Elmana was a strange bird. No warmth towards the people she fed." She looked at Beeslaar and said, "How well do you know psychology?"

"Well enough to know it's overrated, especially when it's used to find excuses for crime," he muttered.

She smiled, looked through her glass at the dying sun. The refracted light gleamed on her skin. "You know," said, "some people say children have rubber hearts. They bounce back, their innocence protects them from trauma. But I believe differently. If you neglect a child, make them feel physical and emotional pain, the scars remain on the inside. Just like the growth rings of a tree. The skin grows over the scar, but it's still there. And sometimes it festers, erupts violently …"

She took another sip of wine, contemplated the dancing light in the glass. "When a baby's born, he doesn't know who or what he is. He discovers himself in his mother's gaze, the way she looks at him. Do you understand?"

Beeslaar said nothing. How did one respond to something like that?

"He sees it in her eyes. Whether he is welcome in this world, loved. Or he sees shadows there."

"Shadows of what?"

"God knows. The pain of her own childhood?"

This time she looked at him pointedly, forcing a response.

"Actually," he said uncomfortably, "I'm not the philosophical type. I just wondered why a youngster like that would become a happy-clappy. You think it's because his mom had issues?"

"Yes," she said with a smile, "that's what I think."

"But what about the dad, then?"

"Good question. In fact, it's a national question, isn't it?"

Beeslaar shook his head, not in the mood for such nonsense.

But Liewe Heksie was on a roll. "What I mean to say," she said, "is that there are no fathers any more. All of you … How can I put it—"

"*All* of us? No, hang on—"

"No!" she insisted. "Your children grow up without fathers. *That's* what I want to say. Two-thirds of the children in this country live without a father. And then you still wonder why there's so much anger and crime?"

"And we men are to blame?"

"Yes. No. Wait, give me a chance to explain. It's, well, it's very complicated. Traditionally, the African father is an important figure. But that position was almost completely destroyed. And without fathers, the boys – they learn how to become men *and* fathers from their fathers!"

"And we've learnt nothing?"

She sighed in frustration. "Yes. It's not that simple, Albertus. I see it here with my – my clients. Children learn from their parents how to become human beings. Nowhere else."

"What kind of clients do you have?" He held out his glass so that she could top it up.

"I'm a counsellor."

"Oh, I thought … Do you mean, as in a *psychologist*?"

"Yes. No, not a formal psychologist. A counsellor."

"Who throws bones?"

215

She laughed. "I'm a registered herbalist, but I have a background in social work and psychology. Really not that different from the work a traditional sangoma does, don't you think?"

"If you say so, I suppose. And you see many fatherless people?"

"What I'm trying to say is, it's a bigger issue than just men fathering children, left and right. Think migrant labour. Think poverty. How does a man feel when he can't provide for his children? Ashamed. Powerless. Angry? Yes! And who does he direct his anger at? The people closest to him, the most defenceless. Women and children!"

"And what does that have to do with Malan du Toit? He's not exactly unemployed – at least not the last time I looked?"

"No, obviously not. But he *is* disempowered!"

"*What?* Good heavens, Maaike, how do you come up with that?"

"*That* father is co-dependent."

Beeslaar was stunned.

"Do you know the story of the dead elephant in the lounge?"

"No. And I'm not really—"

"It weighs five tons. It stinks to heaven. And everyone in the house feels powerless. The problem is too big, you see. Malan du Toit thought that if he ignored it, the elephant would just disappear by itself. We call that denial. Only a very strong man will tackle the problem head-on. I don't think he was, or that he *is*, a strong man."

Beeslaar emptied his glass in one gulp, stood up. "I have to go," he said. "Thanks for the wine. And the wisdom."

49

Ghaap watched as the bunch of excited trackies told Patrick-the-boss about the shooting.

Ghalla pointed to the bullet holes. They smoked, lit one another's cigarettes. Every so often one of them was on his phone. Bursts of laughter, with the odd shoulder thump. More trackies arrived with bottles of Coke. Ghalla opened one and washed down another Grand-Pa.

Ghaap stood apart, his butt resting against the bonnet of Duif's car. Envious, if he had to be honest. Of these guys' camaraderie. He'd been in the police service for a couple of years now, but it was only from the time Beeslaar arrived that he understood how these guys were feeling right then. Like war vets. They'd stood shoulder to shoulder in the trenches. Brothers. It forged an unbreakable bond. Just *maybe*, he thought, this was the kind of bond he had with the grumpy Beeslaar. They'd been in the trenches together. Had dodged bullets together.

And now Ghaap was going to abandon Beeslaar. Because if he left the service now, or if he were forced to leave, he'd have to stay *here*, in Joburg. There was no way he could go home. And *here*, he knew in his heart of hearts, he'd never survive. With the Orlando police he'd already seen his arse. But even if they didn't suspend him, the politics there was too hectic for him. The only dushie at the station. Guys like Mthethwa, so openly racist. Always making him feel unwelcome. He'd be chatting to a tjommie, then suddenly clam up when Ghaap joined them. Or he'd poke fun at him: "Heita, butizi! Here's the kom-ver!" Everyone would laugh, Ghaap too. Until he discovered that a "kom-ver" was someone who came from far, a makwerekwere. A foreigner.

And then it was also this *place*. Never mind the crime. It was too suffocating here. Too many people. Too many different groups pushing, competing for survival. Like hyena cubs: the one with the strongest killer instinct was the one that survived. He'd seen them, the spotted hyenas. The mother only has two teats, and only enough milk for one cub. So it's push or perish. The stronger ones push out the others. The weaker cub lopes off to one side of the lair, and dies.

They had a name for it here in the district: ukutabalaza. To survive. To hustle. To spin, they said. Anything to get your hands on smeka – money. No matter how. You didn't give a damn. You grabbed, you flashed the blades – ukuhlaba! Or you stole the wheels of a slow guy like Ghaap, guys they called a Pentium 1 – a slow computer.

No. He wasn't cut out for this place. Firstly, there was his blue blood, his membership of the Fathers. That's what his people in the Northern Cape called the cops. The darkies here had another name for them: bokgata or Bo 4. The coloureds called them gattas, while white cops were called n'gamlas behind their backs.

And this was, in fact, his second problem: cluelessness when it came to the local lingo. You were either one of the amanyora – a thug – or you were a mampara – a fool.

Ghaap's phone rang.

"Sergeant Ghaap?" It was Uncle Solly, the station commander.

"Afternoon, Colonel!" Ghaap sprang to attention.

"You'll have to come in. I'm recalling everybody who's on leave. We need all hands. Night shift, okay?"

The phone went dead and Ghaap stared at it for a good minute, unsure of what to do next. He suppressed the impulse to phone Beeslaar, to inform him that his luck had changed. With a spring in his step, he walked towards the trackies. Seemed they had to remain at the scene until someone from forensics had arrived to collect fingerprints and evidence. And because a shooting was involved, The Trickster had to square the paperwork with the cops.

Duif extended an arm towards Ghaap, an invitation to join their circle. But Ghaap declined, requesting a lift again. And this time, he added, he *really* did need to get to his workplace.

Duif didn't ask any questions.

The sun had set by the time they pulled up in front of Orlando East police station. Along the way they'd turned up the volume of the police radio: be on the lookout for an old white Mercedes that was last seen heading east out of Soweto. A possible kidnapping, white woman, mid-thirties. Pregnant. A baby in a car seat. Both since dumped, it seemed. The hijackers were last spotted where the shoot-out took place. Warning – armed and dangerous. Approach with caution.

"It's going to be a long night, my friend. And this morning you left half your breakfast on the plate!" Duif produced a brown paper bag from behind his seat and offered Ghaap a piece of droëwors. "There's no rusks at the cop shop. Here's something to chow in the meantime," he said as Ghaap was getting out of the car.

After a moment's hesitation Ghaap grabbed the sausage and then walked into the duty room. He was still in his civvies, but he reckoned that this night it wouldn't matter.

He ran into Mabusela. "You're with me," he said, jerking his thumb at Ghaap.

Soon afterwards they joined the stream of traffic travelling citywards. Tonight Ghaap was the writer, Mabusela said. There was a clipboard in the storage pocket next to him. They were going to the victim's house in Melville, he explained.

"She's thirty-eight years old, white, nine months pregnant, and has her baby son with her. She was last seen at a restaurant near her house, the Lucky Bean. Enter the address for us." He pointed to the GPS on the dashboard, turned down the volume of the police radio. The address he read out was for a house in Seventh Avenue. Ghaap couldn't believe his ears. Could it really be the same street as TV's *7de Laan*? His mom would never believe him. It was her favourite soapie, and she'd probably just finished watching tonight's episode.

Ghaap wondered what had become of Mthethwa and why he wasn't accompanying them, but he didn't ask.

They drove in silence through the residential neighbourhoods. First Orlando East itself, where rows of brick and corrugated iron houses were enveloped in a soft, rosy haze. Everywhere, children were playing in the streets in the last remaining light. People hanging over front gates, chatting to neighbours across the street. Most of the houses and shacks had electric lights, but here and there Ghaap saw the warm glow of paraffin lamps spilling out of an open door. Every now and again, a spaza, consisting of a structure in the front yard with a burglarproof shutter that opened onto the street, where people came to buy basic necessities such as mielie meal, cigarettes, sweets and airtime. Outside, they stood around casually, kids on the hip. Talking, laughing, gesticulating in the squares of light that fell from barred windows. He'd read somewhere that there were more than forty thousand spazas in the Greater Johannesburg area.

As they drove, the thudding beat of music from a shebeen reached their ears. Ghaap noticed a nattily dressed group of gents clustered on a pavement, fedoras on their heads. There were other groups too, men sitting on their haunches in a circle, engrossed in morabaraba, the pebbles and seeds on a wooden board, or just on the ground. Ghaap didn't know the game, had seen it for the first time here in Soweto.

These scenes reminded him of the mellow congeniality of small-town life. A gangsters' paradise? With some of the highest rape stats in the world – and those were just the reported cases. You'd never bladdy say so.

Ghaap snapped out of his reverie, asked Mabusela whether he watched *7de Laan*. His companion shook his greying head. He wasn't in a talkative mood tonight.

They left the tranquillity behind them and merged with the stream of traffic going through the coloured area. All the towns had originally been designed like that by apartheid planners: the whites around the centre of town, where the shops and businesses were. Further away, the coloureds and the Indians. And then the blacks. Far away. Made "kom-ver" by apartheid.

The surroundings became more familiar to Ghaap. They were in Canada Road – where only the day before he'd been footslogging, kicking at stones. It felt like a lifetime ago. His anger returned, and he swore out loud.

"What?" Mabusela asked, his eyes on the road.

"My car," Ghaap said. "It's been stolen."

The older man clicked his tongue in disgust. "Skebengas," was all he said.

"Is that the same as a jackroller?" Ghaap asked.

Mabusela laughed, didn't reply. They'd got stuck in a traffic jam in Main Reef Road, the big east–west artery. Vehicles stood bumper to bumper in all directions, the traffic lights out of order. Mabusela clicked his tongue again, switched on the blue light and pushed his way through. They wove through heavy traffic for several kilometres. The light remained on. As they sped past Helen Joseph Hospital, Mabusela relaxed.

"A jackroller," he said, "is a young guy with only two things on his mind – money and sex. If he's anywhere in the vicinity, families with daughters have to lock their doors. Because when he gets in, he takes everything. He leaves with a smile. The girls he leaves behind walk bow-legged. Raped. And if he feels like it, he just takes the other females in the house too. That's just his way. He's got many names, that guy. He's a playa, a gent, a majita. That's just how things are here in the district," he said.

"So, a skebenga is the same?"

Mabusela wiggled his head from side to side. "More or less," he said eventually, "a heavy criminal."

Melville, Ghaap realised, the *real* Melville, didn't exactly look … But on the other hand, he didn't really know what he'd expected. The main road had a slightly African feel, with KFCs and other fast-food places, a Chinese shop, and a pub where music was pumping.

And in the residential part of the suburb the houses were hidden behind sky-high walls. With some, you'd never guess there was a house behind the wall, he reckoned. Not even a rooftop visible. And it was quiet. Not a soul on the streets. Not even a car driving around. It looked as if the Second Coming had arrived early here. The place had a gloomy, depressed, fearful atmosphere. Obscured by the trees, even the streetlights were dim, he noticed.

The house where Mabusela stopped was visible from the street. It was perched high up, on a slope. In front, a high wall with razor wire as well as electric fencing running along the top. And security gates.

They climbed out. Ear-splitting barking erupted as Mabusela pressed the bell at the gate. Someone answered on the intercom, and Mabusela introduced himself.

"My name is Rebecca," said the woman who opened the front door, eyes like saucers and a yellowish complexion in a stricken face.

She led them down the corridor to a bedroom where an old man was lying in bed. "This is Oupa Matthee. He's Mevrou Gerda's father." A news broadcast in Afrikaans was blaring from the TV. The man ignored the two cops, his eyes glued to the set.

Mabusela requested that the TV be switched off. Rebecca looked anxiously at the old man. "Oupa, we're going to watch the news again later, okay?" She picked up the remote, but the old man struck out wildly. Though she quickly stepped back, his fist hit her hand and the device clattered to the floor.

"Leave it!" he shouted. "Leave it! It's the news, I'm watching the news! Leave it." He glared suspiciously at Ghaap. And then he noticed Mabusela, who was standing to the side. The old man's eyes widened in alarm and he started shouting. "Help! Help! Pattie! Help, it's … it's a … Heeeeeelp!"

Signalling to the policemen to leave, Rebecca bent down to retrieve the remote. She shoved it into the hand of the old man, who grabbed it and turned up the volume.

"Who was he calling to?" Mabusela asked as they followed Rebecca into the kitchen.

"His late wife. Pat. Oupa's very sick," she explained. "He has Alzheimer's. Yoh, he's very difficult. Since yesterday already. The sicker he gets, the more he fights. Or he shouts. He calls for his wife. And then he cries. The only thing that keeps him busy is the TV. Mevrou records the news, on the machine. And when Oupa gets so tjatjarag, we play the news for him. It's always the same news. It doesn't worry him."

She stared at Ghaap and Mabusela expectantly, hoping for advice, it seemed. Or good news, at least.

Mabusela spoke to her in Zulu. She shook her head. She was Tswana, she told him. Then: "Where's my mevrou? And Kleinpietie. That's the little boy. Every day, Mevrou goes to work and I look after the oupa. Me and Xolani. He works in the garden."

"And yesterday?" Mabusela motioned to Ghaap to take notes.

"No. Yesterday I wait, but she doesn't come. So I think maybe she went to the shop. Or to Baz, he's her boyfriend, he wants to marry her. But she didn't tell me anything. Nine o'clock last night, I knew she wasn't coming. I phoned Meneer Baz's place, but nothing. So I didn't know what happened. Maybe the baby came and she was at the hospital. Maybe it happened quickly. I didn't know. I didn't know what to do. Then I phoned the police."

"Where is Xolani right now?"

"No, Xolani, he's gone home. But he works with the garden and maintenance, and he also helps to look after Oupa. He left just now. He had to go home because his child is sick. He's coming back quickly, he said. He also stayed here last night. When our mevrou didn't come, we didn't want to go away. Because the oupa can't be here on his own. He makes a lot of trouble."

She looked at both men, dismay in her eyes. Mabusela asked her when she'd reported the case, and she told them about the constable who'd come by the previous evening. He had promised they would make inquiries at the hospitals, but she hadn't heard from him again.

It was only early this morning, she said, that she'd remembered about the car-tracking company. The woman from next door came to help her, and they eventually found the name of the company and raised the alarm.

"We really don't know what happened to our mevrou. Yesterday she—" Her eyes filled with tears, which she wiped away with her apron.

"How far pregnant is Mrs Matthee?" Mabusela asked.

"No, the baby's time is now."

Mabusela asked where they could find Baz. She gave the name of a restaurant in Melville's Main Road. Ghaap jotted it down. "He wants to marry her," she told them. "But then the oupa will have to go away. And Mevrou, she says no, she's going to look after Oupa until he dies. She tells me, Rebecca, I've lost everything. I can't throw Oupa away. Meneer Baz is cross. He says the oupa must go to the sick place. But Mevrou just keeps saying no." She shook her head slowly, looked away.

Making an effort to compose herself, she gave them the cellphone number of "Meneer Baz". Ghaap called the number, but no luck. Not even voicemail.

Ghaap glanced around at his surroundings. Something was missing, but he couldn't put his finger on it. A neat kitchen, with an inviting table in the middle. The lounge was also a pleasant room, landscape paintings on the wall.

Then it dawned on him: the absence of photos. A home with a baby, a boyfriend, a deceased mother, a dying father. There should surely be a couple of photos around.

He walked down the corridor, past the oupa's room. Next to it was another bedroom. It seemed to be a spare room – with an ironing board and a washing basket in one corner. Two single beds, which appeared to have been slept in the night before. Rebecca and Xolani, no doubt.

He opened one of the built-in cupboards. Sheets, blankets, towels. And children's clothes. Boys' shirts, a pullover with Superman on the front – for a four- or five-year-old, he guessed. He looked for a name tag, saw nothing. Maybe the boyfriend had children of his own. These days, up to three, four different sets of children all lived under the same roof.

In the main bedroom he took a quick peek inside the cupboards, saw only a few items of men's clothing. So the man didn't actually live here.

There were no photos in this room either. He pulled open the drawer of the bedside cabinet, found a baby monitor, a hairbrush, a Bible and a box of ginger tablets. *For the prevention of morning sickness*, the sticker on the outside declared. He opened the box and smelt the contents. Smells like chicken shit, he decided.

An inscription at the front of the Bible read: *To our dearest daughter – for your confirmation. Pa and Ma.* A date underneath: *1990.* He flipped through it, saw a pressed leaf here and there, each with a date: *Neil – 2006. Fransie – 2008.* Old boyfriends? Right at the back, on the inside flap of the leather cover, he found some photos, looked at each one. Examined the pic of a coloured cop. It must have been taken at least twenty years ago. The man had "blougat" stamped all over him. Another one of the same man, maybe a few years older, sitting next to a red-headed woman. Their faces were a bit blurred, but they were laughing, each holding a bottle of beer. Behind them stood a tall dark-haired man, his face turned away from the camera – as if he'd decided to duck out of the photo at the last moment.

Ghaap stared at the photo. He could swear that the tall man looked like a younger, thinner Beeslaar. The broad shoulders and rugby-prop neck were just the same, though. Also the straight nose and the thick eyebrows that met in a frown. Grumpy, even then.

Ghaap shook his head. It was possible. But of all people … He flipped through the rest of the photos. Babies, quite a few of those. The red-headed woman again, with two little boys.

He selected one of the clearer photos of the woman, hesitated, and then slipped it into his shirt pocket, together with the Beeslaar lookalike.

50

Gerda's heart hammered against her ribs. *Not now, sweetheart, now isn't a good time. Someone will soon come looking for us, get us to a hospital. Then you can come!*

She had to keep her head, stay calm.

Next to her, close by, The Beast scratching and whining again. More urgently than before. It sensed something.

Scraping sounds, a man's voice, the same voice as before. The Brute. He was talking to The Beast. Cajoling.

A loud squeaking – a gate opening? A chain dragging, footsteps, scraping. And silence.

More scraping sounds. Strangely tentative.

Protectively, Gerda tried to turn her body away from the door. A white-hot pain shot up from her loins and she groaned.

A whispering voice: "Lady, sh-sh." It was the child, Mpho. He started working at the tape over her mouth, eventually managed to remove it. She swallowed, tried to wet her tongue.

"M ... Mpho. Is that you?"

"Thula! Shhh." He untied her hands, her feet.

"Please, what did you do with my child? Tell me, please!"

He didn't reply.

"Help me, Mpho! Please, they're going to kill my child!"

"No talk, thula. He is angry."

"Why? Why did he hit you?"

Silence. She listened, tried to regulate her breathing.

"He does not like the naughtiness. Is all."

"Who? Who is this man?"

Silence.

"Mpho, are you hurt? Does it hurt badly? Did he hit you with the sjambok?"

"He shapa the naughtiness. I'm all right. I'm big now. No talk. We wait."

"Is it your father?"

No response.

"How old are you, Mpho?"

"Fifteen."

"I think you're nine years old."

"I work for him," was all he said.

Somewhere, an engine starting up. Diesel. A truck? Or a motorcycle?

The sound came closer. The backfiring told her it was an old car with a clapped-out exhaust system. The engine stopped, and two doors slammed.

A voice calling, another responding.

Mpho gave a nervous giggle.

A loud scream, a man shouting. Rapid footsteps, car doors slamming.

Mpho stifled another giggle.

What was going on, she wanted to know, but he didn't reply. It had to be The Beast, she decided. She imagined the man brandishing The Beast. A weapon against uninvited visitors? Perhaps he was some kind of a witchdoctor. Demonstrating his power?

It suddenly hit her! A sangoma. Yes, she was sure. The strange smells and the muttering and the smoke. The rustling sounds, beads? Bones? Which meant that she … Her mind balked at connecting the dots. But she recalled the man's voice. Was it yesterday? *Fifty thousand for the unborn.*

She heard a shuffling outside, the clanking of a chain. Squeaking, and again the padding sounds of paws pacing.

A minute or two later, voices – The Beast was now safely back in its cage.

Panic constricted her chest. She bit into her bottom lip. Tasted the blood, but she didn't stop. She *had* to calm down. She *had* to. For her children. She was the only one who could fight for them now. The sharp pain in her lower belly would not subside. She drew breath, held it a while, concentrated hard, trying not to cry out.

She groped for the boy. "Mpho, they're going to kill my babies. You must help me. The police, they—" Tears overcame her. She sniffed angrily. She couldn't weaken now.

She felt a gentle hand on her shoulder.

"Shhh. Please. Thula. He will hit us. He—"

She grabbed his hand and rolled heavily onto her back. "Where's the baby!" she demanded

"The mother. She's looking after it. She make it sleep."

Oh dear God. Sleeping pills? Kleinpiet wasn't strong enough. He'd …

"Take the blindfold off, Mpho!" she hissed.

"No! You lie still."

"I *can't* just lie here and let them sell my baby!" Her voice rose.

"Thula! We wait. You no thula, I run away."

Voices approaching – The Brute's she instantly recognised. Two other male voices. The boy quickly gagged her again before scurrying away.

Gerda lay motionless, heard her heart thudding. The scraping, then the presence of people in the room, she could feel it. They didn't come closer, but

225

she knew they were looking at her. She didn't move a muscle – what if they saw that her hands and feet had been untied?

"Tomorrow, my brother. Be ready. We do the ceremony."

The voices faded.

51

Beeslaar decided to walk. There was still more than enough time, after all. He'd brave the wind that was tearing at trees and shrubs like a poltergeist with issues. The late-winter wind of the Kalahari was a better bet, any day. Late July and August. Relentless. Merciless, day after day. Right up to the desert coast of Namibia, where it turned day into night and ate away at the paint on your car. It ate away at your nerves, too, eventually. But it had none of this ill-mannered unruliness.

As he walked, he mulled over Maaike van der Wiel's philosophising. About the Du Toit kids. And what she'd had to say about men. South African men, being useless fathers. She was damn right, he realised. Take his own history. Take Gerda's. The histories of so many other people he knew. Blikkies.

No wonder the country was in such turmoil. And that things were falling apart so. He thought of something he'd once seen on TV, an American cop show. One of the cops was talking about the fall of civilisations. It wasn't necessarily the greed and corruption of rulers that caused such downfalls, he'd said. Or enemy invasions. No, it happened when a society lost its values. To the extent that it neglected its own children, obliterating its own future. Children who had no voice. Who stumbled into life with a handicap. Emotionally damaged, a soft target for disaster.

What was it Maaike had said about apartheid and oppression? Apartheid's oppression of the black majority was over. But the oppression of children was still rampant.

He struggled to clear his mind of these sickening thoughts. He was looking forward anyway to a proper drink at Jan Cats. Which reminded him of Blikkies: "Alchohol doesn't solve your problems, but fuck knows, neither do tea and coffee!"

Ahead of him on the street, he saw a woman with a small dog on a leash. A pug, the breed with the gargoyle face. The short-legged animal was straining forward, its pig-like tail a fat curl on its backside. The woman took long strides to keep up, leaning against the wind. On high heels, too.

Beeslaar came up to her from behind. The dog barked.

"Jakob," the woman sharply reprimanded. She looked up apologetically at Beeslaar.

He gave a half-smile and walked on.

"Pardon me," the woman said suddenly. He came to a halt, the dog still barking. Without thinking, he picked up the animal.

To his chagrin, he was rewarded with a rapturous smile. "You're staying at Maaike's place, aren't you?" She patted down her hair, which the wind kept tossing across her face.

He inclined his head. The dog lay grunting, its chin resting on a paw.

She started walking again, the leash still in her hand. "The wind," she called out to him, "always reminds me of my late mother. Whenever I complained about it, she said it was good exercise for the trees – all that dancing in the wind."

She turned in at a house on the corner of a quiet cul-de-sac. A pretty old thatched-roof cottage. No fence, a moss-covered stone path leading to a royal-blue front door. She motioned to him to follow her, dog and all; a picture popped into his mind of the fisherman that caught the shark that had caught the snoek.

Beeslaar deposited the dog in the homely entrance hall. "Just call me Birrie. Come and have a glass of wine," she said, and led the way to a cosy lounge. Two big easy chairs in green pastel shades, Persian carpets, an entire wall covered in bookshelves. The other walls were filled with paintings. A contemporary ceramic vase holding lilies, and several orchids on pot stands.

There was a bottle of white wine in an ice bucket, Beeslaar saw. "Thelema," she said, and half-filled two long-stemmed glasses. "The first sauvignon of the season. One of the best from this area, in my opinion."

They sat down, and the wine was indeed good. He needed to take it slow, he knew. He wouldn't only be drinking Coke at Jan Cats.

"A tragic business," she said, regarding him with gleaming eyes. "The two children attend the school where I teach, you know?"

She was short and athletically built. Tanned, as if she spent a lot of time on the track. Energetic.

He guessed she was in her middle to late forties. Snow-white hair in a bob, the fringe flicking from her forehead in a cowlick. She wore a conservative dark-blue suit, but her high heels and beaded earrings in the colours of the national flag suggested a mischievous streak. She was scrutinising him with delighted fascination, as if he were a rare insect.

"I hear you're the Du Toits' private investigator?"

Beeslaar sighed inwardly, then set her straight.

"I've been in education all my life. But God knows." She twirled the stem of her glass and watched the wine swirl in the bowl. She sniffed at it with evident pleasure and took a dainty sip. Demonstrating her connoisseurship for Beeslaar's benefit.

"An event like this traumatises the children so badly. And believe me, I've experienced many things in the course of my career. But to find your own mother like *that* … In fact, it affects all of us. So, I've been wondering if someone like you … if I may ask you … Would you perhaps be willing to come and talk to the learners?"

Beeslaar almost fell off his chair. "Er, what do you mean?"

"I'm the deputy principal at the high school around the corner. You're an experienced policeman, after all, and you may be able to set the children's minds at ease. Something like this creates unconscious fear among young people. And, er, we've already had an incident today at the school. One of the white kids lost his front teeth in a fight. The kid who punched him just happens to be black. The fight was about some trivial thing, but then the parents got involved, and suddenly it's a race issue."

"You mean the fight had nothing to do with the Du Toit murder, but the parents have turned it into a racial issue?"

"Between you and me, yes."

"It'd be best to ask Captain Qhubeka, she's leading the investigation. She may even be a former pupil of your school."

She shook her head. "I suspect she's too busy if she's in charge of the investigation. And it'd be good if a man were to address the children. Psychologically speaking, a strong father figure may be more appropriate right now. Someone like you," she said, batting her eyelashes.

"Then I'd suggest you ask the station commander, Colonel Baadjies. I'm not really in a position to do something like that." He explained that he was actually on holiday.

She looked suitably disappointed, took a mouthful of wine.

"How well do you know the family?" he asked.

She had the alert eyes of a fox terrier, Beeslaar thought. Missed nothing.

"As well as I know the rest of the families, I'd say. I make it my business to meet all the learners' parents. I believe absolutely that we, as educators, have a big responsibility. The parents tend to expect too much of a school. They forget that *they* are the child's primary educator. But when it comes to this case …"

Her expression changed, became sombre. She picked up the wine glass. "You keep wondering if you might perhaps have *done* something. Because if I had to be honest … Well, there was something wrong with her."

Beeslaar assumed she was talking about Elmana du Toit.

"Most of the parents are involved in the school. There's no alternative, because without the parents' input, if we had to survive on our state subsidy alone, this school would long ago have lost its position. The extra teachers, for one thing. The equipment. Maintenance. Our parents pay for all that." She put down her glass. "There are parents, and then there are parents. Elmana du Toit was one of *those*." She shrugged and picked up the glass again. He wondered how much wine she'd already had to drink that afternoon.

"Ellie is now in grade eleven. It's a difficult stage in an adolescent's life – neither fish nor fowl. But she seems to be – I don't want to say *lost*, that might be an exaggeration. But she's been absent a lot since the beginning of the year."

"Oh?" Beeslaar put his glass down carefully. "Was she absent on Tuesday too?"

She gave him a meaningful look and said, "Yes, she was definitely absent. In fact, we spoke about that in the staff room yesterday. As a school, we obviously have to make a gesture of sympathy, you know? But she hasn't been back since the weekend."

"Did any of you make inquiries?"

She pursed her lips. "It's been difficult, lately. The child had lost weight, dark circles under her eyes, sudden aggressive behaviour. I was convinced she was suffering from depression. We phoned Elmana, of course, a few weeks ago. Because Ellie is actually a star pupil, an overachiever, almost, but anyone could see she was, well, slipping away from us. Elmana shrugged it off as a phase, said it would blow over. She was also like that in her teens, she said."

"So there was no discussion?" Beeslaar thought of Maaike's five-ton elephant.

"No. But all of a sudden she was in hospital, and her classmates said she'd tried to commit suicide. She'd cut her wrists and taken a whole lot of her mother's sleeping pills. But Elmana labelled it an accident, said the child had merely taken the wrong pills by mistake. Now I ask you: even if they had been energy pills ... According to her friends, she'd swallowed about thirty of them. But the mother stuck to her guns."

"And the father?"

"I can't really say I know him. I see much less of him. You know how it is." She widened her eyes to emphasise what was clearly a poor opinion of fathers.

"She was absent from school for about ten days. But when she returned, she seemed even worse. She didn't participate in anything any more. And she was constantly ill, stayed away from school. Then I phoned again, and said I wanted to see the mother *and* the father. But Elmana said the child was having treatment for anxiety. And if I had a problem with that, she'd move the child to another school. You could have knocked me down with a feather!"

It was nearly seven o'clock when Beeslaar arrived at Jan Cats. Qhubeka was already seated, but he could see at a glance that something was wrong. Her face was grey and tired, her head sunk into her shoulders. He caught her eye as he walked in, saw the defeat in her expression. It dawned on him: *that's* what she concealed under the standoffish attitude. Next to her sat a petite, attractive woman with lively green-brown eyes. "This is Charmaine Jephta," Qhubeka introduced her colleague. The one who was an expert on gangs.

The two women had glasses of juice in front of them.

Beeslaar ordered a proper drink: double brandy, on the rocks. It was still too early for Coke.

They clinked their glasses, with Qhubeka proposing the toast: "To the first forty-eight hours! And the major fuck-up of my career." She took a sip of juice. "Oh, and to the biggest bunch of clowns you've ever met. And to the provincial commissioner himself: Long live! Because at this very moment, as we speak, he's announcing the success of this investigation at an international press conference."

"Press conference," Beeslaar echoed. "And what success might that be?"

"The solving of this case. The darkie in the story is already behind bars! And the woman in the story comes across as a total dick. She's been shown by the prov com *himself* how to solve a case. How a *man* does it: chop-chop. Assertively. And he's not one to hide his feelings. He made it quite clear to Prammie that there are certain cases that should be dealt with by a 'man.'"

"So, it's Ndlovu?" ventured Beeslaar.

"The very same. The poor bastard had a set of expensive earrings belonging to the murdered woman in his possession. Ergo, he murdered her, end of story. And you, Captain Beeslaar, can now officially unpack your bathing costume and your beach towel and your bucket and spade and go and relax at the seaside. Charmainetjie and I have a mountain of paperwork to complete so that the powers that be can then fuckin' rubberstamp it all."

The two women clinked their glasses again. Beeslaar jiggled the ice cubes in his drink.

His heart went out to Qhubeka. "Shame, man," he said, "it's a tough break. But you have to steel yourself: this kind of thing will happen over and over again. That's just how this job works."

She looked up at him, her lips set in a tight, grim line.

"If I were you," said Beeslaar, "I'd fight back."

"Out of the question, Beeslaar. The evidence against Ndlovu is strong. He had the earrings in his house. Pricey things, loaded with diamonds. And that's strong enough for detention."

"But did you find the murder weapon at his place?"

"We found fuck-all else that links him to the murder. No gun residue, not a shoe of his that matches the bloody tracks at the scene. No fingerprints, nothing."

"The goods are *something*, of course," he replied after a while, "but it's not enough for a smart lawyer. And, believe me, there'll be a bunch of eager-beaver lawyers clamouring to take on Ndlovu's case pro bono. Especially once it becomes known that Elmana du Toit was an addict – a tik-head."

"I feel like buggering off. Handing in my papers, along with the Du Toit docket. Because I *refuse* to sit around waiting for the lawsuit. Damn, damn, damn," she exclaimed. "It's enough to drive me to drink."

"What exactly is the prov com's story?"

"I think it really just boils down to all the bad publicity we've had lately. All the mishaps. And that forty-six-million-rand case against the department hasn't helped either." She emptied her glass, pulled a face, and ordered a Coke. Then she turned to him: "Do you perhaps have a better suggestion?"

"One thing I *do* 'have' is: we haven't even uncovered the tip of the iceberg in this case."

She raised an eyebrow. "That's for fucking sure." Her voice sounded tired.

"Firstly," said Beeslaar, holding up an index finger, "we know far too little about Elmana du Toit and what was going on in her life in the past three months. After her mother's death. I think *she's* got to lead us to what really happened in that house on Tuesday. Your friend from the newspaper confirmed that she was on the point of losing her position managing the feeding scheme. And she talked about paranoia, claimed that Elmana du Toit had phoned her on the day of her death, wanting to see her. She'd mentioned something about blackmail. Mrs Syster didn't go because the woman sounded drunk to her. My conclusion is that it wasn't the first time she'd experienced this 'paranoia'."

Holding up another finger, he continued: "We don't know enough about her exact relationship with Ndlovu. For example, what if he'd been so harassed by her unstable behaviour that he genuinely developed an ulcer? As I understand it, she'd been quite manic in recent months, *and* according to Veronica Syster, convinced Ndlovu was trying to get rid of her. I don't think poor Ndlovu has the gumption for that. But: how did the jewels end up in his pozzie?"

"He claims she gave him the earrings."

Beeslaar raised his ring finger: "The victim was a typical benzo junkie. All those pills for her nerves and the paranoid behaviour, the tik. Did it make her vulnerable to blackmail? For sure. But by whom?"

The pinky went up: "How far up was she on the ladder of addiction? How desperate had she become? How much tik did she need? And where's the equipment then, the straws? And who were her dealers? Surely she didn't go hustling herself? Or was that, in fact, Ndlovu's job? Did she pay him with her jewellery for his services?"

The thumb: "Ellie." He related what Birrie, the deputy principal, had just told him. His thumb still in the air, he said: "What had been going on in that household? How could that woman have abused so many substances without her family being affected? People like that are unstable. One minute they're normal, the next they're capable of ripping your head from your body. Literally. Was she ever violent towards the children? Or was her *thing* more emotional in

232

nature? The grandmother says she raised the kids like little soldiers. Had she become worse lately? How much worse? We know that she quarrelled with all and sundry, that she believed someone was out to kill her."

"By the way," said Qhubeka, "there was blood on the craft knife we found at the scene. The girl's. And I questioned Veronica Syster again, but she didn't have a clue as to who Elmana was afraid of. I don't think she's shedding many tears about the woman's death either."

"So we need to take another look at the father?" Charmaine said after a while. "You can imagine how ecstatic the prov com will be." She spoke with a typical Boland burr, Beeslaar noticed. Cute.

"The fact remains," Qhubeka suppressed a Coke-hiccup as she addressed Charmaine, "Ndlovu is too *obvious*. You said yourself that the money issue will probably give us a lead."

"That's right," Beeslaar concurred. "There'll almost certainly be a money trail. We don't have anything else on Malan Junior yet, do we? You said there was no gun residue on his hands, not so? And the blood on him came from his efforts to resuscitate the woman. And the children? So, we look at the money. How many people hasn't he pissed off with that development in the valley? What kind of money are we talking about, Charmaine? The estate agent, Henkie, guessed tens of millions."

"Current prices in that area? Starting at five million per hectare, I'd say. The asking price for a big house – guesthouse, actually – is currently twenty-six million. We're talking building costs upwards of twelve thousand rand per square metre. So it's big money."

"Right," said Beeslaar. "And do you know yet what the source of the money behind his project might be?"

Charmaine shook her head and stirred the ice in her drink. "Still working on it. But one thing I can tell you now already: it doesn't come from a bank." She shot a glance at Beeslaar, quickly averted her eyes.

She was shy, he realised in surprise, the tough-nut exterior notwithstanding. Or was that the impression Qhubeka had given him? But here she was, actually blushing as she smiled into her orange juice. Nice teeth, he noticed.

"You see?" he told Qhubeka. "Charmainetjie agrees with me: there are more questions than answers. And what this means is that that docket of yours is still far from complete! So, go back and fight for it!"

Once outside, he walked headlong into the wind.

He'd always scoffed at the notion that this wind could blow people off their feet. But tonight he was prepared to change his mind. He recognised the town hall's stately white columns as he turned into Plein Street. At the corner, he had to stop for a moment to wipe the dust from his eyes. It felt as if he were walking straight into the maw of a raging monster.

At the roundabout in front of the Absa building, he saw a man's tie slapping wildly around his face – as if it were being given electric shocks.

A car hooted behind him.

Du Toit's lawyer, Willem Bester, stopped and gestured to Beeslaar to hop inside.

"Congratulations, Captain," he said as Beeslaar slid into the calm haven of the Mercedes, "I hear you've apprehended the perpetrator!"

"If you're referring to Ndlovu, he's only been brought in for interrogation. As far as I know, he hasn't been charged yet."

They drove in silence for a while. The Mercedes sped across a four-way stop, only to get stuck behind a smoking Nissan bakkie crawling along at about twenty kilometres an hour.

"This is now our famous Black Southeaster, Captain," Bester observed as he put his foot down to overtake the old rattletrap.

"More infamous," Beeslaar said. "How long does it blow like this?"

"Anything from two days to a week. And this is our most dangerous time of year. If a veld fire starts and the wind is blowing like this, it's a disaster. The wind takes it and runs with it, over all these mountains."

Beeslaar grunted in reply.

"Where can I drop you?" asked Bester.

"I'll drive with you to your house. If Mr du Toit is still there."

Malan du Toit was watching the BBC's *Business Report* when Beeslaar and the lawyer walked into the house. He stood up, surprise on his face. "I thought you'd already left."

"I'm still here till Sunday," replied Beeslaar.

The lawyer offered Beeslaar a glass of wine, but he turned it down and requested water instead. He watched as Du Toit busied himself with opening a wine bottle. The process was meticulous: the leaded wrapper around the stopper was cut away with a small knife, then a corkscrew was inserted squeakily, with the cork being pulled out with a soft plop.

The lawyer excused himself, and Du Toit sat down. He placed the bottle on a coffee table in front of him, poured himself a glass, and raised it.

"So, it was Vincent after all," he said. His expression was a mixture of panic and relief. A muscle twitching at the corner of his mouth made it look as if he wanted to smile.

"I think it's still too early to say for sure, Mr du Toit."

"But it's just been announced on the news! Press conference, the whole shebang. Yet none of you thought of informing us, the family. Or is it just another murder to you people? Just another day at the office for the cops?" Du Toit dipped an index finger in his wine and drew it around the rim of his glass to produce a weeping sound from the fine crystal. The sound vibrated mournfully in the large room.

"Were you aware that your daughter hadn't been going to school?"

The sound stopped, but Du Toit didn't look up. Then he dipped his finger in the wine again and resumed the lamentation.

"Mr du Toit?"

His eyes closed. When he opened them again, there was a pleading look, a weariness, in his eyes.

"Ellie was ill," he eventually said.

"And your wife?"

There was a slight tremor in his hand, Beeslaar saw.

"She, er … Can't we just let it rest now, please? Allow me to bury my wife in peace and quiet."

"You'll have to talk about it sooner or later."

"But Vincent—"

"We don't know yet that Vincent Ndlovu is the actual culprit, Mr du Toit."

The man frowned, as if his brain had to calculate something that was beyond comprehension. "I didn't even know that Elmana's earrings were missing. I got them for her in Russia. It's the second biggest diamond-producing country in the world, did you know?"

Indulgently, Beeslaar shook his head.

"More than two carats of flawless stones on each ear. Magna cut, a hundred and two facets each. I don't know if that says anything to you. But you'd have to go far to find a more expensive stone than that. She …" He sighed, looked at the glass in his hand. "Maybe she considered it a worthless present. I seldom saw her wearing them. That's why I didn't know they were gone."

"I'm sure you realise that your children's version of the events of two days ago doesn't exactly make sense, given the fact that Ellie wasn't at school. She must have been home at the time of the murder?"

Du Toit frowned again, his eyes still on his glass.

"But it's … imposs—" He stared at the glass uncomprehendingly – as if he were seeing it for the first time.

Was the man drunk? Beeslaar couldn't help wondering. Or did he genuinely have no idea of what went on in his own household?

"Your daughter has been absent from school frequently in the past months, but on Tuesday she gave you to understand that she'd returned from her music lesson at four o'clock and found her mother's body in the house."

"It was really such a shambolic day. I don't know if she … I had …" He glanced up at Beeslaar with eyes that slowly started to focus.

The lawyer came back into the room. He had changed into shorts and a T-shirt. His bare feet were milky-white, resembling two pale fish. He took the empty glass Du Toit held out to him, waited for his wine to be poured.

"This man claims that we're lying about Tuesday, Wim."

"How so?" Bester directed his question at Beeslaar.

"Mr du Toit's daughter didn't go to school on Tuesday. And apparently Tuesday wasn't Ellie's first suicide attempt. That's all."

Bester frowned. "Isn't this sort of interrogation a bit belated?"

Beeslaar ignored him, his attention still on Du Toit: "Well, *someone* is lying. In your opinion, Mr du Toit, why did Ndlovu have your wife's earrings in his possession?"

"Now that's ridiculous," exclaimed Bester. "He'd stolen them, obviously! She caught him in the act, and he killed her. And he's—"

He didn't finish the sentence because Beeslaar abruptly got up and put his glass on the table. He had heard enough. "Captain Qhubeka will resume this conversation with you, Mr du Toit. But if you'd like to learn more about your kids, I suggest you speak to Dr Birrie Scholtz, the deputy principal at their school. Seems she knows them a bit better."

He strode towards the door. Glancing back, he saw Du Toit pour the rest of his wine down his throat.

52

"We wait."

"The blindfold, Mpho. Take it off, please. I need to see."

"No. The Fatha, he sees everywhere."

She didn't understand. Father? What father? But she refrained from questioning, afraid that he might change his mind and leave. And then, suddenly, she heard Kleinpiet.

"He's crying, Mpho! Please, you must fetch him. Tell your mother you will look after him. Then you bring—"

"Thula!"

"Please!" she whispered. "He's hungry. Maybe he—"

"Shut up! We wait. Wait." His voice sounded tired, scared. And it dawned on her that this child was taking an incredible risk by even just talking to her. Why had he been beaten? Was he badly injured? Those lashes, they'd sounded so vicious.

But he was right, she had to stay calm.

She heard muffled male voices in what sounded like a heated argument. Xhosa, she guessed from the clicks.

A loud laugh. A woman's voice. The "mother", perhaps? It sounded as if they were drinking. Closer by, she heard The Beast pacing. It seemed to be waiting for something to happen, or was it simply relieving stress, like in a zoo? A cheetah ... dear God, could this animal be a cheetah? Whining like that? No.

The woman's laugh started up again, it was coming this way. Gerda heard Mpho scurrying away. Then, the sound of the door scraping. Gerda lay motionless, her breathing shallow.

"Lady."

She felt a warm hand against her neck. The woman was checking her pulse, she realised. The hand moved to her belly, paused there for a moment.

"Hey, Lady." The voice was hoarse, her breath smelling of cigarettes and beer.

Gerda didn't react, feigned sleep.

The hand on her belly moved down, became heavier. Began to feel her lower abdomen. "You keep that baby inside, you hear? Don't think I did not hear you moan. If it comes before tomorrow, you are dead."

53

"How's things, boet?"

Ghaap recognised the voice. Ghalla. The racist Rambo.

"I'm in Melville."

"You don't say!"

Ghaap didn't grasp what he meant at first, but then he remembered that the trackies had police radios in their cars. He and Mabusela had just released the latest details of the Matthee woman and her foreigner friend with the unpronounceable name. Ghaap guiltily fingered the photo he'd pocketed. The one with the Beeslaar lookalike.

"We're looking for the boyfriend. He's some other nationality. Lebanese. No, something else."

"Albanian?"

"Ja, maybe. A name full of z's and things," Ghaap said.

"They're naughty, those Albanians. And you can bet that if there's a contract on that woman, you'll be able to connect it to *him*."

This Ghalla guy was full of fokken prejudice, Ghaap thought to himself. Now there was suddenly a *contract* on the Matthee woman, just because her boyfriend was a foreigner. No wonder Ghalla had left the cops. With an attitude like that, he'd probably been fired.

"Just keep your ear to the ground, boet. You'll probably find the connection when you track down the Albanian. Me and Duif are still stuck here at the scene, but The Trickster and Mo have also gone looking for the antie. We'll be out of here soon, then we'll come check you. But you should go check things out there around the Westdene Dam in the meantime. It's nice and quiet there, they might have gone there to dump the first tracking unit, the dummy. We found the real one here. If the vehicle is from the Melville area, that's where they usually drop it. Or at the Jewish cemetery."

"The *what*?"

"Westpark. That's the big cemetery opposite Melville Koppies. It's got a special area just for the Jews, close to the northern fence. Who're you riding with?"

"Mabusela."

"He'll know what I'm talking about. Tell him you must drive around the back, there where he and the brothers always go and collect the Easter eggs. Okay? Check you!" The line went dead.

Ghaap told Mabusela about the tracking unit the hijackers had left at the mine dump. He explained that the other one, the dummy unit, which the car thieves usually found first, must be somewhere in the area.

Mabusela phoned the station, talked to Uncle Solly – who instructed them to find the Albanian's home address. And to get moving. Every minute that passed was a minute closer to the death of the woman and her child.

On ending the call, Mabusela said he knew the area well enough. He'd worked in Hillbrow for a while, some time ago. Ghaap toyed with the idea of asking him whether he'd known Beeslaar, but thought better of it. Beeslaar had left under a cloud. He didn't know what kind it was. But it was definitely a cloud. A moer of a big one.

Mabusela drove in a south-westerly direction. Crossed Melville's busy Main Road, then up a steep hill. They wove through a few dark, quiet streets, then went down the hill, where a large expanse of black water came into view.

"Westdene Dam," Mabusela remarked, and told Ghaap about the day a bus filled with schoolchildren had plunged into the dam. White kids, he added. A detail that apparently made this tragedy different, Ghaap suspected. Usually this kind of accident happened to black or coloured kids in ramshackle transport. And it was newsworthy for a day or so, then forgotten.

They drove past a row of houses overlooking the dam. At the far end of the street was a parking area, where Mabusela pulled up.

Torches out, they searched the parking area, their eyes peeled. Then he spotted it: a baby's dummy. He called Mabusela, who squatted down and studied the object. "Could be any child's," he remarked. But still, he took out his cellphone and punched in a number. Uncle Solly, Ghaap concluded.

While Mabusela was occupied, Ghaap continued searching. He tried to imagine a hijacker, most likely nervous on account of the woman and baby in the car, stopping here to dump the tracking unit, hoping they were shot of the signal it kept emitting. It's the first thing they do, Duif had explained this morning. While speeding off, they'd begin to dismantle the dashboard to extract the tracking unit. If it was dumped in a white area, the hijacker would think he was safe, because the unit only started transmitting when the car entered an area the client had specified as somewhere he wouldn't usually go. Otherwise, the device was activated by the control room as soon as the theft was reported. And nowadays the tracking companies installed two such devices as an extra security measure. But smart hijackers, the ones who did their homework, were aware of that. Hence they would keep searching until they find the second one too.

So, if the second unit was the one that had almost cost Ghalla his life earlier that day, there was a distinct possibility that the dummy unit would have been dumped here. Or in the cemetery. Or in one of the city's ten million rubbish bins.

"Right, we're staying put," he heard Mabusela say to Uncle Solly. Then he turned to Ghaap and said, "They're sending fingerprint guys. We have to cordon off the scene in the meantime." He took another call. As Mabusela walked back to the car, Ghaap could hear him giving directions to where they were.

"Excuse me," Ghaap suddenly heard from the darkness behind him, and his heart missed a beat.

It was an elderly white man with two dogs, he saw to his relief.

"I'm sorry, sir," Ghaap replied, "but you can't take the dogs to the dam now. We're going to cordon off this area. It's a crime scene."

"That's the reason I'm here. Yesterday afternoon I walked past this spot with Bella and Sweetie. I think, well, I'm not sure, but I think I saw the white Mercedes. It was on the news this evening. The Melville woman who was hijacked. The car was dented. I saw the woman inside. A redhead, if my memory serves me. I can't remember so well any more. But I did see them. There was a man with her. And he was holding a baby."

Again, Ghaap heart's missed a beat. This time because of the adrenaline. A witness. He felt as if he could kiss the old toppie!

"What did he look like, sir? The man? What did he look like? White or black or whatever. Tall, short, fat, thin?"

"No, er, I ..." He shrugged.

"I'm Sergeant Johannes Ghaap from the Orlando East police. My colleague and I are working on this very case. Come," he said, and took the man by the arm.

"No, I don't want to go anywhere, man. I just thought, when I saw the blue light, that I'd come and ask whether—"

Ghaap could barely contain his excitement. He called out to Mabusela, who hurried towards him.

"Warrant Officer Bandile Mabusela," Ghaap introduced a slightly winded Mabusela. "Please tell him about everything you saw, sir."

His house was near the entrance to the dam, he told them, and he passed this spot every day. The previous afternoon he had been there just after two. The white Mercedes he'd seen was one of the big, older models, he said. And the woman inside the car "looked as if she was a bit tired".

Taking out the photo, Ghaap shone his torch on it, but the old man was unsure. "I couldn't see her clearly, she seemed to be asleep. Long hair. Red, as I remember, like I told you. Maybe a bit, er, stout, I'd say. But the man ... There was a man. He stood next to the car, rocking the baby to sleep." And then he apologised, his attention had been on his dogs, he said. And in any case, there were always people around there in cars.

"How long was the car parked here?" Ghaap asked.

"No, gosh, that I really can't tell you. I didn't walk for long before my old Bella got tired. She's old. And so I turned back."

"And was the Mercedes still here?"

"No, I don't think so. But I can't say for sure."

"Were there perhaps other people around here? Walkers, I mean."

He gave a shake of his head, looked somewhat lost as he glanced up. "Man, I can't really ..."

"Please try, sir," Ghaap politely persisted.

The old man played absent-mindedly with the leashes in his hand. An old, weather-beaten hand, Ghaap noticed. Even in the dim glow of the streetlight the liver spots were visible.

"But ... I think I did see Wollie," he eventually said.

"Who's Wollie?" Mabusela asked in a commanding tone.

"A dog, sir. It belongs to the little girl whose family lives at the end of the street. She often brings the dog here for a walk." With a crooked finger, he pointed down the road – at the very moment a Golf GTI with a flashing blue light came round the corner.

Mabusela excused himself and went to meet the car. The occupant, a small, overweight Indian woman, climbed out and took her case from the boot. Once Mabusela had briefed her, he got into the van, told Ghaap to wait as he drove a short way down the street with the dogs and their elderly owner to have Wollie's house pointed out to him.

Ghaap stayed with the new arrival, who was clearly in a hurry. She was wearing three-quarter pants and Crocs. Her long black hair was streaked with grey, and tied up in a practical ponytail. She introduced herself briskly to Ghaap, and asked him to assist her with his torch. He followed her around, stood patiently at each spot where she squatted down to take a photo, and provided her with light.

And then the woman struck gold: she found the trackies' tracking device. In a rubbish bin next to the entrance gate to the dam. It was clear to Ghaap that she'd made similar finds in the past, as she immediately made a call and read out a number printed on the tiny box. The device, Ghaap saw, was about the size of a bar of soap, with ripped wires on either side. It was an absolute miracle that they'd managed to find it.

The confirmation came at once: it was the dummy unit from the hijacked Dolly Parton.

Half an hour later, Ghaap and Mabusela were on the road again. Wollie's owner – the young girl at the end of the street – had confirmed the old man's story,

Mabusela related. But the girl had a rather strange story of her own. According to her, the red-headed woman had looked a bit like a witch. She had black rings around her eyes. And she had pulled a face at the girl.

"*What*? How old is the girl?"

"Nine," Mabusela laughed. "But she said the man behind the wheel seemed very angry. It looked to her as if he was fighting with the woman. And there were two children in the back of the car, a toddler and a schoolboy. She can't remember whether the boy was white or black, but he wore a black school cap."

Mabusela drove back to Melville, heading for the Albanian's home address. Ghaap phoned Duif in the meantime to tell him about the rubbish-bin find.

"Jislaaik, boet. You're a bladdy brick! We've finished up here. We're just going to get some chow, then I'll come your way."

At the Albanian's address, the face of the middle-aged woman who opened the front door for them showed a fair bit of mileage. Her appearance was a far cry from what Ghaap had expected. And she spoke Afrikaans. A Boere antie – and a grumpy one at that.

"I fail to understand why the police keep pestering *me*," she said testily. With her prominent nose and beady black eyes, she looked just like a crow, Ghaap thought. She was holding an unlit cigarette in one hand.

"Mevrou, it's about a car hijacking. A very serious crime. And we have reason to—"

"You have no reason. This is just another way of yours to implicate me and my family in a mess. I have *nothing* to say to you. My son left for Durban yesterday. On business. And no, I haven't had any contact with him since he left. I last saw him on Tuesday. And he's not a child any more. He's a businessman. In his own right."

She stood glaring at them, her hand on the doorknob, her expression unyielding. Mabusela seemed hesitant, unaccustomed to facing down tough white anties. It was at times like this, Ghaap thought, that he missed old hardegat Beeslaar. He cleared his throat and took a step towards the woman – who promptly tried to pull the door shut. Ghaap stuck his foot out, keeping it open.

"Remove your foot," she snapped at him. "I've done nothing wrong. And the whole afternoon I've had to deal with cops bothering me here. Look, I know *nothing!*"

But Ghaap stood firm. "Mrs Rezart, you can get into big trouble if you refuse to talk to us. I don't know how well you know Mrs Matthee, but her life's in danger, and at the moment you're the only person who can help us."

To his surprise the woman opened the door wider, switched on the passage light behind her. Only now did Ghaap realise they'd been talking in semi-darkness.

She turned and led the way through a narrow passage, the two men following wordlessly.

The woman wore a faded dressing gown and shabby slippers, and her long grey hair hung in oily strands over her shoulders. She paused at a doorway and switched on a light, waving them into a dusty lounge crammed with old-fashioned furniture that smelt of stale cigarette smoke. She shuffled towards a small table lamp and switched it on. Then shuffled back into the passage to switch off all the other lights.

She returned, and none of them sat down. Mabusela did the talking in the shadowy room, asked whether she had telephone numbers for staff at her son's business – partners, anybody. People who might know where Baz Rezart was at that moment. She shrugged her shoulders in reply. But Mabusela pressed on politely, inquired about her son's relationship with the Matthee woman. Whether he was the father of the toddler and the unborn baby.

"Humph!" she snorted brusquely.

Ghaap felt his skin crawl. It was the darkness. As if a blind person lived here.

He started when she suddenly spoke again: "Look, I'm very sorry that the woman is missing, and all that. But my son has *nothing* to do with it. And I don't know where you got your information about him. Let me repeat it for the umpteenth time: whatever people may say about him, he's a hard worker. And his business does very well, and that's why the women are always chasing him."

"Gerda Matthee too? According to our information, he intends to marry her."

"Bah! I can tell you *one* thing, she's only after his money. Just like all the others. She pretends to be so independent. A job of her own, a house of her own. But *I* know what Baz spends on her every month, and it's not small change. And she's spinning a web for him. *That* I can tell you!"

Ghaap and Mabusela glanced at each other, both unsure of how to proceed.

"Your son lives here too?" Ghaap asked.

"Yes."

"May we look at his room? He may have phone numbers there. Of his partners, staff, or others, maybe."

"You may look at his room when you come here with the permission of a magistrate. And until then we'll be saying goodnight to each other. Understand?"

"Mrs Rezart, I'm sure your son would have contacted you by now. The disappearance of Gerda Matthee and her baby has been on TV news. All the channels, countrywide. Your son is nowhere to be found. He could be in danger, who knows?"

243

"He's *not* with her. That I know."

"But how do you know that, Mrs Rezart? You last spoke to him on Tuesday. Let me please just check his computer. Maybe we'll find something that'll make it easier for us to contact him. Just to make sure he's safe. Please."

She stood there another moment. Deathly silence. Then she shuffled out of the lounge, followed by Mabusela and Ghaap.

She didn't switch on the passage light. This place was like a crypt, Ghaap thought. It had a sour unwashed-human smell. Cat piss and dirty ashtrays. And dust. He remembered the story someone once told him about an old blind woman who, for a week, hadn't known where her husband had disappeared to. Until they found him in his chair in front of the TV. He'd been dead for four days, already decomposing.

He nearly jumped out of his skin when his phone rang. Hung back to take the call.

It was Duif, jubilation in his voice. "Yes-yes-yes, my man! Good news. We've found that Dolly Parton!" He sounded breathless and bubbling. "Right here in the district, less than a block from where Ghalla took that bullet."

"But the victim? And her son?"

"Negative. But it won't be too hard to find them, I think. There can't be that many *white* blue-bellies walking around in the district?"

"White *what*?"

"Preggies, man."

"So why are you waiting, then? You guys always find what you're looking for, don't you?"

"No, man, we're fokken good, but we're not magicians. But we do have a suspect. Young black guy, spinning lots of stories. I'll call again later!"

Ghaap trotted off to catch up with the two in front of him.

Mrs Rezart unlocked a door that led outside, stood back to allow the two men to pass. The garden had lighting – praise be, thought Ghaap. The men walked down a paved pathway that led to an arched gate in the wall, giving access to the adjacent property. As they walked through, Ghaap glanced back at the house. The door was still open, but he didn't see the woman. He could feel her eyes on his back, however, and hurried through the gate in Mabusela's wake.

This must be a separate property, Ghaap reckoned. Maybe a subdivided section of the original Rezart stand.

The young gent's living quarters were nothing at all like his mother's. An enormous dark pool lay across the width of the property – with pillars that emerged just above the level of the water, serving as stepping stones to the front door. Mabusela cursed softly in Zulu as he and Ghaap carefully made their way across the swimming pool. Ghaap was amused at the situation: here he was, in the middle of Sodom and Gomorrah, and he was walking on water. And dead sober at that.

Baz Rezart's place was clearly geared to the needs of a healthy ego. A huge open-plan living area, with a home gym occupying at least a quarter of the space. Mirrors from floor to ceiling. To the left of this was a sunken lounge – lined with snow-white mohair carpets, one entire wall was a window. On the other side of the glass, underwater pool lights twinkled. To the rear, a kitchen and dining room, and a spiral staircase that led to the floor above. They began to look around. Ghaap noticed the bar in one corner, consisting entirely of mirrors. An ornate little wooden casket stood on the mirrored counter. Inside it lay a slim silver pipe, shaped like the nozzle of a vacuum-cleaner. "Look at this!" Mabusela exclaimed. "The man has his own little Hoover!" Then he shook his head and shut the lid of the casket. Ghaap suspected it was a cocaine stash Mr Rezart kept for his friends. Not wanting to look like an ignoramus, he just shook his head too.

On the top level there was a giant shower and a transparent bath on legs. And another bathroom, but more private. With a toilet.

The rest of the space was a combination of a TV room and bedroom. Deep leather couches, with footrests, focused intently on a huge flatscreen TV mounted on the wall. A double bed was next to a sliding door that gave onto a balcony, with a panoramic vista of northern Johannesburg. Ghaap's jaw dropped as he beheld the view. City lights as far as the eye could see. And trees. He could swear that the trees outnumbered the people in these suburbs.

Next to a wall was an old writing desk – a rolltop. But it was locked. Ghaap lifted a vase that stood on top of the desk, turned it upside down, and the key dropped out. Rolling open the lid of the desk, he saw a MacBook. Somewhat hesitantly, he searched for the power button, cursing as he did so. He didn't exactly feel at home with technology. Mabusela came to assist, and they both started in surprise when the machine came alive with an orchestral flourish.

Ghaap passed the computer over to Mabusela and turned his attention to the drawers of the desk. In one he found two cellphones, both switched off. And in another drawer, a framed photo of a red-headed woman with big green eyes and full lips. Gerda Matthee, Ghaap guessed, and showed it to Mabusela. Underneath the framed photo, he found a cheap plastic album filled with photos. The first showed a muscular dark-haired man participating in a marathon of sorts. His curly black locks were tied back in a ponytail, and his thumb was raised to the camera. A smile like a Colgate advert, and smouldering dark eyes like some kind of slimy seducer in a TV soapie. Ghaap flicked through the rest of the album, but the photos were nearly all the same: the muscleman running some kind of race, always with the idiotic thumb in the air and a smile on his hairy mug.

A player, Ghaap decided, and very much in love with himself.

They left soon afterwards, with the MacBook, the framed photo and the album in hand, walking back across the swimming pool to the mother's house. She kept them waiting a good five minutes before answering, then took them back to the front door, surprisingly nonchalant when they informed her they'd be taking the photos and the laptop along to the station to search for more information. They were still explaining when she'd shut the door in their faces.

Back in the car, Mabusela phoned the office to relay the information.

"I suppose we'd better write a receipt for the stuff we've confiscated," Ghaap said uncertainly.

"And which of us is going to wake up that antie again to give it to her?"

They drove off in silence. For the first time that evening, Ghaap was acutely aware of his stomach. He wondered what he'd done with the dried sausage Duif had given him earlier on.

And thinking of food, what the hell was the "chicken leg" Duif had referred to?

Mabusela laughed at the question. The trackies, he said, had their own lingo. He'd guess that the chicken leg was a gun – a revolver, to be more precise.

54

Gerda tried to heave herself upright, with the boy pulling her by the arm. But she simply didn't have enough strength.

Whatever it was she'd been dosed with, it had affected her entire body. She felt weak and lethargic. When she finally managed to sit up, her feet on the ground, she realised she was still wearing her sandals. The flat ones she constantly wore these days because of her swollen feet.

"Can you walk?" Mpho whispered, so softly that she could barely hear.

"I'm wet. I wet myself."

He said nothing, pulled her by both hands to help her stand up. An unfamiliar pain shot up from her abdomen, and she gasped. "The blindfold, Mpho," she pleaded in a tight voice. Please, I can't see."

"Walk," he whispered in reply.

Her feet hurt. They felt swollen. And she was nauseous; she felt her stomach heave.

She tried to loosen the blindfold, but could barely lift her elbows. She moaned with nausea and pain.

"Shhh." Though his voice was barely audible, the fear in it was palpable.

She was hunched over with the pain in her abdomen, but the boy supported her by the elbows, his breathing in her ear. Rapid, like a terrified animal. She swayed, her legs threatening to give way under her. Panic-stricken, she grabbed at the boy. He groaned. She'd forgotten the sjambok injuries.

Why did he refuse to remove her blindfold? To retain control? Then she realised: it was fear. If anyone arrived, there'd be no time to put it on again.

They began shuffling, inch by inch, across the uneven floor. She could feel her dress clinging to her backside, the wetness down her legs. She wanted to cry. With gratitude. She was going to make it! For the first time in an eternity there was hope.

"Good," Mpho whispered. For a few minutes they walked in what seemed like a circle, the boy guiding her as if she actually was a blind person. At one point they were back at the bed, and he asked her to sit down. She shook her head. No way would she be getting back onto that smelly bed. Not now that she was able to walk. If he didn't come up with a plan quickly, she'd do something to escape. She was uncertain whether she'd be able to overpower him. But how to prevent him from screaming? She'd have to get her hands around his throat.

"Wait," he whispered in her ear. "I'm going now. Do not go before I come fetch you. If you hear—"

He suddenly fell silent. She, too, held her breath, both of them listening to the voices, getting louder.

"The mother. If they come, you lie down, sleep."

"Can the … can the mother help us?"

He said nothing. But she knew: a stupid question. The woman had only recently threatened to kill her if the baby came. She shuddered involuntarily, felt the boy's grip tighten on her arm. "Bad witch," was all he said. "Someone come, you lie down. Sleep."

She heard him moving away. A moment later the familiar scraping sound. A door, for sure. Opening and closing again. What was he up to? She could hear the man, other voices, the woman laughing like a drain; it sounded like a drinking party.

Then she heard a growl, the sound of jaws snapping. Again. And again. Where was Mpho? She recalled his face as he sat in the back seat of her car: the vacant stare, the spiteful smile as he'd aimed the pistol at her and Kleinpiet by turn. And where was Lucky? She hadn't heard his voice at all since regaining consciousness.

What to do? Just stand there, or attempt to sneak out and go looking for her child? Try to escape?

But there was no chance to agonise further: a sudden commotion erupted. Shouts. A voice calling: "Shaka! Shaka!" The sound of glass shattering. A man bellowing in pain.

The next moment Mpho was at her side, plucking the blindfold from her face and pulling at her hands. She could still barely see anything; the room was pitch dark.

"My baby," she moaned. "I'm not leaving without my baby."

"Thula!" Mpho scolded in an urgent whisper. "Here, you take him!"

She felt the soft, warm bundle in her arms and sagged under the weight of it. Her arms and hands were still too weak. Mpho took the baby from her and hurried ahead of her. She battled to keep up. Her legs dragged, but at least she was moving. Her heavy belly complained, and she tried to hold off the contractions.

She had to stop at the door to catch her breath. The door, she saw, consisted of a loose piece of corrugated iron hinged with wire to the wall of the windowless shack where she'd been held captive. It stood close up against a house, an infernal noise coming from inside.

"This way," Mpho hissed. Crouching, they crept round the corner of her prison. In the darkness, she could make out the outlines of a cage – The Beast! But the cage was empty. Only the smell of apples and rotten meat still hung in the air.

Mpho helped her squeeze through an opening in the fence, and then they were in a piece of open veld. It was dark all around them, but there was light ahead. Streetlights. Gerda tripped over tufts of grass once or twice, fell to her knees, but didn't stay down. It felt as if her lungs would burst, her knees collapse, but she held on. Suddenly, the ground sloped sharply, and they were scrambling down to a dry donga. Mpho held Kleinpiet in one arm, helped Gerda with the other. The air cooled slightly as they descended, struggling to keep their balance on the eroded edge. When they reached the bottom, Mpho allowed her to rest. He shifted Kleinpiet, whose head flopped to one side. He was probably still drugged. All the better, Gerda decided.

They rested just long enough for Gerda to get her breath back. But then she felt a contraction and doubled over in agony. Mpho used his hand to stifle her cry.

Several minutes later, she was on her feet again, Mpho dragging her along with one hand. They walked and walked, for what felt like hours, along the chilly donga. Then Mpho led her up the opposite side, and she scrambled on all fours to get to the top. Around them it was dark, but further ahead Gerda saw the bright lights of a highway. She didn't dare glance back, afraid that she might hear The Beast sniffing behind her.

As they approached the highway, Mpho began to slow down. Every now and again he squatted down behind a clump of bushes. He was out of breath, she could hear. Kleinpiet must be a terribly heavy burden for his scrawny body.

"We wait," he said over his shoulder.

"No, Mpho, I can't. The baby wants to come!" She tried to take Kleinpiet from his arms, but he stopped her.

"They find us, we dead."

Letting go of her son, she sagged to her knees when the pain started up again, prayed it wasn't another contraction.

For a while they stayed like that. Mpho nervously looking over his shoulder, and back at the highway again. He seemed in two minds about what they should do: sit here and let The Beast find them? Or press on to the highway and risk being found by "The Fatha"?

Gerda spotted an aqueduct under the road, pointed to it. Stooping, they crept towards the opening, sank down in the cool sand at the bottom of the giant pipe. Gerda held out her hands for Kleinpiet, and the boy passed the child to her.

She held her son so tightly to her that he started moaning. Through her tears she looked at Mpho, who stared at her expressionlessly. Without his cap, his face looked even smaller. He was still panting, she saw, and his top lip gleamed with sweat and snot. A swollen, bloodied line ran across his little face; his brow was cut open to the bone, right up into his hair.

That's what a sjambok did to a person. The lash curled itself around the body, flaying the skin. Gerda looked at his arms, saw they were covered in welts.

"Thank you," she said softly and held out her hand to him. But he didn't take it. Instead, he turned around and gazed at the dimly lit area they'd just come from.

55

Captain Qhubeka's voice was exhausted as she answered the phone.

"It's no fucking use to me," was her response when Beeslaar recounted his conversation with Du Toit and co.

"Captain, don't let those lead-swingers drag you down to their level. You have a PC here in the Western Cape who isn't any less or any more of a doos than the ones the rest of us have to put up with. They all have a master's degree in window dressing. It comes with the territory. You need to keep a cool head. If this was *my* case, Du Toit, his son, his daughter and the bladdy lawyer would now be on my shit list." He had to speak loudly to make himself heard above the wind. "The whole bunch of them have been lying to us – including Ouma. Right from the start."

She said something he couldn't hear, and he ended the call with a promise to phone back later. Picked up his pace as he headed home. He wanted to fetch his car, get something to eat. He was hoping to sneak in quietly, without Liewe Heksie and her noisy menagerie storming him. But Rembrandt heard him, and came rushing to the gate to greet him, ears flapping in the wind.

He had just washed his hands and face and pulled a comb through his hair when there was a knock at the cottage door. His heart sank into his boots.

It was Maaike. There was an uncertain look in her eyes, a hint of anxiety. Rather apprehensively, he let her in. She didn't sit down, fiddled uncomfortably.

"To what do I owe the honour?" Beeslaar prodded.

"I just wanted to know, er, if everything is in order here? Do you need anything?"

"Thank you, I'm quite okay. I was just on my way out, actually. Is there anything I can help you with?"

She sat down.

"Maaike?" He sat opposite her.

"I think … How can I say?" She gave him a searching look. "I can't saddle Vuvu with this. But I heard about the man they arrested. The black man, I forgot his name. And he … it wasn't *him*, you know."

"Vincent Ndlovu," he helped her.

"I think Vuvu's made a mistake. Vincent isn't a killer."

"Oh? And what makes you say that?"

"I, well, I just *know* it!"

Rembrandt jumped onto Beeslaar's lap, flopped down with a grunt.

"I think …" She glanced around nervously, as if she were afraid someone might be eavesdropping. Then abruptly, she said: "But you're finding this a nice little place?"

"Nice, yes," Beeslaar said. "Or is something wrong here? Why are you suddenly so concerned about my comfort?"

"No, not at all! All I mean is …" Her words dried up again.

He waited, his stomach screaming for food.

"It's … the man. The man who stayed here before you."

"Andries April."

She started when he mentioned the name.

"You know him?"

"I ran into him at your gate early this morning. I thought he was a boyfriend or—"

"Oh, no, please! He wanted … It was a professional conversation. *Nothing more.*"

"And what kind of 'professional conversation' would you be conducting with Mr April?"

"That's private, you know! Highly confidential."

"So help me understand correctly: you're sitting here for one reason only – and that's to tell me that Vincent Ndlovu is innocent."

"Yes."

"Thank you very much, then. I'm sure his mother agrees with you."

He stood up, then bent over to put the dog down.

She didn't move.

"Or is there something else, Maaike? I don't want to be rude, but I'm in a bit of a hurry."

She shook her head but kept her eyes averted.

Rembrandt suddenly started growling. He stood at the front door, sniffing furiously, his hackles raised. Beeslaar was about to open the door for him, but Maaike grabbed him by the arm. "No!" she whispered urgently.

She was frightened, he realised. Her eyes were like saucers.

He removed her hand, strode to the door and yanked it open. Rembrandt shot out from behind him and ran barking into the darkness, towards the front gate. Beeslaar had his pistol out and gave chase. As he reached the corner of the house, a car pulled away, its tyres screaming.

By the time he was through the front gate, the car was too far away to make out the number plate. It was an old, cream-coloured sedan. Smoke streamed from its exhaust, and one of the tail lights was out.

Then he heard Liewe Heksie's scream from inside the house.

56

Mercifully, they'd been spared the Jewish cemetery, Ghaap mused. Thanks to the rubbish-bin find at the Westdene Dam.

On their way back to Soweto, Mabusela stopped at a KFC. "Toyota Corolla," Ghaap said when Mabusela asked him what he was going to order. The older man laughed. "For a blougat from the bundu you're pretty streetwise, nè?" He opened the door and got out. "Or is it because of all the time you've been spending with the trackies?"

"I may look a bit dof, boss, but my my brain's tuned in."

There was a queue at the counter, passengers of the many minibus taxis parked outside, Ghaap reckoned, and he meekly fell into line behind them. But Mabusela walked straight to the front, ignoring the dirty looks and odd hiss from the waiting customers.

It turned into an exuberant greeting session with the women behind the counter, with him calling out, "Awe, sista?" At one point Mabusela turned around jovially, called Ghaap to come over to him. "And for my friend, sisi, a Kentucky Rounder. He's a moegoe from the Kgalagadi, where they eat the chicken with feathers and all. And two min'ral, Creme Soda. To go, nè?" The women smiled benevolently at Ghaap, colourful earrings swinging against their dark cheeks. When the bill came, Mabusela turned around and started a loud conversation with someone in the queue. Ghaap gritted his teeth and paid, took the number of their order and walked outside again. It was stuffy inside, with so many people, and also the cooking-oil smells from the kitchen.

He stood watching the stream of traffic, mostly white minibus taxis with tired, dull faces staring blankly out of the windows. The traffic, still heavy, came to a standstill every now and again. A squad of hawkers, selling goods ranging from s'kop – boiled sheep's head – to cheap packs of sweets and salty snacks, darted to and fro among the stationary vehicles.

The traffic lights on this major arterial road were still not working, he noticed. The intersection was blocked with taxis. And where the road narrowed at the Rea Vaya bus lane, they simply ramped up pavements to overtake slower traffic. Or, where possible, drove through the veld.

Further away, he saw the Orlando cooling towers. People bungee-jumped from the top, he'd heard. You had to be off your head to do that, or pissed out of your mind, he decided. Or maybe you did it willingly if you'd lived long enough in this place.

Like a glimmering, pulsating ocean, Soweto lay sprawled in the night. Giant Eskom masts looked like rows of sci-fi giants marching into the township. Here and there you could see long ribbons of bright light – the big traffic routes, Klipspruit Valley Road and Old Potchefstroom Road. All the rest was dim and hazy, brooding under a blanket of smoke that hung suspended in the chilly night-time air. Close by, he saw a group of people clustered around a brazier. Probably taxi drivers, warming their hands and having a quick smoke while their customers were buying takeaways.

He returned his gaze to the sprawling city, the abandoned mine dumps resembling albino Karoo koppies, full of mystery. And the Apollo lights on tall stilts – the sharp, all-seeing eyes, remnants of the apartheid regime, glaring into the smokiness.

His thoughts turned to the Matthee woman and her child. Where could they possibly be in this place? And why hadn't their bodies been found yet? The possibility that they were still alive was very slight. Actually, he knew next to nothing about this kind of crime. Hell, what was there to hijack in the Kalahari? Donkey carts and skedonks? Or the clapped-out bakkies that most of the white farmers drove? And where, in any case, would you hide a stolen car? You had to drive hundreds of kilometres before you—

"Extra chips for the Kgalagadi blougat," said Mabusela, suddenly next to him. He held out the distinctive red-and-white box. Ghaap thought of commenting on his new nickname, but his mouth was watering too much. He wasn't used to eating fast food all day long. For one, it was too expensive – especially when his superiors made him foot the bill each time. Besides, there weren't any fast-food outlets in the Kalahari. Not enough salaried workers to keep them in business.

But the food smelled fantastic. He shoved a handful of chips into his mouth, only to spit them out again because they were as hot as hell.

Mabusela doubled over with laughter.

Ghaap soothed the burn with a long drink of his Creme Soda. His eyes were watering and his temper threatened to boil over. He dropped the box with the chips and chicken burger on the ground and stalked off to the van, too angry to bother about Mabusela's calls.

He called Beeslaar's number. It went directly to voicemail, but in his foul mood he had no desire to talk to a machine. He jerked open the door, climbed into the van, and saw Mabusela come running towards him, a box in his hand. Well, now: he'd actually picked the KFC up from the ground.

Ghaap decided to swallow his anger.

There was a commotion at the police station when they walked in, about half an hour after driving off from the KFC. They ran into S'bu Mthethwa in the passage. He greeted Mabusela loudly – "Howzit, butiza!" – but ignored Ghaap.

Ghaap walked to the office – a six-by-six-metre room crammed with far too many desks, cables lying everywhere, piles of dockets, and chairs of all sizes and ages. Rumour had it that new furniture and desks were on their way. The new kick-ass provincial commissioner wanted only the best for his men. Seeing was believing, Ghaap reckoned, but he kept this thought to himself.

A dushie with an opinion couldn't expect a long shelf life in this joint.

There was a kind of consensus among most of the cops here that made it hard for outsiders to become part of the circle. It wasn't a matter of people of colour being excluded. More an issue of background, Ghaap suspected. The black cops hung out in the shebeens. White guys drank in hotel bars or around a braai. The black cops preferred their pap-en-vleis at twelve rand a plate at one of the hundreds of backyard eateries in the district. That's when they weren't eating KFC, of course. And the white guys steered clear of the pap-en-vleis joints, didn't like eating with their hands. Or at least that's the impression he'd so far gained. Ghaap just fell in with the plans of whoever happened to be his senior officer for the day. Nothing to be done about it, that was the lot of his kind, he brooded, as he sat at an empty desk. Didn't really belong anywhere. Not black enough. But never white enough either. Just spectators.

He gave a long sigh and looked around for a pen. He still had a shitload of paperwork to complete, the fruit of the night's events. No sign of Mabusela coming to lend a hand. He could hear him, however: every few minutes or so, his laughter rang out.

Ghaap's phone beeped.

Duif, he saw on the screen. Did Ghaap have time for a head-office meeting, he wanted to know. *Have to work*, Ghaap messaged back. Hell, *someone* had better start putting the docket together.

57

Maaike van der Wiel was sitting at her kitchen table when Beeslaar rushed in. The table was a mess of blood and feathers. Vermeer the parrot's, alas.

The bird had been decapitated. Together with a severed wing, it lay on a bread board next to the sink. Beeslaar strode past, quickly searched the rest of the house, but found nothing. He returned to the kitchen, where Maaike was sitting with her head in her hands. His heart went out to the poor woman, although he couldn't go so far as sharing her grief about the bird.

"Maaike, I'm so sorry," he said. The dog stood with his paws against her leg and she scooped the animal up, clutching him tightly to her breast. He squirmed, jumped from her arms, sniffed around the kitchen floor, and gave a snort as a feather stuck to his nose.

"Who, Maaike?" Beeslaar asked, believing she knew very well who had been responsible. "Was it Andries April?"

She sniffed, but didn't look up.

Beeslaar opened a broom cupboard in the corner near the pantry, took out a dustpan and started sweeping up the feathers. Maaike sat motionless at the table. Devastated.

He stuffed the feathers into an empty plastic bag he'd found in the broom cupboard, added the bread board with the bird and all, and took the bag outside. Outside, he surveyed the surroundings for a while, the overgrown shrubs and trees. No shortage of hiding places for a thug. He phoned Qhubeka, asked her to drop by if she could.

Then he walked quickly to his own cottage, whose door was still wide open. He rummaged in his suitcase for the brandy. The expensive brand, Flight of the Fish Eagle, which he'd brought along to share with Blikkies.

Maaike hadn't stirred from her seat at the table, he saw when he returned to the kitchen. He put the bottle down, looked for glasses and some ice. Poured them both a generous tot.

With trembling hands, she picked up the glass and tossed the brandy down her throat.

He poured her another.

They sat sipping their drinks in silence. Every so often she gave a sniff, and wiped her eyes with the back of her hand.

"I think you should rather just tell me, Maaike," he eventually said. "Because if I read the signs correctly, there's someone who isn't very happy with you, right?"

She gulped, still looking away.

"And, by the way, I phoned Qhubeka. She'll be here soon."

"No! I don't want the cops here!"

"So you'd rather have someone doing to *you* what they did to Vermeer?"

She blew her nose.

"What's going on? Who are you so scared of? And what is it that they don't want you to tell me? It's April, isn't it? That's why he came to see you so early this morning? He came to threaten you, didn't he, Maaike?"

Almost imperceptibly, she inclined her head.

"So, *what* is it then?"

"He … I think, I … I should go back home," she said in a small voice.

"You mean back to Holland?"

"Yes, it's time."

Beeslaar took a small sip of the brandy, swilled it around in his mouth. Felt the fish eagle soaring. And the gentle landing, right at the back of his tongue.

"It's no longer safe for me here. To do my work." She remained seated a while longer and then stood up resolutely, as if she intended packing her bags right then and there. But instead she went to the kitchen cupboard, took out three plates, knives, forks, a salt and pepper set. Serviettes decorated with jolly Dutch cows. From the fridge she took an aluminium container covered in foil. A stew, Beeslaar saw as she removed the foil and put the dish into the oven.

"Just a few minutes, then we can eat," she said softly. "As soon as Vuvu gets here."

"I hope you decide against staying shtum with her too. She won't go as easy on you as I've done, you know. It's just a friendly word of warning."

Maaike said nothing, merely gulped.

Rembrandt announced Captain Qhubeka's arrival by jumping from his mistress's lap and rushing out the back door, barking fiercely.

Maaike dished up a huge helping of lentil and pumpkin stew for each of them. Beeslaar gazed warily at the steaming mound on his plate, not sure whether he was game for the small brown seeds. The two women noticed his hesitation, and he quickly shovelled a forkful into his mouth. To his surprise, the food was delicious, flavoured with Indian herbs and spices. He and Qhubeka emptied their plates simultaneously, and their hostess wordlessly ladled another helping for both of them, licking a spot of sauce off her hand as she did so.

"Ik heb Andries April—" Maaike began in Dutch.

"English, Maaike," Qhubeka gently reminded her, "my Dutch is rubbish."

"Godverdomme, but I wasn't speaking—"

"Yes, you were."

"Oh. Sorry. I ... I got to know Andries April through the CIC. It's for women and children, domestic violence victims. He brought a young mother and her daughter to us. The girl was raped by gangsters, her own father was a member of the very same gang. We ... Andries and me, we became friends. Many shared interests, you know?"

Beeslaar wasn't quite sure that he could see the shared interests, but he held his tongue and ate in silence.

"He had many plans, projects for the youth. He wanted to help young people stay out of gangs. To teach them about the veld, also about nature ..."

Beeslaar couldn't help himself, snorted involuntarily. The women ignored him.

"He *really* tried. There are so many single-parent families, no father ... unwanted babies, bad parenting. Poverty. What poverty *does* to you ... it takes your human dignity—"

"Okay, Maaike, we get the picture. But what does that have to do with Vermeer and with you? And why is he threatening you? Does it have anything to do with Elmana du Toit's death?"

Liewe Heksie recoiled at the mention of the name, squeezed her eyes shut, and took a deep breath.

"Yoga. I used to teach yoga. And she attended my class, just a few times. Here, at the house."

"Until about three months ago?" Beeslaar asked. He was struggling to visualise Liewe Heksie's dumpy body in a lotus position.

"Yes, I think so."

"Her mother's death," Beeslaar remarked to Qhubeka, who nodded in response.

"And then," Heksie continued, "late one night, very late, I caught Elmana here."

"What? Here, as in here – at your house?" Qhubeka asked.

"No. Yes."

"What on earth did she want from *you* in the middle of the night?"

"Nothing! She was with Andries. At the cottage, you see? He was still living here."

Qhubeka turned to Beeslaar. "The missing link," she said, using another of Blikkies's expressions.

"You're saying April sold her drugs, Maaike? Why didn't you say anything earlier?" Qhubeka's eyes were flashing. "If April killed her ... Hell, man, you were withholding evidence! You can go to prison for fucking ever!"

"No! That I can't say ... that she got her drugs from Andries. I never saw that!"

"But you *knew* there was something between them. And you kept quiet, Maaike? No, man! You may as well have lied, it's one and the same thing."

"Maybe Maaike should tell us about Vincent Ndlovu as well?" Beeslaar said.

Qhubeka snorted angrily, got up to pour herself a glass of water. She drained it before sitting down again, in a calmer frame of mind.

"Maaike," she said with a slight crack in her chocolate voice, "this has been a terribly, terribly long and difficult day. I don't want to end it with you in jail. So will you now *please* stop fucking around and start talking. Why did Vincent Ndlovu come to see you?"

"It was earlier, a few weeks ago. The healer in Kayamandi. The sangoma there. I … He sometimes sends people to me because I've done training, in the Swazi tradition, which—"

"Vincent Ndlovu, Maaike!" Qhubeka reminded her.

"Ag, ja. He was very stressed. And depressed. I tried to help him—"

"Did he say what was causing his stress?" Beeslaar interjected.

"He suffered from insomnia, stomache aches, couldn't eat. Anxiety. But, of course, I also knew that he … well, that he worked for Elmana, you know? I told him to go to Johan Erasmus. Doctor Han, the GP – near Kayamandi. I phoned him and told him why I wanted to send Vincent to him. That's why I know that Vincent didn't … Listen, Vuvu, he's not a killer."

"How on earth would *you* know, Maaike? Or are the spirits of the ancestors whispering this into your ear?" Qhubeka stood up and put on her jacket. "For the first time, I'm starting to believe that we've actually arrested the right man. Who else has a better motive than Vincent? I expect you at my office at eight o'clock tomorrow morning to make a statement, do you understand? And April? Why did he kill the bird? So that you wouldn't tell us Elmana got her drugs from him?"

Maaike looked up with a wounded expression. She inclined her head.

"Well, thank you very much. I have to go back to work. But first we need to get you into bed."

Maaike meekly assented.

Beeslaar got up, taking his brandy bottle and his half-drunk glass along with him. He turned around at the back door. "Just tell us again why you decided to kick April out as a tenant?"

She sighed. "It was not easy. Not very nice, you know? There were too many strange … you know, strange kinds of people that came here."

"What sort of strange people?"

She rubbed her head. "Just strange. I could feel it. The dark auras. I can't have that here, you understand? Especially one person, he used to visit often." She shuddered, said she didn't know what his name was because she only saw him, never spoke to him. He had tattoos all over his face – crosses on his eyelids and teardrops under one eye.

Qhubeka looked at Beeslaar: "A guy with a prison record. One teardrop for each murder, committed for his 'general'." Then she turned to Maaike and said, "Could you identify any other marks on him?"

Maaike shrugged, and Qhubeka gave a soft snort.

At that, Beeslaar said good night, and made tracks.

He switched on a light, a dim one, then sank down into an easy chair and stared at the wild dancing shadows of the trees outside his cottage. Not unlike the thoughts dancing in his mind, he realised.

If Andries April had been her supplier, and not Vincent Ndlovu … Why then did Ndlovu have the expensive earrings in his possession?

And why was April so afraid that Liewe Heksie would identify him as the supplier? Afraid, perhaps, that his political interests in the valley might suffer?

Or was it money? He didn't seem the type of guy who'd lose too much sleep over his public image. And what exactly had he wanted to convey to Beeslaar when they'd run into each other at Maaike's front gate?

He raised his glass, savoured the taste of the expensive brandy as he ran it over his tongue. Angel piss, pure and simple. You didn't adulterate this with Coke. That's something you added to a cheaper brand. Block-and-tackle, as the cops called it. Here in the Cape – or at Jan Cats, at least – he'd heard it called a "stoute Cokie" – a naughty little Coke.

Why keep picking at this thing, he asked himself. It wasn't *his* case. He didn't know this town. He didn't know the people. The only person he did know, was dead. And really, there was no reason for him to hang around here like a lost fart. He had attended Blikkies's funeral service. He'd said his final goodbyes. With an after-tears drink at Jan Cats. In the company of Qhubeka …

Was it she who was keeping him here? Or his own ego? He wanted to be the great hero. For her sake. Acting like a hotshot to impress a pretty woman. Hell, could he be any more pathetic?

But that wasn't the only reason. There was something floating around at the back of his mind. A shadowy thing. Which whispered to him that he had, in fact, already connected the dots. He was sitting right on top of it. It was something he'd seen somewhere. But what? Not at the funeral, not at the Mystic Boer, when he'd got motherless. Where, then? He slowly twirled his glass, and the ice cubes tinkled convivially. Was Qhubeka's boss catching any sleep tonight? Old Prammie.

Qhubeka had said he wasn't the kind of man who bowed easily to pressure from above. But today he'd done just that, and had walked all over Qhubeka in the process.

And he was bound to blow a gasket if he found out that Qhubeka was "consulting" with an outsider. An old-school has-been cop from the platteland, pretending to be Magnum PI in a town he knew sweet blow-all about. In fact, one he'd never even visited before. And where he'd come only because his best friend, hell, his *only* friend, the man who, for the past fifteen years … Could one say it? Could he allow himself to say it? … He'd regarded Blikkies as the father he never had? Annoyed with himself, he pressed the cold glass against his forehead. Why was he digging up the old skeletons? The fact was: he couldn't get the confusion and the contradictory feelings about this murder case out of his mind.

He took another swig. But the eagle was fast losing altitude – the ice was melting from the warmth of his hand. The bottle was close at hand, and so he "spilt" a dash into the glass.

He was startled by a soft knock at the door.

Qhubeka.

He let her in, produced another glass.

"There's no way I'm drinking that stuff," she said.

"What would you like, then?"

"Don't you have any cocoa – for chocolate milk?"

She followed him into the kitchen where he switched on the kettle for coffee.

"How are things over there?" He gestured towards the main house.

"I've summoned a female constable to spend the night with her. But she keeps insisting she never witnessed April peddling drugs."

"So why did she kick him out?"

"The 'strange' people, she says. The guy with the prison tats used to hang around here like a smelly fart. April claimed he was only a bit of a rough diamond. A difficult past – prison, gangs, the usual. He maintained that the guy had turned his life around, was now helping in the community. But Maaike says her antennas never lie. So she told April to leave."

"Do we have a name for the jailbird?"

She shook her head. "By the way, Ndlovu's alibi is supported by Doctor Han. I talked to his receptionist this afternoon. She confirmed it. They were very busy, she says, a long queue of patients. Doctor Han only saw Ndlovu somewhere between three and four on Tuesday afternoon, according to her books, but she remembers that he'd been waiting since the morning. Apparently there was an emergency, and the doctor fell behind. So the alibi isn't watertight, but it may hold up in court."

She took the mug from him, stirred in the three spoons of sugar he'd already added to the coffee.

"And what exactly is it that's wrong with him?"

"The doctor says it's nerves. And the rest he's not talking about, not without his patient's consent. But I bet my bottom dollar it's—"

"The Big Sick?"

"Quite so," she said, then walked back to the lounge, still stirring her coffee. "Which boosts the murder motive."

"It's against the law to fire someone for being HIV positive, though. Still, you're right. If his status were known, it'd make life difficult for him. Apart from the stigma in his community, the man works with food on a daily basis. And what about the earrings? How do you explain that?"

She peered at him over the rim of her mug. "They were found wrapped in a pullover in Ndlovu's wardrobe. He says it's a second-hand jersey of Malan du Toit's he got as a present from Elmana. He had put it straight into the cupboard, without unfolding it."

"Hm. Elmana's plan to get rid of Ndlovu? We know she'd been pretty paranoid lately. Maybe that's the reason she phoned both him and Kokkewiet Syster on the morning of her death, and asked both of them to come to her house. Maybe she'd intended to accuse him of theft in front of Kokkewiet."

She didn't seem convinced.

"And what happens to April now?" he asked.

She finished her coffee, smacked her lips in satisfaction, and put down the mug. "He's not my main problem right now. My problem is my boss, who won't exactly be thrilled that I'm digging up new evidence behind his back – and the prov com's back too, for that matter."

"Qhubeka, you either do this job properly or you go and peel potatoes at the fish-and-chips shop."

"Oh, please, that's the *last* thing the politicians at the top are interested in. Chasing results, the whole lot of them. Another arrest: check. Another murder solved within forty-eight hours: check."

Her eyes gleamed, then she wiped at them in annoyance and looked away. "I feel like I'm totally on my own in this thing. I don't know—"

Beeslaar's phone rang. Ghaap. He didn't answer. "Hang on, let's tackle this thing systematically. Number one," he said, "is to pick up Andries April for questioning. And number two is to find out why the Du Toits are lying through their teeth. You have to rattle them. Up to now, they've been treated with kid gloves. And you shouldn't waste any time either. When your Prammie boss clocks in tomorrow morning, you need to be ready for him. With new evidence. Convincing evidence. And even if the politicians threaten you with suspension, you fight back. But you fight back with new evidence, deliver the goods. Once you've capitulated, your career is finished. Then you could just as well join the speed parras, writing parking tickets for the rest of your life!"

"Anything else, Boss Beeslaar?" She grimaced, though not in a hostile way.

"Someone needs to interrogate Ellie properly – trauma or no trauma."

She didn't reply, and they sat in silence for a while until Beeslaar asked: "Do you know where April lives?"

"Somewhere in the valley. With the group that's refusing to move off the land and is agitating for permanent tenure."

"Where?"

"Up in Assegaaibosch. Next to Cape Nature, the research station."

"And the group, who are they exactly?"

"They're from farmworker families – most of them, anyway. Some are still employed in the valley, others work for the forestry department, and a number of them are just vagrants. They started protesting a few months ago when two families were evicted and moved to the town. The owner of the land wanted to sell, or something. And one of the new owner's conditions was that there should be no workers on the land."

"That's illegal, isn't it?"

"Too right, you are. But when you've got the money for palm-oiling—"

"Palm-greasing," he corrected her.

"Whatever!" Impatient, a hint of the old Qhubeka in her voice. "I mean, the families were given a sort of severance package. But you know how it goes. Money bends the law whichever way it wants. And I suspect that *there*, laws were bent like crazy. The new owner converted the cottages into guest accommodation. And then one of his vineyards burnt down, no one knew how the fire started, et cetera. I'm just giving you the short version. Next, the new owner's car was stoned in the middle of the night as he drove up to his farm gate. The man's face had to be stitched up. Some of the stones were quite big.

"Anyway, our Mr April became active among the group. Suddenly there were protest marches and blocked roads and placards. And April holding forth in the press about the injustices of the whites who want to turn the valley into one big golf estate ... blah blah fish paste."

Beeslaar put down his glass. "So why don't we go and pay a visit to Mr April?"

"*Now?*"

"Let's go," he said and stood up.

58

The boy kept staring in the direction of the place they'd just come from.

"We must move, Mpho," Gerda said as she glanced back too. There was nothing to see.

She found it hard to get her feet, impeded by the dead weight of Kleinpiet's sleeping body. She struggled to manoeuvre him across her bump. And she didn't want to put him down, determined that this child would never leave her arms again.

The air was getting colder. This was typical of the Highveld autumn, Gerda knew. Hot days, but the nights could be frosty. She could see that Mpho was shivering. Perhaps it wasn't the cold so much as his fear of "The Fatha". The boy's bloodstained T-shirt was testimony to that. In places, the fabric was in shreds, which stuck to his scabs. She noted the slight body, the sharply protruding bones of his back, his unkempt hair. Her Neiltjie would have started Grade R this year. And while his build had been more solid, by now he might have been as tall as this boy – who was twice his age.

"Mpho," she said softly, "where are we?"

No reply.

"Mpho!" She repeated the question in a sharp whisper.

He shrugged.

"Where are your real parents?"

The boy didn't turn around. He sat blowing on his hands, his gaze fixed on a spot in the veld, slightly to their left.

"Thula," he eventually said, and looked back at her for a second. She saw the dark skin, and the whites of his eyes seemed to shine out of the little face.

"Mpho, why did you hijack us? And where's your brother?"

"He make jabu pule – very fast. He want the car. Strong car. Sell it. The sharkboys, they—" He clapped his hands together, miming a collision.

"Crash?"

"Ja. They take big smeka. Money. Big mountain."

"You took us because you wanted the car?"

"No, no. The car we sell. The sharkboys, they use that car for the cash vans, the vans with the smeka."

"Okay, so they use the car to … to *crash* the cash vans?" Then it dawned on her: transit heists! "But what about us? What were you planning to do with us?"

"Is business."

"How do you mean, business?"

"Mama, no talk please."

"What business, Mpho?"

"Umlungu business."

"A white man?"

"Yes. No. Look like dushie, but he kwerekwere. He want the business. He pay big smeka for the business."

She understood some of what he was saying, the patois used by black urban youth. She'd heard some of the words at the school where she worked. She asked him who the kwerekwere was, the foreigner.

"No! No more talk."

"The animal, what is it? Why does it smell so—"

"Shaka. He stink. Wash with Colgate shampoo." They sat quietly for a while. But she was itching to get moving, conscious of the persistent pain in her pelvis. Her Lara child was signalling her imminent arrival.

She pushed herself up, levering her weight against the cold concrete as she peered into the darkness of the huge pipe. Maybe there were houses at the other end, some place where they could get help? She was about to suggest this, but he brusquely shushed her. Then, gingerly, she stepped into the darkness of the pipe.

The road above must be very wide, if the length of the aqueduct was anything to go by. She couldn't see an opening at the other end. It was too dark outside, in any case. With Kleinpiet at her hip, she tried to feel her way along the curve of the pipe. But the child's weight soon became too much. She rested a while, resisting the temptation to sit down – she wouldn't be able to get up again. She looked back at the seated figure of Mpho, which was barely discernible in the dark. She wondered what he was on the lookout for. Did he expect that "The Fatha" would pursue them? That he'd suddenly materialise out of the darkness? She herself had a sense that the man could move about soundlessly. She shuddered, goosebumps running down her back and legs. But the thought propelled her to walk deeper into the dark pipe.

She recalled a minor subject she'd once studied, a mere filler. Heavens, that was more than twenty years ago. Anthropology. The dying days of apartheid, and the condescending way in which African beliefs had been described in a textbook. Malignant wizards and witches that practised black witchcraft: abaThakathi, pronounced with a soft "k" – "abaTagathi". She didn't believe the stories. Tales of wizards and witches that rode on the backs of baboons and hyenas at night to do their evil work, robbing graves and creating zombies. Magicians able to transform themselves – into an owl, or a leguan.

UmThakathi. A witchdoctor who'd held her and her child in his clutches these past days. She had sensed the evil in that place. It had emanated from the woman, too.

Gerda's legs began to give way. She was so thirsty that her tongue stuck to her palate. She leant against the cold, curved surface of the pipe, slowly slid down to her haunches. Her heart was pounding against her ribcage. Dear God, she had to hold on. Cautiously, she palpated her belly, Kleinpiet groaning as she shifted him. She could feel nothing. She closed her eyes, tried focusing on the unborn child, as she had whenever she felt depressed in recent months: leaning inward and listening, sensing her daughter. Pink little bushbaby, gently drifting inside her. She could hear her, could even imagine her sucking her thumb, could project the clear golden warmth of her love onto her ... *You're safe, my dearest child. Please just hold on a while longer. Mamma will get us away from the nastiness. Just a little while ...*

She'd make it. The three of them together ... She dropped her head and pressed her son's face against her own. His warm little body gave her courage, hope and strength. She *would* get up again. She *would* walk out of here with her child in her arms. She *would* get help. If she could just make it to the nearest house. Any ordinary house, where you'd find warmth and care and African hospitality. Because *that* was the Africa that she knew. And loved.

Not the scare stories of her youth. No. A thousand times no. Not the delusional phobias of her father.

She nuzzled her child's neck, felt its soft folds, rubbed the rosebud of his ear with her nose. He moaned slightly. He'd been so quiet, maybe still a bit drugged. Normally she'd be worried sick about it, but perhaps it was a blessing in disguise, given the circumstances. "We're going to make it, my boy," she whispered to him. "We've come this far. This far, now we just need to persevere a while longer ... never say die. Try, try and try again. Brave little boer makes a plan. Little ducklings waddling to the dam. The three of us all in a row, there are good people here too. More good than bad, just believe, believe, believe."

The cold against her back intensified. She had to move.

UmThakathi. She *knew* this was no myth. It was this sort of thing that had pushed ... she couldn't bear to even speak his name ... that had pushed him over the edge. Him and Albertus ... when they were colleagues in the dog unit. The horror stories. They never wanted to tell her. But she always knew when they were dealing with that kind of case. Where people had been chopped up for muti. Children, sometimes. That one time, when he ... the father of her sons ... was hitting the bottle. Hard. Didn't sleep a wink, just sat in the dark lounge, waking with a scream the moment he dozed off. She'd tried to get him to a doctor, for sleeping pills, psychological help. But he'd refused. "I don't give in," was all he'd said. "My two friends and I," he'd told her, raising his pistol, his other hand on the head of his dog, Sakdoek. His working dog, who had helped him sniff out corpses. Kept him company on nights like that. "The three of us. We don't give in. Let the fuckers come!"

On days off he'd sometimes occupy himself with the dog to the exclusion of everything else. The children weren't allowed near the animal. "He's a fuckin' working dog, not a toy," he'd snarled once as he chased Neiltjie away.

Once, he'd been drunk enough to tell her. About the child without a head or hands. The "thakathi" harvested the body parts "live", otherwise the muti didn't work. The lips, the ears, the eyes. They'd be sold for thousands. A hand that you'd build into the foundations of a new shop – to beckon to new clients. Albertus and he had gone looking for the child's head. A six-year-old Soweto boy, who hadn't returned from school the day before.

The corpse was found between two pillars of a cement fence next to the railway line. The little body stuffed into a narrow opening. The head had been severed with a tree saw that lay on the other side of the fence, and the tiny penis sliced off.

Later that day her husband and his dog had found the head, its ears, eyes, tongue and lips missing. The brain had been scooped out. The plundered head had been flung carelessly onto a roof, among old tyres and stones.

Gerda shuddered. She had to move, get away. She pushed with her elbows and back against the concrete curve. Halfway up, another contraction wracked her body. She almost dropped the child, stood swaying and gasping for breath. As the pain started to abate, she straightened up again. They had to get moving. They'd been sitting here far too long. It felt like hours. She glanced back towards Mpho, still visible in the distance. She called to him softly, but he didn't stir.

He stood watching. Like a bewitched bird in a trap. She started walking again, picking her way carefully. It was hard going. The pipe was strewn with rubbish, old rusted tins that creaked when she trod on them, papers licking at her legs. She stifled a scream when something scurried over her feet. Rats. She heard their squealing. Keep moving. If her strength deserted her now, the rodents would have no qualms feeding on them all.

She stopped short. A deep growl came from the darkness ahead of her. She held her breath, listened attentively. Kleinpiet began to stir in her arms. Then she heard it again. The ominous growling, from deep inside the chest of a giant animal. This was no dog. *That* she knew. She retreated a few steps, paused to listen. The sound came again. Closer. The Beast! She could smell it!

She spun round and blindly fled back. Towards the dim light. And the silhouette of the child who had leapt to his feet.

59

Qhubeka's van sped along the road leading out of town. Up a slope, past the historic Lanzerac Hotel. The road was quiet, thanks to the late hour. At the end of an incline, Du Toit's construction board loomed, glinting in the light from the scrap of moon that had just risen above the jagged mountain peaks.

Qhubeka turned on the high-beam headlights. "This development will lead to a lot of bloodshed on this land, mark my words." She slowed down. "Look out for a small gravel road to your left," she said. "There are no signboards."

She suddenly veered off and followed a bumpy track up a steep incline. They came to a clearing among some trees. Lights were burning in the two rows of labourers' cottages.

Qhubeka stopped the van, checked her pistol, and climbed out, followed by Beeslaar.

A group of men were sitting around an open fire. When they spotted the van, one of them stood up: Andries April. He didn't come towards them, waited for Qhubeka and Beeslaar to walk up to him and his circle. As they approached the men, Beeslaar smelt the dagga. At the fire, he noticed that some of the eyes were bloodshot. "Hos!" one of the seated men called out. "The boere are paying a visit!"

April stood, his arms folded.

"Mr April," Qhubeka began, "is there somewhere we can talk in private?"

He shook his head.

"Or would you prefer to accompany us into town – to the police station?"

One of the men turned his head to the side and spat. "On what charges?" he demanded, his chin jutting defiantly. Beeslaar recognised the man: black teardrops under his left eye. He had seen this man before. Then it struck him: it was the fellow who'd picked up Rea du Toit's handbag at the murder scene, the one Liewe Heksie had spoken about earlier that evening.

"And who, may I ask, are you?" Qhubeka rested her hand lightly on the holster at her hip.

April came forward. "Sit down, Quentin. They're looking for me."

Qhubeka didn't back down: "I've asked you for your name, or are you deaf?"

"Quentin, mammie, but my true friends call me Swiff – as in spliff, djy weet?" Then he leered at Qhubeka, flicking his tongue suggestively in the gap between his front teeth.

"Shuddup, Quentin," said April, a threatening look in his eyes.

But Quentin was enjoying the limelight. "I have respect for the law, my bru. Respect for the law, which puts our brothers on the floor. Respect for the gattas who call the shots on the Vlaktes!" The rest of the group giggled.

"Your name!" Qhubeka thundered.

"I've mos already told the sisi merrim. Swiff as in stiff!" Balling his fist, he obscenely mimed sexual thrusts.

The next moment, Qhubeka's pistol was out and she had knocked the man to the ground. She put her knee on his back, pinning him to the ground. In a flash, the pistol was back in the holster, the handcuffs out, and closed around his wrists.

She bounced to her feet, yanking the man up as she did so, then marched him wordlessly to the van and bundled him into the back. Quentin was squealing like a pig, cursing in what seemed to be every South African language, and accusing Qhubeka of being a "horrible Xhosa meid" – just one of a string of insulting epithets.

Beeslaar observed the alarm that had come over April's face. As soon as he became aware of Beeslaar's gaze, he looked down, started walking towards the van. He climbed meekly into the back, ignoring his comrade's mocking and moaning.

They drove back in silence, Qhubeka grumpy and stony behind the wheel. And with a heavy foot on the accelerator.

Her office was a modest room on the second floor of the big police station. She shared it with Charmainetjie and another colleague. Atop a steel filing cabinet stood a yellowing plant that was in dire need of water. The rest looked like any office in any police station the world over.

She made coffee, took some rusks from a tin she kept locked up in a cupboard.

Beeslaar helped himself to two rusks, Maaike's lentil dish earlier that evening a distant memory.

"And what if your boss had to rock up now, Qhubeka?"

Her reply was a regal stare – she was in control of her territory again. "He also knew Oom van Blerk, after all."

She gave an instruction for April to be fetched from the cells.

When he arrived, he looked considerably more timid, Beeslaar thought, than he had during their encounter at Liewe Heksie's gate. The man sat staring grimly at his hands in his lap.

"Well, then!" Qhubeka began. "Get wise and tell the gattas where you were between two and four on Tuesday afternoon."

He replied soberly: "Grafting."

269

"And who can confirm that?"

"My boss."

At Qhubeka's command, he supplied the name and phone number of his regional head, a Mr Adams. Beeslaar left the room to call him. After fuming for a while at being bothered "in the middle of the night" for "shit", the man finally confirmed that April had participated in a regional meeting on Tuesday.

"But what's going on? Why are you harassing our people again? Who's your commander? I demand to speak to him. Now!"

Beeslaar sighed and gave him Pram Baadjies's name, but added that he would only be in the office again the next day. The man calmed down.

"Mr April hasn't been arrested, he's helping us with our enquiries into a murder investigation," Beeslaar said.

"Helping? This time of the night? You must be joking!"

"One of our officers will come past your office tomorrow to take a statement. If that suits you? Ja? Then I'll say goodbye for now." Beeslaar ended the call. He wasn't in the mood for an argument, at least not with a guy who sounded as if he'd quaffed a few nightcaps and had already taken out his teeth for the night.

He slipped back into Qhubeka's office and whispered in her ear that Adams had confirmed April's alibi. She nodded, her eyes fixed on April.

Beeslaar went and stood against the desk next to Qhubeka's. He had a clear view of the man's dreadlocks that reminded him of sausage rolls. He became aware of heartburn. Had to be Liewe Heksie's lentils, he decided. Lentils were seeds, and seeds were for the birds.

"Where were you tonight between eight and nine?" asked Qhubeka.

"Nowhere."

"You were at Maaike van der Wiel's house."

"I was at the place where you people came to pick me up. I've been hanging out there from the time Maaike kicked me out."

"Why don't you tell Captain Beeslaar when you started supplying Elmana du Toit with tik?" She motioned towards Beeslaar with her coffee mug.

April shot a nervous glance at Beeslaar, concentrated again on his mottled hands. "Don't know her," he mumbled.

"Excuse me?" Qhubeka raised her eyebrows. "You were her pusher, Mr April. Of course you knew her."

April gave a slight shake of his head.

"That's what you were doing at her house on Tuesday afternoon. But then things went wrong, didn't they?"

This time his reply was two barely perceptible shakes.

"Ag, come on, Mr April. All of a sudden you with your big mouth have nothing to say for yourself? Just let it all out, man, tell us what happened at

Elmana du Toit's house on Tuesday afternoon! And why you shot her. And where your gun is now."

April sat upright in his chair, his eyes darting nervously from Beeslaar to Qhubeka. He took a deep breath and said: "I haven't *got* a gun!"

Beeslaar's blood was up, he could smell the man's fear. "For a weasel like you, you're moerse cheeky with the gattas, hey?" he barked, mimicking the Cape slang. "Or are you looking for a lekker fat snotklap? You can choose, but I bet you Captain Qhubeka here klaps much harder than me."

He winked as he caught Qhubeka's eye, which had a twinkle. "He schemes he's confusing us when he throws the gangster lingo, hey? He thinks we don't get it, so he can mess with our heads! He schemes he's sitting here spinning kak stories to two doosheads, but if he doesn't watch out, he'll see his arse. He can be sure of that, nè, Captain Qhubeka?"

"I've got nothing to do with that antie," April said defensively. "I've only heard some of the skinner from the guys here."

"What sort of stories did you hear?" Qhubeka asked.

"That she smaaks zol. And she's rolling in bucks. That's just what an ou hears, nè, when an ou's tjommies are talking shit and passing around the papsak."

Beeslaar again felt his irritation rise. "It seems to me this man's looking for a PK. Hey, April?"

He shifted in his chair, away from Beeslaar. Qhubeka looked up, puzzlement in her eyes. "It's a special kind of klap," Beeslaar explained. "You don't say the name in front of ladies. But I have to tell you, mister," he said to April, "my hand's itching! Just carry on with this shit and you'll soon know all about it!"

"Let's start again," Qhubeka intervened, "and this time you stop making jokes, and you stop lying, Mr April."

April dropped his head, the dreadlocks hiding his face. "I didn't kill her."

"Volume, April," Beeslaar said. "Use your fokken speakers! And you can also give Captain Qhubeka the names of those okes you were bottlenecking with around that fire!"

A theatrical sigh. "I did nothing. Nothing. And I don't have to talk to you people either. And this is an unlawful arrest, ek sê."

Beeslaar bent down, his breath stirring the fine hairs that had escaped the dreadlocks. "Mrs du Toit was seen visiting your place at all hours of the night," Beeslaar said. "During the time you stayed in Miss van der Wiel's cottage. And now you're going to tell us why she was there, okay?"

"This is intimidation," April muttered.

Beeslaar leant even closer, and turned up his own volume: "EK SÊ, start TALKING!".

"She hassled me. For zol. That's all. But I didn't do anything to her."

271

"I don't want to know about the dagga, April. I'm asking what ELSE there was!"

"Nyaope," he mumbled.

"Kak, man! That's what the darkies from Joburg smoke. Now talk!"

"She schemed she could score a lolly or two from me."

"Tik."

"Tik, yes. But she had the wrong address, I'm telling you! I don't carry the heavy stuff!"

Qhubeka rolled her eyes.

"No," Beeslaar snapped at him, "but you get it from your good friend Swiff-as-in-spliff! Don't worry, we'll get round to him in a minute."

April's leg was bouncing rhythmically. "She probably schemed she … She *did* come there," he said. "But she came to visit the Dutch koeksuster, not me. And why are you tuning *me* now? I know you people have arrested that bantu bro!"

He looked up at Qhubeka from under his woolly locks.

"Your stories are getting too complicated, Mr April. First you say that Mrs du Toit wanted to score dagga from you, and next you talk about koeksusters – are you insinuating she had a lesbian relationship with Maaike van der Wiel?"

April kept mum, his eyes darting around.

"Start over!" she ordered.

"She ambushed me. Stopped me at the gate, offered me a lift. Asked if I had a gwaai for her, you know? Zol. We, er, we smoked some zol. Then she dropped me in town. And she tuned she wanted my number."

"And you considered it normal that someone like Elmana du Toit would want to have *your* cellphone number."

He thought a moment. "I might just be coloured rubbish to you people, but—"

"We know damn well who you are. What we don't know is why you hang out with lowlifes like Quentin. Or is it part of the political action plan there in the valley?"

"He's nothing to me, fokkol! He was just sitting there talking kak with the brasse, smoking with the ous. But me, I've got nothing to do with him. My one and only mission is to protect the oppressed people of the valley, to make sure they aren't once again robbed of their own land!"

"And you do this by burning down landowners' vineyards and stoning their cars?"

He shook his head vigorously.

"So what were you doing there tonight with Quentin and the other zol heads?"

"It's where they live, my clients. And at the moment I'm homeless. So I'm kipping there at night until I go back to Wellington."

"Clients?"

"Of our NGO, for the people who get kicked off the farms. The people with the family trees that go back to the old slave days. And the Khoikhoi. That whole valley. It's not a happy valley. It was land that belonged to the slaves. Like half of all the business areas in this town—"

"Okay, April." Beeslaar felt a burn in the back of his throat, promised himself never to eat lentils again. "Just drop the history lesson. Tell us how helpful the 'friendship' with Mrs du Toit has been to you in the *real* fight: the one against Malan du Toit and his development."

April took a deep breath, looked around, seemingly for inspiration for his next lie. Eventually, he said: "No ways, man, the antie, she was ... lonesome. Wanted to tune a bit of kak with another person. Just have a chat and smoke a zolletjie. That's all."

"She must have been damn lonely if she sought *you* out for company," Beeslaar muttered. "But she was an easy target, nè? You blackmailed her. Extorted money from her, not so? Or was her *husband* the one you black-mailed?"

"No *ways*. Jissus, man!"

Qhubeka stood up, brushed some crumbs from her bosom. "Just say it, April, in plain language. So that we can make progress, because it's turning into a really long night. Elmana du Toit had developed a taste for tik. She couldn't get it from Ndlovu because *he* was too shit scared. Then *you* became her supplier. You were just a *pusher*, not her bosom buddy. A pusher. Is that what you were doing at her house on Tuesday? Making a drop? You schemed you were clever. Hitting Malan du Toit in a soft spot, where you knew you could hurt him?"

"And you used a woman for your dirty work?" Beeslaar added.

April kept shaking his drooping head. He was clearly aware of the two pairs of tired, irritated eyes fixed on him.

"Okay. Her and me, we shared a zol. So what? And then she tunes me that she has to graft so hard. Her energy's finished – she needs a bit of go. If I can maybe hook her up, see? So that she can feel more lively. She wants lollies." He paused a moment, his mouth working as he concentrated. "The Lord knows, I don't *touch* that rubbish myself. It's the devil's own dope, that stuff. Makes you crazy. And *she* – that woman was slowly becoming a heavy disaster area."

"And she paid you well for your services, no doubt." Beeslaar folded his arms across his chest, leant back so that he could see the man's face.

Silence.

"Answer the captain!" Qhubeka said sharply. "We want to go home, not just sit here listening to your performance!"

April cleared his throat. "I've got nothing to do with her husband. I couldn't care what he does. And yes, she was on a mission. But she's a larney goose. She couldn't just jol into the smokkie to get her stuff, mos. And I could help her. I know the tjommas you can score from."

"You call that 'help'? And who was *your* supplier?"

April fidgeted. "I don't even *have* someone like that. I don't do that kind of business. One of the outjies said there's a man who chills at a smokkie there by Idas Valley. Snake, they call him. He's got a snake tattoo on his neck. And that's all."

"You're talking shit, man. For how long did you feed her tik?"

"I didn't 'feed' her anything! I only gave directions. But the koek … Maaike, she's sharp, she checked Miesies du Toit when she came to see me. Next thing, I'm thrown out of my pozzie 'cos Maaike doesn't smaak it when the people come looking for me. And I didn't even do anything wrong. Just ask Appollis and Adams. I work with them. We fight for the surplus people. The poorest of the poor. And the landless. And the reason we're fighting is to keep people away from rubbish like tik."

Qhubeka stretched her back and her arms, and walked back to her chair. "Yes, April. And your tjommie, Mr Swiff? He's not from around here, is he? His tats, they're Mitchells Plain. So, which gang's he from?"

"I don't know him," April mumbled.

"But you sit smoking with him around the fire? Let's try again."

"His name's Quentin. He's from the Flats."

"Quentin who?"

"Quentin Latief Daniels. He just came to score some zol."

Beeslaar bent down to his face, smelt the anxiety. "You mean he came to make a drop. It's from him that you buy the tik, nè? And in whose team is he? Which gang?"

"I don't know nothing about that," April said.

"You're lying, April." Beeslaar straightened up. "Have we taken his fingerprints?" he asked Qhubeka. "Shoe prints too?"

One of the uniformed guys in the service room had already taken care of that, she replied.

April sat hunched over, as if he were about to vomit. The man's nerves were shot, Beeslaar thought, and then asked: "Are you sticking to your story about Tuesday, April?"

A long silence.

Then he gave in: "I did have to make some deliveries, especially lately, when she needed the stuff badly."

"And Tuesday. You were there on Tuesday too. And you probably lit the lollie for her too, didn't you?"

April sat bolt upright, his face pale. "No. Fok, man, I swear I wasn't there. I thought maybe the goose found herself a new dealer 'cos she'd stopped hassling me. I schemed, maybe she'd gone cold turkey, stopped taking the stuff. I wasn't even *near* that place on Tuesday."

"Yes, but your best pal, Mr Swiff, was there!"

"No! I told you, I've got nothing to do with him. Genuine. I'm not lying. You can go check – outside, at the swimming pool pump. That's where she kept her tackle."

"Come," said Beeslaar, "Captain Qhubeka has a lot of work to do. And she still needs to catch a bit of sleep before tomorrow. But first you're going to show us."

60

Warrant Officer Bandile Mabusela fetched Ghaap from the office, where he was still busy with his docket. He wanted him to sit in on the interrogation of the suspect who'd been apprehended in the stolen Dolly Parton.

Just a kid, Ghaap realised in surprise, as he walked into the room, looked barely eighteen.

His bottom lip was split and swollen, one eye beaten to a pulp. He sat, handcuffed hands in his lap, his feet in worn-out trainers, swinging to and fro. So this was what one of Soweto's formidable carjackers looked like? A real live jackroller? Unbelievable …

Mthethwa gave Ghaap a dirty look before he turned to the boy and asked him his age. He received a mumbled reply.

"Speak up!" the cop shouted. He switched to Tswana, but the youth shook his head. He was thin, with greyish patches on his dark skin. Every now and again he licked at the bloody cut on his lip.

"What's your name?" Mthethwa pushed his notebook towards Ghaap, who took it with an inward sigh.

"I did nothing," he replied.

"Your name!"

"Lucky."

"Surname?"

The boy's eyes were downcast, and his small frame seemed to shrivel even further with embarrassment. No father, it seemed.

Ghaap wrote down the information.

"Who do you work for?" asked Mabusela, more restrained than his colleague.

"I did nothing," was all the boy said. He seemed afraid. Afraid of something other than the two huge cops in front of him.

Ghaap sat to one side, notebook and pen at the ready.

"Lucky, why did you hijack the umlungu woman and her child?" Mabusela leant over the table to stress the seriousness of the situation. "We caught you with the very transi she was hijacked in. The big car, man. So don't you tell lies here by us. We don't like it when people lie. Just tell us, where are the woman and her child?"

Lucky stared at his knees.

"Where did you take them? And where do you live? Who's your authi? Does he live with you? Or is your mama on her own?"

One of the boy's fingernails was torn, Ghaap noticed; blood oozed from it. The injury must have happened at the same time he'd taken the blows to his face. His bloodstained T-shirt was torn under the sleeve and at the neck.

Mthethwa snorted and stood up, tapped Mabusela on the shoulder and called him to the door. They signalled to Ghaap that they were going out for a smoke.

Ghaap remained seated, stared at the frail figure that sat rocking dejectedly on his chair.

"So you're one of the famous jackrollers of Soweto?" Ghaap said.

"I didn't do it," said the boy, glancing up at Ghaap through a bloodied brow.

"Who hit you like that?"

"Where?"

The reply caught Ghaap by surprise. He stood up and walked over to the boy, lifted the scrawny arms, handcuffs and all. The skin was covered with scars and bruises, some fresh, others yellowing. The boy flinched in his chair, as if he were expecting a blow to the head. Ghaap lifted the shirt and looked down on a bony back that carried the red welts of a recent beating. A sjambok caused injuries like that, Ghaap knew.

"Who hit you like that?"

The boy shook his head.

"You don't have to be scared, Lucky. I'm not with those two cops. I'm very against beating up people. I'll give you protection."

Lucky stared at him in disbelief, and Ghaap smiled encouragingly. There was a chink in this armour. And if that bully boy Mthethwa were to smoke for long enough, Ghaap might be able to get through to this young man.

"Where's your brother? The little one who helped you to take the white woman and her child?"

Lucky's eyes clouded over but he said nothing, his chin set determinedly.

"You see, we know your brother was with you. Because there are many people who saw the two of you, okay?"

No response.

Ghaap waited, started drawing a picture of a horse in his notebook. The little brother, he mused, might be the instrument he could use to crack this hard-arsed little shit. He sat sketching for a while. The ears were too big. The animal looked like a cross between a rabbit and a donkey.

"Is he safe, your brother?"

Ghaap didn't raise his eyes, but he knew Lucky was looking at him.

"I can give him protection too," Ghaap remarked casually. "Him and you, together. 'Strue's Bob and fo' sho'. What do you say?"

"No, themba," the boy sighed, despairingly. Ghaap felt helpless. What the hell did "themba" mean?

277

Lucky looked at Ghaap, seeming to appraise him. Then he dropped his head and started rocking again, like someone in urgent need of a pee. All the while, he picked at the torn nail. He must have a helluva high pain threshold, Ghaap imagined.

He started on a new drawing of a horse.

"The Fatha," Lucky said softly.

Ghaap's heart jumped, but he feigned absorption in his sketching. After a while the boy spoke again.

"We give him trouble, he kwatile. Angry," he translated for Ghaap's benefit.

"Is he your father?"

Lucky shook his head vehemently but repeated, "The Fatha." He looked around him anxiously, kept glancing towards the door. But Ghaap knew it wasn't Mthethwa that he feared – it was this man he called The Fatha.

"Who is he? Why are you with him, Lucky?"

"He's the Big Man. Big Man. We work for him. We must do the gryps – handbags and things on taxis, trains. Everything."

"What is that? You steal for him?"

Lucky looked down, shifted uncomfortably.

"Your brother too?"

"No! Not him. He is too small."

"Don't be scared, Lucky. We're cool, okay? You're safe here. All the gattas here, they won't let the, um, The Fatha come and beat you. Okay?"

Lucky looked away.

"Where's the woman from the car, Lucky? And your brother? Where are they?"

A vehement shake of the head. Too vehement, Ghaap reckoned, but he let it go for the moment. Started on yet another horse. The previous one hadn't come out too well either. He'd always wanted a horse of his own, even as a child. But his mom had just laughed.

"The car you took, was that for The Fatha?" he said after a while.

A nod.

"Why?"

"Business."

"What kind of business, Lucky?"

"Umlungu business. He very kwata. Vrostana?" he said, and drew his finger across his throat.

"Ja, I think I 'vrostana' what you're trying to say, Lucky. I get it. I'll make sure he doesn't touch you. He won't come here. He doesn't like this place, the bokgatas' place."

"He like it fokkol." His face brightened momentarily.

278

"Where's The Fatha's place, Lucky? That woman and her baby that you guys took. We have to help that woman. You can help us. You just have to talk to us. No lying, nè? No lies. We won't let that man get his hands on you."

The boy sighed. It was an old person's sigh, world-weary.

"Chicken Farm," he heard Lucky whisper.

Ghaap realised he didn't have a clue where Chicken Farm was. But he knew he'd heard the name somewhere, it was a residential area of Soweto.

He stood up, saw how Lucky shrank back in his chair. "Chill, man, I won't do anything to you, nè." He sat on his haunches next to him. "Focus," he said, pointing his two forefingers at Lucky's frightened eyes and then at his own. "I promise you, you're safe. That bastard won't hit you again, 'strue's Bob. Okay? I, Johannes Ghaap, I'm telling you now. You vrostana?"

Big pleading eyes looked at Ghaap as he nodded uncertainly.

"You stay here. I'm going to call our boss and he'll tell you the same thing, okay?"

Ghaap stuck his nose out of the door and spotted his two colleagues, still chatting and smoking at the far end of the corridor. He whistled, and as they looked up, he beckoned to them.

"Where's Chicken Farm?" Ghaap asked when they were within hearing distance.

Mthethwa laughed. "You after some jollies for the night?" he said mockingly.

"That's where the kidnapped woman and her child are."

"Says who – that little shit in there?" Mthethwa sneered. "You don't know the amajitas around here. You think he looks so young and innocent, next thing he slits your throat. I won't believe a word—"

"There's a guy there," Ghaap insisted. This time he appealed to Mabusela. "Sounds like a proper mafia boss or something. Lucky and some other kids – I don't know how many – they work for him."

But Mthethwa refused to budge: "He's talking kak. There's only cockroaches there. Lovas and skebengas."

"What's he talking about?" Ghaap asked Mabusela.

"Thugs and loafers, unemployed people. So, what did you do to get the boy talking?"

"For starters, I didn't hit him," Ghaap said, shooting a glance in Mthethwa's direction. "But he says the man's called 'The Fatha.'"

Mabusela and Mthethwa exchanged glances, then looked at Ghaap. Both cops smiled, and Mthethwa said, "It's just a rubbish story, Ghaap. They say it's an umThakathi."

"A what?"

"Sangoma. But it's rubbish."

"The guy's shit scared as he sits there. But not of you," he said to Mthethwa. "He's scared of something much worse. I don't know if you had a good look at him. You can see he's often beaten with a sjambok. Until he bleeds. Did you see what he looks like? His arms and his legs?"

"The Fatha is an urban legend, Sergeant Ghaap, to frighten the kids when they're naughty. Ask anyone who grew up around here."

"But why would the boy lie to me? And why's he been beaten like that? You can see he's been abused like that for a long time."

"Man, most of the tsotsis in this place look like that. Many of their injuries come from fighting. Knife fights. So, he's spinning you a load of kak, Sergeant Ghaap," said Mthethwa. "And I'll prove it to you."

He pushed open the door of the interrogation room.

Ghaap tried to stop him, but without success.

"Who are the other guys that stole that car with you? And what did you do with the woman and the baby?"

Lucky's face fell. He raised his eyebrows in apparent despair, looked over Mthethwa's shoulder at Ghaap, then looked away.

Mthethwa walked around the desk, grabbed the boy by his shirt, and lifted him from the chair. "Talk, you rubbish! Or do you want a klap?"

Ghaap felt a dark anger surge inside him. He glanced at Mabusela, who simply stood watching, unmoved.

Before Ghaap knew it, he'd walked around the desk and pushed Mthethwa away. "This boy has already been hit enough, Warrant."

Mthethwa blinked in surprise and started laughing. "The dushie mampara from the bush actually thinks he's got rank!" Then he became serious: "But if you ever push a senior officer again, I'll lay a formal complaint. You got me?"

Ghaap nodded but he didn't let go of Lucky.

"And since you're so concerned about a fokken rubbish like this, you can go and make up a nice little bed for him in the cells."

"No!" Lucky called out. "He will find me in this place. Please!" He stretched his handcuffed hands out towards Ghaap. "You make promise!"

"We need to get someone from the Nappy Squad who can take him," Mabusela said. "Ghaap, ask Nthabiseng to help."

Ghaap had no idea who Nthabiseng was, but he took the boy by the arm and escorted him out the door. "And who'll be going to Chicken Farm?" he asked as he walked past Mabusela. But the officer simply shrugged.

"Get the laaitie organised, we'll talk to the Solly man."

"And in the meantime the clock's ticking, nè," Ghaap couldn't help remarking as he left the room.

61

"You make rasa!" Mpho said angrily to Gerda. "Thula!"

"We run," she told him. "I think there's something inside here, in the pipe. Come!"

"No!"

"Come, Mpho. It's inside here!"

"No. You must wait."

"I'm going, Mpho," she panted. "There's something – I think it's that animal, the one from the house."

He shook his head. "He will find us. Everywhere."

"Who, the animal?"

"No. The Fatha. He see everywhere. He walk like the wind."

"That animal is here, Mpho. I can't risk my baby. Please." She pressed the child closer to herself, so close that he whimpered.

"The animal, she is there, in the mkuku." Hy pointed towards the house. "I chase it there, into the house. Shaka, she gets a fright, she is dangerous. She bite your face."

"Mpho, that animal is here. I heard it growl. In there." She looked back at the pitch-dark tunnel. "I know it's here. I smelt it. We must go!"

She saw the doubt in his eyes. Then he grabbed her by the arm and forced her to her knees, Kleinpiet and all. "We crawl. He can't see us, The Fatha." He was more afraid of the man than the animal, she realised.

"But the animal. Shaka. Let's run, to the road. We'll find help," she said urgently.

"Shaka afraid. We go up to the lights, we find a shoe-marker."

"*What?*"

"Shoe-marker. He jabu pule."

She twigged – Michael Schumacher, the racing driver. And the soccer player, of course: Jabu Pule, known and loved for his speed.

He reached out his hands for the baby, his eyes willing her to trust him. She hesitated, her head screaming NO! But her body had reached its limit. Utterly exhausted, she handed Kleinpiet over to Mpho.

Kleinpiet began to fret. Mpho held him against his chest, his eyes widening in fear at the whimpering. "No rasa," he said, and passed the little one back to her. Gerda rocked her son in her arms, conscious of the insistent pain in her pelvis. She took shallow breaths, short, quick gulps of air. But the pain became more intense; her body broke out in sweat. She was unable to stifle a cry when it came again, and her legs began giving way. Mpho tugged at her arm. "Run! We run," he whispered anxiously. "He hear *everything*."

She concentrated on her breathing and the pain subsided. "It's rubbish, Mpho. He just tells you that to scare you."

"No! He is strong. Like snake. He eat the eyes of the vulture. He see very far. He eat the feet of the baby. Make him run *strong*. He kill us, he will eat us. Come!"

Gerda struggled to get upright. "Take the baby, Mpho. You run. You find the Schumacher, go to the police."

"No!"

"I can't, Mpho." Gerda felt the tears. "Please take the baby and get him safe. I can't any more. This one …" She looked down, pressing her palms against her belly.

He said nothing, sank down next to her, as Kleinpiet grizzled in the dark.

Gerda peered down the tunnel. She *knew* The Beast was there. She sensed it. She tried to regulate her breathing. Calm down, breathe slowly, she told herself.

"Mpho," she panted, "who is the boss man, who, who—"

"Many money. He pay only clippas and 'sgodo."

"Clippas?"

"One hundreds. 'Sgodo is the one thousands."

"Umlungu?" she asked.

"Ja. Hair like woman, is long. He make business with us. He give money for the sharkboys. They bring the cars. The Fatha, he make them strong. Like crocodile. Bullets, they fall off. Like water. Police bullets, they no good. This umlungu, he kwerekwere. He pay with *you*."

"What? He pays with *me*?" She felt nauseous, swallowed. Tasted the bile.

"He buy dagga, nyaope."

"Nyaope?"

"Drugs, cheap."

"He pays with me?" She gulped. A white foreigner: kwerekwere. Long hair. "And the sharkboys, who are they?"

"My brother and his gang. They work for him. They clever, take any car."

"Who do they work for?"

"Long-hair man."

"That man, does he wear a ring?"

Mpho held up his pinky.

This time she couldn't contain the nausea. She vomited, over her breasts and belly. No. It couldn't be true. Not Baz. How in God's name was this possible?

When the spasms were over, she wiped her mouth with her hand, the sour smell of her own insides in her nose. She rubbed the hand on her dress and then extended it to Mpho. "Come, we go," she said and took his arm.

"I try help you," he replied, and deposited Kleinpiet carefully on the ground.

Gerda took a deep breath and heaved herself upright with the boy's help. Her head was spinning, but she managed to stand. Mpho turned around to pick up Kleinpiet. He froze as he saw that the child's blanket was moving.

"My baby! Mpho, it's the animal!" she called out.

"Hamba!" he yelled. "Voertsek!" He got hold of a corner of the blanket and pulled furiously, but lost his balance. He fell forward, grabbed at the child, held him out to her, and Gerda snatched him up.

The next moment The Beast had Mpho by his trousers. The boy shrieked, kicking wildly.

Gerda looked around desperately: a stone, a stick, anything. But there was no time. Mpho's flailing body disappeared into the dark.

He'd been dragged off in the jaws of the biggest hyena she'd ever clapped eyes on.

62

On their way to the Du Toit house, he asked Qhubeka to stop at the service station shop in Merriman Avenue. He needed Rennies for his heartburn. April remained seated in the back of the van. Beeslaar bought the biggest pack of antacid tablets he could find, a few sachets of Gaviscon, and a bottle of water.

Back at the van, he saw that April was smoking a cigarette. He flicked the butt out of the window as soon as he spotted Beeslaar, who was enraged. He walked around to the side of the van and stamped out the half-smoked cigarette.

"You're supposed to be such a greenie, yet you couldn't care less where you drop your shit," he barked, yanking open the passenger door.

"Fuck's sake," he heard April mutter, "it's only a stompie."

He slammed the door shut and walked over to the barred window of the van. "It's not just a fokken stompie, Mr April, it's a live ember on a dam filled with petrol!" He unwrapped two, three Rennies, popped them in his mouth, and got back into the vehicle. He chewed furiously, and the sour taste sent a shudder through his body. He washed it down with water. The quickest way to get the stuff into your stomach.

He and Qhubeka drove without talking. Due east. Up Merriman, past the big circle at the intersection with Cluver. Past the expanse of veld that was Jan Marais Park. Beeslaar sat chewing on another tablet, pleased at his growing familiarity with the landmarks en route to the Du Toit house. Qhubeka turned off, towards the river, street names flashing past them. Zwaanswyk, Beeslaar saw. Then she turned into the quiet little street where the Du Toits lived. The house was dark and had an abandoned look. Or maybe it was the garden lighting, making it look like some kind of monument.

They climbed out in silence. Qhubeka unlocked the gates and let them through. She had taken out a pair of gloves, which she handed to Beeslaar.

As they walked along the garden path towards the front door, April stopped short. "I'm not going inside," he said, his eyes wild with fright.

"Relax," said Qhubeka. "We're going *around* the house."

"You deliberately misled me the other day," Beeslaar said as they set off again. He let April walk in front.

April ignored him.

Beeslaar stopped, tugged at his arm. "Ek sê!"

April turned around, his eyes reflecting the pale glow of the new moon.

"Did I?" Innocence itself.

"Yes, you did. You tried to sell me a story about how unpopular Malan du Toit was in the community, and how it wouldn't surprise you if he was to blame for his wife's death. Do you recall that, or does the zol keep erasing your memory, like Alzheimer's?"

"Alzies is for the krimpies," April said, affronted. "And I only smoke a little, anyway."

"You're lying. Come on, move!" said Qhubeka. "You and your tjommie Swiff, you stink of witpyp."

"Aggh," he replied indignantly.

The long, dark swimming pool came into view. It lay like a living being, its surface stirred by the fountain, shimmering amid the garden lights.

They walked around the pool and through a stretch of garden to the pump house. Beeslaar bent down with a torch, which he nearly dropped when something jumped onto him out of the darkness. He bumped his head as he recoiled.

"Cat," April remarked behind him.

He leant over the spherical shape of the pump and shone the torch around it but saw nothing.

"Look under the leaves," April said at his back. Beeslaar bent down further. A good thing he was wearing gloves; the thought of spiders living under the dead leaves gave him the creeps. Spiders were the one thing that freaked him out.

Mercifully, he felt something on his first attempt: a Ziploc bag, inside it a small glass tube with a ball-shaped end – like a miniature test tube – and several disposable lighters. He took his phone out of his pocket and photographed the bag. Then he picked it up and stepped back, shuddering involuntarily at the cobwebs brushing against his neck.

He held the bag up against the light, and April said, "Ja, that's her gear."

The trio walked back in silence to the swimming pool, where Qhubeka asked if she could drop Beeslaar off before returning to the station with the evidence. Beeslaar said she needn't bother, he felt like walking home.

"And what about *me*, sisi? How do I get back to my pozzie?"

"*You*, Mr April, can be grateful that I'm not throwing your arse into jail." She turned to go, flinging a last word over her shoulder: "You can walk off the zol!"

"It's fokken far, man, that place," April complained to Beeslaar, who just shrugged. Not his problem.

They stood like that a while longer, watching the light on the swimming pool water.

"She was finished, that woman. Sif," said April. "I know fokkol about what went on there." He jerked a thumb at the house. "But I can tell you *one* thing for sure: that lady was a fucked-up merrim. Nice and pretty. She looked good. Expensive everything. Jewellery, which she started trading bit by bit …" He shook his head. "And I scheme I wasn't the only one she scored from. Sometimes when she rocked up at my place she was already doped up. Man, then she was reckless. Reck-less," he emphasised.

"And you were only too happy to take her money."

"My bru, I only got paid in troubles."

At the bru-ing, Beeslaar felt like shaking him.

"At first I thought I'm scoring big time. A larney cherry like that, best reverse in the world," he leered. "And she knew it, always wearing those tight jeans. And when I heard whose wife she was … jirre, my bru. Then I stepped proudly, like a show horse." He fell silent, shoved his hands into his pockets.

Beeslaar unwrapped two more Rennies.

"You know," April went on, "my big thing is Mother Nature. A valley like that, like a woman's womb. It's a special place. You won't believe it, but there's still a wild leopard roaming in these mountains. The last of the last."

He looked up at Beeslaar with sad eyes. "Same story as the old Cape lion that used to roam around here. A five-hundred-kilogram thing with *teeth*. And heavy as a fokken cow. Saw his arse here – the farmers with their guns and the march of progress. Moer toe. Poof, gone! All that's left is the type of shit we took out of the pump house tonight. The rest is gone, or it's dying. You could say the valley is one long funeral parlour. The only song the birds sing there nowadays is ka-ching ka-ching."

"And you want to stop it all by making a big noise?"

April sneered. "Progress and jobs, that's what Mr du Toit and his tjommas say. But it's a living thing they're fucking up. Every grand castle is like a new little cancer in the mother's womb. And the first peoples, *my* people … They have to watch from the sidelines. The first man who got land here was Marquart, a freed slave. Now I hear they're going to call the new project Marquart."

"I thought the place was called Jonkers Valley."

"No, man. That's just for now, it's the trust's name."

"Okay. But the name of the place isn't something you or I can do anything about. Not at this time of the night. Let's go, I want to get some sleep."

Beeslaar started walking. His heartburn was finally buckling under the onslaught of the Rennies. "Anyway," he said to April over his shoulder, "the issue here isn't so much who the original owners of the Jonkershoek Valley were. It's about a mother of two children who was murdered."

"And if it was a black developer? Or – God protect us – a coloured one? What would you and the sisi have done then?"

"Just shut your mouth, won't you, April?"

286

"Ja, Baas Beeslaar, and if it was a Mr Kunene who wanted to cover the whole valley in buildings, you and the sisi would have been onto it like flies on shit."

Beeslaar stopped and said, "We're not interested in property issues."

"Listen, our NGO's head office is in Wellington. Our law boys there have checked out the title deeds. They're all squeaky clean, nè?"

"So? What did you expect? That a man like Du Toit doesn't know what he's doing? And out of spite, you set the place on fire!"

Qhubeka clicked her tongue in exasperation and walked past the two arguing men, disappearing around the side of the house, her torch still in her hand.

"No ways, man. It wasn't our people who did that. But all of a sudden there were moves here. Heavy moves. A lawyer woman came to see me. Her client, anonymous, who's looking for kak with Du Toit and his gabbas. She tunes me there's been tampering with the archives, old servitudes and other stuff. Dating back to the time of the slaves, she tunes. When *my* people still owned something."

"Look, Mr April, my heart bleeds for the people. But now I'm going home. I want to go to bed."

"These are facts, my bru. Have you checked the conservation larneys of this town? Pillars of society, the whole lot. I sent the law antie to them. They've got big bucks. Retired proffies, people like that. *They'll* be able to pay for the lawsuits. Not that I'm walking with them. Now they're all of a sudden so concerned about history, but where were they in apartheid?"

Beeslaar turned to leave.

"Wait, wait, hang on, my bru."

Beeslaar's shoulders sagged as he stood there.

"What I'm going to tell you now … It's dangerous. And I want to stay anonymous. Okay?"

"Just talk, man."

"You have to promise me, my bru."

"Spit it out," Beeslaar said irritably. "And drop the bru business. I'm giving you one minute."

"This man's money," April cautiously began, pointing at the house and lighting a cigarette. He took a pull, but then he nipped it between his thumb and forefinger and put it back in his pocket. "You know how many farmers tell me they'll sell their land for development? And they'll do this happily. It's too expensive to farm. Only the okes with the big bucks can get in here. Ernie Els and the Ruperts and types like that."

"So, what are you really trying to say? That Malan du Toit doesn't have enough money? The land's already *his*, my man."

"Sharp-sharp, my bru. Ja, he's got a lot of bucks, but he also *doesn't* really have that much."

"And how would *you* know, April? You're a bladdy dope pusher that hides behind an NGO!"

April laughed, began to walk again. "Where there's money, there's tracks."

Beeslaar followed behind. The fountain was off; it probably worked on a time switch. The pool lights were off too, but the water rippled restlessly now that the wind was rising again. In the distance, the sound of the river softly babbling. What an absolute paradise, he thought. Who'd imagine that it concealed so much unhappiness.

"Who sent the lawyer to you?" he said to April.

"Now you're getting clever. But let me first educate you a bit. 'Cos that's the thing about the Cape archives. They go back hundreds of years, man, to the first peoples. *My* people. No one knows any more what their names were, but this is where they lived."

They walked towards the front gate, April talking all the while. "Today the owners are in the pound seats, they sell off the places to fat-cat foreigners. Like Lanzerac, that larney hotel; sold for two hundred mil, they scheme. Original slave land. An outjie they called Schrijver. Him and three freed slaves. It's *old* history, and—"

"Right, and that's where we're going to leave it, April!"

"Ag no, man! That's *exactly* what it's all about! Jonkers Valley's first owner: Antony de Kaffir. He was a freed slave, that man. But what do his descendants own today? Fokkol! And Mister Antony's will, that gave his descendants access to the river—"

"You're wasting my time, man." Beeslaar dipped under the police tape, and as soon as he was outside the front garage, he began to lengthen his stride.

"Wait," April called out. "You must give me a lift, my bru."

"If you call me your fokken bru one more time, you'll be getting that PK, okay?"

April kept his mouth shut and followed Beeslaar to Maaike's house. The car was parked at the gate. He unlocked the doors, impatiently gestured to April to get in.

They drove into the valley in silence. The scrap of moon cast just enough light for the Pieke to be etched against the horizon.

"Just look at that," April said as they drove past the Lanzerac's wrought-iron gate. "And us klonkies, we get chucked out. 'Cos the colour of our blood is still not good enough. First our Khoi ancestors—"

"Good God, man! Just stop with the political sermons for a change. I'm not bloody interested. We're just interested in catching a killer!"

"Copper wire and beads, my bru. When they didn't want to take the beads any more, the guns were turned on them. But then came the shortages. Big disaster, the whites didn't have wyfies. But the Khoi antie was kwaai lekker. Then the land was gone, stolen from under us. And just as we were pulling ourselves up again, they hit us with apartheid. My own grandpa had a shop in Stellenbosch. He had enough money to give my two oldest uncles an education. But then the whole lot of us were thrown out of the town. Our school, our churches, our houses. Overnight, we had nothing. Fokkol. And no rights in those days. No constitution. It broke my grandpa, made us poor. My pa became a gangster. I'm telling you!"

"And I, April, am praying that you will shut up."

"But that's the thing! You and the sisi must check out the gangsters that are bankrolling Jonkers Valley. The Mocha Java Diamonds from the Cape Flats. These days, they buy property. Invest in partnership with Boere like Du Toit!"

Beeslaar's phone rang. Ghaap, he saw before he answered.

"Right, let's hear it," he said in a bored voice.

"You alone?"

"No, but I wish I was."

"There's big kak here. Real bad. I need to ask you about something."

"I'm going to sleep now, ouboet. I'm getting ready for bed."

"Please. Phone me if you get a chance. It's urgent," he said, and the line went dead. Beeslaar wondered what was up with Ghaap. What the latest mess was he'd got himself into.

Next to him, April had resumed his tale. But Beeslaar's thoughts were with poor old Ghaap.

"Are you listening, my bru?"

"No! And I want you to shut your damn mouth right now, okay?"

63

Ghaap sat fidgeting. He just *knew* Lucky hadn't lied to him.

Mabusela and Mthethwa were still laughing as they left. "O pambene wena," were Mthethwa's parting words. An index finger at his right temple, he'd signalled that Ghaap was crazy.

When he decided to call Duif, the familiar voice said, "How's things your side, boet?" Duif sounded half asleep.

"How well do you know Chicken Farm?"

"It's a bad place, my friend. You don't walk around there at night. Even the chickens will gang rape you."

"Do you know the dokotelas of that place?"

"Eish, man, have you been smoking zol? There are no dokotelas in Chicken Farm. It's a backward place. You only get – but do you even know what a dokotela is?"

"A witchdoctor, I know!"

"No, man, they're the *real* doctors. The ones with the surgeries. That's what the tsotsis call them. All the gangsters have their own dokotela, who sews them up when the cops have shot them to pieces. But I don't know of any witchdoctors in Chicken Farm. Why do you ask? Is it anything to do with that kid we found in the Dolly Parton?"

"He says there's a guy in that place. A guy they call 'The Fatha.'"

Silence.

"You still there?"

"Still here, my friend. Now you're talking about the tokoloshe. It's just a story to make people scared."

"Well, the kid is scared shitless. Serious. But the bosses here just laugh at me. They say it's an urban legend. But ..." Ghaap thought for a moment. "What if The Fatha is actually something else, maybe someone who wants to show how powerful he is? And so he calls himself The Fatha?"

"Eish, man. We can go and check it out. I haven't been there for a while now. The people in that place are too dof to steal cars. They're still stealing rocks – the brothers love those white chickens, you know."

"What if the laaitie's telling the truth, Dawid? What if that woman and her child are really there?"

"Must I come pick you up?"

"I'm on duty, bru. And I'm already in the shit."

"Look, if you guys could send a vehicle in there. Not a van, the streets are too narrow. A starter pack, maybe. And you ask around there. But it's got to be someone who can speak the lingo, those Chicken Farm people don't talk to outsiders."

"What's a starter pack?"

"A small car. Golf, anything like that."

If you hadn't been born here, it seemed to Ghaap, you were permanently at a disadvantage. "Okay, shot," he attempted his own lingo, and ended the call.

He decided to check whether Nthabiseng had finished with Lucky. She was from the child protection unit, and was supposed to clean him up and bandage his wounds before getting him to a place of safety.

He tracked her down in an office where a light was still burning. She was at a computer. Missing persons' records, she told him; she was hoping to trace Lucky's identity. But so far her search had been fruitless. "What did he tell you about his name?" she asked.

"Just Lucky. And that he lives with a man called The Fatha."

"The Fatha." She pushed her chair back and crossed her legs, hands folded across her belly.

"I know," Ghaap said, forestalling her. "Everybody tells me it's an urban legend. But I'm just telling you what the kid told me. Where is he, anyhow?"

Lucky had been taken to a hospital by a social worker, she explained. Some of the wounds on his back were septic, and should actually have received medical attention a long time ago. He was also malnourished. And paranoid. The latter perhaps as a result of his drug use.

"Tell me about the legend."

"Oh, the usual thing. If a child is naughty, the mother tells him: 'The Father-man can see *all* the naughty children!' He's a powerful wizard, umThakathi. Not like sangomas, but bad stuff. Very bad stuff."

"So what does he do when he catches the children? Body parts?"

"That's not what the mothers tell their children. I, for one, would rather klap the taaikop child. I find it cruel to scare children with stories of the magriza. That's old women," she said when she saw the bewilderment on Ghaap's face. "But the story goes that the Bad Father turns himself into an animal, a baboon or a hyena. And he takes the child away and makes him a zombie."

"A *zombie*?"

"Of course, there aren't any such … people … things. But in the old days people believed that a bad sangoma, the thakathi, has workers – you know, like slaves. They dig up the fresh grave of anyone who's been cursed. And they turn the dead body into a zombie. You can recognise a zombie at night because you can see it. It's white. And it hasn't got eyes. But it can smell you. Just rubbish!" she exclaimed dismissively.

But Ghaap listened, intrigued.

"These days you don't need the thakathi or the zombie to harm children. The parents sommer do it themselves. All the runaways we deal with. Eish."

"But people still believe in it all?"

She grimaced. "Stupid people, yes."

Ghaap ventured to ask. "Have you ever been to a sangoma?"

She looked at him as if he were crazy. "Hayibo! No ways," she said, and laughed.

"But seriously," said Ghaap, "why would a … tha-whatever, a bad sangoma, want to hijack a car? As I understand it, those guys don't do things like that?"

"No, you're right. Maybe it's the customer. Gang boss. Or car theft syndicate. The sharkboys that they employ to steal the cars, they wear the muti that turns police bullets into water." She smiled. "They say even the soccer teams do, each player has his own sangoma, you know, to win the game. He talks to the ancestors, burns mphephu for them and slaughters a …"

"Rock," Ghaap said helpfully, and she laughed.

"Yes, a chicken. That's what the ancestors want, a sacrificial chicken …"

She continued working on the computer.

"Can this computer … Does it have internet?" asked Ghaap.

"Of course, yes."

"The white woman, Gerda Matthee, she's got no history."

"What you mean?"

"In her house. I've been through that whole house, but she has no photos. She lives with her father, she's got a young child, and she's pregnant. She has a boyfriend. He's not the father, but he's done a jabu pule – run away."

Ghaap was pleased at the smile his Soweto slang elicited. "He's gone. Like piss in the wind – disappeared. The strange thing, sisi, there's no photos in that house. Not nowhere. He's in the system. But she isn't. Can you get her maybe on the net? Facebook, or something."

He watched as she typed in the name, corrected her when he saw she'd spelt Matthee with only one "t".

There were millions of entries, Ghaap saw, but the first ones all referred to a well-known author.

"Put in her first names. She's Gerda Johanna – double 'n', nè. Then Elisabet." He helped her with the Afrikaans spelling.

She glanced at the computer to check the progress of her search and asked: "Did Lucky tell you who he works for?"

"He was too scared," said Ghaap.

"I asked him too, and he wouldn't say." Clearly irate, she said, "He's never been to school. Doesn't know his surname. He's not even sure how old he is. But he's got septic wounds on his lower back and his backside."

"And on top of that, he was beaten again soon after his arrest," Ghaap added.

"Auwe," she sighed. "Some people … This whole place. You know how many dead children we have every year? Here in Soweto? It's a disease, my brother. It's bigger than Aids, I tell you. And it's not even Easter yet. Come school holidays, the numbers jump."

Leaning closer to the screen, she said, "Woza …" Then read the first entry she'd clicked on: "Jassas! This woman … Oh, my God. Oh, my God. The poor lady. She's already lost two children. Two little boys!"

In a strangled voice, Ghaap said, "I've seen their clothes – she's still got the clothes at her house." He stood up to read over her shoulder, saw *The Star* headline: *Cop shoots sons, himself. Pregnant wife escapes death.*

There was a photo of the woman. Rather blurred, but recognisable. It was Matthee.

"Good God. It says here that after his dog died, her husband snapped. He'd been depressed and was drinking heavily. The woman wasn't at home at the time, she was visiting a friend. God! You come back, your home is a slaughterhouse."

Ghaap read along with her. The report ended with a "no comment" from the neighbour.

His name: Inspector Albertus Beeslaar!

64

The heartburn was gone, but he felt hungry again. He wouldn't be able to sleep, in any case; there were too many ghosts wandering around in his head.

His phone rang: Qhubeka.

It reminded him – he'd forgotten to call poor old Ghaap back.

Qhubeka told him she'd just finished interrogating Mr Swiff, aka Quentin Latief Daniels, who they'd brought in with April earlier that evening. The guy had an impressive charge sheet. And he'd already served two jail sentences, in both cases for attempted murder. Seemed to be the floating trophy of the 28s gang operating in Cape prisons. His membership of the 28s was confirmed by his tattoos – one of which was of a setting sun. The tattoo of a hand on his throat also marked him as a member of the gang. He was, moreover, probably in the top echelons of The Firm, one of the most notorious gangs operating outside the prisons.

He wasn't just anybody. According to Charmainetjie, they called him The Fixer – his job was to put guys in their place when they showed disloyalty.

"But he's walking around freely?" Beeslaar observed.

"Yes, he's been out since January."

"And what's he doing here?"

"This isn't his territory. But his fancy little lawyer who's waiting down below will no doubt inform me," she said, before ending the call.

Beeslaar drove back to Liewe Heksie's house. It was in darkness, he noted gratefully. And then, on the point of sneaking around the corner, he heard her voice: "Albertus?"

He stood still. "I thought you were sleeping."

"But how can I?" She was sitting on the front stoep, just visible in the dull light from the street. One hand rested on Rembrandt, who lay in her lap. Also, she was smoking – something that smelt suspiciously sweet.

"Where's the constable who's supposed to guard you?"

"Sleeping."

She took a drag, the smoke drifting away as she spoke in staccato tones: "I think … that I … should … go home."

"Was that the message Andries April came to deliver here tonight?"

"It's not just Andries. It's this country, godverdomme!"

He watched her as she took another drag, waited for the long exhalation.

"You're wrong about Andries." A thin plume floated from her mouth, and then she said: "He's *not* a man of violence."

"Oh? So who butchered your, er, *Vermeer* like that?"

"It wasn't Andries."

"Who, then?"

"It was those people, the ones he's fighting against."

"Sorry, Maaike, but you're not making sense. How much boom have you smoked tonight?"

His eyes were adjusting to the darkness and he watched her stroking the dog on her lap, rubbing its floppy ears. "Andries is not a bad man, Albertus. He is working hard to heal his community."

"Well, he has a very funny way of healing."

She said nothing, kept fondling the dog.

Beeslaar was on the point of saying good night when she suddenly spoke again.

"Andries wants to keep the boys out of the gangs. Really. He teaches them cricket, soccer, rugby. To keep them away from the strong attraction of the gangs. Drugs and crimes. I thought ..."

She searched for words, her eyes staring uneasily into the darkness. "I thought I could make a contribution, that I could help. Because I see what is happening around us, you know? The children ... And the women. The people who come to our halfway house. So ... broken." She sniffed, and Beeslaar was surprised to see a gleam of wetness on her doughy face.

She flicked away the zol, wiped her nose with the back of her hand.

"I was so stupid. So naive! I thought I could make a difference. But this country ..." She gulped, wiped at her cheek. "The damage is too great, you know? Too great." Another tear slid down the side of her nose. "The scars of poverty ... of years and years of violence. People robbed of their dignity. Until they *themselves* believe that they're inferior. The frustration, all the anger. And then, who is it that suffers the most?" Bloodshot eyes looked at him accusingly. "The vulnerable, the women and the children, of course."

"Maaike, I hear you. But unfortunately that's our history. That's just how it is. There's nothing you or I can do today to change the past."

"No," she said after a while, "but we ... you people ... the whites here ... you Afrikaners. You *still* don't understand. You think the blacks and the coloureds, you think they have forgotten. But the wounds, they're still *very* raw."

No doubt this was true, but it wasn't something he wanted to debate at that moment.

"Remember the question you asked: Why would a teenage boy become so obsessed with religion?"

He folded his arms, waited for her to finish. "I'll tell you why. And it's not just him, you know. It's *all* of you."

"Oh," he said, totally gobsmacked.

"You're grabbing at a ridiculous god, an American fantasy. Fanatical. Hallelujah! We're speaking in tongues! God will save us! Because our own fathers betrayed us, they abandoned us. Look, we're not racists, you all say. Apartheid wasn't our fault. No, our fathers are to blame, the church, the whole patriarchy of politics."

Her eyes glistened with tears. "I used to hope that I could make a difference here … here in Africa. Help a few children, at least, to escape from the vicious cycle." Her voice lost the battle against the emotion that was threatening to overwhelm her; her bottom lip began to quiver.

Beeslaar shuffled uncomfortably. He suspected that what he was hearing was alcoholic blues. "I'm really sorry about your parrot," was all he managed to come up with. "And I think you should try to get some sleep. You'll see, tomorrow you'll feel much better. Okay?"

She didn't move.

"Come on, Maaike. I'll wait until you're inside. Until I've heard you lock the door. Understood?"

She stood up, the dog under one arm, and walked to the front door. Before opening it, she turned towards him again and said: "Andries and I talked a lot about this, you know? He also wanted to make sense of it."

"Of what, Maaike?"

"The violence in this country. The anger. But I'm a foreigner, a kwe … kwe …"

"Kwerekwere," said Beeslaar, not sure if that was the word she was looking for.

"Yes! Andries used to say if we could get the boys … So many of them don't have fathers, you know? And fatherless children … they often have more emotional problems, aggression, teenage pregnancies, juvenile delinquency. Ag, everything. Andries and I, we just weren't strong enough. The current of anger, it's too strong."

"It's sad, Maaike. That's just the way things are in this country. But maybe you shouldn't take it to heart the way you do. It's not as if you personally can—"

"I know that, yes! But it's *you*, you men. Open your eyes, Albertus. Look at the children: ignorant, damaged, abused. It's a crisis, I tell you! Bigger than Aids! There are no proper fathers any more. No role models for them. No one who can nurture, who can protect them and guide—" She broke down in tears.

"Oh, Maaike." He came closer, intending to comfort her.

"No!" she exclaimed. "Don't touch me. I'm leaving. It's all too harsh, too *violent* here for me. But for you who come from here … It's inside you, in your flesh and blood and bones. It's been burnt into you, branded – the violence!"

"Please, just go to bed now, Maaike."

She opened the front door, and gratefully, Beeslaar began to walk away. Then she spoke again, less vehemently, at least. He paused without turning around.

"This society is like one big dysfunctional family. Lumpenproletariat! Free from apartheid, yes … but no self-respect. No job, no brains, no education. Ashamed of itself. Ashamed of being black, because that equals being poor and stupid! And full of anger …"

Beeslaar strode off. Let her preach to the fokken wind, he thought. He's had enough sermons to last a lifetime.

65

The walls were pressing down on him, Beeslaar felt. And there was a racket in his head; Maaike's outburst refused to let him alone.

He could have told her long ago that she wasn't the first do-gooder from Europe to become disillusioned in Africa. And she would certainly not be the last. You had to be made of steel if you wanted to survive here in a way that made sense.

He got out of bed, put on his fleece and set off on foot; it was way past midnight, but he might just find a hamburger at the Mystic Boer. Apart from a few barking dogs, the suburbs were dead quiet.

He walked west, heading for the town centre. The wind at his back propelled him forward. On either side of the road there were big houses, set far back on their stands. Elegant wrought-iron gates, lush gardens. This was what you might call a beautiful place, he decided again. Unlike the environment he'd grown up in. The modest mining houses of the East Rand on their tiny stands, just enough room for an old car up on bricks and a garden gnome in front. Theirs was called Bruno, he remembered. There was a Pablo, too. Up on the front wall of the house, the Mexican figure dozing under his sombrero, leaning against a cactus.

It was so much nicer, then. Koefie was still around ... Their lives relatively whole.

But he was determined not to dwell on old wounds, even though the Dutch woman had reopened every single one. He found himself in a wide street with picturesque Victorian streetlights, old houses with little turrets and broekielace and all.

He thought of April, what he'd talked about earlier on. The centuries-old disputes about land. The first people who had lived here. The arrival of a bunch of Dutchmen who didn't belong in Africa, according to Maaike. The new arrivals who had moved into this territory – sailors, slaves, farmers. Who'd taken the land and were now using their wealth to hold on to it.

Looking around, you'd never believe you were in Africa. This was still a lily-white town full of umlungus – sea scum, the Xhosa term for white people. It was as if the mountains kept everything out, protected the place against the ... What was it she'd said? The lumpenproletariat. Political rule by scum.

The Mystic Boer was still open, he was pleased to find. He ordered a cane and Coke. A double. Blikkies's late-night dop. Spook and diesel, he remembered, the "spook" being the colourless cane. Sometimes you asked for twins: still a light dop. But in times of need you'd order triplets: half a bottle of cane to one can of Coke.

He took a swig. It sent a shiver down his spine. Someone walking over his grave. The spook hitting the wrong spots, perhaps. The pivotal moments. Where everything in his life suddenly changed. The streak of blood on the gravel road. Koefie's crumpled bicycle.

He signalled to the barman that he was ready for a refill, chewed an ice cube while he waited. He studied the menu. Hamburger and chips, or hamburger and salad. He ordered the one with chips.

Twice, his life had been ruptured like that. Got a *before* and an *after*. The time with Koefie. And then with Gerda: *before* the time of Gerda. And the chaos of *after*.

The violence of that day. And time, which stood still.

Fouchétjie, he remembered him too. Seeing his former colleague's brains spattered across the Goofy wallpaper of the kids' room. Boetatjie, half his head shot away. And the older one, Neiltjie. On his stomach, in his favourite sleeping position. The hole through his—

Beeslaar pushed the drink aside, called the barman, ordered a double brandy.

"Met eish?" the guy asked jokingly.

But Beeslaar's sense of humour had been flattened. That's what you get from remembering, he berated himself. From listening to the sob stories of Dutch anties who suddenly woke up to reality. In Africa!

He watched the students, clustered around tables or smoking in groups outside on the stoep. For them, the night was far from over. He was the only adult among them. It made him feel old. A krimpie. Someone who'd seen far too much for one lifetime.

He felt his phone vibrate in his trouser pocket, decided to ignore the call. It was fucking one o'clock in the morning. And he was supposed to be on holiday, thought he'd be learning how to handle a fishing rod. Yet here he sat, once again trying to make sense of the many ways people managed to harm each other. The list was endless.

Bashing a corpse's head to bits with a Brahman bull. It was *way* too absurd.

His drink arrived. Not strong enough, he felt, so he requested another double.

When he glanced up again, he was looking straight at the face of Ellie du Toit. She seemed far from dazed and fragile. Her long, shiny hair was hanging loose. There was colour in her face, and her mouth was violet-rose. The sad eyes were rimmed with black make-up. She was standing with a shot glass in one hand, a cigarette in the other. She tossed the drink back and slammed the glass on the counter, her eyes fixed defiantly on Beeslaar. A boy in the group she was with pushed another glass in front of her, and she repeated the trick.

Beeslaar's blood boiled. He jumped up, rushed at the girl and grabbed her by her drinking arm. She screamed and lashed out at him; the glass flew from her hand. And then he grabbed her other arm too.

"Woo-hoo!" yelled the boys, their eyes shining with excitement. And then an exclamation, "Watch the old toppie!" as Beeslaar unsteadily moved closer.

"Sit down, kid," he snarled at the youngster and pushed him roughly away.

"Leave me alone!" the girl screamed as she delivered a vicious kick to Beeslaar's shin. "Let me go, you perv!"

Beeslaar didn't release his hold. He twisted her arms behind her back and half carried, half marched her out of the door and onto the pavement. She yelled and swore at him, but he paid no attention, just kept pushing her out in front of him. Some youths on the stoep approached threateningly, and Beeslaar reached under his jacket for his pistol. "Police!" he bellowed. "If one of you brats take one more step, I'll have him locked up! This girl is a minor."

He saw the militancy fading from the would-be rescuers' eyes. They turned around, slunk off with their tails between their legs. The girl kept yelling; he yanked her, grabbed her by both shoulders, and gave her a good shake.

She hung her head and started crying uncontrollably, a curtain of hair veiling her face. Beeslaar gathered her in his arms and felt the sobs racking the thin body. He waited until she'd cried herself out, his hands big and clumsy around her tiny frame.

The make-up streaking her cheeks accentuated the helpless confusion he read in her gaze. "Ellie," he said, bending down to look her straight in the eyes, "*what* are you doing—" The rest of his sentence was drowned out by a new fit of weeping.

"It was *me*," she spat out suddenly.

Beeslaar knew instantly what she was talking about. But his mind struggled to come to terms with what he'd heard.

"It was you who did *what*? Ellie!"

She fell forward against his chest; the top of her head barely reached his breastbone. "It was *me*, Oom. It was *me*," he heard her sobbing into his jacket.

Beeslaar felt paralysed. For a moment he lifted his head and wanted to pray, pray that this child was lying to him. Suddenly he was back at that stop sign. The dark stain in the dust … The inability to think Koefie back to life. The Goofy wallpaper … The stain of violence and disgrace he'd carried since that day. Gerda … Gerda putting down the phone. "There's too much memory between us …"

He wrapped his arms around the girl's shoulders and pressed her close to him, just for an instant. "It's all right," he heard himself murmuring, perhaps more to himself than to her. "It's all right, all right."

Once she had calmed down, he led her to a car parked across the pavement. He sat her down on the bonnet and handed her a Gary Player tissue from his pocket. She took the big tissue but made no move to use it, stared vacantly into space.

"What happened at your house on Tuesday, Ellie?" he asked warily.

She didn't reply, her eyes empty and dim.

"Ellie?" He took the tissue from her hand and wiped at a mascara streak on her cheek. His touch jolted her from her daze.

"I killed her," she said. "My mom. It was me who did it. Me."

"Why, Ellie?"

"I was ... My mom was out of it again. She'd freaked out." She fell quiet, and Beeslaar could see she was losing focus. He lifted her chin to get a better view of her face.

"How did she freak out, Ellie? What happened?"

"It was so ... She was crazy," she said with a shrug. "She talked about the gangsters, said they wanted to kill her. They were outside in the garden, we had to ... we had to lock everything. She screamed that it was the 28s, that they were coming to kill her. She ... she had the pistol. She was so freaked out, Oom. She'd gone crazy. She even had a security door installed on the stairs. We had to ... My dad ... We had to lock our doors from the inside. My dad ... She said the gangsters worked for him. They were coming to kill us."

She looked up at him with a lost expression. She'd started shivering badly, Beeslaar saw. He took off his jacket and put it around her shoulders, wrapped it tightly around her body and pulled her close to him.

Then he phoned Qhubeka.

66

Gerda was battling to haul her body up the slope that led to the highway. She couldn't allow herself to think about Mpho, whether he was still alive ... or about The Beast.

Help. She had to get help. Otherwise all four of them would perish.

She prayed, aloud. That the contractions would stop coming. They drained her, she was no longer able to carry Kleinpiet. She shifted his weight. Prayed. Dear Father, help us.

She inched upwards, step by step, on all fours. One step. Hoiked the child up on her hip. Rested. Another step. When the pain came, she waited. Breathed. Then onwards again: one step. Using her hand, her knees, as she hauled herself up the slope. Her toes were bleeding. Somewhere along the way she'd discarded her shoes, pulled off her dress. To be able to move more easily.

Where was the hyena? *Was* it a hyena? It wasn't possible, surely ... One step. It didn't matter what kind of animal it was. She had to get to the top, get help. If not for herself, at least for this child of hers. For Kleinpiet. Dear God, help him, at least. Just him. Just this one child.

She was almost at the top; she could hear the roar of traffic. Or maybe it was the dizziness in her head. The little one moaned when she shifted him again. She muttered a prayer of thanks. At least he was still *alive*.

Then she was at the top, slid Kleinpiet under the metal railing and onto the shoulder of the highway. By now, he was crying lustily, thank God!

She pulled herself up against the rail and glanced back anxiously into the night, hoping she'd see Mpho, that he'd be okay.

Her legs buckled under her and she sank to the ground.

She heard sirens in the distance, beyond the open stretch of veld through which she and Mpho had fled. Saw blue lights flashing ... too far away.

A traffic light flickered to her right. A single car cruising through the red light, its indicator signalling that it was turning away from her.

"Help!" she shouted and waved her arms. "Help me!" She strained to get up, she needed to walk into the road. Her head spun and the black night threatened to envelop her. She kept sitting. "Help ..." she muttered, bone-weary.

With dismay, Gerda saw that the car had begun to move away. Hoarsely, she shouted, stumbled into the road. The occupants didn't see her. She had to get closer to the traffic light, but she sagged to the ground, felt the chill of the tarred road against the dampness of her thighs. She lifted an arm but didn't have enough strength to keep it raised. She closed her eyes, sat huddled on the road.

It was only then that she heard the oncoming car, a flashing light homing in on her.

67

For the umpteenth time, Ghaap tried to get hold of Beeslaar.

Nthabiseng had, in the meantime, managed to track down Mabusela and Mthethwa, whom she'd briefed. Uncle Solly too.

He'd taken another look at the photo – the one he'd taken from the Matthee woman's Bible. Now that he was aware of the connection, he could barely believe he hadn't immediately recognised Beeslaar.

His phone rang: "Yes, Sergeant," he heard Ghalla Kruger's voice. Sounded like a dog that had been chasing a hare. "Are you sitting down?"

"Go, Ghalla, I'm all ears," Ghaap said wearily.

"We've just picked up that antie, the one with the little boy."

"Genuine? Where?"

"Like you said, at Chicken Farm!"

Ghaap's mouth fell open.

"We had to drive like hell to get her to a hospital, the tannie was about to drop her baby. Right there – in Duif's car, nogal."

"Where was she?"

"In the road. In the middle of the road, boet. Old Potch Road. Not too far from where you whacked that jackroller the other day."

"But where is she *now*?"

"Bara, boet. The biggest hospital in the whole wide world." Then he added wryly, "Also the biggest fokken mortuary in the whole wide world. But that was the best we could do for her, given the situation. She was *so* close to popping, I swear that baby was on the point of marching into the hospital by itself."

"And?"

"I scheme they're okay, boet. They had a bit of a rough ride, but the tannie held on till we got there. You should have seen old Duif. His two headlights on bright all the way! Scared shitless 'cos he had to hold the other baby. I just handled the wheel." He paused for a moment and Ghaap suspected it was either to gulp down a Grand-Pa or to light a cigarette. Or maybe both.

"Did she tell you where she'd been?"

"Not a chance, bru. She was too busy there on the front seat, one moment pinching to keep that baby inside, and the next she was screaming. With old Duif telling her from the back that she had to breathe. Meanwhile that other baby was screaming loud enough to buckle the wheels of the car."

"But how did she get to the road?"

"I told you mos, bru. There was no time for chit-chat. I kept calling the cops on the radio. But at least there were two brothers from the Pimville cop shop who cleared the road for us. Jirre, we floored it, bru. Fuck *Gone in 60 Seconds*! Then we dumped her at the hospital one time."

"Dumped? Dumped! Don't you have any respect? That woman … she's … she's bladdy related to me, man. And is that how a *white* man should speak?"

"Hey, sorry-sorry, man. We've all just had a bit of a fright."

Ghaap calmed down. "So she's okay now?"

"No, we're still waiting for news about her, bru. You don't know this place. Here the meide sommer have to give birth in the corridors, any old way. There's half a million patients but only three thousand beds."

Ghaap's felt his anger rise. Bladdy whitey that still talked about "meide". "Where are you guys now?" he said, trying to sound composed.

"We're hanging loose here, man. We've handed over the rest to the cops. So we're staying here, because you never know. Maybe it's twins. She was big enough for that, the antie. Sorry, bru. How's she suddenly related to you?"

Ghaap said goodbye without answering the question. He phoned Mabusela, reached his voicemail. Then he tried Beeslaar again: same story. So he wrote an SMS: *Gerda Matthee. Just found alive. So far the babies are OK. Phone me ASAP!!!!*

Then he called Duif.

"How do I get to you?" he asked. "We've got to go look for that lowlife that kidnapped the Matthee woman."

"The cops are already there, I think. Me and Ghalla went looking for the guy in Chicken Farm. We tracked down one old sangoma, but it wasn't him. This one looked like he's totally had it. Aids or something, I scheme. Begged money for info. And Ghalla kept tuning him that he should ask the ancestors!"

"Did he know about The Fatha?"

"Those are old wives' tales, my friend."

"They say he's a shape-shifter. So, how would you know that the one you were talking to wasn't in fact *him*?"

Duif snorted. "Dammit, Ghaap. Suppose there really was a rubbish like that. The cops would nab him chop-chop. The place is crawling with cops as we speak. At the moment there are more cops than lice in that joint. Every dick with wheels. Wall-to-wall blue lights and sirens. So, even if a heavy like this existed, he'd be in Sandton by now. Or wherever. Or maybe he just jumped onto a v8 broomstick." He cackled at his own joke, then said he had to go. "The larney cops had arrived, the okes with copper on their shoulders. If a bomb exploded here right now, Gauteng's top structure would be totally moer toe," he said cheerfully and ended the call.

Mabusela and Mthethwa came sneaking back into the office. "Where the fuck were you guys? You've been away more than half an hour," Ghaap said. "That jackroller kid was fokken right after all. She *was* in Chicken Farm!"

"Shut up, dushie," Mthethwa snapped at him and sat down behind his desk. "We've got the radio, my friend. Yesterday's news."

"So Lucky was right about everything," Ghaap persisted. "That lady could have been fokken dead."

"You just go back to sleep," said Mthethwa. "Leave the police work to us, dushie."

Ghaap grabbed at Mthethwa. Tonight was the night he'd donner the living shit out of this guy, even though he was a senior officer.

But Mabusela intervened. "Wait-wait-wait! You've got it wrong! We *did* go check it out. But we couldn't go far enough in. And we had to wait for back-up. It's fucking dangerous, that place! So, sit down, for God's sake."

Ghaap lowered his fists and sat down.

"That place is very, very dangerous. No way you go in there on foot – not without back-up. They'll panga you without blinking an eye. You don't know that place. It's dark. No electricity. No nothing. The roads are dongas, full of dead things and sewerage. So, we—"

Right then, Ghaap's phone rang, and his ears cut out when he saw who was calling: Beeslaar.

68

There was a veritable Babel around her, and dazzling lights. It had to be a hospital. But where?

Gerda could barely recall how she'd landed up here. There'd been sirens, blue lights. She remembered half-sitting in the passenger seat, gripping with hands and feet to anchor herself and to combat the pain. And then they'd suddenly emerged into the light. People milling around. They'd dragged her into the building by her arms. She'd cried out for her baby, but a stout nurse with perspiration on her face had taken her in hand. She'd lifted Gerda's chin and told her firmly: "Thula. Thula, mama. You're going to be fine." They'd hoisted her onto a gurney, started wheeling her through the throng.

Gerda gazed at the lights above her head as she was wheeled along. Some were out, she noticed, and she began to count the neon tubes dangling from the ceiling. She soon stopped, though, as all around her were people – wherever she looked: along the walls of the long corridor; on either side of the moving gurney, a blur of faces, grim and sick.

"Basop," she heard the nurse yelling at a figure with a blood-soaked cloth clutched to his head who'd grabbed her arm, appealing for help. Gerda tried calling out for Kleinpiet. But she could scarcely hear herself in the hubbub, and had to fight a black dizziness. "Stay with me, mama, stay!" she heard the nurse shout. Felt the light taps on her cheek. She had to focus. Look, keep looking at the lights. At the people lining the walls of the corridors. Some shrouded in blankets, eyes sunken and mouths gaping, as if they were already dead. Others lay on the bare floor. Staring blindly, eyes dulled by pain and fear that they wouldn't be helped in time.

Straining, Gerda searched for her child in the surrounding chaos.

"My baby!" She reached out a hand to the nurse. "Where's my baby! Please don't take him again. Please!"

"Woza," the perspiring nurse said as she stopped. "Listen. Look at me!" She gripped Gerda's face with both hands. "Your baby is taken care of. Do you *hear* me? He's with the doctor. He looks dehydrated, but he will be fine. Now you work with me, you hear? You *work* with me. We take care of the one that's coming, okay? Do you *hear* what I'm saying, mama? Nod if you can hear. *Look* at me! Focus!"

Gerda nodded, her body gripped by another spasm. She groaned, the sound coming from deep down in her belly, drowning out the noise around her. She couldn't breathe, was aware only of the pain. And far away, the booming sound of the sister's voice. "I need a ventilator," she heard her bellow. "Someone bring me a ventilator. Stay with me, mama, *stay* with me! Don't close your eyes. Breathe!"

Gerda felt her throat close up.

"Over here!" she heard the woman calling. "Here! Boniswe! It's coming fast now. We're not making it. Push her against the wall, give her some privacy!" And then softly, "Thank you, my darling, you are my star tonight!"

The warm voice was at her ear.

"I'm Sister Lucy. You're doing good, you're going to be fine. But you must tell me: Are you z3?"

Gerda frowned, not understanding the question.

"HIV. Is your baby safe?"

She shut her eyes as she nodded, feeling her abdomen contracting again. This time, her groan became a drawn-out wail.

"No-no-no! Don't scream. What's your name? *Look* at me! Lalela – listen!"

Sister Lucy's face floated close to her, she could feel the woman's breath on her skin. "The pain," she whispered. "I need something for the pain, Sister. The pain ... the pain!"

"Noooo. Sorry, mama. You need nothing now. Your baby is almost here. I will help you, nè? Tell me your name?"

"Gerd ... a. Gerd ... a. Johanna. Elis—" She struggled to say the name. "Matthee. Gerda ..."

"Whoa. Okay. Put your hands there." Taking Gerda's wrists, she pushed her hands firmly under her buttocks. "You keep it there. You focus there. And you push. Don't scream, it wastes your energy. You need it for the baby. Okay? Come, lift your forehead. Now. Push. Push. Push. *Push!*

Gerda pushed for all she was worth, taking deep breaths as she did so. With every push the pressure in her pelvis intensified.

"I need a delivery pack. *Now!*" Sister Lucy called out. "Bonni, my darling, go! Delivery pack and a drip. Quick-quick. She's had a rough time. She's bleeding all over, so hurry, my star!" Then she turned towards Gerda again. "You don't worry now, mama. Sister Lucy has delivered thousands of babies in this place. You're doing fine. When the pain comes, you push! You close your mouth, nè? Lift your face. Don't scream, nè? You push the energy down *there*. For the baby. No shout. Now. Again! Push! Push! Push!"

Gerda pushed with the last bit of energy she could muster.

"Yes!" the nurse exclaimed excitedly. "It's coming, it's coming, you're doing g-o-o-o-o-d. One more push. One more!"

And then, suddenly, it was all over.

"Beautiful!" Sister Lucy called out. "We made it! Yoh-yoh-yoh!"

For a moment Gerda was enveloped by a merciful darkness. She slid comfortably into a blissful peace that had come to carry her off. But she was jolted awake when the sister slapped her gently on her cheeks.

"Stay with me, Gerda. Look down there! Just look. It's a girl. A beautiful, healthy, sweet baby girl! Laduuuuma!" she triumphantly cried, as if Gerda had scored a goal.

69

"Captain Lelieveld of the Nappy Squad is with the girl," Qhubeka said as she entered her office. "And a doctor. I think that girl has finished talking for the night. We got all there was to be had out of her tonight. She's in such a state. Now she's in their hands. Next thing, the dad and his lawyer will be arriving."

Beeslaar was sitting in the visitor's chair opposite her desk, rigid with shock after the news he'd just had from Ghaap.

"Helloooo?" She waved her hands to get Beeslaar's attention. "I just can't face briefing Prammie right now. He'll have a heart attack." Qhubeka sat down dejectedly, pulled the Du Toit docket towards her. She suppressed a yawn as she flicked listlessly through the contents, and with a frown between her brows she took out a few crime-scene photos.

Beeslaar looked at her but couldn't tear his thoughts away from the image in his head of a pregnant Gerda. Flushed, peach pink, her green eyes shining. But that had been *before* the tragedy. What state was she in now? Why hadn't she told him? How far advanced was her pregnancy? Whose child—

"Captain! Are you sleeping, or are you praying?" Qhubeka smiled, her cheeks dimpling.

Beeslaar looked up smartly. "Sorry," he muttered.

"Is something wrong?"

"Not at all." Then he asked, "What do you make of the girl's so-called confession?"

She gnawed at her bottom lip and replied, "Hell, man. I'm not so sure that it's making things less complicated. It certainly doesn't make a lot of sense. If Ellie du Toit *did* shoot her mom, how did she get hold of the pistol? God knows, she's been rambling. Claims she doesn't know how it got into her hands – but she must have taken it from the mom. The question is: how?"

"Also," said Beeslaar, "if her mother was really paranoid, there's no way she'd have handed the weapon to that young girl."

"So you think it was the father, after all?"

"No. Ellie's exact words were: 'My mom was out of it again.' Meaning she was high on drugs. Again. She claims she was lying on the sofa, watching TV, when her mom came in from the back garden."

"She wasn't alone, if I understand correctly?"

"I'm not sure. The girl says it sounded as if she was talking to someone. But there was no one there. And when she saw Ellie, she started screaming. Called the kid a 'lazy slut', tried to chase her out of the house. Ellie had been decorating her thigh with the craft knife. The same one I found among the cushions, remember?"

Qhubeka didn't reply. She looked long and hard at the photos of the murder scene, then said: "Okay. Maybe she lost her temper, threatened her mom with the craft knife." She gave him a quizzical look. "Sounds a bit far-fetched to me, Beeslaar."

"Not necessarily. Take a look at the forensic report – the amount of tik. You said yourself it was enough to fell an ox. So, she was on a very bad trip. Thanks to Mr Swiff-as-in-spliff Quentin Daniels, nè?"

"Okay," said Qhubeka, "so when did the pistol change hands? Come on – you're so damn clever. What you're saying is: she *did* murder her mom. But we don't know exactly how?"

Beeslaar sighed. "Yes. And no. I *do* think there was a quarrel. Mother and daughter. She said her mom had been constantly on her case, especially lately. Unusually aggressive. Maybe she'd tried to go cold turkey. But then, on Tuesday, she'd buckled and taken a hit that made her go bananas."

"And then the kid shot her? But what did she do with the pistol? God, what a mess! We didn't even think of testing her hands for gun residue on Tuesday. How can this be possible, hey? Shit! Fuck-shit! We just *assumed* it was a robbery that went wrong and ended in murder. Allowed ourselves to be led by the nose, because of what the family and that Willemse lawyer of theirs told us!"

"Bester," Beeslaar corrected her.

"*What*?"

"Willem Bester! That's the flippin' lawyer's name!"

"Okay, okay. They all sound so similar."

There was something about the name. The way Qhubeka kept getting it wrong. It bothered him somewhere at the back of his mind, but he couldn't put his finger on it.

They sat in silence for a while. She took another photo from the docket, slid it towards him. He looked at it, gave it back to her. She returned it to the stack, then began to go through all the pictures, one by one.

"See how the bonsais were thrown all over the place. Could a thin, delicate kid like that fling them around with so much force? Or was she also high on some of mommy's meths? Out of control and in a rage?"

He didn't respond. "Beeslaar! I'm *talking* to you!"

"Okay, Qhubeka."

"But you were *there* on Tuesday. You saw how hysterical she was. Sweet Jesus, man. She jumped out of the fucking window. How could we have been so stupid? And you! I thought you're so fucking clever!"

She stood up, kicked her chair backwards against a steel filing cabinet. A towering pile of dockets scattered to the floor. Again, Qhubeka swore and kicked at the cabinet, dislodging the last few files, which fell too. Then she turned around and strode out of the office, still swearing.

Beeslaar had sat motionless during the entire performance, his thoughts one thousand five hundred kilometres away. He hadn't been *there* for her. How long had she been held by the kidnappers? And what about Kleinpiet? Ghaap's story, it still didn't make sense to him. The strange disappearance of the Albanian apeman, on the very day that Gerda was hijacked. Pregnant. God, she'd been *pregnant*!

The old, familiar pain settled in his throat, choked him with renewed vigour. She had said nothing to him. Nothing. "I'm making a new life for myself, Albertus," were her only words the last time they'd talked. He'd been drunk and lonely, and the drink had made him reckless. Telephonitis, it was called. He simply *had* to hear her voice.

She was asleep when he phoned, but he didn't give a damn. It had been a rough day in the Kalahari: a two-year-old that had drowned. They'd tracked down the mother, who was drunk.

Gerda hadn't been angry with him. He'd half expected a scolding. But she'd lost her fire a long time ago. She'd just listened quietly to his outpourings, as he lay his wounded love at her feet.

"Albertus," she'd gently said, "you have to move on. You have to find peace. Please. For *my* sake. And for ..." She'd remained quiet for a long time. "My life is different now. There's no violence any more. I'm finished with that old life. And I want to forget. Please. Grant me that ..."

Beeslaar stared at the phone in his hand. And the child? Was it the apeman's? Was she already pregnant the last time he'd seen her? Her mother's funeral. That evening in his hotel room. He felt the sudden sting of tears behind his eyes. He sniffed unselfconsciously and wiped his hand over his face. He had to leave. And he needed a drink. Surely there was something open, somewhere? But he didn't get very far.

"You can't leave," said Qhubeka as she walked in again – having calmed down considerably. "Malan du Toit and his lawyer are on their way. So is Pram. And he's not exactly happy."

"You don't need me, Qhubeka. You and the colonel will have to handle the father. He'll be spinning all kinds of stories to keep his daughter out of prison."

"Do you think it's *him*?"

"Rather tell me this: hasn't your Charmainetjie perhaps bumped into Swiff in her investigations? Picked up some kind of connection between him and Malan du Toit?"

Qhubeka shrugged. "I know it's part of a bigger thing, a case she's been working on for a long time. Every now and again she works with the guys from the commercial crime unit."

"Phone her," said Beeslaar.

"Not this time of night."

"Just phone her."

"And tell her what? That Swiff Daniels and his lawyer are camping out here? She knows that already. She and the unit guys are investigating about ten of the biggest gangs on the Flats. She's not likely to get excited about a cockroach like Swiff, a guy we've got nothing on, really. No fingerprints, nothing."

"But he was *there*, that day. I saw him among the crowd of rubberneckers, I'm sure of it. The tattoos on his face and arms—"

"It still doesn't make him guilty of murder. And besides, the girl has as good as confessed. What more do you want?"

"Then what is Mr Swiff doing *here*? In the valley? If he's supposed to be a Flats man, what's he doing in this town?"

"Business? His lawyer insists that he's visiting family and friends."

"Family as in grannies and grandpas? Or family as in the brotherhood … The Firm? Charmainetjie would be able to tell us, not so?"

"That's a sharp observation. Maybe. For a dumb dick like you." She smiled at him. "They're going big these days, the gangsters. Do business internationally – directly with the Colombians, the Chinese. Everything on iPads and cellphones and things. They've got their own accountants and full-time lawyers, have wormed themselves into the legit business world. Hotels, casinos, property, stuff like that."

"Then you have enough ammunition for Du Toit, don't you? You don't need me any longer, Qhubeka." He made a move, but she stuck her arm out.

"We're *so* close now." Her big eyes were pleading. He saw how exhausted she was, the dark circles under her eyes. "It's not only the Du Toit guy. It's Prammie, too. He's spitting fire about tonight's developments, says we're making him look like a doos. You have to help me convince him. Would you?"

He groaned inwardly. His heart was urging him to get away quickly, catch a plane to Johannesburg. To Soweto. Where he wanted to … do *what*, exactly? Catch another man's baby? Bare his soul once again? Just to be abandoned like a ghost?

He put his hands on Qhubeka's shoulders. "All right, then. One for all and all for one. To protect and to serve, isn't that so?"

"Captain!" A high-pitched voice yelled at her.

Instantly, he recognised the short, stocky man who came rushing up the stairs: Old Prammie. Beeslaar dropped his arms to his side.

"What in *God's* name do you think you're doing?" He strode up to them, a bag of rusks in one hand, a cellphone in the other. "And *you* are the famous Beeslaar!" he barked.

"That's right, Colonel," Beeslaar replied, holding out a hand that the man ignored.

"My office," the man ordered and marched past them.

Qhubeka shot him a quick I-told-you-so glance and followed her boss. As did Beeslaar.

Once in his office, Qhubeka immediately began to speak: "Colonel, the girl has made a provisional statement. Captain Beeslaar did the same. And Ndlovu has enlisted the help of a man from Legal Aid, who's threatening to take us to court. He's upset about the press conference, says his client was convicted in the press before he was even charged." She stood with her feet planted solidly, hands in her pockets, eyes fixed on the small, agitated man behind his desk.

And small is what Colonel Prometius "Prammie" Baadjies decidedly was. In his mid-fifties, Beeslaar guessed, his walrus moustache already sprouting white. Everything about him was small. The shiny, smooth toffee-brown face, where a small mouth hid under the bushy moustache. Small ears on either side of a virtually bald head, small hands. But they were strong, Beeslaar noticed. The man obviously lifted weights, could even have been a bantamweight boxer in his younger days. He had a Rambo-like look, the neck almost non-existent, sunk into his muscular shoulders.

"And you and Beeslaar go and arrest a man because he irritated you. Why the hell was *that* necessary? Don't we have enough shit as it is? I'm phoned at midnight by the prov com who wants to know if we've lost our marbles!" His phone rang and he aggressively answered: "Yes!" He listened for a second before barking at the caller: "You're wasting my time. Captain Qhubeka had all the right in the world to detain your client! You can pick him up tomorrow. Tomorrow, Mr Patel," he said firmly, and ended the call. Then he again directed his irritation at the two of them: "I'm *waiting*," he said, his knobbly little hands indicating that they should speak.

"Colonel, this is what happened," Beeslaar calmly began to explain. "Late last night, Captain Qhubeka had reason to go and question a suspect in the Jonkershoek Valley – after an incident of, er, housebreaking, damage to property and assault at the home of Ms Maaike van der Wiel in Karindal. She had good reason to suspect that Andries April and Swiff Daniels were responsible for the offences. Since I'm a lodger at Ms van der Wiel's house, I offered to accompany her – for questioning of the two gentlemen. But when we arrived there, we found a whole group of men around a fire. By then they were already far gone. Captain Qhubeka addressed their leader, Mr April, but then one of the other chaps started interfering. He threatened Captain Qhubeka—"

Prammie's phone rang again. This time he answered in a calmer tone, gestured to them to leave the office. Probably the provincial commissioner, Beeslaar reckoned as he closed the door behind them. He seemed to be a man who didn't get much sleep. His strings were being pulled from somewhere. At all hours, it seemed.

Back in her office, Qhubeka picked up the files from the floor.

Her desk telephone rang. She listened wordlessly. "It's Du Toit," she said to Beeslaar when she put the phone down. "He's here. He and the Willemse man."

"Bester. Willem Bester," Beeslaar said wearily, earning a withering look for his trouble.

"The lying bugger and his lying lawyer. Let them wait," she decided. "I need something strong. A mug of tea. How much sugar do you take?" She sauntered out of the door without waiting for his reply. Her footsteps disappeared in the carpeting of the boardroom next door, and then there was the clatter of crockery.

He phoned Ghaap, who informed him that no one could find any trace of the man who'd held Gerda and Kleinpiet captive. Their evidence was shaky, mainly allegations about a witchdoctor in the Chicken Farm squatter camp.

"And?"

"No trace."

"You guys are searching in the wrong way," Beeslaar said. "Not a single soul in that place will open his mouth if the cops rush in there with their sirens blaring. Where's Mabusela?" Beeslaar struggled to remember more names from his time in Soweto. It was a long time ago. The turnover of cops was high in that district.

"Him and Mthethwa have gone out to an accident scene," Ghaap replied. "Three pedestrians in a hit-and-run in Orlando West."

"Killer Road! That's the name for Klipspruit Valley Road. At this time of night it's a race track for the young cheese boys."

"The *what*?"

"Spoilt rich kids, pretending they're Michael Schumacher. But that's irrelevant. You must ask someone to take you to Nkosi Zonda, he's a sangoma in Meadowlands East, Zone 5."

"And how am I supposed to get there? My tackies are moer toe. I'm travelling Johnnie Walker style, or have you already forgotten?"

"Concentrate, boetman. Okay?"

"The witness talks about The Fatha, but the brothers laugh at me. They say it's a shit story. How do I—"

"What's that about The Fatha? Why didn't you tell me long ago?"

"You haven't exactly been answering your phone, have you? When you see it's just old Ghaap, you ignore him."

"Stop talking shit, Ghaap. If The Fatha is your man, you guys had better find him ASAP. Because he vanishes like mist."

"They say he's a shape-shifter. Changes himself into baboons and things."

"That's nonsense. But he *is* bladdy bad news. His real name is … Wait, I'm thinking. Hlanganani. But that's not important. He calls himself uBaba – the father. And he's truly your worst nightmare. The guy deals in body parts. We … I pursued him years ago, when we started finding mutilated kids' corpses. You need to act quickly, Ghaap. The last time he just vanished; we lost his trail somewhere in the bundu in Zululand. Go and ask Nkosi Zonda. He'll know. Tell him I sent you: Mkhulu Umfana, Big Boy. That's the name he knows me by. And then tell him who you're looking for. In Chicken Farm. Nkosi Zonda is almost eighty, he knows that place and its people like he knows his chickens. He's in Twala Street, very close to the Phefeni train station. You must hurry! And phone me if you hear anything about Gerda—"

But Ghaap had already ended the call.

Qhubeka stuck her head around the door. "You have to come," she said urgently. She was holding two mugs of tea, one of which she held out to him. "And the Pram wants to sit in on the interview. He's just let Swiff go. At the insistence of the prov com," she said, clearly annoyed.

In Colonel Baadjies's office, Du Toit's pale lawyer was engaged in a heated argument with the station commander.

"My client *absolutely* insists that we speak to her. She needs her own people now."

"You'll be able to see her shortly. But first we're going to talk," Prammie replied resolutely.

The sinews were taut in his short thick neck, Beeslaar noticed.

"She's on heavy medication, *in no way* criminally responsible. You simply cannot detain her," the lawyer declared. "And I *absolutely* insist that she gets legal representation. At once!" He glared angrily at Baadjies.

Du Toit put a hand on the lawyer's arm. "Wim, shut up. I've come here to make a confession, even though it's so late. I'm more than willing to tell the whole story. *I'm* the one who's responsible for Elmana's death. No one else."

"B … but Malan!" Bester stammered. "That's not true! Your wife's killer is *not* your daughter. And it's definitely not you either. It was a house robbery. Her jewellery was stolen. And the culprit is already—"

Baadjies intervened. "No one's been charged yet, Mr Bester. And maybe you should give your client a chance now. To tell the truth, this time."

Du Toit immediately began: "Elmana *was* still alive when I got to the house. Things happened exactly the way I told you originally. Dawid-Pieter phoned me, said there'd been a burglary and that Mamma ... Elmana had been seriously hurt. Ellie was inside the house when I arrived. Everything ... The house was locked. I tried to break a window, but it's safety glass. I kept calling, calling, ran around to the back of the house. I told Dawid-Pieter to wait at the front gate. The police ... ten-triple-one ... I myself phoned ADT, our security company. I didn't know what the situation was inside the house. I rushed like a madman—" His voice broke off.

"Malan ..." the lawyer cautioned him, but Du Toit ignored him.

"Maybe the assailant was still in the house, I thought. And then I saw ... I was at the sliding door on the back stoep. It wasn't locked. But I could see Elmana's body inside."

"How?" Qhubeka asked sharply. "She died on the floor! You wouldn't have been able to see her from outside!"

"She ... I could see there was chaos. And she ... I saw the blood. The TV blaring. Lots of blood. For a moment I thought she was again ... again—"

"High on drugs," Qhubeka interjected. "Please just accept that we know about that. We've found her equipment, just this evening. At the pool pump, where she'd hidden it."

Du Toit gave her a sideways glance, a strange light in his eyes. Then he hung his head. "Yes, she was—"

"A tik-head." Qhubeka again. She dragged a chair from Prammie's conference table over, and seated herself next to Du Toit.

"But she wasn't dead, was she, Mr du Toit?" said Beeslaar. "She was at most unconscious?"

"Yes. No! That was ... I was furious, yes." He rubbed his forehead, pressed his palms over his eyes, wiped away the wetness. "She'd changed overnight, in an instant, after her mother's death. She was fearful. Didn't sleep, didn't eat. Terrified. She locked herself in her room. The children and I ... We lived on pizza from Debonairs. When I pleaded with Elmana to get help, she'd get hysterical. I begged her, berated her, threatened to have her certified. Things would improve for a while. And then again, the children would phone me one day ... she'd thrown them out of the house. They'd be outside, standing in the street with their school cases, with Elmana barricaded inside. And on Tuesday. On Tuesday it was again ..."

He shut his eyes tightly, tried to get his quivering chin under control. "But ..." He rubbed his face again, pressed hard with his thumb and forefinger on the thin bridge of his nose until his breathing calmed down. "When I reached her," he continued, more composed, "she was sitting with the pistol. She was demented … Said she'd shoot if *I* came any closer. As if … as if I had come to …"

"So how did the pistol get from her hands into yours? And where is it now?"

"I … lied, earlier. I inherited the pistol from my father. A Luger."

"What model?"

"It was old. I don't know much about firearms—"

"What calibre Mr du Toit?" Beeslaar had to work hard at suppressing a desire to shake the man.

"It … my grandfather … He brought it from Germany after the war. It was a sort of family heirloom. I never got as far as … It's very valuable. But after my father's death, I never registered it. It was in my safe at home. But—"

"What *calibre!*"

"P08," he whispered.

Qhubeka and Beeslaar exchanged glances. It could well be the murder weapon as the P08 used 9 mm ammunition, the same bullet that had caused Elmana du Toit's death.

"And where is it now?" Qhubeka sat back, waited for his reply.

"It's been *stolen!*" The lawyer's contribution. "And without it you can't prove anything against my client—"

"Ag, go home, Mr Bester. And take Du Toit with you." Beeslaar could no longer contain his irritation. "Ellie told Captain Qhubeka the whole story. And, to be honest, it's laudable what you're trying to do. But it's too late."

"Besides," Qhubeka added, "Mr du Toit's daughter is already asleep. She's under medical supervision, and there's an outstanding person watching over her. Tomorrow she'll show us where she buried the pistol. Isn't that so, Colonel?"

"Er, yes," Baadjies said and came to his feet.

But Du Toit remained seated. "I'm not leaving. My child is innocent. She has *nothing* to do with this!"

"That's not what she told us," said Qhubeka. "She's already made a statement. In the presence of an official from the child protection services. So you'd best go home now. Your son needs you."

"Yes," Baadjies affirmed. "We'll talk further tomorrow. And then, perhaps, you can see your daughter too."

70

Gerda came to, felt the warm breath of Sister Lucy on her face. For a moment she didn't know where she was. Then she felt the little bundle nestling at her side. Gratitude flooded her heart. The memories of the previous night started coming back.

"The child ... Mpho—"

"Sh-sh-sh-sh," Sister Lucy said comfortingly. "You'll soon feel better. You did very well. Your baby is beautiful. Don't worry. She's fine."

"Mpho ... You must help him. The hyena, it took him. Please help him."

"Shhhhh. You're going to be all right. You've got your drip, nè? Soon—"

"No!" Gerda tried to lift her head but it weighed a ton. "The boy. There was a boy, sisi. He helped me ... He ... I left him there." She began to sob.

"Sh-sh-sh-sh. Thula, thula. Shhh."

"Please! You must help the boy. There was a boy ... His name is Mpho. He's injured."

"Where was this boy?"

"I don't know. On the road. Where ... the people found me. I left him there. I'm so sorry."

"Yoh-yoh-yoh." She wiped Gerda's face with a damp cloth. Her forehead, cheeks. Her neck. "Don't cry. It's not your fault. Tell me, where is this child?"

"In the donga. Under the road. The ... the animal bit him."

"What animal? The one that made you sick? Cut you here, by your breasts? Come, drink some water," she said and lifted Gerda's head, her arm strong and steady as she held a plastic mug to Gerda's lips. She took a sip and coughed. Then another, the water running down the corners of her mouth, into her neck.

"I didn't see," she said between sips. "But you must hurry. Please. It was ... I think it was the ... Don't know where. Squatter camp. By the railway line ... A big hotel. I could see it from the road. Please, please, send someone for the child. He's so small. And alone."

71

Ghalla Kruger arrived to fetch Ghaap. Duif would be joining them too, once he'd finished tending to his pigeons.

They drove west, at breakneck speed. Ghalla flicked a cigarette butt out of the window. "It's starting to get chilly here in the district," he said with a yawn as he closed the window. "A sleepy little village, when you see it lying here like that. The brothers must be exhausted tonight. From all the jigga-jigga."

Ghaap leant back in his seat. "What's jigga-jigga?"

"Making babies." Ghalla yawned again, his foot pumping the accelerator.

The road was dark, few streetlights. The shacks and matchbox houses shot past in a dull grey haze. There was little traffic. Still too early for the first taxis. Ten past four. Ghaap felt nauseous from all the coffee and Coke he'd drunk that night. And the frustration. He'd eventually been forced to call Ghalla for a lift – all the vehicles were out on other jobs.

"Yup," said Ghalla as he sped through yet another red robot. He flicked on his strobe lights, narrowly brushed past a donkey cart with two seated figures huddled against the cold. "That's the thing about the lingos of the district. They've got a word for every damn thing you can think of. You've heard of a starter pack, haven't you?"

Ghaap didn't reply. His head was feeling far too dull for a lecture.

"It's the street name for a small car like a Golf, or a Tazz. But it's also the thing they use to unlock Golfies. Another name for it is a snake. The manufacturers scheme they're soooo clever, always coming up with new antitheft technology. Soon enough, though, the hijackers figure out how to unlock it, laughing their bladdy heads off. When the cops pull a vehicle off the road, that's one of the first things they should look for – that starter pack. But today's cops! Just a bunch of lazy buggers."

He was all innocence when Ghaap gave him a murderous glance. "I swear!" he said. "Whenever you see a bakkie drive past with a neat cover over the back, you should stop it sommer then and there – you'll find either the spares the guys are transporting from the chop-shop, or you'll find the snake. They've got many names for those things, the brothers."

He gave a chuckle, braked sharply for a stray dog and sped off again.

"Every place, every gang. They all have their own lingo and words, and every day they add new ones. Every day, boet, every single day. Especially for the important stuff, like money, sex and dop."

He slowed slightly to swing the car around a traffic circle, then accelerated again, the engine protesting. He sat back in his seat. Mister Cool. "Yes," he continued. "You get the tiger, nè? Ten rand. The half-tiger is five. Two tiger for the twenties. And so on. While a hundred rand is a clip. As in a money clip, see?"

"How far is it still? I thought you said it's just around the corner from here."

"A kay or so, bru. Almost there. Look, there's the station."

Ghaap's nerves were frazzled. He was fuckin' crazy, he thought, to be speeding around here at this time of night. And with *this* guy too. Ghaap suspected he had brain damage, or something. Maybe from his days of driving cash-in-transit vehicles. He drove as if the devil were on his tail, ignoring red lights and stop streets, braking and swerving around the potholes. Time and again it felt as if the car would roll. If a tyre had to burst … And you could barely see anything around you. The smog was pinned low to the road by the cold.

"Now you must keep your eyes peeled," Ghalla said as he slowed down abruptly, then braked and swung the car at an angle onto the pavement so that the headlights illuminated a neat brick house behind a vibracrete wall.

They jumped out, the engine still idling.

Ghaap knocked at the door. All nerves.

An old man in a T-shirt and pyjama pants appeared, his eyes narrowed against the headlights. Ghaap wasted no time: he told him he'd been sent by the Makhulu Boere to get the man's help in finding out where uBaba was. "Sorry, nkosi," Ghaap said, "I've forgotten his real name. But that Makhulu Beeslaar, he said I must tell you it's The Fatha, you know him."

"Yes. Hlanganani. He's back?"

"We believe he's in Chicken Farm. He held a woman captive there. A white woman. We're looking for that mthakathi, but he's disappeared."

"Au-we!" the old man exclaimed. "That man, he's very, very dangerous. You must go to Mama Mahlatse. She's the sangoma there. Look for her house by the railway line. Tell her I sent you."

"Which house, nkosi? I don't know this place."

"You keep right, nè? As you come in it looks as if there's no road, the shacks are so close together. But you keep on with that road. It's a bad road, but it will take you there. To the railway line. You will see her house. It's the only one there made of bricks. It's got a spaza in front."

"I think I know the place," said Ghalla. "Let's go!"

"I have to notify my colleagues," Ghaap called out as they pulled off, tyres screaming.

"Relax, boet," Ghalla said. But Ghaap felt far from relaxed. He was musing about a shape-shifter …

321

They skidded round a sharp corner, went through a red light, with Ghalla braking only slightly. At a big intersection they turned right. "It's a straight road all the way from here. Klipspruit Valley Road. Now it's one time, boet. One time. Quick-quick."

Ghalla already had his Beretta out, cradled between his legs as he controlled the wheel.

Ahead of them, a high building rose from the hazy horizon. "What are all those lights?" he asked.

"It's the new Kliptown – a moerse development around Freedom Square. Hotels, flats, the works!"

Ghalla slowed and suddenly swerved off the tarred road, to his left. His headlights revealed a sea of flat-roofed shacks. To Ghaap, the place looked like a vast scrapyard. Rusted corrugated iron, wooden planks, wire. And it was pitch dark. He spotted rats as big as spring hares, their eyes red in the headlights.

"Ai," Ghalla grumbled to himself, "your brothers have trampled this place dead, boet. You should have seen it earlier tonight."

Ghaap sank lower in his seat and unbuckled his seatbelt, ready to jump and run if the car got stuck or had a flat. He kept his eyes open for any sudden movement. The shacks stood shoulder to shoulder, wedged tightly against each other on either side of the car. In one place the track was so narrow that Ghalla had to reach out of the window to push washing hanging from a line aside. Then he veered off to the right, and the track became even narrower. Someone's "garden gate" hung open: a rusted bundle of wire and wood. Ghalla nudged it closed with the nose of the car.

"Have a look on the back seat," Ghalla said in a hushed voice. "Take out the long gun. So that you've got something to hold on to, boet. But you don't have to worry too much. These people are snoozing. The cops wore them out tonight."

Ghaap couldn't imagine how Ghalla managed to stay so cool. He himself had seldom been so scared. Not so much of the environment as the things he couldn't see. A guy who could bewitch you from out of the darkness. Who cut people to pieces while they were still alive. Talk about a chop-shop! He shuddered. Shape-shifter. He couldn't get the word out of his mind.

"Look in the cubbyhole," Ghalla said softly and stopped the car. The track seemed to come to a dead end against a wall of shacks. "Get the torch." The stench of sewage, smoke and rotting meat hung in the air. To their left, a dilapidated concrete wall separating the houses from a railway line. Further on, Ghaap saw the lights of the hotel that stuck out from the rubble like a sore finger.

"There," said Ghalla, pointing to one of the ramshackle houses next to the railway line. "Ma Mahlatse's place." They climbed out of the car. Ghalla left the lights on.

"You hold the gun," Ghaap said. He didn't want to knock on the antie's door with a rifle in his hand, seeing that he came in peace.

A young girl opened the door.

"I'm looking for Mama Mahlatse," said Ghaap, his voice barely audible. His mouth felt dry.

"Wait," the girl said and closed the door, as if the request were the most natural thing in the world. He could hear her calling softly to wake the Mahlatse woman up.

The front door opened a chink. "No police," the girl said this time.

"Tell her I'm looking for uBaba. The Fatha. Tell her Imi … Imikosi Zola sent me."

The next moment, the door was yanked wide open. "What you want? Hamba, man! Voertsek from this place. You making trouble here in our location. Hamba!" As the woman shut the door, Ghaap stopped her.

"Imikozi Zola sent me!"

"Nkosi!" she sneered. "Imikhosi is fruit! And it's Nkosi *Zonda* who sent you. Why you harrass me? Go away!"

"I'm going nowhere," Ghaap heard himself say, full of bravado. "You show me the place of uBaba. Now! Or I—"

"What's your story, Mama?" Ghalla said behind him. He had the gun slung casually over his shoulder, a placid grin on his face. Just like a guy from an American cop movie. "You now show us that house, okay?"

The woman gave them a hostile look, then turned around and showed them inside. Ghaap lowered his head as he entered the dark room, saw a row of people lying on the floor, one or two of them stirring or snoring. He switched off the torch. They stepped over the row of bodies, Ghalla behind them with the rifle under the arm.

The house was stuffy. Smelt of human odour. The woman stepped through an opening behind a curtain. Inside, a candle was burning. The girl who'd opened the door sat wide-eyed in a corner of the room. Against one wall was some kind of altar, with various bowls and tins and a bundle of smouldering twigs in a saucer. It looked like saltbush, Ghaap thought. The same greyish colour. But he knew this was some other kind of plant. It was mphephu, used for making the smoke that summoned the ancestors. A shiver ran down his spine.

The woman knelt at the little altar; producing a Bic lighter from under her clothing, she relit the smouldering bundle. She started rocking her upper body rhythmically as she chanted in a low, urgent tone. The only word Ghaap could make out was Makhulukhulu, uttered each time she took a breath. He knew it was the Zulu name for God.

323

The girl in the corner had by now joined in the chanting, softly beating out a rhythm on a small cowhide drum.

Ghaap peered cautiously around the room, uncertain of how long he wanted to wait for the ancestors to arrive. There were goat skins on the floor. Rows of shelves along the walls, crammed with bottles and tins and plastic bowls. Her herbal medicines, he guessed.

He cleared his throat, itching for the woman to finish.

This place gave him the creeps.

"Makhulukhulu," she finally said, "siyabonga kakhulu." Thank you very much, God. She came to her feet, the smouldering bundle in her hand. She waved it in front of Ghaap's face and again began to chant. Moved it around his shoulders and along his sides and down his back. She did the same to Ghalla, who brought her ministrations to an end with a melodious, "Thank you."

"I burn the mphephu for you," she told Ghaap, all traces of irritation gone from her face. "It cleanses you. It will protect you. But you must be very, very careful. Ubaba! He's a powerful doctor. You don't go alone. You'll find him there on the other side, nè? Not far from here. In the veld. But you must ... Oooeee," she moaned suddenly and bent double. The girl in the corner started speaking, but he couldn't understand a word, and then she jumped up and wrapped her arms around the woman. Took the mphephu from her hand, waved it all around her.

"Oooeee, the pain. The pain. He's killing me," the woman cried out. Her arms flailed wildly, as if an invisible hand were shaking her.

Ghaap took a giant step back, his skin covered in goosebumps.

"Oooeee! Yoh-yoh-yoh-yoh! It's *him*. He's here!"

Ghaap retreated another step, poised to flee. From the corner of his eye, he could see Ghalla lowering the barrel of the rifle.

"The address, Ma! Tell us the address!" he said, the rifle aimed at the two women. "You! Help her tell us. We're wasting time!"

The girl kept waving the mphephu furiously. "It's here," she called out, helping Ma Mahlatse to sit down. "That way, there, in the veld. Number seven three nine. You go now. Go! You have brought his evil here. He's attacking her." Ghaap didn't wait another second before turning around and rushing to the front door, with Ghalla bringing up the rear.

They ran outside. Both men had their phones out, and began to summon the troops.

72

"You know," Qhubeka remarked as she got into her van, "we should perhaps have kept Du Toit here. Who knows what nonsense he might get up to tonight."

"Get some sleep, Qhubeka." Beeslaar stood next to the van in the chilly wind, his hands in his pockets. He had only one thing on his mind: making a phone call. "It's almost dawn and today's going to be a helluva long day for you. Your case is far from done and dusted."

"And what about you?"

Beeslaar waved her off, started walking. "Go to bed," he called over his shoulder. "I'm okay."

She drove away and the moment her rear lights had disappeared round a corner, he whipped out his phone.

"We've *got* the bastard! We've *got* him," Ghaap answered excitedly.

But that's not what Beeslaar wanted to hear. "Gerda," he said. "You must see to it that she gets out of Bara. Get her into a private clinic. I'll pay. Please just make sure that she and Kleinpiet are moved out of there and taken as quickly—"

"Beeslaar, I *can't* do it right now. I swear. We're in Chicken Farm. I did as you told me. At this very moment, we're on our way to an address because we *know* now where that fucker hangs out. But I'll call you later. Over and out!"

Beeslaar cursed, resisted the impulse to smash the phone against an oak tree. Mister Soweto had more important things to focus on right now than the life of a woman. *His* woman.

He launched a fierce kick at a cement bin on the pavement. It wobbled for a moment and he kicked again, but the thing still didn't fall over. Then he grabbed the bin with both arms and lifted it, strewing rubbish over himself in the process. Howling with rage, he hurled the bin into the darkness. As far as he could. It hit a pole with a thud as it broke into pieces. Beeslaar bent down and grabbed one of the cement chunks, flung it against the snow-white wall of a historic house. It made a sizeable hole in the brittle plaster. Panting, Beeslaar observed his handiwork for a while.

Then he headed off into the wind. He walked up Merriman, past the university buildings, the hospital. Saw the Pieke in the distance, and the morning star.

He tried to banish the image of Gerda Matthee-Fouché from his mind. Somewhere within the mazes of that dreadful hospital. In labour. Would she have the luxury of a bed? Not likely. She was lying somewhere in those corridors – between the front entrance and the mortuary. On a mattress, if she was lucky.

If only there was someone he could phone. Who'd go there to fetch her. Wherever she was ... Ten kilometres of corridors – spread over at least four hundred buildings, but still too small. The masses of patients, daily. The hospital only had enough beds, enough staff for three thousand – in a community of close to five million people.

And Gerda ... Just thinking of her made him want to smash something.

How the hell could the bladdy trackies have dropped her there, of all places? Were they out of their minds? Milpark Hospital was just a few minutes further at most, *and* it specialised in trauma!

Beeslaar kicked wildly at a takeaway box that the wind had blown against his leg. And where was the father? The hairy Albanian. Mister New-life-for-Gerda!

He lengthened his stride, bent into the wind. A bergie pushing a supermarket trolley appeared suddenly around the corner of a building, hitting him on the side of his thigh.

"Watch where you're fokken going!" Beeslaar bellowed and kicked viciously at the man's trolley. It toppled over, catapulting a mass of empty bottles and other detritus onto the pavement. The stunned trolley proprietor stood staring for a moment – at the scattered shards of his bottles and the enraged giant who'd caused the damage.

"Sorry, my larney," he stammered. "I didn't expect anybody so early. Sorry, sorry."

The fear in the man's eyes brought Beeslaar to his senses. He shoved his hand into his pocket to find his wallet, saw the man duck instinctively at the movement.

Beeslaar pressed a hundred-rand note into his hand and walked wordlessly around the glass-strewn pavement as he walked homeward. He had probably sown enough infantile chaos for the night. Maybe he should waste his energy on something more useful. As Blikkies used to say: "If you want to fix the world by using your balls, you'll end up unmanning yourself. Just take it from an old man who tried to make a career out of that. Who beat up suspects until they told me what I wanted to hear, believing it's the only language a criminal understands: war-war, instead of jaw-jaw."

The idea of being unmanned sparked a new thought. Qhubeka was right: they should never have let Du Toit go.

He began to walk faster, his arms pumping. Fuckwit! he berated himself. The solution was *so* damn obvious. Handed to him on a platter earlier that night. He quickened his pace, the adrenaline urging him on. After the Merriman circle he veered right, in the direction of Malan du Toit's house. He broke into a trot. He should have thought of it earlier. But his head had been in Soweto … He should have gone with Qhubeka. And they should have anticipated Du Toit. He phoned Qhubeka.

"Go and pick up Swiff and April," he gasped into the phone. "I'm on my way to Du Toit's house. I think I know what happened to the pistol. *And* who pulled the trigger!"

She didn't argue or ask any questions, just said, "I'm on it like a comet."

The front gate was hanging open. And the house itself was dark.

Beeslaar raced around the side of the house, past the fountain, the swimming pool. Stopped a moment to catch his breath in the murky dawn. He moved stealthily down the steps to the green garden behind the pool. There was a sudden movement in the shrubs to the side of him. He took out his pistol. "You can come out, Mr du Toit! I know you're there," he shouted.

Silence.

Beeslaar stepped forward slowly. "Du Toit!"

He took another step, called out again. Beeslaar couldn't make anything out in the dense curtain of foliage. He stood as still as a mouse, straining his ears. Then he heard it. The breathing.

"It's over, Du Toit," he said, "you can stop hiding now."

"No one's hiding," the man replied, emerging from behind a shrub.

He had his hands in the air. Empty.

"Relax," said Beeslaar. "Do I have to guess, or are you going to tell me yourself what exactly you're doing here?"

"It's Ellie's cat. I came to look for her cat. When I see her, she'll want to know how it's doing. And … I've forgotten about the—"

"What does it look like?" Beeslaar interrupted, sitting down on the top step.

"It's a cat, man. A cat."

"How sure are you that she's actually got a cat?"

"I paid for the thing, dammit!"

"Yes. But there's a difference, see? It's one thing to write out a cheque for a fancy cat, but quite another to know whether it still exists – if it ever did."

Du Toit didn't reply. He just stood there.

Beeslaar regarded the man's exhausted figure. The lines on either side of his mouth had changed into furrows overnight, he'd grown a bit of stubble, and the wreath of hair around his bald spot stuck out every which way. His eyes were bloodshot.

"You're not looking for the cat, Mr du Toit," Beeslaar said, and stood up. "I think you were so deep in denial about what was going on in your own house that you wouldn't recognise that cat even if it had to jump out of your pocket.

You know as little about the animal as you know about the members of your own household, not so? You didn't know that your son had suddenly become a Bible-basher. You didn't know your daughter had been bunking school for months. Because you weren't there to witness the disintegration of your family. Right?"

Du Toit sank down onto a step, sat huddled at Beeslaar's feet. He rubbed his hands roughly over his eyes, leaving streaks of mud on his cheeks.

"Yes. You're right. And yes, *I* killed her, Beeslaar. It wasn't Ellie."

He stared vacantly into the darkness. His shoulders were sagging.

"Bullshit." Beeslaar pulled his jacket closed; the wind was icy on his sweaty body. "It wasn't you. And I suspect it wasn't exactly your daughter either."

"What? Man, don't you understand?"

"I think I understand only too well, Mr du Toit. Who are your financial backers for the Jonkershoek development?"

Du Toit's head jerked up, fear in his eyes.

"Come, now. It's cold out here in the garden. And in any case you haven't found the pistol, have you? Because *I* think it was removed long ago. The big question is, by whom? You lied to us, didn't you? You *don't* own a pistol. But you did find a pistol at the scene on Tuesday. You and your son buried it here in the garden."

Du Toit didn't react. His head hung on his chest.

Beeslaar bent down to help him to his feet. "Come," he said, "let's go find some warmth. Do you have keys for the house?"

Du Toit looked up at him in alarm. He was afraid of seeing the murder scene again, Beeslaar realised.

"We're just getting out of the wind," he reassured him. "So that we can talk, okay?" He took a bunch of keys from the man, led him by the arm round the side of the house, unlocked the front door, and switched on the lights. Du Toit trailed behind him like a somnambulist. Beeslaar sat the man down on an old riempie bench in the entrance hall and stood opposite him, leaning against the railing of the staircase.

"It's not true," said Du Toit, his voice husky. "What you said outside …" He took out a handkerchief, wiped his mouth and face with a trembling hand. Stared with surprise at the mud.

Then wearily he said, "You have to let my daughter go. I'm to blame for everything."

"You're probably right, Mr du Toit. But there's a difference between culpability and actual complicity. Because it's for the latter that I'm going to lock up your lackeys."

Du Toit shook his head. "I can't carry on any more, Beeslaar. I can't. God knows … I have …" His bottom lip began to quiver, and once again he rubbed his palms across his cheeks.

"This time you have to believe me. It *was* me. I cracked up. I was at the end of my tether. I took the pistol from her and—"

"Stop right there! Try again. And this time you tell me the truth. I think I already know, but for your own sake and that of the children, it's better that I hear it from you, okay?"

"You *must* promise me first that you'll let her go."

Beeslaar shook his head. "I'm a cop, Mr du Toit. Of the old school. I don't make deals when I already know what the truth is. Because you'll try to lie to me *again*. To keep your daughter out of jail."

"Please, Beeslaar. She's a … She's not strong. She won't make it."

"She's much stronger than you think, Du Toit. Your daughter will pull through. But it's *you* I'm worried about. Because your life won't be safe if it's known who your *real* pals are, not so? And that's why you actually want to go to jail for a murder that you definitely didn't commit. Rather tell me about your so-called business partners."

Du Toit hung his head. "My business has nothing to do with this."

"It's got *everything* to do with it, man. In fact, it's not really your daughter you're so concerned about! You're trying to save your own skin, aren't you?" Beeslaar took out his phone and called Qhubeka. "Can you please send someone to pick us up?" he asked. "And Charmaine had better come in as well."

"Right," she said. "Anything else?"

"There is something else, yes," Beeslaar said, "the man you caught so much flack for. The municipal official you'd arrested for drunk driving. Willemse, or something like that – the guy who died in custody."

"Williams!"

"The very same. Charmainetjie should get his bank statements. I believe *he's* our missing link."

73

"That oke has just joined the amaDlozi," said Ghalla Kruger, and lit a cigarette. Along with Ghaap, Mo van Schoor and Duif Vermeulen, he was leaning against Mo's black Lancer. They'd just heard shots being fired in Hlanganani's house.

For a moment there was silence – and then an unearthly wailing. It sent shivers through Ghaap's body, from his heels, along his back, right up to the top of his head. It sounded like a cat that had been hurled into a fire, then changed to a roar, and a gurgling howl, as if a person were drowning in a sticky substance.

Ghaap peered at the umThakathi's house through the haze. His hands itched to storm in there himself with an R5. But he was forbidden to join his colleagues: too junior, and also semi-suspended.

And now everything was suddenly over, it seemed. This was clear from the calls of a commander inside the house. He could see it in the lowering of the cordon of rifles around the house.

He'd seldom felt so useless. By rights, he was the man who should have led the raid on the house of Hlanganani, aka uBaba, aka The Fatha. Not just standing around like a lost fart, rubbernecking with the civvies. Because *he* was the one who'd finally cracked this case. Admittedly, with Beeslaar's help, but still … He hadn't deliberately lost his service pistol. They could at least have given him an R5. He couldn't believe his ears when Mthethwa banned him from the action.

That would teach him to go by the book. All he'd got for his efforts was for his slapgat colleagues to grab the credit. A slimeball like Hlanganani … How many times in your career do you come up against someone like that? *How many times?*

He kicked furiously at a stone. Missed. Glanced up to check whether anyone had noticed. All three trackies looked away; their cheeks were quivering as they struggled to suppress their laughter. Which made Ghaap even more the moer in. And then he sullenly asked: "What's this fokken 'amaDlozi' thing anyway?"

It was Ghalla who replied. "The ancestors, bru. The ancestral spirits. It's tickets for that brother inside that house. He's just had his last meal. But *you,* Sergeant Djannie, *you* sniffed out the fucker single-handedly. You may not be the SAPS's number-one kicker, but you sure kicked ass – big time. You made history tonight, boet. That's befok, ek sê!"

"Ag, whatever," Ghaap mumbled, suddenly embarrassed. Ghalla leant into the window of Mo's car and grabbed a pack of cigarettes from the dashboard, offered it to Ghaap.

"Thanks, man," said Ghaap and put a cigarette in his mouth.

Ghalla offered him a light, then yawned and stretched. "I wonder how the antie's doing there in Bara?" he asked. "I scheme she's probably calved by now."

"Ghalla, my friend, I don't want to tune you, but you're really crude, man. That woman … She's family, mos."

"Family? Serious? And you didn't say anything!"

"I did, but nobody wants to listen to me!" He told them about the Beeslaar connection. How Beeslaar had been the one who ultimately put him onto Hlanganani-The-Fatha's trail.

"Old moerbroer," Mo squeaked. "I'd heard of him. A big guy, with anger issues. He bliksemed one of his superiors, if I remember correctly. I thought he'd have become a bouncer or something by now. Joined the private sector."

"No way," said Ghaap, "these days he runs around the Kalahari. He's my boss."

Mo gave Ghaap a slap on the shoulder. "Kwaai," he said.

Day was breaking, and the four of them started moving towards the witchdoctor's house. Ghaap was itching to see what he looked like.

An ambulance had arrived. Two young men climbed out in a leisurely manner and took a stretcher from the back. No urgency at all; they clearly knew that they were collecting a corpse.

The inside of the house was badly damaged. There was blood on the wall of the front room, a lounge that now resembled a war zone. There was an upholstered two-seater couch, a boxy old TV on a coffee table, and an overturned display cabinet that Hlanganani had probably used as a shield in the gunfight. It couldn't have helped him much – he was totally fucked.

The body was slumped against a wall, with bloodstains arced around it. A cushion was propped under the man's chin – a fruitless attempt, perhaps, to staunch the bleeding. A bullet must have split open his throat. Ghaap crouched down and peered in under the cushion, saw the whitish tube of the severed windpipe. That was the gurgling yell he had heard: Hlanganani choking and drowning in his own blood.

Half of the face was shot away, the upper teeth protruding through blood and tissue like old ivory. It was difficult to estimate his age. But he was a big man, stomach bulging over a belt, thick legs sticking out of his shorts. The one knee was torn away; yellow fat and splinters of bone protruded from the wound.

Whichever of the bullets had hit him first, Ghaap thought with satisfaction, one thing was certain: the shape-shifter had died a brutal death. Then he stood up and took a last look at the corpse. On the man's left wrist was a woman's watch, barely visible in a bloodied tangle of strips of leather and beads.

In another room, the body of a young woman lay curled up in a pool of blood. She, too, had a wound to her neck. But, Ghaap realised, that was no bullet wound – it was as if a bear had bitten her.

In the back yard there was a small, windowless corrugated-iron shack, with a mattress on the floor. And ropes, which in all likelihood had been used to restrain Gerda Matthee.

Behind the shack was a kennel.

But no trace of a dog.

When Ghaap had finished looking around, he found Ghalla waiting for him.

"Duif said he'd organise some chow for us. He had to let his feathered friends out for a while, otherwise they'll croak. So we're having breakfast at his pozzie!"

Great, Ghaap thought glumly, thinking of the smell of Duif's pigeons. Aloud, he said: "But what about Gerda Matthee? Beeslaar says we have to get her out of Bara."

"That's okay by me. But I doubt she's ready to cruise yet. We don't even know if the baby's come. All the more reason for a visit. Anyway, she's family!"

Outside the window, there's the gleam of the early-morning sun through the haze of cooking fires in the township. A soft orange glow. It was at times like these, Ghaap thought, that it was possible to believe that there was a God in heaven. And goodness on this earth.

"Oh hell," said Ghalla, "my wife'll be spitting fire. She'll have to drop the laaities off at school *again*, this morning."

"You've got kids?" Ghaap asked in surprise.

"Check here," said Ghalla, producing a photo from his shirt pocket.

Ghaap held it at an angle, to catch the pale light. "Ha, ha," he said, "moerse funny." It was a photo of two little black boys.

"Genuine!" said Ghalla. "They're my laaities! Trevor and Fikile."

"Stop joking," said Ghaap, annoyed. "These kids are black."

"So? I mos suffered some damage. During that last cash-in-transit robbery the motor got a bit smashed. Can't make babies. But these two I picked up. Not too far from here!"

"Kak, man."

"I'm telling you, pal. You can ask old Duif. I was on my way home one evening when I saw something moving in the veld. I sat waiting for the robot – minding my own business. But then I heard the laaitie. It was my Trevor."

"What kind of a name is Trevor in any case for a Boer like you?"

"He's a bit dark, the laaitie. I couldn't call him Frikkie. His pals would mock him!"

Ghaap handed back the photo, a smile on his face, and also in his heart.

He read the name outside: Chris Hani Baragwanath Hospital. He'd heard many stories about this place – third biggest in the world, they said. But nothing could have prepared him for what he saw. The reception area was already packed with sick people waiting to get help.

Ghalla walked past a long line of people and spoke to a clerk at a counter. "Come!" he called out to Ghaap. "Looks like they had an Eskom moment here. Lights out! At four this morning they had to lock the doors for an hour to stop the masses from stripping the place. All these people had to queue outside. And they'd had a shift change too. It doesn't look quite as bad as this every day!"

They landed in a corridor that seemed to stretch into eternity. As far as the eye could see, there were people sitting or lying or milling around. Ghalla walked through confidently, pressing Ghaap against a wall whenever a gurney emerged from a side corridor, carrying some poor sod.

At one point they had to clamber over a number of people. "Askies, mama. Askies!" Ghalla kept calling out as they made their way through the throng. Then they passed through a set of swing doors and found themselves in relative calm.

"Now we have to look for her," Ghalla said. They walked for a while before spotting Gerda. She lay on a sponge mattress against the wall, a smaller figure than Ghaap had expected. Her face was pale, her lips cracked and raw. Her russet hair was drawn back, a damp bundle at her neck.

They squatted next to her. Ghalla gently pushed a strand away from her forehead.

She gave a wan smile, turned her head towards him and slowly opened her eyes. For a moment she looked puzzled, then she recognised him from the night before.

"Hey you," Ghalla whispered, "you're the bravest cherry I've ever seen, you hear?"

The smile broadened. For a while she just looked at Ghalla, her green eyes swollen and red.

She lifted her hand. It was a slim hand, two of the fingernails broken and bruised to the quick.

She touched Ghalla's arm, then lifted the blanket that covered her body. Showed them the tiny pink face lying next to her.

"Wow!" Ghalla exclaimed in a low voice. "And that's the prettiest little thing I've ever seen." He beckoned to Ghaap. "Boet, come check the little kiddy!" With a broad grin he exclaimed, "It's the most beautiful baby in the whole wide world!"

The woman lowered the blanket and tried to say something, but no sound emerged. Ghalla brought his ear to her mouth. Listened, then explained to Ghaap: "Sister Lucy. I think it's the nursie."

Ghaap turned around to go in search of the nurse. But he found himself blocked by the huge bulk of a woman who had blood on her uniform and lightning in her eyes.

"*What* are you doing here!" she thundered.

Ghalla jumped to his feet. "Sorry, Matron, we've just come for a quick—"

She silenced him with a raised hand. "There's no time," she said. "You must go back to the place where you found this lady. She says there's still a child out there!"

"Her child? But we brought the child. A doctor took him—"

"Don't be stupid, wena! It's an African boy. She says he's the one that saved her life! He's still there, under the road. Right by the place where you found her and the little one! Go quickly!"

"Is he okay? The picaninny?" asked Ghalla, pointing to Gerda Matthee behind him on the floor.

"It's a *she*. And she's fine, but you're wasting time. Now get out of here and go do your work!"

74

After he'd spoken to Qhubeka, Beeslaar phoned Ghaap.

"Can't talk now!" said Ghaap.

"Hey! Lis—"

"I'll call you back!"

The line went dead.

Beeslaar took a deep breath. Frustration burnt in his throat.

His phone rang. Rea du Toit. He brought the phone to his ear reluctantly, glanced across to where Du Toit was sitting with his head in his hands.

"Albertus, I can't get hold of Malan. You have to help. I think Dawid-Pieter is in trouble."

Beeslaar gulped. Dear God, was there no end to this infernal case? They'd all been awake since … for ever? Dully, he said, "What kind of trouble, Tannie Rea?"

"The police must go look for him!"

"Where? What's going on?"

"It's his church friends. They've been receiving strange SMSes from him, since four o'clock already. They've tried to call Malan and Ellie, but they're not answering their phones!"

"Where is he, Tannie Rea?"

"That's what I don't know, Albertus. Apparently he's got a firearm! You have to help us, please."

"Who phoned you?"

"It was his frend, Francois! He told me Dawid-Pieter had SMSed him to say goodbye and to ask for forgiveness. He sounded confused, he said!"

"Send me his number – immediately!" An image flashed through his mind of the boy who'd pressed the card into his hand. When was that, again? It felt like days ago. Years. Another lifetime.

By now Du Toit was standing, alarm on his face. He felt around in his pockets, failed to find his phone, and ran to his office. And then the sound of a high-pitched voice, making a call.

Beeslaar, in turn, phoned Liewe Heksie – there was nothing else for it.

She answered at once. "Maaike speaking."

"Maaike, it's Beeslaar. The card I showed you yesterday afternoon. The one from the Jesus freaks? I need the phone number on it. It's urgent, please!"

"Just a moment," she said. He heard barking, the sound of doors opening and closing. Then her voice: "Got it," and she read out a number.

Beeslaar scribbled it down on the wall next to the stairs, called immediately. Voicemail. He left a message. Then he rushed to the office and shouted, "Have you found anything out yet?"

A wild-eyed Du Toit was sitting behind his desk, a tremor in the hand that clutched the phone.

"Who are you calling?" asked Beeslaar.

"Wim. He says Dawid-Pieter isn't in his room. He must have slipped out."

"When last did you see him?"

"Last night, when Wim and I went to the police. He'd woken up, insisted on coming with us. He wanted to pray for her or something. He was distraught, wanted to phone a preacher to, er, intercede for us with God. He kept talking about … God, have we all gone mad? He said Elmana had given her heart to the devil. And that's why, that's the reason everything happened. We managed to calm him down before we left and Wim's wife took him in hand, said she'd look after him."

Just then, Beeslaar's phone chirped again. A please-call-me SMS, with a number. He phoned at once.

"Albertus …"

His heart lurched. He tried to say something, but his voice was gone.

"Albertus, you have a daughter. We're …" Her voice faded, then came back. "We're okay. In Baragwanath. It was Baz, Albertus. *He's* the one who's responsible … It's *him*."

"Gerda!"

The line went dead. He redialled the number, his hands shaking as if he had the DTs.

"Êhê! Sister Lucy here!"

"Is she all right, please …"

"She's fine. I'm a bit worried about the mother. But we've got a drip coming. You can call again before I go off duty, okay?"

"Thank you! Please, please take good care of—" But she'd already put the phone down.

A daughter. He, Beeslaar, had a daughter.

The phone rang again, and he listened intently.

"Oom, it's Francois. Oom must please look for Dawid-Pieter—"

"Do you know where he is?"

"Oom, he SMSed that we must pray for him. Satan has destroyed his family. He's said his final prayers … God has turned his back on the Du Toits and—"

"*Where*, Francois, *where* is he?"

"I don't know."

"Where do you *think* he may be?"

"Oom—"

"Think!"

"Yes, Oom. I think … the suspension bridge, maybe. We—"

"Just keep thinking, and let me know. We're off to the suspension bridge."

Malan du Toit was already in the doorway. "I'll get my car," he said.

Beeslaar phoned Qhubeka, informed her about the latest developments.

There was a gate at the entrance to the bridge. Locked. Beeslaar recognised the area. It was near Liewe Heksie's house, at the edge of the town, on the banks of the Eerste River. Du Toit was already climbing over the two-metre-high wire fence, calling out his son's name.

Beeslaar spotted a smaller, unlocked gate and ran through it. The first rays of sunshine were breaking behind the mountains and the wind had come up with renewed fury. Both men kept calling out as they ran. Ahead of them was a cemented ford, a pedestrian bridge alongside it.

The bridge was a contraption suspended from steel cables attached to poles on either side of the river. The boy sat in the middle of it, his legs and arms hanging casually through the railing. As he sat there, apparently musing, or merely bored, a pistol dangled from his right hand.

Beeslaar stopped at the bridge, blocking access, and shouted the boy's name. There was no reaction. The boy's father stood pressed up against him, and shouted, "Let me through!" Beeslaar held him back. He called out to the boy, who slowly turned his head towards them. He said something, but his words were drowned out by noise of the wind and the water rushing over the ford.

Beeslaar called out again.

"Keep away!" came the reply. Dawid-Pieter was holding the pistol in both hands. Beeslaar jumped forward and landed with his full weight on the bridge, which began to wobble.

The boy grabbed hold of the cable with one hand, the pistol dangling in the other.

"Listen, Dawid-Pieter! It's *not* your fault, okay?"

The boy said nothing, stared vacantly. Beeslaar inched forward and the bridge rocked from side to side. He had to clutch at the cable to keep his balance. The entire bridge was in motion, rocking the boy who was sitting in the middle of it. He called out something to Beeslaar and held the pistol aloft – a P08. Beeslaar tried to see whether the safety catch was on. Malan du Toit was pushing from behind to get past him, making the bridge sway again, and throwing Beeslaar off balance.

The boy shouted again, telling them to keep away, and lowered the pistol to the level of his face. Beeslaar took two long strides and the bridge bounced.

The boy grasped instinctively at the cable; the pistol flew from his hand, disappeared into the rushing water.

Beeslaar stormed forward, the bridge like a trampoline under his feet.

Then he reached the boy, bent down, and grabbed him by his collar.

By the time they had shepherded Dawid-Pieter away from the bridge, Qhubeka was on the scene.

Unceremoniously, she bundled both father and son into the back of the police van. Ordered Beeslaar to drive with her.

"My car," Malan du Toit complained from the back of the van. "My car is unlocked!"

"You should have thought of that earlier, dammit," Qhubeka snapped at him and slammed her door closed, but she waited nonetheless while Beeslaar went to lock the vehicle. Lights flashing, they drove through deserted, dew-fresh streets. Beeslaar phoned Ghaap's number again. He reached voicemail, left a brief, irate message.

"What *is* with you and that phone?" Qhubeka asked in annoyance.

"It's ... nothing."

Apparently deciding not to pursue the matter, she told him instead that Prammie himself was accompanying the task force team that had been dispatched to pick up Swiff and Andries April.

"The chickens are coming home to roost," Beeslaar remarked distractedly, his eyes still on his cellphone screen.

"That's for fuckin' sure, ouboet," she said with a tired smile.

75

Ghaap and Ghalla found themselves stuck in traffic. Directly opposite the hospital entrance was a taxi rank as big as a soccer field, with milling passengers and a multitude of minibus taxis.

"Ag no, man," Ghalla muttered under his breath, "the brothers are busy again today."

"What's up with you and all this brothering?" asked Ghaap. He was famished and dog-tired, his eyes were burning, and he was so thirsty he could drink a dam dry.

"It doesn't mean anything, boet. It's just the lingo around here."

Too clapped out to reply, Ghaap switched on his phone and saw the string of missed calls from Beeslaar. For once in his life the bugger can wait a while, he decided. He phoned Mabusela, who seemed to be holed up in some kind of raucous establishment. He informed him of the situation with the child, told him that he and Ghalla were on their way back to Chicken Farm. Mabusela said he and Mthethwa would come too.

Ghalla switched on his strobe lights, swung the car onto the rumble strip, and gained some ground by racing along the dusty gravel, the oncoming traffic hooting at him as he did so. At a big intersection, they pushed through the red traffic lights and skidded off in a southerly direction. The traffic was lighter in this area. Ghalla turned off again, into the quieter streets of a residential neighbourhood. His foot flat on the accelerator, he hooted at the sight of a pedestrian and had a couple of close shaves through a series of red lights. Ghaap marvelled once more at the patience of the other motorists.

Here and there, Ghalla took a short cut across an uneven patch of open veld. Ghaap's head kept bumping against the roof of the car and he clung on for dear life, ignoring his phone when it rang. Probably Beeslaar again, but he was certainly not going to look now. They swerved through another maze of narrow streets, and Ghaap swore he'd soon kick a hole through the footwell, he was braking so hard.

Suddenly they were out of the neighbourhood and on a wider road. Modjadji Street, Ghaap read on a curbstone. Ahead was a big set of traffic lights and he recognised the surroundings, saw the huge block of the Soweto Holiday Inn. Ghalla swerved onto Klipspruit Valley Road. Behind them lay the run-down buildings of Kliptown's business centre, and then the railway line came into view.

The traffic thickened, and for long stretches Ghalla drove off the tar, racing along the rutted strip alongside the road. They dashed across the railway line, with Chicken Farm just ahead. But this time they didn't drive in. They sped on to the crossing with Old Potch Road, swung to the left. After about a hundred metres, Ghalla brought the car to a halt.

"I scheme this is the spot, boet. Right here. You take the long gun," he said, "and don't forget the torch!"

By the time Ghaap was out of the car, Ghalla had already disappeared down the steep shoulder of the road into a thicket. He followed, scrambling down the slope. As they ran, the vegetation became more and more dense. Ghaap spotted a red sandal and pointed it out to Ghalla, who nodded: it had to be the Matthee woman's.

A short distance along, they suddenly found themselves at the giant pipe of an aqueduct.

Ghaap shone the torch into the dim passage. The first thing he noticed was bloodstains in the dry sand. He cocked his gun and passed the torch to Ghalla, who had his pistol out. Ghaap crouched down at a large bloodstain, studied the strange-looking tracks.

"Wolf," he said softly.

"*What?*"

"Shine the light here, man! Take a look. The tracks." He took the torch from Ghalla, shone it deeper into the pipe. The beam illuminated litter that had been washed up here by years of rainstorms. "It took something, here. Look at the trail. Must be a moer of a big thing."

"What kind of a thing, boet?" Ghalla cocked his pistol, aimed it into the dark.

"Hyena, a big one. Must be a female. Look at this." Ghaap showed him the tracks. "Look, you can see here. Big paws in front, little ones at the back. First, they walk out of the pipe. And then they drag something back in." He pointed to the mouth of the aqueduct. "Seems to me that the animal was here first. It must've stalked the woman and the child …" The torchlight caught something that dried Ghaap's words in his mouth. A child's foot. He stood up, raising the beam higher because he couldn't see the body. The foot seemed to be growing out of the sand and litter. He'd have to go closer. He motioned to Ghalla to come.

Then they saw the rest of the body. A boy's body. One arm covered in blood, the bone and sinews visible in the light from the torch.

Ghaap sank to his haunches next to the boy, felt for a pulse at the neck.

He was alive!

76

Beeslaar gratefully accepted another mug of rooibos tea. Luckily, it contained no milk. Plenty of sugar, though, which he needed desperately.

He was itching to be out of this place. On a northbound plane. Qhubeka had asked him so nicely, but still he'd protested: "There's not a single reason for me to stay."

She had looked up at him earnestly, the fear and uncertainty of the night before written all over her face. God, was it really the night before?

"You … Listen, I'm not going to beg. But you said it yourself: all for one – didn't you?" Her gold-flecked eyes entreating him, seemingly defenceless.

He cursed himself for succumbing to his perennial weakness – another's vulnerability.

Maybe it was the news from Johannesburg. It had left him raw, as if his skin had been peeled off. He needed to pull himself together. This vulnerability was dangerous. The weakness of caring; you lost your shell, opened yourself up once more to the pain.

"An hour," he had said. "Then I have to leave for the airport. Urgently. There's something … something up north that I have to sort out."

They waited together for the lawyers to arrive. In the meantime, Qhubeka had sent someone to fetch the grandmother from the old age home and bring her to the station. And Prammie had obtained a warrant for the seizure of the contents of Malan du Toit's office – at work as well as at home. He came to tell them the news, and stayed on when Charmaine rushed in with two senior officials from the National Prosecuting Authority in tow. All three of them were frantic with worry: the Du Toit case threatened to derail an investigation of many years into the affairs of a well-known Cape "businessman". Charmaine had become involved after the NPA guys began to suspect that a certain Leonard "Pannevis" Davis, one of the Cape's top six gang bosses, was extending his "domain" into the platteland – in other words, Stellenbosch.

Davis, Charmaine told them, was a "respected citizen" with a swanky house on the slopes of Plattekloof – a view of Table Mountain – and an array of legal businesses, including a restaurant in Sea Point, several loan shark agencies, a petrol station, minibus taxis …

"That's just his profile on the surface," Charmaine said. "But his real business is with a Chinese organisation that supplies methamphetamine and heroin in exchange for perlemoen and rhino horn. He's the main link between the Chinese and the five-hundred-man syndicate, The Ninja Boys."

"How does it tie in with Malan du Toit?" asked Beeslaar.

"Look, we've kept the investigation very quiet, thus far. That's why I haven't really been forthcoming with info, Vuvu. Sorry, but we had to be careful, all the walls have ears. What we know for sure is that Pannevis is eager to become legit. We believe that Du Toit's development presented him with a golden opportunity. He's sitting on mountains of cash but has no legal outlet to launder it. It's *Mission Impossible*, nowadays. Before the 2003 FICA legislation, South Africa was the money-laundering capital of the world. But today the banks throw you out, even if you roll up with the little pile of cash you'd earned from baking bread. They refuse to deal with cash deposits that exceed five thousand rand. Many gangsters were knee-capped by this legislation in the past – like the late Rashied Staggie, former boss of the Hard Livings gang. But it never takes these okes long to come up with a new plan." Charmaine's eyes sparkled with excitement.

"Property?" Qhubeka contributed.

"Right on, Vuvu. That, I believe, is the link between Davis and Du Toit."

"But how exactly?" asked Qhubeka. "Just give us the short version; we're all dead tired."

"Yes, ma'am! The one link is Shane Williams – a municipal official – also known as the late Shane."

"Williams!" said Beeslaar. "I *knew* he was the link."

"Indeed," said Charmaine. "He was involved in the approval of dodgy construction deals, his palms being greased by developers as well as moneylenders. Poor sod was buckling under the pressure, in the process of turning 204 and cooperating with my two colleagues here as a state witness when he was tragically killed in our overnight facilities. The man who'll go to jail for the murder is one Michael 'Snoekie' Smoog – a warden who's suddenly driving around in a brand-new Fortuner, compliments of Pannevis Davis himself."

"And the other link?" said Qhubeka.

"A middle-aged woman: Myrtle Johns," Charmaine explained. "She's a client manager at the bank where Davis and his wife *and* Malan du Toit save their cents. She's a very unlucky online gambler, borrowing money from all sorts. Her story didn't end well, of course. So that's how she wound up in Davis's clutches. Okay?"

"Wait a bit," Qhebeka said, "that name rings a bell. Isn't that the woman whose daughter was attacked with battery acid?"

"Well done, Vuvu. That's *exactly* how Pannevis keeps his 'teams' in line. But we're working on her 204 status. We stumbled across her—"

"But you never said anything, Charmaine!" Qhubeka frowned at her.

Charmaine just shrugged, then continued. "When I started digging into Malan du Toit's financial affairs ... *that's* when we struck gold, see. Because

342

Du Toit had paid the deposit for the Jonkers Valley land from his company's funds. To get the rest of the money, he literally had to beg, steal and 'borrow'" – and with the last word, two fingers on each hand theatrically mimed scare quotes. "Among others, from 'investors'" – fingers up in the air again – "one of these being Hope Holdings." She stressed the company name, paused, then fixed her eyes on each member of her audience in turn, ensuring that she had their full attention.

"Hope Holdings exports local arts and crafts to the United States via Bermuda and other dodgy places. The company also engages in a lot of 'charity work'." She raised her eyebrows meaningfully as she used the phrase. "You know the kind of thing – feeding schemes in Manenberg and Bonteheuwel, a number of nursery schools, building soccer fields, et cetera."

She paused, her brows furrowed. "That's the problem with these new thugs. The connection between them and a multitude of smaller street gangs and syndicates is hard to prove, mainly because of a lack of information. The community doesn't want to say anything to incriminate someone like Pannevis – because in so many poor households, he's the one who literally puts the food on the table."

Qhubeka listened calmly, fully in control once again – something Beeslaar envied her right then. Eventually she asked: "So what's your problem, Charmainetjie? How are we pissing on your parade with this case?"

"Has Du Toit made *any* kind of confession?" Charmaine asked Beeslaar. She dunked a rusk in her tea, chewing quickly as she waited for an answer.

"Not yet formally. He insists that *he* was the one who pulled the trigger. That it was just domestic trouble – nothing to do with his business."

Charmaine and her two NPA colleagues exchanged glances. One of the men, who had been introduced as Cebo, took over from Charmaine: "Look, it's of vital importance that your Mr du Toit remains alive in order to assist us, because we're really after Pannevis. What we're afraid of is that Pannevis will get to Du Toit before we do. His life isn't safe at present, especially in custody. Pannevis's troops will get to him – and I'm talking about warders as well as inmates. And when word gets out, there's no way either of us will be able to keep Du Toit safe, see?"

"So, what are you actually saying?" Qhubeka's eyes flashed and she leant forward belligerently: "Are you telling me I should suspend my investigation for the sake of *your* case? As we speak, there's already a whole bladdy army of lawyers on the ground floor. Who can't *wait* for me to remove their clients' bangles and send them home with a lullaby. Hey? And then, what about the murder, man? What about the murder of Elmana du Toit?"

"Whoa!" Charmaine raised a hand. "Vuvu, all we're saying is that you should also keep the bigger picture in mind. That's all. Whatever happens to Malan du Toit now – whether he's charged or whatever – Pannevis knows he can kiss his 'investment' goodbye. It's eighty-five million rand, more or less. He's prepared to fight for it, okay?"

Qhubeka pursed her lips in frustration, glanced at Beeslaar.

He shrugged. "It's your decision," he said. "And, er, your boss's."

"So, what do *you* propose?" Qhubeka asked Cebo.

"What *we* would like to propose is a deal with Du Toit: information in exchange for safety. Otherwise Pannevis is, for the time being, a free man. And Du Toit's a dead man."

Prammie massaged his temples and said: "I hope one of you has something logical for me to convey to the prov com in an hour's time. Because at this moment it seems to me that we're trying to fish without a rod. Isn't that so?"

When no one offered an answer, Beeslaar took up the thread of the discussion: "Colonel, if I could perhaps say what I'm seeing here from an outsider's perspective. Maybe Shane Williams's death was the trigger for everything that's happened. I think Du Toit must have been scared out of his wits by the ease with which Williams was eliminated. Maybe he started getting cold feet. Hence the presence of Quentin Swiff Daniels in Stellenbosch - to keep Du Toit in line. Not so, Charmaine?"

"You're right, but he's small fry. Along with a number of officials higher up in the food chain. We want to nail the *big* fish – Pannevis."

"And what about Andries April?" asked Qhubeka.

"Nothing," said Charmaine. "He's the poor prick who unknowingly served as the decoy. We suspect that his NGO was financed by Pannevis."

They sat in silence for a while – mulling over the thought.

"April," Beeslaar resumed eventually, "told me last night in so many words that Malan du Toit's development is being financed with money from the Cape Flats. He mentioned a name ..." Beeslaar racked his tired brain. "Mocha Java – Mocha Java Diamonds. That's what he called them. They buy property to launder their money."

"So you're saying April is an innocent bystander?" said Qhubeka.

"It makes sense," said Charmaine. "It also makes him a valuable witness – for *our* investigation into Pannevis Davis. And if we want to keep him alive, we'd better separate him and Swiff Daniels." She stood up. "I'll organise it," she said and disappeared, leaving a piece of rusk floating in her tea.

Colonel Baadjies stood up too, but with less enthusiasm. He had to phone the provincial commissioner. The two NPA men followed him out of the room.

Qhubeka's desk phone rang. It was a service clerk, informing her of the arrival of Du Toit's lawyers *and* those of Quentin Daniels. She asked Beeslaar to wait in the conference room while she fetched Du Toit's legal team.

The time for "trading shit for shit" had arrived, Qhubeka said, managing a weak smile: it was another of Blikkies's sayings.

On his way to the conference room, Beeslaar tried Ghaap's number again, but it went straight to voicemail, like before. Same thing with Sister Lucy's number. He tried to book a flight to Johannesburg. Seats were available on Kulula, the twelve and two o'clock flights. The latter landed at Lanseria – within spitting distance of Soweto.

Just then, Willem Bester arrived with his colleagues – two of them, for good measure. Bester introduced the newcomers as he put his briefcase on the conference table and opened it. The soul of businesslike efficiency. He was freshly shaven, but there were bags under his eyes.

"Our offer," he began, brandishing a memory stick, "is full disclosure of Malan du Toit's financial affairs. In exchange for indemnity and protection for our client and his children." The two colleagues produced a document, which Bester pushed across the table towards Beeslaar and Qhubeka. "This is a signed instruction from our client to handle the disclosure on his behalf. With certain conditions, though."

Qhubeka picked it up, frowned, and passed it to Beeslaar, who didn't even bother glancing at it. He said: "Your client is in no position to impose conditions, Mr Bester, seeing that we've seized all his computers, all his financial statements, all his financial transactions. Everything. We don't have to negotiate about a thing."

Bester gave a nod. His colleagues produced more documents.

"Surely you don't think my client would have left information of this nature lying around on his office computers?"

"It doesn't matter where—"

Qhubeka silenced Beeslaar by holding up her hand. "We want all possible evidence of the transactions that have taken place between your client and one Leonard Davis – better known as Pannevis. As well as names, bank accounts – the whole caboodle. Failing that, you can bargain on—"

"Our client has various partners in the Jonkershoek Valley development. Legitimate companies. All the information is here." He held up the memory stick again, gave it to Qhubeka when she held out her hand.

She stood up. "I need to consult with my SC, Colonel Baadjies. Hang on."

As soon as Qhubeka had left the room, the three lawyers started conferring with one another in hushed tones.

Beeslaar used the opportunity and quickly called Ghaap.

Still nothing.

In exasperation he stood up, felt like flinging the mug against the wall, but walked out of the door instead. Qhubeka was standing at the end of the passage, in deep discussion with Baadjies. Remembering his fleece jacket, Beeslaar slipped into her office where he'd left it. He was sure Qhubeka could handle the rest of the case on her own.

There were more important things on his mind right now than all the Pannevisse in the world. He couldn't even *think* the word: a *daughter*. His mind still refused to believe it.

His phone rang, and he almost dropped it in his hurry to put it to his ear. Ghaap.

"Talk to me!" he almost shouted. "And you'd better talk properly, or I'll stick my finger in your eye and dial your face to a nought!"

"We were just in time," Ghaap panted into the phone. "He'll lose his arm, but he's breathing."

Beeslaar's blood ran cold. "What were you in time for, Ghaap? Jissus, man, stop with the riddles!"

"The boy. The one that nearly ended up as hyena breakfast!"

Beeslaar slumped against the wall, his mouth dry.

"As for Hlanganani, alias The Fatha, it's over and out for him too. They shot him to hell and—"

"Does she know yet? Have you told her yet, about the boy?"

"She's very weak, Beeslaar. We don't want to upset her for now. The dogs have taken over here – to track the hyena. You should've heard them yelping when they caught that smell. As if they'd sniffed lion. They're busy—"

Beeslaar's ears cut out. Kleinpiet losing an arm? Jissis. How much was *one* woman expected to endure in a lifetime?

"You still there?" Ghaap inquired.

"You know, she's already lost two."

"Yes, I know," Ghaap replied. "That's why I'm so glad that these two kids are at least okay."

Beeslaar felt his heart lurch. "But the boy's arm ... Who's the boy that was hurt by the hyena?"

"A local youngster. It was him who saved your Gerda and her kids."

Beeslaar's head was spinning. This was becoming too bizarre. "Ghaap, listen to me. The boyfriend. Have you managed to find him yet?"

"Negative," Ghaap replied. After more assurances that Gerda and her children were safe and well, they ended the call.

For a couple of minutes after Ghaap's news, Beeslaar stood rooted to the spot, unseeing. He was aware of the bustle around him, the footsteps of people in the passage, but all of it sounded far away. Here, inside him, there was quiet. There was relief. Gratitude. And hope – heavenly, invigorating hope, that made his blood rush.

And anger too: at the gorilla with the bedroom eyes. Baz. Who'd better prepare himself, because he was going to hunt the cunt down. And once he'd got his hands on him, he would just disappear – hair and all.

Qhubeka tapped him on the shoulder. "Confession time," she said with an excited smile. "Andries April has just signed a statement that links Quentin Daniels to Pannevis. Not a peep out of Swiff himself: loyal to the end. Anyways—"

"Qhubeka," Beeslaar said. "From now on you're flying solo. I really do need to get to Joburg. Now."

She looked up at him, her eyes soft. "Is it bad?" Her voice was warm. Sympathetic. But he didn't want any sympathy right then. Couldn't afford it. Overcome with emotion, he stepped away from her.

"One last favour," she said. "Malan du Toit."

Beeslaar glanced impatiently at his phone. It was already nearly ten o'clock. "Half an hour, max," he grunted and followed her, back to the conference room. "And it'll cost you," he said on the way. "The old guy at Great Gables whose Krugerrands were stolen, Oom Arnold Sebens – please pay him a visit. I promised him."

She gave him a murderous look, but Beeslaar was unperturbed. He knew she'd go. That's just the way she was. One of the good guys.

Malan du Toit was seated among the three lawyers when they walked in. He looked the way Beeslaar felt: buggered. Worn to a frazzle.

"Well, then," Qhubeka began. "Captain Beeslaar is here, so you can start talking. And for once, forget about all the other stories. We want to know *exactly* what happened on Tuesday afternoon when you arrived at the house."

Du Toit took a deep breath and glanced at his lawyer. When Bester gave the signal, he began: "Dawid-Pieter phoned me. Said he thought Elmana had been hurt. That Ellie was still inside the house, and that she refused to open the door for him." He swallowed a few times.

Qhubeka stood up and poured him a glass of water from the tea table.

He half-emptied the glass, then resumed his account: "I could see at once that Elmana was dead. She lay on the floor, her eyes open. Blood all over her head. Ellie was sitting on the … the stairs, there was blood on her."

He gulped down some more water. "She simply sat there. I don't think she even saw … She wasn't even aware of me. I couldn't … I asked if she was okay. Ellie, I mean. She … she said no. She was quite calm. Completely calm. Said that she'd … killed Elmana, killed her by accident. They'd been fighting again. Elmana had slapped Ellie. Because of the ugly names. She'd called Elmana a … She'd called her a dopehead and a hopeless c-cunt. Plus some other bad names.

347

"When Elmana slapped her, she lost it. She slapped her back. Elmana exploded, grabbed the Brahman statuette, intending to throw it at Ellie or something. She was completely ... Ellie said she was crazed. Mad. Berserk. Ellie had taken one of the bonsais, trying to defend herself. Those trees were precious to Elmana. They were the one real passion in her life. I guess ... I guess she wanted to save the tree. But with the heavy statuette in her hand ... She must have lost her balance, hitting her forehead against the table as she fell."

He rubbed his eyes. There were no tears. Beeslaar suspected that the man was way beyond tears.

"Ellie said Elmana had some kind of fit, convulsions. She was frightened, tried to help her mother. But the blow to the head and the tik convulsions ... Elmana stopped breathing. That's when Dawid-Pieter arrived at the house. And phoned me."

Du Toit finished the rest of his water.

Qhubeka refilled his glass and said, "So then *you* decided, in your wisdom, to disguise it as a house robbery?"

"Everything was so confused. It happened so quickly. The chaos, the two kids, the blood. Ellie was hysterical. She kept saying: 'I killed Mamma, I killed Mamma.' And Dawid-Pieter ... He was trying to shake his mother awake, shouting that she must ask God for forgive – I didn't know what to do, so I fetched the pistol. I had to do it so that it'd look like she was shot from behind – to conceal the wound on her forehead. I grabbed some gardening gloves of hers and put them on. I was convinced she was already dead."

"Then you staged the scene with the statuette, throwing the other bonsais around, stealing the money from your own safe. And Dawid-Pieter was supposed to dump the pistol somewhere or bury it?"

Du Toit screwed his eyes up, as if to blot out the recollection, and Qhubeka continued: "Except that he didn't get rid of it, did he?"

"We were panic-stricken, the three of us. The past few weeks had been very hard on all of us. Things were unbearable with Elmana. Traumatic. I sent Ellie to her room to wash the blood from her body, told my son to hide the tik equipment. And to go bury the pistol. The rest you know."

He paused. "The damn pistol. Which I ... when Pannevis Davis started threatening me, terrorising me, I started keeping it by my side. For years it had been locked away in the safe. But I ... I had no control over those scumbags, they were calling the shots. Ever since the death of Shane Williams. They ... I knew at once that they were behind his murder. Williams had phoned me. He demanded money to shut up, or else he'd take his information to *Akkernuus*. I was at the end of my tether. It was all such a mess." He stared intently at the wooden table top, as if watching a replay of the events in his head.

Qhubeka prompted: "And Tuesday, Mr du Toit? How did this lead up to Tuesday? Why were you so desperate to prove it was a robbery gone wrong? I mean, it was an accident, after all. The law would have been lenient, in the circumstances. But you killed your wife all over again, moved the body, messed up the scene. Why, for God's sake?"

"I *had* to," Du Toit said. "For Ellie. For my family. Even though it was so late in the day. I had been so paralysed, so weak in standing up to Elmana. And Davis, who'd become more and more menacing by the day. After the business with Williams, I told them I was finished with them, that I was going to take my family away from here, leave the country. Ellie's cat. They killed the cat, had the head delivered to me at the office. A gift-wrapped parcel. The body was sent to our house, addressed to Ellie. Elmana opened it, of course. She went really crazy."

He paused, screwed up his eyes.

"I was mad with fear. And Elmana was slipping deeper and deeper into the abyss. She was either sleeping or raving: there were snakes in her bed, the kids and I were trying to kill her. All three of us were walking on eggshells."

Du Toit glanced at his lawyer. Bester blinked his eyes, signalling that what he had said would suffice.

It was close to ten-thirty when Qhubeka eventually let Beeslaar go. "It's a pity you have to leave. You may not have noticed it, but the wind has died down – the best time of year to be in the Cape."

"Old Blikkies didn't do a bad job as far as you're concerned, Qhubeka," he said in reply.

There was a twinkle in her eyes as, unexpectedly, she stepped forward, put her hands on his shoulders, and planted a quick kiss on his unshaven cheek. "He didn't raise you too shabbily either," she retorted with a smile.

Beeslaar was sitting in the departure lounge at Cape Town International, his flight due to leave in forty minutes. He ordered a coffee at a restaurant, gazed at the masses milling around him, looked through the window at the distant Hottentots Holland Mountains, with Stellenbosch behind. He stretched his back and arms, suppressed a yawn. The coffee would pep him up. In fact, he should have ordered champagne. It was customary, wasn't it? A man in his position … cigars and champagne.

But he wouldn't be able to celebrate in style, he knew. Because first he had a moerse bone to pick with a certain Albanian, who, according to Ghaap, may have fled the country. Yet the world wasn't big enough, he resolved; that gorilla would have no place to hide. He, Beeslaar, was going to find the fucker. And then it would be just him and Mr Baz.

He stirred three spoons of sugar into his coffee. But maybe he should at least consider a small brandy. Just to add to the coffee. To celebrate.

Which suddenly reminded him: the scattering of Blikkies's ashes tomorrow! He had to notify Tertia. Blikkies's one and only. Faithful right to the end to a father who hadn't known how to love her.

He would phone her from Johannesburg.

But in the meantime. In the meantime, he wanted to mellow out. Use the time to attune his mind. To the faint gleam of hope. His one chance. Dear God, just one possible chance to be a real man. And a father.

To his daughter.

Acknowledgements

Many thanks to my publisher, Fourie Botha, for his kindness and wisdom in the production process of this book. Also to the team at Penguin Random House South Africa who helped to put it all together.

I had the privilege of working with two fantastic people who did the translation and the editing from the original Afrikaans: Linde Dietrich as translator and Lynda Gilfillan as editor. Together they formed a formidable team that managed to mould a book from one language into another without it losing either its character or grit. Respect.

Thank you also to Isobel Dixon of Blake Friedman Literary Agency for offering important advice and guidance in giving final shape to this novel.

The original book was written with the help of numerous people who generously shared their knowledge and expertise:

Gareth Crocker, a writer I greatly admire, helped me in gaining access to the Johannesburg company Tracker and its capable team of anti-vehicle theft experts. Those involved frequently put their lives at risk in tracking down hijackers and vehicle thieves. Stan Davis, Stroppie Grobbelaar and Piet Kruger took me into their world of night-time patrols in the streets of greater Johannesburg and Soweto. Under the leadership of Leon Bothma, they provided me with a unique perspective on the war on crime in this country. It was, at times, very scary, and also rather unreal. Thanks, guys, it was a hell of a ride – literally.

In addition, I encountered the unstoppable energy of Captain Patrys Rautenbach of the West Rand SAPD, who gave me important insights into the difficult, often dangerous and unacknowledged work that ordinary policemen and -women do on a daily basis. Richard Brussow of the National Hijack Prevention Academy helped me to get inside the head of those who hijack cars. Rolinda Nel of Business Against Crime shared her knowledge and experience, and I also owe Virginia Kepler, *Beeld*'s top crime reporter, a big thank you for sharing her time with me, and for prompting the idea of a high-speed car chase where a woman in labour is an unwitting – and unwilling – passenger. My thanks are also due to Liezl Thom, a Pretoria journalist who also shared her knowledge and experience with me.

On a more personal level: Dr Liesbet Botha and her wife, Jomari Dick, thank you for providing accommodation, as well as transport, during my research trips. I am grateful also to Hanret Snyman of Seventh Avenue in Melville, Johannesburg, who generously provided accommodation, often waiting up for me with a cup of warm coffee and beskuit after a night of high adventure with the boys from Tracker. Dineke Volschenk occasionally played taxi driver, fetching me from the airport, and transporting me to places all over Gauteng for research purposes. Estelle Bester, who worked in Soweto for many years as a civil servant, and knows all the different varieties of Kasi-slang and iScamto, thank you for unlocking a fabulous city and its thriving culture, its warm heart and its unique rhythm. Estelle also introduced me to several wonderful sangomas who allowed me the privilege of undergoing sacred rituals.

In Stellenbosch, Johan Laubscher, my brother-in-law and a respected developer, assisted me with information on the intricacies and difficulties of the property market in that part of the country. So, too, did Karine Swiegers, who is a top property agent with Pam Golding. Thanks also to another brother-in-law, Kobus Swart, for his constant willingness to give advice on anything concerning weapons and shooting.

Elsabe Retief, former editor of *Die Eikestad Nuus* in Stellenbosch, gave valuable advice on the workings of small-town newspapers, and Linde Dietrich provided useful information about the history of Stellenbosch during the apartheid years.

Journalist Pearlie Joubert of the *Mail & Guardian* shared her research on the gang culture of the Western Cape, and General Glen Schooling, formerly a policeman and later head of the Stellenbosch Buurtwag, helped with information on white-collar crime in the area.

To my friend and mentor of many years, Hettie Scholtz, thank you for your sharp eye and acute intellect, your expert guidance and constant friendship. You're a brick. I'm also grateful to Dr Etienne Bloemhof of NB Publishers, editor of *Onse vaders*, the Afrikaans version of this book, for refining the final product from its rather ramshackle beginnings.

Further thanks are due to Fahiema Hallam for the text design and typesetting, Georgia Demertzis for the cover design, and my friend Ansie du Toit for the author photograph.

Last but not least: thank you to my husband, Rien, the rock in my life, my best friend, and my loyal companion – the person who helps to make it all possible.

In the making of this book, I made liberal use of several books and internet sources:

For South African slang, www.watkykjy.co.za

Lebo Motshegoa's wonderful dictionary, *Township Talk* (Juta and Company)

For Your Own Good: Hidden Cruelty in Child-rearing and the Roots of Violence (www.fsgbooks.com)

In ons bloed, compiled by Hilton Biscombe (University of Stellenbosch Sun Press)

Nog altyd hier gewees: Die storie van die Stellenbosse gemeenskap by Herman Giliomee (Tafelberg)

Spots of a Leopard: On Being a Man by Aernout Zevenbergen (www. laughingleopard.co.za)

Home Invasion by Rudolph Zinn (Tafelberg)

Baba: Men and Fatherhood in South Africa by Linda Richter and Robert Morrell (HSRC Press)

Teenage Tata: Voices of Young Fathers in South Africa by Sharlene Swartz and Arvin Bhana (HSRC Press)

Fruit of a Poisoned Tree: A True Story of Murder and the Miscarriage of Justice by Antony Altbeker (Jonathan Ball Publishers)

Iron John: Men and Masculinity by Robert Bly (www.randomhouse.co.uk)

WEEPING WATERS

A troubled cop. A vicious killing. A community's secrets laid bare.

Inspector Albertus Beeslaar has left the ruthless city, only to have his hopes of finding peace and quiet in the Kalahari shattered by the brutal murder of artist Freddie Swarts and her adopted daughter. But Freddie's journalist sister Sara is not convinced that this was a typical farm attack. Amid a spate of stock thefts, Beeslaar must solve this high-profile crime, all the while training his two rookie partners, Ghaap and Pyl. After more murders, the disturbing puzzle grows increasingly sinister, as age-old secrets and hostilities surface, spurring the local inhabitants to violent action. No one is above suspicion, not least the mysterious Bushman farm manager and falconer, Dam.